LoveHampton

a novel

LoveHampton

Sherri Rifkin

St. Martin's Griffin ⚞ New York

LOVEHAMPTON. Copyright © 2008 by Sherri Rifkin. All rights reserved. Printed in the United States of America. No part of this book may be used or reproduced in any manner whatsoever without written permission except in the case of brief quotations embodied in critical articles or reviews. For information, address St. Martin's Press, 175 Fifth Avenue, New York, N.Y. 10010.

www.stmartins.com

Book design by Ralph Fowler

ISBN-13: 978-0-312-38021-2 .
ISBN-10: 0-312-38021-6

First Edition: May 2008

10 9 8 7 6 5 4 3 2 1

LoveHampton

Summerhouse Guidelines
*** 2007 ***

1. Each person is assigned a bedroom, either alone or paired with a roommate, depending on the level of share you bought, for the entire summer. Note: there will be no room switching.

2. Since everyone has their own assigned space, please respect one another's privacy. That means not going into other people's rooms or using their belongings without their permission. Even if the person is not out for the weekend, it is up to that person's discretion whether or not they want to let someone else, either a house member or another member's guest, sleep in that room for the weekend. (See Attachment A: The Guest Policy for more.)

3. Everyone has a full share, meaning you're all allowed to come out every weekend between Memorial Day and Labor Day. You will not be refunded for unused time, so like they say about the FLEX plan, use it or lose it.

4. The house is available for you to use during the weekdays. All house guidelines still apply. You won't be guaranteed weekday time alone, as the house is still a share house, even during the week.

5. Please keep the common areas neat and clean up after yourselves. It shouldn't be that hard to

put your glasses and dishes in the dishwasher
(BTW, putting them in the sink doesn't count).
And if the dishwasher is full, here's an idea:
turn it on!

6. I will be taking care of all the finances and
   paying our bills out of a house fund everyone
   contributed to in the cost of their share. I
   will also purchase basic house supplies such as
   paper goods, bath soap, laundry detergent, etc.
   If you see that we're running low on anything,
   please write it down on the list I will be
   posting on the refrigerator. NB: Food, alcohol,
   and Red Bull are not included.

Season Preview

Hamptons Unwritten Rule #1:
There is no other place to be between
Memorial Day and Labor Day.

I'm standing outside of Dos Caminos, the original one on Park Avenue South, my hand frozen on the cool bronze *C* of the *DC*-shaped door handle, my breath shallow and heart pounding. This should be easy. All I have to do is pull the door open and go inside—but I can't. Even the name of the restaurant—which I've translated, using my ninth-grade-level Spanish, as "two roads"—seems to be taunting me. Why did I decide to do this again? Is this total immersion thing really necessary?

But it's too late. *I need to get a life. Now.* Because I haven't had one for almost two years. For better or worse, I've already embarked on this particular road—not necessarily by my own choice, but for my own good.

And this road continues with tonight: having dinner with seven complete strangers, only one of whom I've been in contact with, and that was via e-mail. It's far worse than a blind date and not because it's like being on seven simultaneous blind dates, but because no matter if we love or hate one another after this evening, we all have committed to a very intimate three-month-long relationship.

We are going to be sharing a house in the Hamptons for the summer.

I look down at the sidewalk and focus on a crack by my foot, trying to employ a breathing technique I learned recently to help calm
me down. I start by closing my eyes, taking deep, rhythmic breaths,
pulling fresh air—as fresh as it can be in New York City—into my
diaphragm and exhaling to the count of four. Before I can finish my
first round, the heavy glass door swings open from the inside as a
group of people push their way by me without so much as an "excuse me," knocking me back several paces from the door, causing
me to stumble into an older couple passing by.

"Watch it!" the man shouts at me while his wife grabs his arm
and stage-whispers, "She must be on drugs!"

Clearly, this is no time for meditation. I might as well get this
over with.

I raise my head, straighten my back, turn up the corners of my
mouth into a semblance of a smile, pull the door open, and step
through.

Hamptons Unwritten Rule #2:
First impressions—especially when made
at the Pre-Summerhouse Dinner—last a
summertime . . . and then some.

The small bar is packed even though it's a Sunday night. I scan the
crowd, looking for a group of people who could be my housemates,
but unfortunately, I have no reference point for recognizing them.
When I exchanged e-mails with Leah earlier in the week and she
told me about the dinner, I forgot to ask what she looked like. The
plan was to meet for drinks in the bar at seven o'clock with the dinner reservation set for seven-thirty. My predinner panic attack set
me back by only ten minutes, so theoretically everyone should be
here *and* I avoided being the first one to arrive.

After one more fruitless look around, I ask the hostess.

"I seated them ten minutes ago. Let me bring you back."

Strange, I think, as I follow her into the loud, cavernous restaurant. She abandons me at a table filled with a comely crowd.

A skinny woman with beautiful long blond hair and a great body but not a particularly soft or pretty face shoots out of her chair and stalks toward me in a suede miniskirt and sheer white fitted blouse, unbuttoned just enough to reveal a flawless, possibly surgically enhanced cleavage. "Miller! Where have you been?" She looks like the kind of girl Molly Ringwald would instantly be intimidated by in a John Hughes movie. I just wish I was feeling even as remotely confident as Molly Ringwald would be in this situation.

"It's Tori, actually. Are you Leah? It's so nice to meet—"

"What happened to you? You're so late! We thought you were bailing on us."

"Only by a few—well, ten—minutes, right?"

"More like forty." She throws back her blanket of straight multitonal blond hair over her shoulder, then cocks her head to the side so her tresses fall right back into place. Perfectly.

"I thought your e-mail said drinks were at seven."

"That was the *original* plan, but then everyone wanted to start earlier, so we decided to move it up to six-thirty. Didn't you get my e-mail today?" She blinks at me several times.

"I don't check my e-mail on the weekends. It's against my religion," I joke.

Blink, blink. "Well, the important thing is that you're here now. And your check cleared." She flips her hair again. "Kidding! Seriously, you're going to have a great time this summer. It's going to be *mad fun*, if tonight is any indication. So. Let me introduce you." She spins around on her high heels, causing her hair to fan out in a wide circle and leads me toward three girls at the end of the table, all of whom are wearing versions of the perfect we-know-it's-Sunday-night-but-this-is-still-an-important-social-occasion outfit, noting with relief that I'm in the same fashion camp, thanks to a little recent outside help.

"Abigail, Cassandra, Stacy: meet Miller."

"Hi, it's great to meet you all. Actually, my name is Tori. I know it's confusing, since the name on my e-mail is Miller at MillerWorks dot—"

"Do you live really far away, like in an outer borough or something?" Abigail gives me a limp, clammy hand to shake. She, unlike Leah, is naturally very pretty, but the scowl on her face is not doing her any favors. As much as I am apt to project that her frown is for my benefit, I get the feeling she is cursed with a permanently displeased expression, since it seems to fit perfectly with her nasal tone.

"No, I came straight from home, a little bit farther downtown. Why?"

"Well, it's just that you were so late."

Now it's my turn to blink.

"Miller says she doesn't check her e-mail on the weekends," Leah answers Abigail. This time, I don't bother correcting her about my name.

"I didn't know anyone still did that," Abigail comments, still frowning. Talk about a conversation ender. I shift on my feet, unsure of what to say or do next. I'm woefully out of practice meeting and socializing with new people outside of business situations. Speaking to my three best friends, two of whom work for me, is one thing. Trying to create new friendships when you've been sitting on the bench for two years is another matter entirely. I was kind of hoping that this was one of the things that was supposed to be like riding a bike, but now that it's happening, I'm not too sure.

"Hey there, I'm Cassie." She reaches across Abigail to shake my hand with a cool, confident grip. "I am so coveting your blouse! It's fantastic. I hope you plan on bringing it out to the house. We look to be about the same size. . . ." She gives me a wide, welcoming smile.

I feel my shoulders start nudging down from my ears for the first time since I left my apartment. "Thanks. I . . . it's new."

Stacy pops up out of her chair and gives me the kind of hug that little kids give. She's much shorter than the other three girls and has a head of massive shoulder-length dark brown curls, big brown eyes to match, and a face full of freckles. "Hi, Miller! Did Leah tell you we're going to be roomies? Isn't that great? We're going to have so much fun together! I have a car, which you're welcome to use anytime because I heard you don't have one. And if you ever need a ride out there, I can totally drive you—"

Leah cuts her off. "Stacy, Miller still needs to meet the guys. You'll have plenty of time to bond with your new *roomie* later."

Leah leads me around to the other side of the table until we're standing in front of three very good-looking men. My heart starts pounding. They will be the first straight, unmarried, non-work-related men I've spoken to in two years.

"Guys, this is Miller. Miller, this is Michael, Andrew, and Jackson."

In response to their chorus of friendly greetings, all I can do is nod. And then there it is again: the abhorrent, awkward silence.

"Cat got your tongue or something?" Michael asks with a heavy Long Island accent.

Suddenly they're all staring at me. Maybe I can make a run for it. All I'd have to do is push Leah out of the way, jump over that baby stroller at the next table. . . .

Just then, Andrew stands up to shake my hand. "Hey there. I'm Andrew Kane. Welcome to the nut house." He's solidly over six feet, has dirty-blond wavy hair—slightly longish for a guy but not hippie-ish—a strong chin, hazel eyes, and underneath an untucked striped button-down shirt and well-fitting dark jeans, a seemingly built body. Celebrity He Most Resembles: Simon Baker. But the fact that he resembles anyone famous means that he is definitely out of my league.

"Nice to meet you," I choke out as casually as possible.

He leans in and stage-whispers, "You seem like a nice, normal person. You might want to run while you still can." He pushes his chin in Michael's direction, who is too busy CrackBerrying to notice.

Does this guy read minds? "I was actually just considering that very thing, but I thought I'd give everyone a few more minutes before deciding whether I'm going to need to exercise that option."

He narrows his eyes at me and then laughs. Score one for Tori, I mean, Miller.

"You know, it's really bad that you were late . . ."

Et tu, Andrew? "But, I wasn't—"

". . . because you missed happy hour. I wouldn't recommend experiencing this awkward presummer ritual sober. What can I get you?"

"How about a margarita on the rocks, no salt?"

"A fine choice. I'll just order it at the bar. We currently seem to be without a waiter. Be back in a few." Andrew ambles away.

Michael puts down his BlackBerry. "Hey, Miller, why don't you take a load off?" He cocks his head toward the empty seat next to him.

"Isn't that Andrew's chair?"

"He can find somewhere else to sit. Besides, I didn't pay all that money for a share to hang out with guys, if you know what I mean." He pats the chair. I sit. He is good-looking but in a way completely opposite to Andrew. Michael's dark curly hair is clipped short, which is not doing such a good job of hiding a bald spot that's beginning to appear on the crown of his head. His best feature is his blue eyes. The only thing detracting from his looks is that he's a little puffy all over, as if he recently put on some extra poundage and it didn't know where to settle, so it distributed itself evenly from head to toe. He leans in and not so casually drapes his arm around the back of my chair.

"So, how do you all know one another?" I ask Michael, beating him to the punch.

"I know Andrew through work. I'm an investment banker, and Andrew was the lawyer on some of my deals. We got to talking at a couple of closing dinners and figured out both of us are into tennis, so we started playing out at the beach last summer. I was in another house not too far away from where he was. Then he invited me to the famous birthday bash that he throws for himself every August, which is where I met Leah. Now that was a killer party! That guy knows more people than God. I'm sure he'll do it again this year."

"I hope I'm invited."

"You're funny," he says without laughing. "Andrew and Leah randomly ended up in the same house three years ago and then they organized a house last summer, so this is their third summer together."

"I thought Leah was managing our house alone."

"She's large and in charge for sure, but Andrew helps out by bringing in people. I guess I think of it as his house too, since he was the one who asked me to join."

A huge margarita appears in front of me, delivered by the most beautiful man-hand I've ever seen adorned by a chunky silver Rolex. "I hope your cocktail is to your liking," Andrew says, "even though you stole my seat."

"I'm sorry! Michael said—"

"Don't look at me. I was just sitting here minding my own business." Michael edges away, as if I've suddenly been diagnosed with a communicable disease.

"Let me find another chair," I say.

"No worries. I should probably go spend some quality time with the other female members of the household." Andrew strides over to the other end of the table, where the girls happily make room for him in the middle of their klatch.

"I'm starving and they haven't even taken our order yet." Michael cranes his head to look around the restaurant. "I'm going to see if I can find any signs of life. If a waiter comes over, don't let him leave!"

I look across the table at Jackson, who until now has been so quiet I almost forgot he was there. He is staring at me with an amused look on his face.

"So, how do you like us so far?" he says, his voice tinged with a welcome touch of sarcasm and an unexpected British accent.

"Um, good, I guess. I mean . . ."

"Try not to worry yourself too much. We're not all Neanderthals. Some of us even know how to read."

I'm not sure whether to laugh or not, since he doesn't smile or give me any sense that he's kidding. "Good to know."

. . .

After we order and are settled with fresh drinks, the group's attentions turn back to themselves and thankfully away from me.

I'm the most intrigued by Jackson, who remains quiet but I can tell keenly tuned in. As he made a point of saying, he so clearly, even visibly, is different from the rest of the housemates. He has brown wavy hair that is longish and falls into his face, like Michael Stipe circa the late 1980s, causing him to repeat the fruitless gesture of raking his hand through it to push it out of his eyes. He wears wire-rimmed glasses, which successfully—and I'm going to guess deliberately—give him a studious look. He's medium height and thin, bordering on gaunt-looking. Jackson clearly hasn't shaven today, if at all this weekend. His clothes have the air of being expensive, possibly even custom-made, but upon closer look, are well worn and frayed. Since there's no smoking inside, he has excused himself more than once to "nip outside" for a cigarette. Even though we haven't said more than a few words to each other, I imagine him and me to be the two outsiders of the group and feel comforted by that.

By the time the dishes are cleared, I'm more than a little buzzed (three margaritas apparently will have that effect) and feeling emboldened, albeit artificially. So when everyone seat-hops, I follow suit, situating myself next to Cassie. The best way to describe her is a superstylish former ballerina. She has shiny chestnut-colored hair that's pinned back into a loose, messy knot. The few, well-positioned freckles on her nose only help to emphasize her deep brown eyes. We're probably about the same height, but she's clearly more graceful than I could ever hope to be. I wonder how she appears to be so comfortable with her long legs and arms, when I always feel like my appendages are something I have to fight to keep under my control. Besides being genetically blessed, Cassie has what I consider to be one of the most glam jobs: she is a beauty editor at *Elle*. Ironically, she wears barely any makeup, not that she needs it, which is probably why she doesn't bother with it.

I'm fairly certain that I've been thoroughly embarrassing myself for the last half hour by asking her a million questions about her job and gushing about how exciting it must be. "Enough about me! I'm even boring myself. I can't imagine how excruciating this must be for you. Save me from myself and tell me what you do. It's got to be more interesting and meaningful than writing about colored wax and powder every day."

"I don't know about that . . . I'll let you be the judge. I recently started my own business called MillerWorks. It's a TV on-air promotion production company."

"Okay, I have no idea what that is but it sounds good. Tell me more."

"You know those TV commercials that say stuff like, 'Watch our new show every Thursday at nine, eight central or you will be woefully clueless at tomorrow's watercooler!' or 'Coming up next, later, or tomorrow night at eight—you can't afford to miss this very special episode of the latest acronym-named medical drama/derivative criminal procedural'? We create pitches about what those should be, and then once a cable network buys into one of our concepts, we write, produce, shoot, and edit it. Sometimes they just air the spots on their own channels to drive tune-in, but if they're doing a big marketing campaign around a new show launch, they run them on other networks like regular commercials."

"That is so totally cool!"

"I think what you do is much cooler."

"Are you kidding? You have your own business. How great is that! Even though I work at a women's magazine, I still technically work for 'the man.' I'm so jealous that you get to work for yourself. And in television! That just seems so much more relevant."

"Actually," I respond, feeling genuinely proud, "it does feel pretty good. I love what I do."

"Well, good luck with your venture. I'm sure you'll be successful, especially if you're doing something you love. Here's to being in charge of your own destiny!" We clink glasses. My margarita sloshes all over her hand, but she doesn't flinch. While she dabs at the spill with her napkin, I notice her catching sight of her watch.

"Woops, I better get going. I don't want to be late for my date." She hurriedly gathers up her belongings, including a patterned shawl and a butter-colored leather handbag that looks like it cost more than my couch.

"You have a date on a Sunday night at nine-thirty?"

She checks her face in a sleek black Chanel compact. "Marco just flew in from Rome tonight."

"Is he your boyfriend?"

She laughs. "Not so much. He's just one of the guys I currently have in rotation. I'm not the settling-down type, I'm afraid. I think I'm cursed with a touch of Dating ADD. It was so nice meeting you, Miller! I'm really looking forward to sharing a house together. See you next weekend!" She gives me a double-cheek air kiss. "You should help yourself to my water. It will help soften the blow of the tequila later, trust me."

I take her advice and start downing her glass of water while signaling the busboy for a refill.

Hamptons Unwritten Rule #3:
The rules you really have to watch out for
are the ones you didn't even know about.

Before dessert comes, I end up sitting between Andrew and Michael, who have commandeered the end of the table after Jackson went out for his last smoke. When Jackson returned, Leah extended what I thought was a bit of an obvious invitation—since she had been watching the door like a hawk until he reappeared—for Jackson to sit next to her. Between the two of them, there is a whole lot of hair-futzing body language going on: her flipping to his raking.

"I'm so glad Jeff and Rachel didn't end up doing the house this year. This group is much better," Michael is commenting to Andrew.

"I know, they're nice people, but they would've thrown off the whole house vibe we seem to have going on," agrees Andrew as he digs his fork into the communal flan in front of us.

"Jeff was more fun before he started dating Rachel," Michael adds. "Now he's just whipped."

"Who are Jeff and Rachel?" I ask.

"They were in my house last year. They didn't come in as a couple, but they left as one," responds Andrew.

"And from what I hear, Jeff totally choked on the August First Rule," Michael says, aiming his fork at the last bits of flan. "He was lucky it didn't backfire on him. That could've been a disaster."

"I'm lost. What's the August First Rule?" I ask.

"Should we tell her?" Michael asks Andrew. "The information could be dangerous in the wrong hands."

"Good point," Andrew answers, sitting back to size me up. "We don't know her very well. . . ."

Even though I switched to water halfway through my third margarita, the tequila is still yielding its influence over my actions. "Come on, tell me! See! Look at these hands! So not dangerous!"

Andrew leans forward to pretend-inspect my hands. "It's okay. She's clean."

Michael turns back to me. "The rule is that you should never hook up with anyone in your summerhouse before August first. Think of it as a social safety net. Let's say you fool around with someone in June, and then you decide you're not going to keep things going for whatever reason—you were just horny and drunk when it first happened and you don't really like the person more than as a friend, or you meet someone you like better, or you just want to date around—whatever. For the rest of the summer, it can make things awkward in the house. And then if you meet someone else, you feel weird and guilty about bringing them around."

That makes some sense, but a part of me can't help feeling somewhat dismayed that people actually police themselves in this regard until a certain date and are comfortable being so blatant about wanting to keep their options open. And that there's a rule for it. *A rule with a name.*

"I think we freaked her out," Michael says to Andrew.

"No, I'm just trying to understand," I say. "So, what if you really like someone in the house? You have to wait until August first to do anything about it?"

"Yup," Michael answers. "It actually works out much better to wait. It gives you a chance to get to know someone first as friends. And it's not as if they're going anywhere—they're going to be in your house all summer—so what's the rush? Not to mention, the Pre-August Hookup isn't great for the house dynamics all-around. When something happens in the house, it becomes everyone's business, whether you like it or not. I've seen situations like this spin way out of control. One summer, these two people in my house hooked up, just once but on Fourth of July weekend. Within a week they stopped talking to each other, and it even caused a rift in the house for the rest of the summer, because the girls took this girl's side against the guy. It became a major drag for everyone."

I narrow my eyes at them. "Is this a guy thing? Because you think girls can't handle being casual? It sounds like you're implying that it's always the girls who get upset."

"No, not necessarily," Michael answers. "It works out for both sexes. I mean, yeah, nine times out of ten, it's the girl who's looking for more and is all bummed out when the guy wants to keep things cool, but if everyone just waited until August to act on their impulses, then the chances of a situation imploding are far less. Or, at least, even if it implodes in August, you only have a few weeks left to suffer the consequences."

"Sounds like you've broken the rule once or twice," I posit.

Michael and Andrew exchange inscrutable glances. "Nope, not me. I wouldn't be that stupid," Michael replies taking a last swig at his beer. "I never shit where I eat."

"Andrew? How about you?" I ask.

"Me?" He laughs. "Sorry, ma'am. I don't kiss and tell."

2.

Destination Transformation

I decide to walk home in the hopes that the fresh air will both stop my head from spinning and make me slightly less tipsy. But neither of those things seems to be happening, as evidenced by the fact that I almost got run over by a cab. I go into a deli to buy a bottle of water, guzzle down half of it, and set back out on my journey downtown.

Since it's such a warm night, there are still some people out and about in Union Square, so I make a detour into the park. I walk over to the dog run in the southwest corner and sit down on a bench nearby. At this time of night, there are only a handful of dogs and their owners in the run, but I still find it soothing to watch them as they chase after tennis balls and sniff each other.

When my best friend, Alice, and I lived together on Fourteenth Street, we used to get iced coffees and position ourselves outside the fence surrounding the run to watch the tableau of canine antics. We especially loved seeing how the dynamic changed every time a new dog joined or exited the run. Sometimes we would give the dogs voices and make up their conversations. The dog owners probably thought we were insane, but Alice and I considered ourselves to be downright hilarious. We always knew how to entertain ourselves and make each other laugh.

Sitting here, it occurs to me that ever since Alice got married and moved to the Upper East Side—realizing two of her biggest life goals—we haven't done our doggy-talk routine in probably almost four years, although admittedly for the last two, I haven't done much of anything with anyone.

Which is how this whole summerhouse-with-a-bunch-of-strangers thing came about in the first place: as a drastic measure to get me back into the game of life. But even that required a more extreme measure on the part of my three best friends, namely the Animal Planet Intervention. It feels to me as if all of this happened overnight, but it's been one week. I guess considering how long I've been out of it, relatively speaking a week *is* overnight.

The Animal Planet Intervention commenced last Sunday afternoon, when Jerry and Jimmy—who are also the sole employees of my company, MillerWorks—led by Alice—who has a penchant for acting like our boss even though she doesn't work with us—appeared unannounced at my apartment. They had jointly decided that it was time for my two-year-long self-imposed "Personal Hiatus" to end. The timing of their visit seemed arbitrary at first, but I should've known better. These three are anything but arbitrary.

They found me wearing what Jimmy, the dedicated slave to fashion among us, called my Depression Couture Collection: Old Navy "Just Bottoms" pajama pants, a ratty tank top, and a Camp Beverly Hills sweatshirt from the 1980s that had come out on the losing side of a short-lived fixation with *Flashdance*. I was watching an *Animal Cops: Houston* marathon on Animal Planet, even though I had already seen every episode multiple times. The color of my hair, which used to be brown, had grown increasingly nondescript, not to mention the fact that it hadn't been cut since Alice and Scott's wedding two years prior. And since I pretty much hadn't washed it any more recently, it was hanging halfway down my back in my new favorite hairstyle: the lifeless, greasy ponytail. Food had become nothing more than essential fuel. As a result, I was at my all-time thinnest, which I don't think my friends even realized, since all my clothes were about two sizes too big.

My apartment was in equally appalling shape. From my religious TV viewing, I had been sucked in by the promise that all the various cleaning wipes would provide ease, convenience, and protection against vast arrays of bacterial microbes, meaning that actual water and soap entered into my home-care routine these days infrequently at best. Had my friends come later that evening, they would've found me sitting by candlelight, because most of my lightbulbs had blown out and I hadn't bothered to replace them, despite the fact that I lived across the street from the Astor Place Kmart.

I'm ashamed to admit that this all had become absolutely normal to me, but it hadn't always been this bad. Luckily during the first half of my voluntary house arrest, I went through a compulsive phase, scrubbing the bathroom and the kitchen until it was sparkling almost every night as a therapeutic release of nervous energy but more pathetically, as my sole source of entertainment. But in the last year or so, probably around the same time that I officially started MillerWorks, any energy I had funneled away from domestic upkeep went toward starting up my business. My friends, however, had not witnessed the alarming downward spiral of my home until last Sunday. None of them had been to my apartment in quite some time, because whenever we hung out, I'd always go to their places. Jerry and Jimmy, who lived together in the West Village, had DVR and a monster flat-screen HDTV, so I'd go there to watch *Ugly Betty* with them. And on Sunday nights, I usually had dinner at Alice and Scott's.

But having the three of them standing in my living room slack jawed and speechless—and I could tell, not a little bit grossed out—and seeing the tableau through their eyes made me a wee bit horrified. I had become weird. And now my weirdness was being outed.

After Alice ordered me into the shower—"Wash, rinse, repeat!"—she directed me to the couch. She and Jerry sat on the coffee table in front of me, forming an impenetrable barrier (and, I noticed, blocking the television, which they had turned off and covered with a TVLand beach towel).

Alice started the proceedings. "Tori, you've turned into one of those socially phobic, depressed people in that prescription drug commercial."

"You mean the one where the loser person is staring out the window at the next-door neighbors having a party in their backyard? I think that's Paxil," Jimmy said as he poked around my living room, picking up things between his thumb and forefinger, sneering at them in disgust, and then dropping them right where he found them.

"I thought that was the commercial for Zoloft," Jerry replied.

"No, Zoloft is the one with that circle animation thing that looks like a sperm with a face—"

"You want me to start taking psychotropic meds?" I asked.

Alice covered my hand with hers. Her engagement ring looked like it had just been cleaned and shined. As I stared at it, I felt like Superman being weakened by the mere sight of Kryptonite. "No, but we *do* think you need to make some drastic changes, and we're going to help you."

"What are you going to do? Call Time Warner and get my cable disconnected?" I attempted. My normally quip-happy friends didn't laugh or even smile. Suddenly, I was nervous. These people meant business.

"I'm afraid we're way past that point, sweetie." Jerry removed his Elvis Costello–inspired glasses and pinched the bridge of his nose, a clear sign that he was pained.

Just then Jimmy, who had wandered into my bedroom, came running back into the living room holding my pink Rabbit Habit Vibrator with a wad of tissues. "Tori No-Middle-Name Miller! I cannot believe you! What are you thinking?!"

"What's wrong?" Alice asked, panic in her voice.

"There are no batteries in this thing!"

Jerry and Alice gasped.

"It's worse than I thought," I heard Alice whisper to Jerry, who nodded solemnly.

. . .

Looking back on the last two years, I'm amazed at how easily and quickly I was able to slip right out of my own life, retreat into that hiding place. My life seemed to go from so good to so bad so quickly, that I never even put up a fight.

For the year leading up to what became the Big Slide, I was enjoying what I call the Early Thirty-Something Hum. Over were the seemingly endless identity searching, money scraping, and social seesawing of my twenties—or so I thought. It was as if the present I got from the universe for my thirtieth birthday present was a clue. And with that, I was able to recognize and appreciate how everything had finally fallen into place.

After spending an absolutely miserable year and a half of working at a network I called Heinous TV, I was offered a more senior position at what was one of the most lauded network start-ups in cable history, Dream Job TV, as I affectionately called it. After Alice moved out of the apartment we shared on Fourteenth Street and in with Scott on East Seventy-seventh Street, I found an amazing rent-stabilized one bedroom with much-coveted southern exposure on Fourth Avenue just north of Astor Place. A month before my thirty-first birthday, Alice and Scott were getting married and I was going to be her maid of honor.

To top it all off, things were going strong with my first serious boyfriend, Peter, whom I had been with for a year and a half. Not only was Peter Bernstein the first guy I had ever exchanged the L-word with, but also being with him made me understand for the first time in my life how people know in their heart of hearts that they've found The One. It wasn't that before I met Peter I didn't believe in the existence of The One, but based on my relationship history, my theory was that not everyone gets to find it, just like not everyone can win the lottery or land a part in a blockbuster movie or live in a penthouse apartment or be tall. But with Peter I was convinced that I had at least won the relationship lottery: we were best friends, spent all of our free time together, laughed all the time, liked each other's friends and families, and were thoroughly attracted to each other. With Peter, there just never seemed to be any questions; there were only answers.

Thirty had turned out to be so good that I couldn't wait to see how thirty-one was going to top it.

Turns out, I didn't have to wait until my birthday to find out. In fact, I only had to wait until ten minutes after Alice and Scott's wedding reception. That's how long it took for Peter and me to hail a cab. And for him to break up with me.

I never saw it coming.

Sure, Peter had been acting a little off that night, but I didn't think much of it. He had been the model of patience while I had attended to my myriad M.O.H. duties in the months leading up to the wedding and had even volunteered to help orchestrate Scott's bachelor party, since Scott's two best friends lived out of town. So even though he was spending more time in the hotel lobby than in the ballroom, I wasn't about to complain.

Eventually, the band played their last song. After a quick stop at our table to grab the bouquet of flowers I had carried down the aisle, I went to collect Peter from the lobby. The doorman at the Pierre Hotel hailed us a cab, and soon Peter and I were heading downtown. He was quiet as I chattered on about the wedding.

Then he said my name. "Tori." Since he only ever called me "honey" or "sweetie," I knew something was wrong right away. I froze. He began to speak in a strained voice. "After seeing Alice and Scott tonight, it occurred to me that while I care about you a great deal, love spending time with you, and think you're an amazing person, well, the thing is, I don't think I can marry you, and I thought I should tell you as soon as I realized it. So, I think we should end things."

I'll never forget the cabdriver's name, because I kept staring at his license in an effort not to burst into tears: Slohim Sloham. Or maybe it was Sloham Slohim. Whatever it was, I remember thinking that his name sounded like "You win some, you lose some."

So in my state of shock, the only thing I said in response was, "You win some, you lose some." And then, despite my careful, practiced staring, I buried my face into the flowers and burst into tears. He put his hand on my leg, but that just made me cry harder. I must've completely freaked Peter out because he didn't say another word until we pulled up in front of my building, when he asked Slohim Sloham to wait because he wanted to continue on to his apartment on the Upper East Side. Then Peter got out and came around to open my door.

"I'm so, so sorry. I know this is for the best." He kissed me on the cheek, gave me a loose hug, and then slid back into the cab. I watched as the taxi sped to the corner, made a left turn on Ninth Street, and disappeared.

I realized much, much later that I never asked Peter *how he knew.*

I stood there for some time, alternating between silent shock and full-on sobbing, still holding the crushed bouquet in both hands. I prayed that the Slohim Sloham would loop his cab back around the corner and deposit a chastened Peter at my feet, who would plead temporary insanity and beg me to forget his ludicrous pronouncement. But of course that didn't happen. When I could finally breathe and see again, I held the flowers aloft to hail another taxi to take me to Jimmy and Jerry's apartment in the West Village. Then I threw the flowers into the street. I imagined I felt them being crushed by the tires as we pulled away from the curb. Or maybe that was just my heart.

So the Big Slide went like this: ten minutes after my best friend's wedding, I was dumped by the love of my life. Thirty minutes after my best friend's wedding, I was at Jimmy and Jerry's place, bawling every last internal organ out of my body all over my pink taffeta bridesmaid dress, inconsolable until midmorning the next day. Three days later, I peeled myself up off my bedroom floor, where Jimmy and Jerry had deposited me, and dragged my sorry ass back to work. Fifteen days after that, I turned thirty-one, alone and miserable.

Five weeks later, Dream Job TV—aka the only thing keeping me going—announced that they were so sorry (join the club), but they had to lay off the thirty-five most recently hired people. I was number thirty-four. They sent me on my way with one week of severance, three weeks left on my health insurance, and, inexplicably, my stapler.

Five and a half months after that—and a mere two weeks before my unemployment was up—the management company for my apartment building sent me a letter saying it was going condo and I needed to pony up $400,000 to buy my apartment or be out within three months.

And that wasn't even rock bottom. I'm actually not sure when I sunk to my lowest low, but I'm told by my life-support staff that I became erratic at returning their phone calls, stopped showering and changing my clothes as frequently as I should, and all but ceased going out anywhere other than to Alice and Scott's on Sunday nights for my only meal of the week that wasn't delivered by someone on a bicycle.

Eight months had gone by since Peter had dumped me when one Sunday night after dinner Scott, bravely ignoring the fact that I hadn't showered all weekend, sat down with me to study my finances—at Alice's behest, of course.

"Tori, what's this? You have eighty-four thousand dollars just sitting in this account. Did you know about it?" Scott asked.

"I knew I had something. I inherited some money when my grand-mother died, but I don't remember it being that much."

"That's because it was like half that thirteen years ago."

"But I can't really touch it. My parents said I should save it for a rainy day."

"I don't know if you've looked out the window recently, but it's *pouring*. This could help you with your down payment and then some. And you seem to be getting decent freelance work these days."

"Yeah, in fact, I just got a new project from A&E and asked Jimmy and Jerry to help out on it on the side."

"Have you ever thought of starting your own business? Don't look at me like I'm nuts. The truth is, you kind of already have, and it would help you with taxes and insurance if you incorporated, especially if you plan to hire Jimmy and Jerry more often." After a few more Sunday evenings sitting next to Scott in his home office, staring over his shoulder at spreadsheets with numbers on them that I couldn't believe had anything to do with me, MillerWorks was born and a down payment was made on my apartment.

One would think that having a renewed purpose in life—and some security that home ownership affords—would lift a person out of their emotional quagmire.

Not so much.

What it did do was give me something into which I could throw myself while studiously ignoring the fact that I had for all intents and purposes flatlined my social life. I scared up as much business as possible and then persuaded (read: begged) Jimmy and Jerry to give up their current perma-lance jobs to work with me. Then we killed ourselves to come in early and under budget on every project to improve our chances of being hired again and start establishing a solid reputation for MillerWorks.

More than a year had gone by since Peter dumped me. My personal grooming habits hadn't improved much nor had I taken any steps to wrench myself out of social hibernation. But everyone, including me, rationalized that those things were the result of my being so engaged with my business as opposed to being any scary signs of actual depression.

It wasn't until Peter was gone that I realized how small my social circle had gotten, especially now that I wasn't working with a large department full of people who were always up to something fun after hours. In the interim, most of my college friends had gotten married and moved out of the city. When Peter and I were together, we had spent much of our time with his friends, many of whom were couples, going out to great restaurants, attending dinner parties, and heading out of town for long weekends. After Peter disappeared from my life, so did his friends and my active social life right along with him. Still, despite this growing awareness of how disconnected I was, the last thing I wanted to do after months spent building my business from scratch was to rebuild a social life. So I didn't bother. And no one gave me any kind of marching orders to that end.

Until last Sunday night's Intervention, which is when Jerry, Jimmy, and Alice finally told me it was time to get over it and get the hell on with it. And they were there to share their brilliant plan to help me do just that: they wanted me to join a summer share house with other single people in the Hamptons. Their argument was that doing so could be the most expedient path to an instant social life. And since it was the middle of May, they reasoned, the timing was more than opportune.

"Okaaay," I countered, "let's say I'm willing to consider this outrageous plan of yours. You two"—I pointed a crooked finger at Jerry and Jimmy—"besides being the most married-unmarried couple I know, are doing your share on Fire Island again this summer. And you, my dear Alice, are not only actually married, but also will be hiding out in your private love shack in the Berkshires with the

Hubs. Do you people know anyone doing a house? Because I sure
don't. And I'm certainly not about to go into one of those god-awful
Westhampton party houses that are always posted on Craig's List
with a bunch of lunatic twenty-three-year-olds. Besides the fact that
my twenties are thankfully a distant enough memory, you know I
took that vow after graduation to never again drink beer from a
funnel."

"We've got that covered," Alice replied, as efficient as ever. "A
woman Scott works with has a friend whose cousin is running a
house in Sagaponack." She handed me a piece of paper with the
name "Leah Brewster" and an e-mail address written on it. "I already did some preliminary research. The people in the house are
single, in their thirties, and from Manhattan. Not everyone knows
one another, so you won't be the only newbie. Someone dropped
out at the last minute, so there's one spot left. This Leah person is
expecting your e-mail to work out the details. And whatever you
can't afford to pay, Scott and I will float you."

I was stunned into silence. And submission.

"Can I tell her the even bigger surprise?" Jimmy asked. Jerry nodded. "Tori, you know our wacky friend Ms. Percy from our
summerhouse in Fire Island? He and two other guys have been cast
for a reality show pilot on Hurrah! It's a makeover show called
Three-on-One. And guess what? They want you to be on it!"

"As what? Their fag hag?" I joked.

"Not exactly. They want you to be the first person they make
over," Jerry said cautiously. "You know, little things: they'll cut and
color your hair, get you some new clothes, maybe fix up the apartment a little. They won't be doing anything major—no identity-
changing plastic surgery. Put it this way: after you're done, you
won't have to get a new picture for your driver's license. You'll still
be you."

"Only better," Jimmy adds. "With maybe a few more highlights.
And some blush."

"Now I'm beginning to think you're the ones who should be taking drugs. I might-maybe-*possibly* be willing to go through with this share house nonsense, but I am not about to humiliate myself on national television!"

"Right now, it's just the pilot. The show hasn't even been picked up as a series yet. And you know how these things go; chances are it will never even see the light of day," Jerry reasoned in the soothing tone he usually reserved for talent when they became petulant and irrational during long, exhausting shoots.

"Plus, you'll get loads of free clothes and a complete head-to-toe makeover, or 'Transformation' they're calling it," Jimmy said, "and honestly, you could use both. Desperately. Not to mention, could the timing be any more perfect to get yourself all spruced up for your big Hamptons debut?"

"It's not like I've never *been* to the Hamptons before. Alice and I did that house in Amagansett six or seven years ago," I argued.

"That rat hole? We only rented it for a month with four other people we knew from college and none of us even had a car. I don't think that really counts," Alice responded.

"More importantly, getting involved with the show could give us the break we need for MillerWorks," Jerry added, "especially considering how long we've been trying to get business from Hurrah! since they rebranded and became the 'It' cable network. Ms. Percy said that he would get us a meeting so we could show them our reel and pitch them our business." Jerry, I noticed, being my soul mate of sensitivity, had a miserably guilty look on his face, because he knew full well he had painted me into a corner. And I knew that at that very moment, he hated himself for it. "It's time to take Miller-Works to the next level. We've been doing well, considering we're only a year into it, but we need to land some bigger projects. We were only hired to do one upfront sales video presentation this year. Next winter we should have so many lined up that we need to bring on freelancers."

"And you think we can't do that if I don't get a makeover—sorry, *transformation*—from Ms. Percy and his band of merry men?"

Jerry looked down while Jimmy looked away. Meanwhile, Alice just looked lost.

"What?" I insisted. "Is there something I should know?"

Jimmy elbowed Jerry and mumbled, "Go on, tell her. She needs to know."

Jerry grimaced and then reached out for my hand. "Some people were talking at the NBCUniversal Cable Entertainment upfront party. They said . . . they said this business is all about image, and that ours—well, yours—isn't exactly an image they want to project. That if we want MillerWorks to succeed, we have to walk the walk, not just talk the talk."

"But our work is stellar!" I cried.

"I know."

"Jimmy's graphic design is the most inventive in the business! And your editing is so lyrical it's like poetry."

"I know and thank you. But that's what they're saying, kiddo. The three of us have sacrificed so much to get this company off the ground. Can't you at least consider making this one small concession so MillerWorks can grow and ensure its future, *our* future?"

"Sounds like fate to me," Alice said, slapping her hands on her thighs. "How often does something like this fall out of the sky, not to mention at the right exact moment that could benefit you professionally and financially in the long run?" To her credit, Alice sounded like she was trying to convince herself as much as me.

"I don't know, you guys. . . ." Before I could begin listing the at least dozen reasons why this was clearly from the Planet of Bad Ideas, the door buzzer cut me off. "Who the heck could that be?" All of a sudden, the expressions on the faces of my three friends went from ballsy to sheepish. Correction: Jerry and Alice looked contrite; Jimmy actually appeared excited. "Oh no . . . Please tell me you didn't . . . they're not here right now, are they?"

Oh but they were.

A few minutes later we were sitting before the newly minted Transformation Trio: TO-mas, the hairstylist/herbalist; Frederique, the makeup artist and ayurvedic skin-care expert, and Percival Alexander Woodhouse III, aka Ms. Percy, the fashion stylist/spiritual advisor/life coach. Ms. Percy explained how the Trio and their production company were scheduled to begin shooting the pilot for their show the next day, but their original victim had come down with the chicken pox (or chickened out, I thought was more likely). It was too late to reschedule the shoot, and Ms. Percy thought I'd be "purr-fect" to replace her.

I still wasn't convinced. After all, recent downturns in my personal appearance and lifestyle aside, my paychecks came from being the person behind the camera, not in front of it. As much as I loved TV, I had zero desire to ever actually appear *on* it.

After twenty solid minutes of pitching, Percival Alexander Woodhouse III bore his dark brown eyes into mine and said, "Girl! You got to *drive the bus.* Whatcha gonna do? Be a passenger forever? Or worse, keep missing the darn thing? You have to stop wasting your most precious resource, honey, the one even *we* can't help you with. Do you know what that is? It's *time.* You ain't ever gonna get that back. No amount of shooting up Botox or nasty drastic plastic surgery is gonna turn back the clocks, but you're still too young for all that, so don't get me wrong. What Ms. Percy is saying is that Mother Time is doing her thing: marching on, with or without you. So, now listen up good. Are you listening? Climb up those steps, sit that bony, white, never-gonna-be-J.-Lo's ass down in the front seat, and *drive the bus,* girl. *Drive the bus.*"

If anyone knows about the contrived nature of television and especially how unreal reality shows are, it's me. I've been working in packaging and selling shows for almost my whole professional life. I knew these dudes were nothing more than three handsome, fashionable, and semientertaining gay guys from Chelsea who didn't

possess any magical powers, but when I heard Ms. Percy say "drive
the bus," something inside me snapped. What had I been doing to
myself for the last two years? Where did I go? How did I manage
to lose myself so completely that I required not only an intervention from my best friends but also the help of self-professed pro-
fessionals?

"Have I really gotten that bad?" I gasped through a sudden rush
of tears.

Six heads nodded in response.

I nodded back and mouthed "Okay" as Jerry, Jimmy, and Alice
launched forward to fold me into a protective group hug.

. . .

After the Intervention, everything moved at warp speed. By Monday morning, the preproduction team had taken over my apartment, setting up cameras and lighting equipment while one of the
producers preinterviewed me and had me sign numerous release
forms. Tuesday, Wednesday, and Thursday were spent shooting:
the first day in my apartment, which was practically dismantled and
fumigated—come to think of it, that's what they did to me too; the
second day out in the "field" at stores, spas, and salons; the last day
back in my apartment for the big reveal. And on the fifth day, they
saw that all was good and so they rested.

After three days spent being sized up and clucked at ("That the
Down-in-the-Dumped Diet you've been on has done wonders for
your figure and kept that pesky BMI down. And you're certainly
taller than the average girl—what are you, five seven? Five eight?
But what's with those knocky knees and elbows? It must've been
awful being this gangly in junior high! I bet you tried the whole
ballerina thing but were just too clumsy to pull it off, am I right?"),
snipped and colored ("Was this bucket-of-water-after-washing-
Daddy's-Beemer-in-the-driveway the color you were going for, or
can we give you a richer brown with some auburn highlights? This

lovely little natural wave will be the thing to save you. I'm thinking of something Shalom Harlow-esque in last year's Tiffany ad
campaign."), stripped, primed, and painted ("As the Lord above is
my witness! Boyfriends! Will you take a look at those eyes? Am I a
handsome southern gay black man or are those eyes almost *green*?"),
and finally my closet raided and reassembled beyond recognition
("Where are my rubber gloves? Really, Tori, *eight* pairs of Old
Navy cargo pants?! Why not just buy a box of Hefty bags; they're
even cheaper, you can buy in bulk, and they come in the same
palette you have right here."), as I sit in Union Square watching
the last dog being led out of the run, I reassure myself that the
whole humiliating yet thankfully secret events of the past week
just may have proven to be an invaluable dress rehearsal for starting
my new summer share house, which, after my experience at the dinner tonight, I suspect isn't going to feel much different from being
a regular on a reality show. And, for my trouble, I scored a mini
summer wardrobe almost worthy of a Hilton sister, a few pieces of
which I wore tonight in the hopes of convincing my new housemates that I'm one of them. Or, at least, that I got the uniform
right.

As I start walking the rest of the way home, I push aside the nag-
ging thought that beyond the off-camera, preproduction pep talk,
the Trio didn't spend any airtime on my internal transformation.
But after seeing the look of dire concern on the faces of my beloved
friends last Sunday night, I accept the fact that the time has come.
It's do or die, ready or not. I can't disappoint my friends, because
doing that means failing at living my life. And I can't afford to do
that for one more minute.

With the help of the Transformation Trio, I know I look the
part.

At the urging of my friends, I know I have to play the part.

What I'm not sure of is how to *be* the part.

When I voiced my concern to Alice before I left for dinner tonight, she said, "Don't worry! Just be yourself." I wanted to ask, But what do you do if you have no idea who that is anymore?

I guess I'll just have to keep my fingers crossed that since I'll be wearing this season's correct mix of ethnic and metallic, no one will notice.

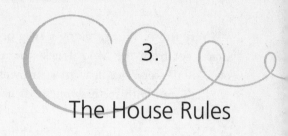

3.

The House Rules

Hamptons Unwritten Rule #4:
The faster you know who you're dealing
with in your summerhouse, the better
off you'll be.

The next morning, I'm slumped over the conference table at Miller-Works seriously hung over. Thank god for the Krispy Kreme doughnuts, also known as the official foodstuff of our weekly Monday morning meeting.

"I still don't understand. Why was Leah calling you 'Miller'?" Jerry asks.

I have just told Jerry and Jimmy, among other salient details about last night's dinner, how not only had Leah insisted on calling me by my last name, but also how now everyone in the house thinks that's my name. "Maybe because my e-mail address is 'Miller at MillerWorks.com'?"

"But not one other person has made that mistake since we started the business."

I sigh. "I know. I corrected her about ninety times, but it was as if she just didn't hear me."

"Or maybe she didn't *want* to," Jerry says, arching an eyebrow.

"I can't keep all these crazy house people straight. I need to visualize this." Jimmy goes to the white board, uncaps a purple erasable marker, and writes "Miller's Housemates" across the top.

"Very funny," I say, taking a swig of the now lukewarm coffee that I got from the Mud Truck, the mobile coffee vendor that's parked in Astor Place near my apartment.

"Let's start with the easy ones. Michael is 'Captain CrackBerry,' right?"

"Absolutely. He didn't put that thing down all night other than when he was trying to make the moves on me. At least, that's what I *think* he was doing, but I sure hope not. Jim, that Magic Marker reeks. It's making me more nauseated than I already am."

"Look, Ms. Hampton-Pants. Who told you to drink last night like Lindsay Lohan on her eighteenth birthday? What kind of first impression is that? At least you didn't say anything to embarrass yourself. Or did you?"

"Not to my knowledge, but you don't have to keep waving that thing in my face."

"Easy people, let's not get excited here," Jerry says. Unfortunately, he is quite used to refereeing sibling-esque spats between Jimmy and me, mostly due to the fact that Jerry is eight years older than we are. "Let's make the clearly fabulous Cassie the 'Fashionista Socialista.' And your *roomie* Stacy can be what, the 'House Mouthpiece'?"

"I hate to make fun of her, because honestly, the girl couldn't be more well meaning, but after Cassie left, she talked my ear off. She spoke so fast, I could barely keep up. And before you say something snarky, Jimmy, it's not just because I was drunk. That girl's body must be producing a natural form of speed."

"I don't really care about the girls so much," Jimmy says, rolling up the sleeves of his brand-new lilac-and-white-checked Paul Smith shirt to protect it from the marker. "The boys are *far* more interesting." His comment is met with a stack of mini Post-its hitting him in the side of his head. "Really, Jerold. Was that necessary?" Jimmy's hand flies up to smooth down his dark brown gelled hair.

I think the reason the three of us act like siblings (though never in front of clients or colleagues) is because, in a way, we grew up together. We met more than ten years ago when I was still trying to figure out a career direction and was temping at various entertainment companies in the hopes of narrowing down the choices and making rent. Eventually I was placed in a long-term assignment in the On-Air Promotions department at Nickelodeon as the creative director's assistant. Desperate and short staffed, they soon offered me a full-time position, which I happily accepted. I was nothing more than an underpaid gopher, but eventually I started pitching concepts and writing scripts, even though I had neither been asked nor was I expected to do so at my level. But my boss always mawed on and on that he didn't care where the good ideas came from, as long as they came, so whenever I nailed a pitch, he let me run with the spot.

Not only was Nickelodeon the hallowed place of my career awakening, it was also where I met Jimmy and Jerry, who weren't yet dating but who were already bickering as if they were. Jimmy— or James Bradley Cabot III, originally from Virginia and a recent graduate from the School of Visual Arts—was an adorably smug junior on-air graphic designer and clothes-whore-in-training. Jerry Bloomberg, a skinny, bald, nervous Jewish man from the Bronx known for his signature oversize black plastic glasses that we used to joke he was born with, was "slumming it," as he called it, producing and editing promos while he waited for his big break directing documentaries, which sadly never came. Jerry would act as if he was suffering our youth, immaturity, and inexperience, but it was obvious he was never happier or laughed more than when he was with us. And that Jimmy was the perfect, sarcastic, yet bravely outspoken foil to his more serious, retiring demeanor.

"Now, Jackson: Hugh Grant?" Jerry asks.

"Hugh Grant before he got cheesy, bitter, and saggy or now?" Jimmy counters.

"Definitely before, but with better teeth," I answer. "But I think we should go with 'The Wild-Card' for Jackson. I haven't quite figured out how he fits in, but he's the one true anomaly. And you can put Abigail down as 'Absentee Abby,' because the House Mouthpiece told me that Abigail's parents not only own a huge house in Southampton, but also she has a new boyfriend whose family has an estate on the water in Connecticut, so chances are she will never be at the share."

"We love that kind of housemate," Jimmy says as he writes.

Jerry rubs both his hands over his shiny bald dome as he squints through his thick glasses at the board. "And, of course, Leah has to be 'Queen Leah, the Imperious.' "

"Although I'd probably drop 'the Imperious' during casual conversation," I joke.

Jimmy's lips move as he takes silent inventory of the board. "So, that leaves . . ."

"Andrew," I supply. "I got this one." I take the marker from Jimmy and write in large block letters: THE MAYOR.

"Really!" Jerry says.

I describe how Andrew spent the evening expertly working not only our table, but also two other tables filled with people he knew, like a young Frank Sinatra on a Saturday night in Vegas. "He's cute, charming, smooth, nice, smart, and everyone worships him, even the guys. A real man of the people."

I catch Jerry giving me his concerned look, which I've become rather used to recently. "Seriously, sweetie, how are you doing with all this? A lot has happened to you in only a week. Last night can't have been so easy for you."

"I was *fine*. I mean, yeah, I was nervous. That's why I think I drank so much, for the social lubrication."

"How many margaritas did you have?" Jerry asks.

"I stopped halfway through my third and switched to water."

"That would be two and a half more than you've had in the last two years total," Jimmy points out.

"What my life partner is not so subtly implying is that you might want to tread lightly around these new people until you get to know them better and vice versa. It may sound as if we're giving you a hard time, but we're just looking out for you. We might've fallen down on that job before, but damned if we're going to let it happen again. You now have a prime opportunity there for the taking, and these people sound like they're going to be highly entertaining and be just the thing to draw you out of your hiding place. You look better than you have in years, thanks to the Trio. Now we just want you to have a truly fantastic, fun-filled summer. You deserve it."

The trepidation I was feeling on the walk home last night threatens to well up in my chest again. I stand up and go over to the window, looking out at what Jimmy calls our "million-cents view": the backside of the brick building across the air shaft. But as I look outward, something catches my eye. There's someone else staring out the window. It takes me a second to click into the fact that that person is *me*. How could I not recognize myself? The old me is still there, mostly around the eyes, but as I stare at my reflection in the glass, I truly begin to see the new me for the first time. And you know what? This Miller person doesn't look half bad. Ms. Percy was right: it's time for her to climb up those steps, sit down in the seat, and start driving the damn bus already.

I turn around and face my partners in crime. "Look, if the Transformation Trio managed to turn me into a presentable human being again, then I can at least not waste their hard work. And as the two of you and Alice brilliantly suggested, what better place than the Hamptons to try out a whole new me?"

"That's the spirit, *Miller*!" Jimmy says.

Jerry smiles broadly, the worry gone from his face. "You're going to knock 'em dead."

Hamptons Unwritten Rule #5:
The "Summerhouse Guidelines" may
not be etched on stone tablets, but you
better treat them as if they were.

To: SummerHouse2007_contacts
From: Leah.brewster@morganstanleybank.com
Date: Tuesday, May 22, 2007
Re: Summerhouse Guidelines

Hi Everyone,

It was good seeing you all at dinner Sunday night. I hope you're as excited as I am for a great summer. Thanks to my hard work, we have a solid group and a killer house. Having run shares for the last two years, I've found it's best to lay out a few simple guidelines to ensure everyone is on the same page before the season begins.

1. Each person is assigned a bedroom, either alone or paired with a roommate, depending on the level of share you bought, for the entire summer. Note: there will be no room switching.

2. Since everyone has their own assigned space, please respect one another's privacy. That means not going into other people's rooms or using their belongings without their permission. Even if the person is not out for the weekend, it is up to that person's discretion whether or not they want to let someone else, either a house member or another member's guest, sleep in that room for the weekend. (See Attachment A: The Guest Policy for more.)

3. Everyone has a full share, meaning you're all allowed to come out every weekend between Memorial Day and Labor Day. You will not be refunded for unused time, so like they say about the FLEX plan, use it or lose it.

4. The house is available for you to use during the weekdays. All house guidelines still apply. You won't be guaranteed weekday time alone, as the house is still a share house, even during the week.

5. Please keep the common areas neat and clean up after yourselves. It shouldn't be that hard to put your glasses and dishes in the dishwasher

(BTW, putting them in the sink doesn't count). And if the dishwasher is full, here's an idea: turn it on!

6. I will be taking care of all the finances and paying our bills out of a house fund everyone contributed to in the cost of their share. I will also purchase basic house supplies such as paper goods, bath soap, laundry detergent, etc. If you see that we're running low on anything, please write it down on the list I will be posting on the refrigerator. NB: Food, alcohol, and Red Bull are not included.

The guidelines go on for several more pages, covering everything from smoking, laundry, garbage, house phone usage ("Don't bother giving out the number, because no one wants to deal with other people's calls"), suggested parking configurations for the driveway, and where the spare house key is hidden. The Guest Policy Addendum alone is two pages long. She concludes with a warning:

If for some reason following these guidelines doesn't fully ensure you a seamless experience and you find yourself having an interpersonal problem, please note that I'm only organizing the house and its accompanying logistics, not playing referee, resident advisor, relationship coach, or UN peacekeeper. Please take all measures to deal with your issues directly with the person(s) involved, as that will be the most efficient and yield the best possible outcome.

Now let's have fun!

Ciao, Leah

"Holy shit!" Alice exclaims as she flips through the pages I've printed out and stuffs a California roll in her mouth. We're at our favorite sushi restaurant, East, on Third Avenue, which we lovingly refer to as The Happiest Place on Earth, because it has a conveyor belt that constantly ferries small brightly colored plates of sushi rolls around the sushi bar. It's the ultimate in instant gratification. " 'Guidelines,' my ass! These are hilarious!"

I, however, am not laughing.

"Stop it," she commands, pointing her chopsticks at me. "You're freaking out. You can't possibly be taking this seriously! Rules-schmules." She tosses the guidelines aside, causing her dish of low-sodium soy sauce to splash onto the paper. I snatch them back and dab at the brown stains with my napkin.

"In our old summerhouse, we never had rules, much less a nota-rized twenty-page document."

"That's because the house was so crappy, it didn't matter what we did. The landlord was just thrilled that someone was actually willing to pay him to rent his shit hole."

"I liked our house. We had a great summer there. We were a family—the good kind."

"I'm not saying we didn't have fun, but we were in our twenties, and not only did we not know better, we couldn't afford better. From the photos I saw, this house looks about a hundred times nicer than even the house I grew up in, and Leah probably just wants to make sure that you guys don't lose your security deposit because some asshole trashed the place."

"I suppose, but it's just so different now! Going to the Hamptons used to mean spending the summer hanging out with my closest friends. Now it means living with a bunch of strangers who don't seem to be anything like us, complicated rules, a fancy house, al-ways wearing the exact right outfit, and having cute boys around twenty-four/seven."

"Sounds awesome to me. This is going to be so good for you, I know it." Then a serious look crosses her face. "And this just *has* to work. Otherwise I don't know how else to fix what I did."

"What did you do?"

"I know I've never admitted this to you before, but I can't help but feel like it's my fault you ended up depressed and alone."

"Are you kidding me? Why?"

"Because I'm the one who forced you to go out with Peter in the first place, and then he broke up with you because Scott and I got married."

"That's not what happened, and you know it."

It was true that I went out with Peter, who played in Scott's tennis league, because Alice strongly recommended that I do so. I resisted the idea for months, having come to despise blind dates ever since a particularly horrible incident in high school involving a guy with a braided rattail, black Capezios, and a red Camaro. It was also true that from the way Alice described him, I was worried that Peter was more her type—aka the Marrying Kind—than mine—aka a Struggling Blank, as in a Struggling Painter, a Struggling Musician, etc., whom I had favored in my twenties.

But after a particularly long dating drought and, truth be told, a fair amount of pressure from Alice, I gave her the green light on the condition that we double date. Because we were trying to get together around the holidays, the only night that all four of us had free was New Year's Eve 2004. We decided to go to a party being held by some of Scott's business school friends who rented out a grungy industrial loft in a still godforsaken part of downtown.

It wasn't love at first sight, not because Peter wasn't good-looking, nice, and tall—he was. Since I couldn't help but go into the night holding tightly to the preconceived notion that he was going to be as straightlaced, serious, and—I'm ashamed to admit it— boring as Scott, Peter was already starting from a deficit before he even walked through the door. But then he pleasantly surprised me by playing against type: he stole one of the last bottles of champagne from the bar (very un-Scott-like) and used it as bait for me to join him in the back stairwell. While we passed the bottle back and forth, we fell into an easy banter, and before long we were actually flirting. I noticed he was smart and quick-witted. He got all my pop culture references and was interested in hearing about my job. He knew a lot about a lot, but not in a pompous way. Granted, he lived on the Upper East Side, worked at an investment bank (at least it was on the Internet side), was seven years older, had perfect manners, and didn't like to dance—all contributing to Alice's Marrying Kind standards—but still had enough edge to be reminiscent of my beloved Struggling B.'s.

By the time midnight came, I wanted him to kiss me. Badly. But Peter only gave me a polite, friendly peck on the cheek. I thought perhaps I had misread the signals. It wouldn't have been the first time.

We stayed at the party for a couple more hours. Then he offered to take me home. Since there were no cabs to be found, we took the subway, which was packed with other taxi-less revelers. He got off at my stop and walked me to my building.

It had turned cold, so we pressed our bodies together to keep warm. We weren't exactly hugging, since our hands were shoved in our respective pockets, but there was a distinct lack of personal space, the good kind. His breath smelled like wintergreen Tic Tacs.

"Have you made any New Year's resolutions?" he asked.

"I thought I might join a gym."

"I expected something slightly more original from you."

"Wait, you already have higher expectations of originality from me and we just met . . . uh . . . five hours, twenty-six minutes, and seventeen seconds ago? I don't know if I can take that kind of pressure."

He laughed. He had a good laugh. "Well, isn't being original a requirement for your profession? You're lucky my standards aren't even higher!"

"*I'm* lucky!"

"Actually, scratch that. *I'm* lucky to have met you tonight. I thought I was going to be on the worst, most awkward blind date of my life."

"Thanks a lot!"

"Like you weren't thinking the same exact thing! You gotta love Mr. and Mrs. Cupid. They are a very sweet, well-meaning couple, but come clean, you didn't have a lot of faith in their matchmaking abilities, did you?"

I giggled. "I thought you were going to be like Scott."

"Which is what?"

"Oh, no you don't. You're not getting me to rag on Scott! How do I know that you won't go back and implicate me?"

"You think I'd rather get on their good side than yours?"

I had nothing to say to that. So he kissed me. A real, deep kiss. Our noses and lips were cold, but the inside of his mouth was warm and minty. And curiously sweet.

. . .

Now Alice says to me, "I spent so much time feeling horribly guilty about what Peter had done to you. By the time I realized how bad things had gotten, I felt so helpless, like there was nothing I could do to help. . . ."

"You're helping me now. And you and Scott did so much for me over the last two years, not the least of which was Scott saving me from homelessness. And you suffered plenty of weekends with me in the Berkshires. I can't imagine hanging out with Gloomy Gus was too much fun for either of you."

She smiles. "I hated that you were sad, but I loved being able to spend so much time with you. You have to promise to come up this summer. Scott still can't get your secret trick for s'mores right. He pouts when the chocolate isn't melted perfectly. It's pathetic. And sad." We both laugh. "As much as it pains me to say this because I'm going to miss you terribly, it will be good for you to find some new, well, at least single friends to hang out with." She stuffs her last Mexican roll in her mouth.

"Are you pushing me out of the nest?"

She nods as she finishes chewing. "Fly. Be free."

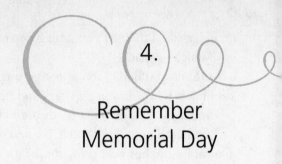

4.

Remember Memorial Day

	May					
Su	Mo	Tu	We	Th	Fr	Sa
		1	2	3	4	5
6	7	8	9	10	11	12
13	14	15	16	17	18	19
20	21	22	23	24	25̸	26̸
27̸	28̸	29	30	31		

Hamptons Unwritten Rule #6:
Getting there is half the battle on a
typical summer weekend, but the whole
battle on a holiday weekend.

I'm scrunched up in the corner near the train door, straddling my huge suitcase. There are about fifteen other people squeezed into the vestibule with me, also in various luggage-straddling poses. The sweat that was trickling down my back earlier is now dry, leaving my skin clammy and shirt damp.

Believe it or not, this is progress.

It's been so long since I've done the Hamptons Trek that I had forgotten what a zoo Penn Station can be on a summer Friday afternoon.

44

On top of that, I didn't leave enough time to actually get to the station and I missed the Cannonball, aka the express train, which would've only taken me two hours to reach Bridgehampton. I managed to catch the one after it, which was scheduled to take at least forty minutes longer than the express. My biggest misstep was when we arrived at Jamaica station in Queens, where you have to switch trains: because I had taken a seat in the middle of the car on the first (and shorter) leg of the trip, I was among the last to board the connecting train across the platform. I think I saw a child actually get trampled as the hordes of khaki-clad Wall Streeters and ruffled miniskirted twenty-somethings pushed their way through the doors to score seats first, leaving those of us who were slower on the uptake to stand as a huddled mass in the vestibules for the remaining part of the journey east.

Finally, the train begins making the stops for Fire Island and the cars start to empty, freeing me to not only stand up straight again, but even change position. When we reach the first few towns in the Hamptons, Volvo station wagons and BMW SUVs spill out of the parking lots, as beautiful, relaxed, uncrumpled women line the platform holding the hands of their children, who look as if they just came from a photo shoot for Ralph Lauren. Every station is a tableau of heartfelt family reunions: kids running toward their arriving dads, who scoop up their genetically blessed progeny and greet their wives with a kiss. A perfect picture of privilege.

No one is waiting for me in Bridgehampton. It didn't even occur to me to try to coordinate traveling with my housemates or ask any of them to pick me up from the train. A lonely feeling washes over me as people hustle past on their way to do something that's surely fabulous.

"Where ya goin'?" A rather large woman is talking to me. "Do you need a taxi? I have one more spot."

"Oh, uh, Sagaponack, Sagg Main Street. They said it's just south of the highway?"

"Get in." Somehow this woman has unwittingly saved me from my own despair, which, as it turns out, isn't as far away from the surface as I was hoping.

. . .

Finally, after dropping off the other five people who were in my minivan-cum-taxi, we pull into a gravel driveway surrounded by twelve-foot-tall hedges that leads us to a driveway-cum-mini-parking-lot in front of a white shingled house that wasn't visible from the road. It's nearly seven-thirty.

After paying the driver an absurd amount of money for what should've been a four-minute ride, I walk into my new summer digs. I find myself in a vast, high-ceilinged room that looks like it was once a barn. The living room, dining room, and kitchen all occupy the main space though are separated by half walls or bookshelves. The ceiling is the original exposed wood underside of the barn roof. In obvious contrast to this rustic look is the lush-looking furniture, which is eclectic in style but clearly all expensive. The wall at the far end of the room and directly opposite the front door is made up entirely of glass, which overlooks a gleaming pool nestled in the U between what looks to be the two wings of the house.

"Hello?" I call out. Silence is the only reply, which isn't surprising, since there weren't any cars in the driveway. The kitchen looks as if a stampede of elephants has trampled through, stopping to empty several bottles of white wine and leave their dirty glasses behind. I wonder if Leah is aware of this flagrant infraction of the house guidelines only minutes into the beginning of the summer.

The Trimline phone on the kitchen counter suddenly rings, making me jump.

"Miller? Hi, it's Stacy, your roommate! Where are you?"

"Didn't you just call me at the house?"

"I mean, why aren't you at the restaurant? We were waiting for you to get here before we ordered dinner. I left you two messages on your cell. Didn't you get them?"

I ask her to hang on while I go back to the front hall to retrieve my cell from the depths of my tote bag. The little screen is blank except for the time. No messages. But also, no signal. "I must not have reception out here."

"We're at a place called Alison in Bridgehampton on School Street. Leah isn't too happy because she convinced them to let us sit down even though we weren't all here because she told them you were on your way." She tells me there are numbers for taxis on the side of the refrigerator. "You can dump your stuff in our bedroom—it's the yellow one in the North Wing. Hurry!"

I have no idea which way is north, so I rush through the living room, picking up my bag where I left it, and speed down a hall full of closed doors. The first room is green, a variety of men's clothing and sports equipment strewn across the bed. The next door reveals a similar room, but painted brown and not yet occupied. At the end of the hall is the most palatial bedroom I've ever seen. It has a king-size four-poster bed that is so high off the ground it probably requires a ladder to scale it; a fireplace; an enormous walk-in closet that's almost as big as my bedroom at home; and a bathroom replete with two sinks, a Jacuzzi tub that could fit four, and a free-standing glass and chrome shower. Much to my disappointment, not only is the room blue, but also there's evidence of male occupation.

Clearly, I'm in the wrong wing.

Back around the other side, there's a cheerful room with two full beds, but it's covered in periwinkle and white print wallpaper. At the end of the hall is a mirror-image of the master suite on the other side of the house, only it's mauve and the closet is filled with a stunning array of expensive women's clothes and accessories.

A room that's fit for a queen, if you ask me.

Two doors left: one is a laundry room and right next to it, across from the bathroom, is a room that's not much bigger than the laundry room. Two twin beds with prim white coverlets are crammed side by side, separated by a narrow nightstand. This room is the smallest by far. And it's yellow.

As I rifle around my suitcase in search of my toiletries kit, I find myself making a silent prayer that the House Mouthpiece doesn't work the midnight-to-eight A.M. shift or it's going to be a very long summer.

. . .

"Look who finally made it! Ms. Chronically Late to Everything!" Leah exclaims over the chatter-filled din of the restaurant, causing the entire table of my housemates to stop talking and stare at me. Déjà vu. Leah, who is kitted out once again to the nines with the most amazing Pucci miniskirt and gold and wood high-heeled slides, her legs long, lean, and self-tanned, strides over to me. "But I'm sure you'll make it worth the wait," she says loud enough for everyone to hear, even though she's right next to me. "We're *starving*, but Stacy insisted on us waiting for you. It's so cute how your roommate is watching out for you, isn't it?" Hair flip.

"I missed the Cannonball and my cell seems to have terrible reception out here."

"No worries. But the hostess had to take the chair we were holding for you, so you'll just have to squeeze in. 'Kay?" One more hair flip signals that she's done with me.

Thankfully, Cassie waves me over to her end of the bench along the wall, where she makes just enough room for me to squeeze in, as long as I stay balanced on one butt cheek. I find myself greeting her as if she were an age-old friend instead of someone I've only technically met once. Now I understand why the place is so loud: over-enthusiasm.

"Hey, you!" She gives me a double air kiss. "How's the house? Does it live up to the pictures Leah sent around? I had every good intention of stopping there first, but the traffic on the L.I.E. was such a disaster that I had to come straight here, even though I look like a fright." She looks nothing but amazing in a khaki skirt and gold knit tank top.

I describe the house to her. We figure out that the room she and Abigail are theoretically sharing is across from mine and Stacy's.

"Leah told me we're in a separate wing from the guys, as if *that's* going to stop the shenanigans from happening," she says.

"Do you think that's what she was trying to do?"

"No, I'm just kidding. I think she did it for more optimal bathroom-sharing purposes, which I fully appreciate." She suddenly leans across the table to throw her arms around the neck of a very tall, dark, exotic-looking stranger. "José!" I make room so she can squeeze out past me. "How *are* you? I had a feeling I was going to run into you. You'll be at Johanna Stern's dinner party tomorrow night, right?" They chat for a few minutes. "Miller?"

It takes me a second to respond, given that I'm still getting used to my new Hamptons alias. "Yes?"

"I'm sorry for cutting our conversation short, but I haven't seen my friend for months. Do you mind if I just grab a quick drink with him at the bar?"

"Not at all," I say, feeling slightly disappointed that she didn't invite me to join them.

"You're a doll! I'll be back in a few." José puts his arm around Cassie's waist and steers her toward a stool at the bar that's just being vacated.

With various housemates needing to slide out to go to the bathroom or say hi to the new people streaming through the door as frequently as planes landing at J.F.K. Airport, it's not long before Stacy and Leah end up across from me.

"I'm still trying to keep everyone in the house straight! A couple of people aren't here, right?" I ask them. "Will Abigail be out this weekend?"

"She's up in Connecticut at her boyfriend's place," Leah responds.

"How does she fit into the group?" I ask.

"She's one of my best friends," Leah says. "I can't even remember how we met, it was so long ago. She used to stay at her parents' place in Southampton, but this year she wanted to do a share because she had just broken up with her boyfriend and wanted a more social situation. But in typical Abigail style, she started dating this new guy a few months ago, so I don't think we'll see much of her."

"I'm sorry to hear that. I mean, I'm glad she found a new boyfriend but I'm sorry that you won't have your best friend here with you."

"Eh, whatevs. I'm used to it. She's been a serial monogamist as long as I've known her," she says, taking a sip of her cocktail. "That's why I'm so glad I recruited Cassie."

"Have you known Cassie for a long time too?"

"Actually, no. I didn't meet her until last fall, when she was dating a friend of someone I was going out with. She and I hit it off better than either of us did with the guys. Eventually, we both ended up getting rid of the men but kept in touch with each other. But with our crazy-busy schedules, it's been almost impossible to get together. We finally managed lunch a few months ago. When I told her about the house and she realized she already knew some other people who were doing it, she agreed to be in it on the spot, especially because it will make it so much easier for us to hang out."

Cassie, I notice, is still being chatted up at the bar by José and another tall, dark, and swarthy type. She doesn't look like she's headed back to our table to hang out with either Leah or me anytime soon.

Stacy, having only semipatiently waited for her turn, pipes in. "And the way Leah and I know each other is because she and my sister went to business school together. My sister and her new husband stay at her in-laws' house in Bridgehampton, so they didn't need to do a share house. And a bunch of my friends ended up in a big house with like twenty-five people in Quogue. But I didn't want to do that because I knew it was going to be a total twenty-something party house like it was last year. All they do is drink beer out of kegs, stay up late being really loud, skinny-dip in the Jacuzzi, and then sleep off their hangovers by the pool. Most weekends they don't even go to the beach! And there are always random people all over the place because everyone brings guests out or hooks up. And I kept getting my stuff stolen! I've outgrown that sort of thing."

"Your roommate is our token twenty-something," Leah says to me, as if Stacy isn't sitting right there.

"How old are you?" I ask Stacy.

"Twenty-six *and a half*," she says, unwittingly proving at least one difference between people in their twenties and those in their thirties: after people leave their twenties, they stop counting in half years, if they even continue counting at all. "But I much prefer the vibe of a thirty-something house, so my sister called Leah to ask if I could be in this house. And here I am!"

"It sounds like it all worked out," I say.

"Totally. I'm really excited." But the look on Stacy's face belies her words as she quickly casts a glance rife with uncertainty at Leah.

"I haven't see Jackson. Is he coming to dinner?" I ask.

"He's not coming out until tomorrow morning. When I spoke to him earlier, he said that since he hates traffic and couldn't get out of work early enough to beat it, he decided to wait and just lay low in the city tonight," Leah answers.

"How did he come to be in the house?"

Leah narrows her eyes at me. "Why are you so curious about him? Are you interested in him?"

I have a sudden flashback to the Pre-Summerhouse Dinner of Leah and Jackson competing for the Gold Medal in Hair Flipping and begin smelling the shit I might've just stepped in. "No! Nothing like that! I just didn't get a chance to talk to him much when we met, so I was just curious about how he fits in, that's all."

The muscles in her neck relax. "Abigail and I met Jackson last winter at the launch party for that book *Raging Mania*—you know, the one that was on all the best-seller lists by James Cheever? It was genius. Anyway, Abigail knows James from growing up in the city, so she was invited to the launch and took me. Turns out, Jackson is James's editor at Farrar, Straus & Giroux, so when James introduced us to Jackson, Abigail and I thought that they'd be great people to add to the mix."

"So, are they both in the house?"

"Unfortunately, no. James said he has to rewrite his new book this summer thanks to Jackson's apparently heavy-handed edits. But Jackson, well, let's just say, he had a couple of very good reasons to join this house." She concludes with a hair flip and a self-satisfied look on her face.

I sit back, confused. So, does that mean that the August First Rule Andrew and Michael told me about is only a guideline, not a rule? I guess I'll find out soon enough.

. . .

I awake to my very first morning in the house, accompanied by my very first Hamptons hangover, courtesy of a very late night out.

Last night, as I followed in the wake of my housemates as they touched down at every nightclub in Southampton Township, including Stereo by the Shore, Pink Elephant, and Dune (in search of what exactly, I never found out), our posse grew in size due to the bevy of pretty girls who were vying for the attentions of Michael and Andrew. A couple of these girls—Blonde and Blonder—followed us home for an impromptu after-hours party. Almost immediately, a new female hierarchy established itself. The Visiting Team Girls easily trounced the Home Team in the male attention competition, causing the Home Team to throw in the towel and retire to the North Wing with minimal protest.

After making myself semipresentable (it occurred to me it would feel weird to walk out in my pajamas in front of a bunch of virtual strangers, especially guys, so I got dressed), I now stumble out into the living room to find my housemates up and about. People are strewn around the living room, including Blonde, who is idly flipping through *Star* magazine on the couch next to Andrew, while he peruses yesterday's *Wall Street Journal*. It's unclear what if anything happened between the two of them last night. The TV is set to News 12 Traffic & Weather, which endlessly loops alternating two-minute-long local traffic and weather reports, but no one seems to be paying attention. The remnants of our late-night munchie fest are gone. I pour myself a glass of water and guzzle it down while I look longingly at an inert Braun coffeemaker.

Leah strides into the kitchen. "We just sent Michael out to Twice Upon a Bagel in Wainscott to get coffee and bagels. He should be back soon."

"Oh, thank god," I say, which actually produces something resembling a half smile from Leah.

"Look who's up!" Andrew calls out to me as I walk into the living room. "It's about time, sleepyhead."

"I must not have heard reveille."

"Next time we'll make sure to blow the bugle a bit louder." Blonde, who doesn't seem the least bit self-conscious that she's wearing last night's clothes and isn't in her own house, doesn't bother looking up.

The front door swings open to reveal Michael, arms laden with a bag of bagels and a cardboard tray filled with Styrofoam cups of coffee, and Blonder, who not only doesn't bother helping Michael but instead steps across people's legs to deliver coffee only to her friend. After planting herself practically on top of Blonde, the two of them sip their drinks in tandem and point at things in the magazine and whisper to each other as if they were the only two people in the room.

I look at the House Mouthpiece to gauge whether or not she has the 411 on where and with whom Blonde and Blonder might have slept last night, but Stacy is too busy watching Michael and looking disappointed to notice me trying to get her attention.

"Consider this feast to be an opening weekend treat," Michael says, putting everything down on the table for us to grab. "Just don't drink my coffee. It's the jumbo one."

Hamptons Unwritten Rule #7:
It is essential to loudly denounce
Hamptons magazine, especially when
caught reading every single word
and studying every photo.

After I score a coffee and schmear low-fat cream cheese on my sesame bagel, I sit at the table next to Cassie, who is reading the thick Memorial Day weekend issue of *Hamptons*, the free seasonal weekly magazine focused primarily on gossip, celebrities, fashion, and party pictures supported by ads for outrageously expensive luxury items.

"You caught me," she says sheepishly. "It's such a rag. I know it has zero editorial merit, but I can't help but look through it every week. It's my secret vice. You won't tell my snobby bosses at *Elle*, will you?"

"Your secret is safe with me, as long as you let me see it next."

She begins flipping through, stopping to point herself out in a handful of party photos. "Most of these were taken last summer but there are some from parties in the city this past spring." She looks thoroughly gorgeous in every photo, accessorized with at least one handsome man by her side, but never the same one twice. I scan the captions, trying to recognize the names of the people she's with, but it is—and I am—hopeless. I've always been aware that there was a scene in New York and by extension in the Hamptons, but

I've never known anyone who was in it or how I'd gain access if I wanted to. And now, I live across the hall from someone who not only has access, but also seems to have a VIP membership. "God, why am I even boring you with this silly crap?" She sighs, slapping the magazine closed and pushing it away. "So, how was the rest of your night?" Cassie had begged off joining the rest of us on our after-dinner nightclub tour.

"It was fine, I guess." I tell her how Michael seemed to know the doormen wherever we went, so we didn't have to wait in line too long and got in without paying the cover. In order to actually sit at any of these places, you had to order bottle service, so for the most part we just stood around, trying to talk to one another, but usually the music was too loud to hear anything. "I don't know if night-clubs are really my thing," I conclude.

"I'm with you, kid. I can't stand that whole thing: the self-important bouncers, the fake guest lists, the overpriced, watered-down drinks . . . not to mention, anyone decent that you might remotely want to talk to is hiding in the VIP section anyway. I'm not sure I see the point, at least for me."

"What did you do after dinner?"

"I met up with a few friends for a drink at Prime 103, but I was home pretty early, which was just fine with me. Besides," she says with a catlike stretch, "it's a marathon, not a sprint."

"What is?"

"The summer."

. . .

Later in the day, the house settles down as people go off to play tennis, hit a spin class, or walk around East Hampton, since it's mostly sunny but too chilly for the beach. Still feeling woozy, I decide to settle myself in a chaise by the pool for a nap. Luckily, the patio area is protected from the breeze by the U shape of the house, so it feels much warmer in this spot than it does anywhere else outside. Piping through the outdoor speakers I've got on WEHM, which has been touting itself as "Progressive Radio for Long Island," even though they've been playing the likes of Neil Young, Bob Marley, and Steely Dan more than any single artist from this decade. I put my head back, close my eyes, breathe in the fresh air, and relax for the first time since I left New York.

. . .

"I hope you have some sun protection on that lovely pale skin of yours," says a deep, English-accented voice.

I open my eyes to see a silhouetted head wearing mirrored aviator sunglasses and a straw fedora. "Jackson, hi. When did you arrive?"

"Just about an hour ago." He makes himself comfortable in the chair next to me and lights a cigarette, careful to blow the smoke in the other direction. "Been here since last night, have you?"

"Yup."

"And how's that working for you?" He gives me a half smile, as if he already knows the answer. "Let me guess. You feel like you've been abducted, brainwashed, and relocated on alien soil." He takes a long draw on his cigarette.

"Actually, it was a tornado and my house landed in a strange land, killing a witch."

"She's dead, is she? Well, that's a relief. Thanks for doing my dirty work for me." I look at his face to try to figure out if he means someone in particular or if he's just playing along. All I can see is my transformed self reflected back in the twin mirrors of his glasses. "So, did you keep up with the professional party chasers last night?"

"How do you know *I'm* not a professional party chaser?"

"I know."

"Is that right? What else do you know?"

"I know you've got a good story, but I haven't quite figured out what it is yet."

"Really."

"Let me rephrase that: perhaps it isn't *good* in the happiest, most positive sense of the word. More like *good* as in interesting, intriguing. Something life changing, even. Something that has given you obvious character and depth."

"It gave me *some*thing, that's for sure."

"So I was correct."

My stomach does an involuntary flip-flop. I lean back against the chaise and look up at the sky. I knew this would happen eventually, but I was hoping it wouldn't this soon. So far, it's been easy for me to keep the direction of the questions flowing outward, to get information out of my new housemates without giving anyone the chance to cross-examine me, since most people love talking about themselves. I did too, until two years ago. For weeks after Peter broke up with me, I could barely have a conversation about the weather or what to have for lunch without crumpling into tears. Eventually, that raw sadness burrowed its way deeper below the surface, but even so, I didn't have all that much to say, especially with people outside of the inner circle. And now? I'm not so eager to share my tale of heartbreak and woe, recent status as an outcast of society, or, most importantly, my potentially televised Transformation. What if they think I'm cheesy for having been on a reality show or pathetic for having no life other than the one this summerhouse is affording me? Besides, I think that with Jimmy, Jerry, and Alice I've beaten to death the topic of the irksome inexplicability of my getting dumped.

Jackson sits up and puts his hand on my arm. "I must apologize. It's my naughty little pastime, figuring out what's going on behind the scenes with people, or at least those people who I can tell have a modicum of depth, but I need to remind myself that it's not always as much fun for my subjects. I can be a horribly impatient chap. I conveniently forget that there's this pesky little bit of actually trying to become worthy of someone's confidence and trust." I laugh. "Please forgive my impertinence."

"You're forgiven. Just don't do it again." I wink so he knows I'm kidding.

He salutes me. "Consider your healthy boundaries established and understood, Captain! Well, I'm sure you're already tiring of my hollow English charm, so I will leave you be. Thank you for humoring me. You're very kind." He snubs out what's left of his cigarette and stands up.

"Where are you off to?"

"I'm going to meet up with some mates for a beer at a fairly good replica of an English pub up in Sag Harbor."

"Already? What time is it?"

"Does it really matter?" He takes off his hat and runs his hand through his hair. "Remember what I said about the sunscreen. It may be cool out here, but the sun, like most things in the Hamptons, is deceptively wicked this time of year. Trust me."

Hamptons Unwritten Rule #8:
For singles of a certain age (not a minute
over thirty), Cyril's is the place to be for
Saturday afternoon happy hour. For
everyone else, it can be hell on earth.

Around four, I'm pulled out of my afternoon stupor by the shushing sound of all of the showers in the house running followed by a chorus of blow dryers (even, surprisingly, from the boys' wing), which are so loud they actually drown out the radio. I sluggishly trail into the house in search of the Mouthpiece to find out what's happening.

She's in our tiny room, fighting with a brush and a hair dryer to tame her wildly curly chin-length hair. I say something but she doesn't seem to hear me. "Stacy!" I shout, just as she turns off the dryer. She practically jumps.

"Miller, you scared me!"

"Sorry, but that thing is deafening! How can you use it?"

"I keep meaning to buy a new one, one of those quiet ones, but I never remember when I'm in the store. So I thought I'd bring this one out and leave it here, hoping that will force me to get a new one at home. But maybe it will annoy you too much. Will it annoy you too much? Because if it will—"

"No, it's fine. I just wanted to know what's going on. Why is everyone getting ready now?"

"We're all going to Cyril's for happy hour. Do you want to come?"

"Isn't Cyril's that divey, roadside seafood shack on the way to Montauk? I thought it was like forty minutes from here. Why would you go all the way out there?"

"Because it's the big après beach hangout for Saturday happy hour. I think most everyone is going. You should come! Isn't that what we're here for?"

It's only four-thirty and we barely stopped drinking twelve hours ago. What happened to lazy summer afternoons? But then it occurs to me that if everyone goes to Cyril's and continues on from there without coming back for me, I will be stranded here alone without a car or plans. Is that what I came here for?

"I can be ready in fifteen." I grab my towel from the hook behind the door and scurry into the steamy bathroom.

Hamptons Unwritten Rule #9:
Once you're out here, the preferred method
of travel is via the Luxury Car Caravan.

Forty-five minutes later, Stacy and I are in her BMW following Leah and Andrew in his brand-new gray Range Rover Sport. Michael is leading the pack in his black Porsche Boxster convertible.

The four of them looked at me like I was insane when I suggested we try to fit into one or two cars. I shut up after that and dutifully followed Stacy to her car so she wouldn't have to ride alone. She was nice enough to explain that though we're all going out together, we might not all stay out together, so people like to take their own cars to keep their options open, even if it means leaving their vehicles overnight in a parking lot and calling a cab if they're too drunk to drive.

As we approach Cyril's, we see people spilling out of Hummers and Lincoln Navigators parked bumper to bumper along both sides of Montauk Highway at least a quarter of a mile from the bar, which Stacy says means the place is going to be packed. This makes her excited. This makes me nauseous. Suddenly, Michael makes a U-turn. Andrew does the same, and Stacy almost kills us trying to stay behind him, cutting off oncoming traffic that's going at least fifty.

"Sorry!" she chirps as I pry my hands off the dashboard. We follow our caravan to the end of the line of cars to park behind Michael. We join up with our housemates for the ten-minute hike to Cyril's along the shoulder of Route 27. It's completely freezing, since the sun has disappeared behind some large clouds and the breeze is whipping strongly across the dunes. I can hear the pounding music and see the fratlike party happening just ahead. No wonder Cassie bowed out of coming. A dinner party with José hosted by Johanna Stern, whoever she is, sounds like it's much more her speed. And right now, mine as well.

At the door, a large, steroid-filled man in a muscle shirt asks for my ID. He eyes me against the picture on my driver's license about three times, as if I were trying to crash a party at the Playboy Mansion. I think about telling him that I look different because I've recently been "Transformed," but he doesn't look like he would think that was funny or interesting. Finally, he clamps an orange plastic bracelet on my wrist too tightly. I catch up to the housemates. Someone hands me a plastic cup with lukewarm beer that tastes like cat piss. I manage to find a spot in the corner where I'm only jostled every thirty seconds instead of every ten. The majority of people here seem to be in their twenties and already drunk. For the men, the uniform seems to be T-shirts with the sleeves cut off, backward baseball hats, cargo shorts, and dirty sneakers. For the women, tight tank tops revealing a roll of pale belly fat over too-mini miniskirts is clearly de rigueur.

As I stand shivering and stupefied against the wall, an anxious feeling begins to creep over me, making me think that I'm shivering not only because I'm cold. Could I be having a panic attack? What if I faint? Will anyone notice? Or will *everyone* notice? Do I really care if a guy wearing Teva sandals and a YOUR MOM'S IN MY TOP 8 T-shirt sees me pass out? This is bad. I need to calm down.

Call Alice, that's what I'll do. She'll say the right thing. I dig my cell phone out of my handbag and jab at the speed dial, but all I get is that sad, droopy, call-failed *da-doop* sound. I press the key harder, because of course sheer effort will help get my call connected. *Da-doop*. I try three more times before I realize I have no signal. It's the story of my life.

Suddenly, the crowd surges and I'm pushed back against the wall. A guy who is trying to squeeze by me loses his balance and knocks into me, sloshing both of our beers down the front of my shirt.

"Sorry, lady," he says insincerely before making a clean getaway.

As I fight to control tears from springing into my eyes, a familiar voice from beyond the beyond reaches my ears, pulling me out of my spiral. The voice is calling my last name. My eyes focus to find Andrew standing in front of me, solid, sturdy, real, and grinning. I must look odd because he immediately gets serious and asks me, "Is positioning yourself in the corner your thing?"

"What do you mean?"

"You sat in the corner at the table last night and barely spoke to anyone. And here you are again, all alone." His eyes avert from mine and flick down to my chest. I can't even bear to look down to check if my T-shirt has become transparent. "I see the problem. It's obvious."

"I can't hold my beer?" I attempt.

He laughs. "That and a girl like you shouldn't be drinking this crap beer in the first place. I think we need to do something about that right now." He offers me his hand, which I take. Suddenly, I feel calmer. He weaves us through the crowd toward the bar, barely turning his head as people call out greetings to him.

"Tony! Long time, no see!" Andrew clamps hands with the surfer-cum-bartender.

"Yo, dude! It's Mr. Andrew Kane, esquire! Was wondering where you were! It wouldn't be a Hamptons summer without you," Tony says. After a brief conversation, he produces three cups for Andrew. "On the house. Consider them your welcome back present."

"You rock, Tony, as always." He throws down a five-dollar bill. Andrew turns to me. "Try this." He hands me an opaque pink drink and a cup of seltzer without ice with a wad of dry napkins. For my shirt, he indicates. "If that doesn't take care of it, I've got a clean shirt in the Rover. It's not as cute as the top you're wearing, but it's dry."

"Thanks," I say, feeling myself slowly coming back to the surface.

"Just promise me you won't hide in the corner all night. Deal?" He squeezes my arm and heads in the direction of Blonde and Blonder, who I didn't even notice were here. I mop at my shirt with the club soda and pat the whole thing dry as best I can with the napkins. Feeling slightly better, I go off in search of Stacy and Leah, who I can bet are nowhere near a corner.

Hamptons Unwritten Rule #10:
The thrill has to be in the chase, because
no matter what you're doing, there's
always something better going on.

From Cyril's, our caravan makes a pit stop at La Fondita, a take-out Mexican joint in Amagansett for mounds of chips and salsa, beer, and fish tacos. Back in the parking lot, I stand amazed as I witness

an impromptu Mobile Device Ballet: each person either has a phone
up to one ear or is typing furiously on a handheld. Without even
looking up, they're circling one another, somehow managing never
to bump into one another, as if they've been practicing this elaborate dance for months. After a few minutes conferring with the
group, they break from their huddle (I half expect them to clap,
bump chests, and grunt) and return to their respective vehicles.

"It's too early to go to the clubs—they really don't get going until eleven-thirty or twelve—so we're going to stop by a couple of
house parties in Wainscott, which is just past East Hampton," my
personal Mouthpiece, Tour Guide, and Driver informs me.

I start doing the math: if we started the evening's activities at five
and we're just hitting the clubs at midnight then that means we're
not getting home until . . . no wonder these people guzzle Red Bull
like it's Gatorade. "Whose parties are we going to?"

"Someone Michael knows told him about them."

"Is it all right for him to bring all of us? Was he invited, or does
he just know someone who was invited?"

"I'm sure it's fine," she says, backing up the car and getting back
in line behind Michael's Porsche, which is currently burning rubber
out of the parking lot for no apparent reason other than because he
can. "They sounded like they were open things."

It is now nine-thirty as our caravan heads westward. We turn
right off Route 27, the primary single-lane road that traverses the
Hamptons and is typically clogged with traffic, into a neighborhood
just north of the highway that is filled with several new, prefabri-
cated houses. Even from my one summer in Amagansett I was
aware of the Civil War–type distinction between North and South
in the Hamptons. For most residents and renters, houses north of
Route 27, aka Montauk Highway, are typically less desirable because they are farther from the ocean beach, which is south of the
highway. Land north of the highway tends to be much hillier and
woodsier than the land south. The strict zoning laws south of the

highway have also kept development to a minimum, meaning property is worth a ton more—not that any of it is exactly affordable.

When we get closer to where the first party is supposed to be, there aren't many cars parked on the street and people are driving away in the ones that are. Michael pulls over so he can talk to some girls who are leaving.

Almost immediately, Stacy's cell phone beeps with a new text message. "This party's over but there's another one a few blocks away, which is supposedly still going strong," she says. Soon we're parking our car and joining several people heading toward an overflowing mini-McMansion at the end of a cul-de-sac.

Outside on the deck, there must be at least seventy-five people standing around the pool. The crowd is thankfully older than the one at Cyril's, and the people seem to be more interested in chatting with one another than doing Jell-O shots. Within minutes, my housemates resume their now familiar party stances: the guys go hunting for women and the girls stand in a circle, pretending to talk but, it seems to me, waiting to be hunted. A coterie of female admirers has instantly formed around Andrew as Michael tries to horn in on the action in search of any spillover.

So Andrew doesn't see me in a corner again, I force myself to join Stacy and Leah, even though they are talking to people I don't know. At first, no one acknowledges my presence, but then a girl next to me introduces herself and we chat for a little while. Though our conversation doesn't extend beyond where are houses are and how many shares we've been in, I begin to get into the rhythm of the party patter.

My conversation partner soon excuses herself to go join the ranks of Andrew Admirers. I can't blame her. He is like a magnet. Almost everyone who comes outside knows who he is and goes right over to him, as if they were seeking to gain admittance into his court. I notice a high proportion of his fans are predominately thin, well-coiffed women who bestow affectionate kisses on his cheek and stay close by his side, although there are also a considerable number of guys in the fan club. It's as if his job is to entertain newcomers to the party, effortlessly performing the duties as the Mayor of the Hamptons.

A position he seems born to hold.

Hamptons Unwritten Rule #11:
Even when you're not in the Hamptons,
you need to be talking and thinking
about being there.

Alice and I are on the phone first thing Tuesday morning for our first round of Weekend in Review.

"How was it? Tell me everything. Start at the beginning."

So I do. "And get this: I found out Leah and Michael fooled around a couple of times last summer!"

"No! Who told you?"

"Stacy Mouthpiece told me, of course. They hooked up at Andrew's supposedly famous annual birthday party last summer—aka *the first night Leah and Michael met!* And then Stacy said they got together one more time after that, but that seems to be it—or at least, as much as Stacy knew. Poor thing."

"Why 'poor thing'?"

"Stacy didn't admit anything to me but it's pretty obvious from the way she followed Michael around all weekend that she's jonesing for him big-time. But if I had to guess, despite whatever happened with Blonde or Blonder, I'd say Michael is still holding out hope that this summer will be his opportunity to be with Leah again, which is so not going to happen because Leah couldn't be more about Jackson."

"The scandal! The intrigue! The only action we get in the Berkshires is when they run out of pies at the farmers' market. That's when the shit really hits the fan." We laugh. "So overall, how do you think your first weekend went?"

"Pretty well, other than being completely wiped out by Monday. As the weekend went on, I definitely began to feel more comfortable." I decide not to tell her about my near panic attack at Cyril's. "I think I figured out the trick. All you have to do is go with the flow. Everything just sort of happens organically."

"Just by being there, you're included."

"Exactly. At first I was worried that I'd be more on my own, but in fact you actually have to make an effort to do something by yourself. It's like there's this tacit understanding that because we're housemates, we're going to do everything together. Except Cassie. For the most part, she did her own thing, especially at night, but no one was mad or took it personally. Except maybe for Leah, but she would never say so."

"Leah's ego aside, it sounds like it was a fun weekend, and even better, that you're fitting in and enjoying yourself. I think this is the first time since you were with Peter that we are both happy at the same time."

"Alice! Did you have to choose now as the time to bring up he-who-I-told-you-shall-not-be-named?"

"I'm sorry, but now I feel like he is definitively past tense. Don't you? You've never seen him since, well, you know, that time after the wedding, you never hear from him, and you *certainly* won't have to spend one second worrying about running into him out there."

"That's true." In addition to espousing the endless benefits of the city in the summer, Peter always thought the Hamptons were overpriced and overblown. He claimed to hate the crowds and the traffic and that the people who went there cared more about the scene than the scenery.

"Let's rewind ten seconds and forget I even mentioned him."

"Done," I respond, suddenly feeling deflated. "How was your weekend?"

While she describes her bucolic weekend in the Berkshires with Scott, I feel a tug pulling me back to the safety and anonymity of their spare bedroom—bigger than the one I'm paying $7,500 to share with Stacy—and the comforting sounds of Scott turning the pages of the newspaper and Alice making coffee, even though I know that that's their life, not mine.

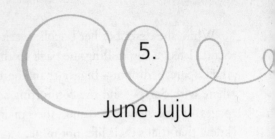

5.

June Juju

May	Su	Mo	Tu	We	Th	Fr	Sa
			1	2	3	4	5
	6	7	8	9	10	11	12
	13	14	15	16	17	18	19
	20	21	22	23	24	25	26
	27	28	29	30	31		

June	Su	Mo	Tu	We	Th	Fr	Sa
						1	2
	3	4	5	6	7	8	9
	10	11	12	13	14	15	16
	17	18	19	20	21	22	23
	24	25	26	27	28	29	30

It's official: I have a social life.

Or, at least, I have the in-box of someone with a social life.

Only a few short weeks into the summer and I've noticed a decidedly sharp increase in the amount of my daily personal correspondence. I love watching the e-mails fly back and forth as plans for the weekend are suggested, evaluated, and then either rejected or confirmed. Most weeks we can count on an e-mail from Absentee Abigail, who informs us she's not coming "this" weekend, except for once earlier this month when she actually made an appearance at the house. However, despite her much-anticipated arrival (by Leah), A.A. spent the entire time scowling because she kept missing calls from her boyfriend, who was on a business trip in Hong Kong.

I'm combing through my in-box one Wednesday morning, devouring my personal mail before getting to the work-related ones, when I see an e-mail from Cassie arrive:

To: miller@millerworks.com
From: Cassandra_Dearborn@ElleMagazine.com
Date: Wednesday, June 13, 2007
Re: Want to come with . . .

> . . . me to a party on Saturday night?
> c.

Every weekend so far, Cassie has stayed true to the pattern of having an enviably packed social calendar that's mostly separate from whatever the rest of us are doing. She has been nothing but friendly to me whenever she has been around, but she has never asked me to join her in any of her reindeer games. Despite Leah's pronouncement about how sharing a house was a surefire way for her and Cassie to hang out more frequently, I haven't seen much evidence of that happening beyond them going to an occasional spin class together when Leah isn't suffering the day-after consequences of her lavish drinking habit. Some people just like flying solo, I figured.

"Guess who Cassie just invited to a party on Saturday night?"

"Don't you mean the Fashionista Socialista on whom you have a secret Sapphic crush?" Jimmy, holding a fresh cup of coffee, comes up behind me to peer over my shoulder at my computer.

"I do not." I minimize the e-mail screen before he gets a chance to read it.

"Okay, right. You just rave on and on about how effortlessly gorgeous she is and how fabulous her clothes are and how she's always dashing off to dinner parties and how handsome, debonair men are constantly falling at her feet because you *don't* have a mad crush on her."

I backhand Jimmy's stomach, causing coffee to slosh out of his Gay Pride Month 2007 mug.

"Hey, there, k.d. lang, watch the new Ferragamos!" He makes a big show of inspecting his tan suede driving shoes for nonexistent coffee stains.

"The invitation sounds like a very positive development," Jerry says. "I knew Cassie would eventually come around to seeing how you're her perfect Hamptons Wing-Woman."

"So where's the party, big shot?" Jimmy asks. "Is it at a house or a nightclub or restaurant or what?"

"I don't know."

"What kind of party is it? Cocktail party? Fancy sit-down affair? Casual BBQ?"

I frown.

"Well, maybe you can find out just a tweensy bit more information and then I can see what I can do about getting more excited." Jimmy spins on his leather heel and strides back to his desk. "Don't give me that look. What if she's planning to drag you to her sixty-five-year-old boss's boring annual family BBQ somewhere icky, like Westhampton?"

I open Cassie's suddenly inscrutable e-mail and try to read between the lines. Westhampton or Georgica? Genuine invitation or sucker offer? Obligation or opportunity?

"Don't listen to him," Jerry soothes. "It will probably be something fabulous. As soon as you tell her you're in, I'm sure she'll fill you in on all the delicious details."

Jimmy rolls his eyes. "Now can we puh-lease talk about the BuzzTV branding project? We haven't even begun addressing their notes, and we're supposed to present our ideas to their SVP of marketing on Friday. I heard TrainTrax is also pitching the business, and I'm not about to let that bitch Colin Campbell win the gig over us."

"First of all," I say, "it's time for you to get over the fact that Colin has won more Promax/BDA Awards than you have, and second, we'll get the changes done. Just give me a second to send this e-mail." I turn back to the computer, click reply, type "Cassie, That sounds great. I'd love to join. Can't wait to hear the details," and press send.

Hamptons Unwritten Rule #12:
Always hold out for the best offer, even
if it comes at the last possible minute.

But the response with all the "delicious details" never came. In fact, I never heard a peep after I replied to Cassie's e-mail on Wednesday. As the week went on, I began to think that perhaps I imagined the whole thing—and maybe it was better to operate as if I had.

Cassie didn't show up at dinner with the housemates on Friday night at Bamboo, an upscale Japanese restaurant in East Hampton. Jackson was also a no-show, but I had learned that coming out on Saturday mornings was his shtick. ("My poor old jalopy can't take the traffic on the L.I.E.," he explained when I asked him why.)

I don't see Cassie until late Saturday morning. A bunch of us are sitting at the table outside, eating our own personally acquired breakfasts and sharing newspaper sections. She sits down in an empty chair at the other end of the table with half a grapefruit and a large cup of coffee, chatting with Leah about who taught the spin class she went to and how many people were there.

After twenty minutes, most everyone has meandered back into the house, except for Leah, who has settled herself with a magazine on a chaise on the other side of the pool. Suddenly Cassie is at my side. "Hey, you!" she says in a stage whisper. "Are we still on for tonight?"

"Yeah, sure, sure."

"Great! We'll leave here around seven-thirty." She's still whispering.

"Why are we whispering?" I whisper.

She looks over at Leah to see if she's paying attention to us and then leans in a little closer. "The thing is, I only invited you. The party is at my friend's house on the beach. He throws it every summer. But it isn't a bring-your-share-house kind of thing. It's more . . . adult."

"Gotcha," I say, flattered at the news that I'm the only housemate she chose to invite and relieved that I'm not her mercy date to an obligatory event.

"It'll be fun. I better get in the shower. I'm going over to a friend's house for her birthday. She's having the girls over for lunch and hired a manicurist to come do everybody while we hang by the pool. Now *that's* the right way to throw a birthday party. See you later!" As she heads inside, she passes Stacy, whose arms are filled with a stack of reading material, bottles of sunscreen, a beach towel, and a giant, purple, adult sippy cup of iced water.

Stacy arranges her towel on a chaise next to Leah and dumps everything else on the table beside it. "I am not moving from this place for the next several hours."

"Sounds like the ideal plan," I say, gathering up my breakfast dishes.

"By the way, we're leaving around seven to go to that BBQ I told you about yesterday."

"I, uh, thanks, but it turns out I can't go with you guys after all."

"Oh. Are you feeling okay?"

Leah looks up from *The Economist*, unabashedly tuning into the conversation. I can't see her eyes behind her opaque Dior sunglasses, but I can feel her looking at me.

"Yeah, totally fine. It's just that . . . I have other plans." I should've guessed from Cassie's whispering that extricating myself from the group wasn't going to be as easy as I thought. It must be one thing if you start out as a member of the Independent Party, like Jackson or Cassie, but to abandon the House Majority and switch loyalties midstream is apparently not as readily acceptable.

Stacy looks like I just told her that I gave away the last of the free puppies and she missed owning one by ten minutes. I have a feeling

Stacy has enjoyed us being "roomies" and playing the role of my Hamptons Tour Guide. Meanwhile, Leah is smirking like the Cheshire cat who adopted the last puppy—and ate it.

"But thanks for including me. I just have this other thing. I'd bring you all along if I could, but someone else invited me." I can practically hear the motor whirring in the Queen Bee's brain. I have a feeling that she knows exactly what I'm doing tonight and with whom.

And I know that she knows that she hasn't been invited.

Leah reaches over and puts her hand on Stacy's arm. Her head may be turned toward Stacy, but I know she's directing what she's about to say at me: "Stacy, you'll be with us tonight. And Michael knows of a party afterward. We're going to have a great time. There's plenty of fun to go around."

. . .

After I get back from the beach with the housemates, it occurs to me that I don't know anything about the dress code for tonight, so I knock on Cassie's door.

"Come in!" When I walk in, there are three different gorgeous outfits laid out on Abigail's unused bed. One is a flowing, layered chiffon cocktail dress with a bold print; one is a silk skirt paired with an embellished tank sweater, and the third is a pair of crisp white pants with a flowing floral tunic I recognize as Trina Turk from my Trio-chaperoned shopping trip. "Hey, you! Just in time. You can help me pick. Which one do you like best?" She starts holding up the outfits in front of her, alternating between facing me and the full-length mirror.

"They're all amazing. I'm afraid I don't have anything nearly as perfect to wear."

"You can wear something of mine." She nods toward her open closet, which isn't nearly as cavernous as Leah's, but is as full of beautiful, colorful clothing, shoes, and bags.

"No, I couldn't. Besides, your stuff would never fit me, though you're the sweetest for thinking I'm as skinny as you are."

"Don't be ridiculous. We're the exact same size. Here, try this." She hands me the most adorable silk jersey cocktail dress I have ever seen, which is also Trina Turk.

I hold it up to my body and turn to look in the mirror. "Cass? I got the feeling that the other girls were upset they weren't invited to come tonight."

"They'll be fine. We're all big girls. They've got places to go, and it's not like we're leaving anyone alone."

"I know. I just feel bad."

She turns to look at me. "Do you not want to come with me so you can go with them? It's okay if you do—"

"No! I mean, no, I definitely want to join you. I really appreciate your inviting me."

"Good. I wish I could bring everyone, but as I said, it's just not that kind of party. We'll invite them the next time. Now go try the dress. If it works, you're wearing it."

Hamptons Unwritten Rule #13:
Going to a fabulous, invite-only cocktail
party is the most expedient way to
becoming a "somebody."

Cassie maneuvers her brown mint-condition vintage Mercedes convertible ("It looks great but secretly it's a lemon. It was my dad's in the 1980s, and every year I have to dump more money into it just to keep it running for the summer," she told me when I was in the throes of cool-car envy the first weekend) into a long, hedgerow-lined driveway that leads up to a beautiful, white, wood-shingled house that looks like it could be on a vintage Hamptons postcard. Fancy cars line the gravel drive feeding into a tight parking formation

on the grass beside the house. A man jogging up the driveway signals us to leave our car by the front door. Valet parking.

As we enter the front door, we are immediately met with a stunning view of the Atlantic. Servers in crisp white shirts hand us *moji-
tos* and direct us outside to the expansive deck, where there are
clusters of couches and chairs covered with overstuffed white pillows and a fire roaring in a stone fire pit in the center. There's a live
jazz trio playing, not so much competing as harmoniously mingling
with the sound of the ocean crashing onto the beach behind them.
There are already groups of people, many of them older and more
obviously well-heeled than any other crowd I've seen out here thus
far, milling about. The atmosphere is mellow, sophisticated, and decidedly adult, just as Cassie described.

I love it.

"Cassandra Penelope Dearborn! Now the party can really start!" A
tan, handsome man looking to be in his early forties with dark wavy
hair streaked with some well-placed gray and wearing a navy blue
sport coat with a crisp white button-down underneath and pressed,
expensive-looking khakis, is holding his arms toward Cassie in an invitation for an embrace.

"George, you know I wouldn't miss it for the world. You must
meet my newest friend. Miller, this is George, one of the most wonderful men in the tristate area, if not the entire East Coast, and
that's including Palm Beach."

"Miller, it's a pleasure," George says, shaking my hand. His eyes,
which are such a dark brown that they're almost the same color as
his pupils, lock onto mine with unmitigated intensity. I shiver.

"Cassandra, where have you been hiding your newest friend?
Why is this the first time I'm meeting her? The summer's almost
half over!" He's still looking into my eyes and smiling at me. I can
feel myself blushing.

"George, don't exaggerate—we're barely halfway through June.
Besides, Miller and I have only known each other since the beginning

of the summer. And she has been flitting around like a social but-terfly all month, it was almost impossible to get on her calendar." This is better than birthday cake, I think, mentally licking the plate. "But I begged her to come. I told her she just *had* to meet you."

"It's true. I actually had to cancel plans so I could be here."

"Then I must do everything I can to make coming worth your while. Let's get your drinks refreshed, and then I'd love for you to meet some of my other guests."

George proves himself to be the consummate host, introducing us around and making sure we're taken care of with ample food and drink. I try not to gawk at the famous people I recognize: a couple of local news anchors, one broadcast network morning show host, an actor and an actress best known for their roles in a few indepen-dent films, and Hamptons scene staple Russell Simmons. I notice a small group of young models who couldn't look more jaded and bored, but who, Cassie asides to me, are consciously crafting that expression to hide the fact that they're barely legal, never mind legal drinking age, and haven't quite figured out how to completely mask their fear of this bizarre world far from their homes in the Midwest or Eastern Europe.

Heeding the warnings of my Homeland Security Council, I'm areful-cay not to overindulge on the ocktails-cay, as I've slipped a little too easily into doing the past few weekends with the house-mates. Even without the cocktail crutch, any nervousness I had ini-tially slips away, and as the evening progresses, I could almost say I'm downright comfortable. A small contingent of good-looking single men in their late thirties and early forties wearing outfits sim-ilar to George's have appropriated Cassie as their token female, shamelessly flirting with her and tripping over themselves in their efforts to impress her. "My boat is docked up at East Hampton Point. I'd love to take you out tomorrow," says one. "I'm one of the partners in Madame Tong's in Southampton. I can put you on the guest list anytime you want," offers another. I strike up a conversation with one guy, but as the sun retreats over the dunes, I find myself scanning the deck for a glimpse of our host, hoping I'll get another chance to talk to him.

Happily, George reappears and asks me if I'd like a tour of the house. Knowing that I will need to relay every detail—including what kind of toilet paper he uses—I agree. I feel an electric spark when George takes my hand and walks me inside the house, which is illuminated by seemingly hundreds of tea lights. I let myself be led around, floating behind him through doors and into rooms as he tells me the saga of the renovations or points out special pieces of furniture and art in each room. His house isn't as big as some of the others we passed on the way here, but it's perfectly proportioned and designed to incorporate its stunning surroundings. We end the tour standing alone in a den-slash-study, which has a stunning view of the pink-and-red striped sky and the dunes to the west. He's telling me he bought the house about fifteen years ago. It had belonged to an elderly couple who were the original owners.

"Why did they sell it? Didn't they have any kids?"

"They had three kids, but they had all moved out west to work in the movie business, and they just didn't want the burden of a house out here that was in need of major renovations. They also knew they'd have to put a ton of money into it. I had just done very well on my first big business deal and scraped together the money to buy the place. My family thought I had lost my mind. I was living in a rented studio apartment and instead of trading up in the city or putting my money into the market, like a sane person would have, I bought this house, even though it was practically eroding from mildew and the sea air. I saw it and fell in love, hard. I knew I wouldn't have the money to fix it up for a long time, but I didn't care."

"It's really wonderful," I say. "It must be worth a mint now."

"I try not to think about how much it's worth because I never want to sell it. I hope to have a family who can enjoy it with me, retire out here, and then pass it on to my kids. It's become a part of me."

We stand quietly, gazing out at the stars beginning to appear over the ocean. He turns to me. "Miller, I should probably get back to my guests, but I've really enjoyed talking with you. I know you must have a million and one engagements, but perhaps you could fit me into your hectic schedule and allow me to take you out to dinner sometime?"

"Yeah, a million and two, actually . . . wait, you're serious?"

"Well, hopefully not too serious in general but about dinner, yes, fairly serious. Why, is that a problem?"

"No! I mean, yes, I'll allow you to take me to dinner. What I meant to say is: dinner would be great." I recite my cell phone number, which he types into his BlackBerry.

"I'll call you this week. Speaking of busy schedules, I think I remember mine being a little full this week, but perhaps we can do something out here next weekend." Then he takes my hand again as we walk back out to the deck. He kisses me gently on the cheek and mouths the words "I'll talk to you soon" as he walks away.

On the way home, I tell Cassie that George asked me out. "I hope that's all right."

"Of course it is. Why wouldn't it be? I knew he'd like you."

"I just wanted to make sure I wasn't stepping on any toes."

"Not at all! I've known George for a long time now. There isn't anything more than friendship between us, nor has there ever been any hope of more than that."

"Those guys we were talking to are cute. Any of them a contender to join the current rotation?"

"They were fun, but most of them are still puppies. But there was this one man there who might have potential. Did you see him: tall, gray hair, parted on the side?"

"The old guy?"

"He wasn't *that* old, Miller. He's probably forty-eight, fifty max. But that doesn't bother me. In fact, I prefer older men."

"Really? It doesn't creep you out?"

"Not at all. They're the best! Usually they have already divorced their first wives, whom they ignored while they worked their asses off, and now they want to find someone they can share the fruits of their labors with. When they're that age, they really know how to treat women. And if they are past say, forty-five, they're even a little bit old-fashioned, which I find very charming. They like going out on proper dates, away for long weekends and on luxurious vacations . . . and best of all, they usually don't try to sleep with you after they paid the tab for one measly dinner like so many guys our age do. They like having someone they can have a real conversation with."

"See, I would've thought that they dated younger women, you know, for the sex."

"Well, the good ones know to bark up a different tree for that. But getting back to you: I think it's great that George asked for your number. He's only in his early forties and hasn't been married before, but he was brought up well and certainly knows how to behave, as you can see. I think you'll enjoy going out with him. And it would be nice to see him with someone real for a change."

"As opposed to what?"

She thinks for a minute as she steers the car along the back roads around a large cornfield. "Sometimes George tends to let the stars get in his eyes, going for flash over substance. But I have a feeling George is in the zone now, or soon will be. If you play your cards right, you just might find yourself in the right place at the right time."

. . .

Sunday morning is bright and warm, promising a perfect beach day. Though Stacy had continued acting wounded throughout most of yesterday, she awakens today cheerful and unaffected, immediately her chatty self once again. She can't wait to give me her full report about last night.

Wild Card Jackson and Queen Leah got drunk as skunks and flirted like mad—which has turned out to be not unusual behavior over the last few Saturday nights. The Mayor spent his evening in the midst of several female admirers but was seen leaving the club with one girl that looked "sort of familiar" to Stacy, though she doesn't know what happened after that.

Stacy wraps up her account with an admission: she has a crush on Michael. "He and I have so much in common. Did you know that we both grew up on Long Island and we both went to George Washington? Not that we were there at the same time, but still. That's a shared experience, right? And I just think we'd be really good together. I know he likes to party and go out all the time, but at some point he'll be ready to settle down. This year he turns thirty-five, and my sister says that after men turn thirty-five, they start getting serious about their futures." I nod as if I know what the hell she is talking about. "But please, please don't tell *anyone*."

I don't need a minute to figure out that by "anyone," she means Leah. Though by the way Leah and Jackson have been carrying on, I doubt Leah could care less about Michael at this point and might even be happy to have Stacy take him off her hands. However, I don't say any of this to my young roommate. Stacy then proceeds to recount every single thing Michael said to her last night to get my opinion about whether or not the feeling might be mutual. As my penance for ditching her, I listen dutifully to the entire endless recitation until she finally stops to come up for air.

"I think it's okay to be cautiously optimistic, but you might want to gather more evidence before you do anything," I say, thinking of Michael's allegiance to the August First Rule.

She blushes. "Oh, I wasn't going to do anything . . . I was kind of hoping he would make a move."

"And who knows? He probably will, but you might want to prepare yourself for the possibility that he may wait until later in the summer."

Her eyes widened.

"Why do you think that? Did he say something to you?"

"No, nothing, I promise. But things can get complicated quickly when you live in the same house. It's just good to be patient," I say, feeling vaguely like a fraud for both giving advice about something I don't know the first thing about as well as upholding a rule that I originally thought was suspect and contrived at best but am now starting to understand.

When I get to work Monday morning, I immediately call Alice, since Jerry and Jimmy have yet to arrive, ignoring the several un-opened e-mails in my in-box from the BuzzTV creative director, no doubt asking for a million more changes that the SVP wants without officially awarding us the project. I just want a few more minutes to savor my weekend victory.

"You will not believe what happened," I tell Alice. When I get to the part about George asking me out, Alice is doing her quiet, office-appropriate squeal of delight—a reaction I haven't been the recipient of in quite some time. I forgot how much I've missed it.

"You are such a rock star! Three weeks into the summer and you've already not only met a guy, but a guy with beachfront prop-erty! He sounds perfect!" I can tell she's already picturing a barefoot beach wedding. "Has he called yet?"

"No, but Hamptons people don't really call one another on Mon-days."

"Well, excuse me. Was that a rule in the house guidelines that I missed?"

I smart at her snide tone but decide to let it pass. "No, not a rule, just a pattern I've noticed. He'll probably get in touch midweek to make plans for the weekend. And I almost forgot to tell you . . ." I give her the rundown about how hurt Stacy was when I told her I wasn't going out with her and the housemates and how Leah seemed pissed that Cassie had invited me, not her.

"I'm sorry they were upset with you, but I kind of don't blame them," she says.

"Why? Cassie could only bring one person. And besides, it's not like we left anyone home alone. They all had stuff to do and people to do it with."

"If I were you, I would just be careful that you don't alienate them by running off with Cassie every time she asks."

"Let's not go crazy here. This was the first time Cassie asked me to do *anything*."

"I know, but you had fun together, right? And if she likes you well enough to have invited you to an exclusive party and introduced you to her friend, I'm sure she'll make plans with you again. All I'm saying is maybe you shouldn't put all your eggs in Cassie's basket. It sounds to me like she has her own agenda. You still need your housemates. They've been inviting you along since the very beginning, even though they didn't have to."

I stare down at the dial pad and see a mental image of Alice wagging her finger at me. "Whatever you say, *Mom*."

"Come on, Tor. You know what I mean. None of this is a slam dunk yet. It's only June. You still need them more at this point than they need you."

"Thanks for your vote of confidence. I thought you were supposed to be on my side."

"Of course I'm on your side. I just thought it might be helpful for you to consider it from *their* side. I don't want it all to come bite you on the ass after Cassie has found her ideal sugar daddy and disappeared, but you've blown off the housemates one too many times for them to bother with you anymore."

"Cassie's not like that. She's totally cool. You'd like her. And she's been really generous to me."

"As she should be. She's lucky to have you as a friend. They all are. You're wonderful and special. But you should be with people who deserve *your* friendship. They have to earn it, not the other way around."

"I hear you." Suddenly I want nothing more than a change of subject. "How were the Berkshires? Did you guys go to that antiques fair?"

"Yes! It was on the cutest little farm! We made friends with the owners, and they gave us a private tour. . . ." I let her ramble on for a few minutes, relieved that the most obvious diversion tactic in the world—turning the conversation to be about her—worked. Thankfully, Jerry and Jimmy bustle into the office, diving for the Krispy Kremes it was my turn to bring and waving their arms to get me off the phone.

"Al, sorry but I have to run. The boys just got here, and we really have to review the feedback we just got on this big potential project. I'll call you later." We say good-bye and I hang up.

"Wait 'til we tell you about Pedro," Jimmy sings.

"Who's he?" I ask.

"Let's just say that Pedro is our new favorite summerhouse guest," Jerry says with a smirk.

"More like, Frank's and Tommy's and Sean's new favorite houseguest, if you catch my drift," Jimmy says.

I reach for a doughnut, happy to hear about someone else's summer shenanigans for a change. "Do tell!"

6.

Love ~~Heals~~ Kills

May

Su	Mo	Tu	We	Th	Fr	Sa
		1	2	3	4	5
6	7	8	9	10	11	12
13	14	15	16	17	18	19
20	21	22	23	24	25 ✗	26 ✗
27 ✗	28 ✗	29	30	31		

June

Su	Mo	Tu	We	Th	Fr	Sa
					1 ✗	2 ✗
3 ✗	4	5	6	7	8 ✗	9 ✗
10 ✗	11	12	13	14	15 ✗	16 ✗
17 ✗	18	19	20	21	22 ✗	23 ✗
24 ✗	25	26	27	28	29	30

Hamptons Unwritten Rule #14:
The only direction to date is UP.

It's late Friday afternoon and Stacy and I are in our room. Since the rest of my housemates all seem to have summer Fridays, I declared an early closing at MillerWorks and jumped on an earlier train, which was only marginally more civilized than the 4 P.M. Cannonball. She's lying on her bed, flipping through *Hamptons* magazine. I'm standing in front of my closet, studying the same three things that have been hanging there since the beginning of the summer, trying to understand why they haven't magically proliferated into more cute outfits.

"Do you want to go to Prime 103 for dinner tonight?" she asks. "Leah made a reservation."

"Actually, I have, well, I guess it's sort of a date tonight," I say, silently hoping that a date gets a different kind of consideration than having separate plans with only one other housemate.

"Really? That's great! With who?"

Yes, a date is definitely different. "He's a friend of Cassie's. I met him last Saturday night. He was the host of that cocktail party we went to." Just as I predicted, George didn't call on Monday. He called on Tuesday evening, which was perfect: just enough time so that he didn't seem too eager but not so long that I'd have to start getting antsy about *if* he was going to call. We didn't chat long because he was on his way to a business dinner, but we had a nice conversation during which he asked me out for tonight. I pretty much floated through the rest of the week.

"Soooo, what's his name? What does he do?"

"His name is George. He does some kind of real estate thing. Development, maybe? I think he's pretty successful—he owns this great house on the beach near Mecox." I answer her next few questions as best I can, realizing that I don't actually know that much about him. Hopefully I'll get to know him more tonight.

"What did you say his last name was?"

"Daniels, I think. Why?"

"Oh my god, it's such a small world! I don't actually *know* him, but I know *of* him. You haven't heard of George Daniels before?"

"Not until Cassie introduced me to him. Why? Is he famous?"

"Not exactly. He's just one of those guys *everyone* in New York knows. I've never met him, but I know my sister has, and I've heard Leah and Abigail talk about him. He's from a wealthy family— they're in real estate too. He grew up on the Upper East Side, went to Dalton and Princeton. He's practically the male equivalent of a socialite. Is there such a thing? There should be a word for it or maybe they just call the guys socialites too? That's so cool that you're going out with him!"

"Yeah, well, you know, it's just a first date." I turn back to my closet, praying that even if something new to wear hasn't suddenly appeared, maybe the modicum of confidence that I was clinging to three minutes ago that just flew out of my body might be hiding somewhere deep inside.

. . .

The front door opens, causing me to jump out of my skin.

"False alarm," Stacy says. "It's only Andrew."

"Well, well, well," he says as he walks into the living room—smartly dressed in half of a very nice suit—and lets out an appreciative whistle. "Nice dress. Got a hot date? Or are you just happy to see me?"

It was nerve-wracking enough knowing that I was about to go on my first date in years. Then I had to go have that date with a guy who sounds like he's in the running to be New York's Most Eligible Bachelor. On top of that, not only do I have an audience, but now the audience has doubled. A veritable high-anxiety troika.

"I'm just going to a cocktail party with a friend. No big deal." My hands shake as I lift the water glass to my mouth, belying the casual tone I was attempting to convey.

"You mean the guy who just drove up in the sweet silver BMW M6 convertible?"

"Oh shit," I say under my breath.

"This is going to be fun," Andrew says, putting down his weekend bag. He turns back toward the door, as if he's going to open it. "Do you want me to do the father-interrogating-the-date thing? Ask him about his intentions? Tell him what time to have you home, young lady?"

"No!" Stacy and I yell at the same time. Stacy hurls a couch pillow at Andrew, which then lands at the feet of my date for the evening, who has just come in the front door.

"Oops," Stacy says. "Sorry, Miller."

"George, hi!" As I jump up, I somehow manage to knock my

thigh into the corner of the glass coffee table. Hard. Pain shooting into my leg. Literal stars before my eyes.

"Are you okay?" they ask.

"Fine, I'm fine." I say, rubbing my thigh furiously. "I'm ready if you are!" I limp toward the door as graciously as I can. "See you guys later." George takes my elbow and helps me outside as I lope along beside him. "George, I just realized that I didn't introduce you to my housemates. I'm so sorry! Should we go back in?"

He has what seems like an amused smile on his face. "No, please, don't worry about it. Besides, I don't want to risk being hit by another pillow or have you injure yourself further."

"Now I'm officially mortified." What makes me think I can pull this off? Not only am I a total fraud, I'm a nobody. And he is so completely out of my league.

"Miller." His hands are on my bare upper arms. They feel strong and secure. His dark eyes are looking directly into mine. He is definitely smiling now. "Let's start over. Hi. How are you? You look very pretty this evening."

I swallow hard. "Thanks."

"Breathe, Miller."

I try but instead burst out with a loud nervous laugh-yell that sounds like "Bah!"

He grabs my hand and leads me to the passenger side. "Why don't you get in, I will drive us to the party as fast as possible, and we'll have a drink in your hand in less than fifteen minutes."

Soon we're driving with the top down, rolling smoothly over sun-warmed blacktop. He's chatting about I'm not really sure what, but the sound is soothing and he doesn't seem to need me to do anything but nod and say "Uh-hunh" and "Oh, really." I can't shake the feeling that I'm Cinderella on the way to the ball and like her, I'm running the very real risk that at any moment I will be exposed as the cleaning lady. So while he talks, I try to concentrate on the gorgeous scenery: the vast cornfields bathed in the warm orange glow of the sinking sun—my favorite light of the day—and the inviting smell of pregnant soil, ready to yield the future. I start to relax and tune in.

"We're going to my friend Louisa's house. She lives out here full-time. She's a relatively famous painter. She's got a great old house—a converted carriage house from an old estate. It's also her studio. She's just having a few friends over for cocktails. Should be very cas."

"Sounds great," I say, easing back into the leather seat and crossing my legs in what I hope to be a demure way. Out of the corner of my eye, I see that my little sex-kitten trick has worked: his eyes are definitely on my legs instead of the road.

"You poor thing. That bruise looks like it's going to be a doozy."

I look down to see the beginnings of the ugliest, most ginormous green and purple bruise forming on my lower left thigh.

But George just smiles, eases the hem of my skirt down over the evidence of my clumsiness, and places his hand gently on my thigh. I can feel the warmth of his skin through the material. "It will be our secret."

. . .

The multitude of cars parked in the driveway is my first clue that my definition of "cas" and George's are polar opposites. We follow the luminarias lining the stone walk to the back of the house and find ourselves standing at the edge of an immense brick patio filled with what looks to be a hundred people. The setting is stunning, picture-perfect wealthy yet tasteful Hamptons.

The air is chilly but sweet. George hands me a glass of white sangria filled with fruit, takes my hand in his, and leads me over to an earthily beautiful woman in her early sixties, who's a dead ringer for Lauren Hutton. "Louisa, I'd like you to meet my friend Miller. Miller, this is Louisa Schwimmer."

"What a pleasure to meet you, Miller. Welcome. I see you two already have cocktails. Aren't those the greatest? Pierre can never wait for summer to begin so he can continue to perfect his sangria recipe."

"Where is Pierre?" asks George. "I haven't seen him yet."

"I think he's futzing with something in the kitchen but should be out soon. The caterer has been very patient, though I know she's dying to kick him out." She laughs. Just then, the screened wood back door suddenly *thwaps* shut to reveal a very young, very handsome man carrying a tray filled with pitchers of sangria. He's at least my age or younger, putting him at a good thirty years younger than our hostess. "Pierre, come say hi to George and his friend!" Louisa calls happily.

Pierre places the tray down and then comes over to give George a hearty handshake. George then introduces us.

"Miller, hello! Nice to meet you. How do you like my sangrias?" Pierre has a French accent and a beautiful, dimple-flanked smile. He could easily pass for Antonio Sabato Junior.

"It's delicious. I hear it's a secret recipe."

"Not so secret as much as never the same thing twice. So more like a surprise than a secret, yes?" he says. "I must replenish the ice. Will you excuse me?"

"Darling, the caterers can take care of . . ." Louisa calls out after him. It's too late; he has disappeared back into the house. "He never relaxes." Louisa sighs. "But he sure makes my life easier. Please help yourself to some of the delicious snacks. I need to go play hostess, but I'll be back!" and she's off with a flourish of her ethereal peach-colored silk tunic blouse.

"She's gorgeous," I say. "And so nice. And what an amazing house! Pierre seems sweet too. Well, at least, great at making sangrias."

"You're dying to know their deal, right?"

"Guilty as charged. I hope that's not rude of me."

"I figured you were curious. Believe me, we were all curious when he first arrived on the scene. Louisa, while an enormously generous and kind person, is extremely private. She was alone for years, as long as I can remember. Most people just figured she was a lesbian, since she often had young women spend the summer as her apprentices. But then about four years ago, Pierre showed up. I think he's the son of a friend from France, so we thought she was doing whomever a favor by having Pierre be her assistant. But then, he never left. They live here together year-round. They kept a low profile for the first few years, but I guess the shock wore off or people got used to them being whatever they are, so they finally started entertaining at the end of last summer. What happens inside that shingled house, no one really knows for sure, but let's just say her close friends hope she's enjoying the arrangement."

If I were her, I know I'd be.

Just then some people come over and George makes introductions. I stand by his side while he chats with them. Every once in a while he puts his hand on the small of my back, which makes me feel that even though I'm not the focus of his attention, he's aware of me.

Eventually we say thank you to our hosts (this time I get a double-cheek kiss from the sangria-making Frenchman) and head back to the car hand in hand.

"I hope I'm not being presumptuous, but I made dinner reservations at Savanna's in the hopes that not only you'd be hungry, but also that you'd be willing to spend a couple of more hours with me."

"That's so sweet. I'd love to."

"Excellent." Before reaching down to open the car door for me, George leans toward me. His lips are soft and carry a hint of fruit and wine.

I try to relax into him as the ghost of Peter—the last man who kissed me so long ago—hovers somewhere above me, above the cornfields and the wide blue ocean, not yet completely gone. But almost. Almost.

Hamptons Unwritten Rule #15:
Beware of the Hamptons Potato Field Killer.

After George drops me off at home, I walk in to find the house deadly silent and dark. I realize I've never been here alone at night before. Having been a city girl for so long with constant noise, light, and people around at all hours, I'm a little spooked by the stillness and the vast amount of unoccupied space, so I turn on almost all of the lights as I work my way through the house toward my room. I'm a little too giddy from the success of my date to go to sleep, so instead of putting on my pajamas, I change into a sweatshirt and a pair of shorts and walk barefoot outside to a chaise. I look up to see that there are billions of stars, but the lights from the house are obscuring their brilliance, so I go in and bravely turn off the lights and come back out to study the cloudless and moonless sky, settling comfortably back against the chaise.

"It's beautiful out here at night, isn't it?" I jump a mile off the chair at the sound of a male voice coming out of the darkness.

"Who is that?" I ask, frightened. What if there's a share house stalker who has been waiting at the house until a female housemate comes home alone? The back of our house faces onto an overgrown field and is totally hidden from the road or any neighbors. This isn't good. Well, I mean, not good for me. It's more than good for him. He can just kill me and throw my body in the field and no one will find me until fall!

"You don't know who I am, do you?"

"No! Identify yourself immediately!"

"I'm the Hamptons Potato Field Killer!" the voice says menacingly. How come Leah didn't include the threat of death by a deranged, embittered East End farmer in her fucking house guidelines? I hear the screen door by the South Wing creak open, swing shut, and then slow footsteps approaching. I grope around beneath me for something—anything—to use as a weapon. It's so

dark I can't see a thing. My hand lands on the smooth plastic surface of what must be a sunscreen bottle on the ground. Okay, here's
the plan: when he gets close, I will squirt Coppertone Sport Sun-
block in his eyes. I just pray it's a high SPF with PABA.

"Don't come any closer!" I yell into the dark. "I've got a weapon!"

"Yah, right." The stalker laughs. "Miller . . ."

"Oh my god, how do you know who I am?" I recoil, pressing
myself against the back of the chair, as if that will protect me, when
really, I should be running into the house and locking all the doors,
even though the phone line has probably already been cut.

"Because I'm your goddamn housemate, that's why!"

"Andrew?"

"Yes, of course. Who did you think it was? Owww!" I've thrown
the plastic bottle at him and have clearly succeeded in hitting him.
"What the hell was that for?"

"For scaring the shit out of me!"

He sits down on the edge of the chaise, and only now can I make
out the edges of his face and body. He is rubbing at his temple
where I clocked him with the Coppertone. He stops and looks at
me, laying a hand on my leg. "Are you shaking? You were actually
scared? I thought you were just playing along! Didn't you recognize
my voice? Who else would be coming out of my room?"

"The . . . the . . . Potato . . . Hamptons . . . Killer . . . Guy
Man!" I stammer. He starts laughing. "Andrew, it's not funny!" He
laughs harder. Then I start laughing. The more he laughs, the more
I laugh. It's totally one of those contagious laughing things until
we're both gasping for air.

"I knew you had a sense of humor in there somewhere," he says
after catching his breath.

"Are you kidding me? I am fucking *hilarious*," I say defensively.
This causes him to start cracking up all over again. "Okay, now
that's really not funny," I say. "What are you doing here anyway?
It's still pretty early. Are the others back?"

He regains his composure. "No, just me. I had a really intense week at work and I just had it for the night. How was your big date?" He stretches out.

"It was good." I tell him about my evening, leaving out the part about the kiss.

"Well, I'm glad you had fun. You certainly looked great."

"I did? I mean, thanks."

"So, what's his name? How'd you meet him?" he says in his best imitation of a Jewish mother.

"George Daniels. He's a friend of Cassie's."

"Uh-oh."

"What?"

"Is he a member of Cassie's famous International Coalition of Mr. Bigs?"

"No. He's from New York."

"Well, he could be from the local chapter. I realize I don't know you that well, but I didn't take you for a player in the major leagues. I know that's Cassie's bag—she's been doing it forever, and it's what makes her who she is—but I have to say, I didn't think you'd fall for that kind of guy."

"I haven't fallen for *any* guy, much less that kind of guy. I've only been on one date with him."

"Don't get defensive. I'm not criticizing or judging. I'm just making an observation."

"Well, Mr. Mayor, it sort of feels like you're judging."

"Did you just call me 'Mr. Mayor'?"

"Yes. You're like the Mayor of the Hamptons. Everyone knows you, you know everyone, and they all fall at your feet the minute you walk into the room while you just eat it up."

He sits up and leans toward me. "Is that really how you see me?"

"No, I just wanted to give you proof that I have a fabulously wacky sense of humor."

"Really. You were just kidding."

"No, I guess I wasn't. Let's just say I've made some *observations* of my own."

"Well, then. I guess that means we have the rest of the summer to either live up to each other's preconceived assumptions about the other one or dispel them entirely."

"Are you that interested in the answer that you're willing to wait the entire summer for it to reveal itself?"

He stands up. "So far, Mrs. Daniels, I am. Or, at least, until August first."

Hamptons Unwritten Rule #16:
You can never be too rich or too thin,
but you can be too eager.

"Another stellar beach day!" Stacy plops herself down on the front doorstep to wipe the sand from her feet.

"I feel like a perfectly toasted marshmallow!" Cassie says, outfitted in her south-of-France in the 1960s beach ensemble: a sheer lilac tunic, a floppy straw beach hat, big black Jackie O sunglasses, and gold thong sandals, a perfect showcase for her bright red toenails.

Earlier today, Cassie and I snuck away from the gang for a long walk on the beach so I could fill her in on my date. She wanted to know every detail. She thought it was a good sign that George asked me out to dinner afterward. "I love the unexpected date extension when things are going well—it means he wanted to spend more time with you and get to know you better, since you probably didn't get a chance to talk one-on-one at the party. And he made a reservation so you wouldn't have to wait for a table. What did I tell you? Older guys know what they're doing."

"Remember," Stacy now says for the seventeenth time today as pushes open the front door with her overstuffed beach bag, "the event starts at seven so we don't want to get there much past seven-thirty. Last year they ran out of parking!"

My housemates seem to love nothing better than a free party, so I was surprised when everyone agreed to shell out $200 each to go to tonight's Love Heals at Luna Farm charity event. But from what Stacy described, this party is known to attract lots of young, single people as well as movers and shakers in the fashion and entertainment worlds, which were probably major draws. They might have also been swayed by Michael, who said that he heard that since this year's theme is "Viva Las Vegas," the cast of *Ocean's Thirteen* was going to make a surprise appearance. Cassie, who I was surprised to learn is also participating in this group activity, laughed it off as pure rumor, though I was still secretly hoping to see George Clooney in the flesh.

I suspect Cassie was always planning to go on her own but figured it might come across as too much of a dis if she didn't go with the gang once she found out that we were all attending. I'm just relieved that I don't have to choose between hanging with her or the housemates tonight.

"It's only four-thirty, Stacy, I think we should be fine," Cassie says, with the slightest hint of true annoyance.

Stacy misses it completely and plows ahead. "Well, I know how long everyone takes to get ready. I just want to be sure. And I know my sister will be pissed if I, I mean we, show up late." Stacy leans down to get something out of her bag, missing Cassie rolling her eyes. "I'm going to put my towel out back to dry. Anybody want me to take theirs?" We both hand her ours and head into the North Wing.

"Holy Mary Mother of God! You would think this was the first Hamptons benefit she's ever been to. They are so no big deal. You've been to one, you've been to them all."

I decide not to tell Cassie that this is the first Hamptons benefit that I've ever been to. I have noticed in my dutiful weekly reading of *Hamptons* magazine that there are at least three big charity events on the calendar every weekend, with huge price tags attached to their tickets. There seems to be a charity for every disease and non-profit organization under the South Fork sun: the Southampton Hospital, the many museums and performance theaters, ovarian cancer, breast cancer, ARF (the cutely and aptly named Animal Rescue Fund), and of course, several for AIDS—from those organizations trying to cure it to those trying to ease the lives of the people who already have it. Galas, auctions, dances, cocktails, clam-bakes, picnics, softball games, polo, and even discount shopping are all held in the name of philanthropy. These events provide sexy, exclusive, and sometimes star-studded opportunities for socializing with other well-heeled types while allowing everyone to feel good that they've contributed to the bettering of society while not having to miss a beat in their personal hedonistic pursuits.

"Stacy's older sister is a chairperson, so I think that kind of has her on edge," I explain.

"That could be," she says, signaling me to follow her into her room and close the door. "I like Stacy, don't get me wrong; she's a sweet kid. But she's a little too eager, don't you think?"

"I guess. But she means well."

"I'm sure she does," she says, hanging her hat on the hook behind the door. "But, she's young. She seems like she's still at the age when she's trying just a little too hard to be accepted. That's what's great about being in our thirties. You just know who you are, good, bad, or boring."

Or, at least, one hopes you know who you are, and hopefully it's neither of the latter two options.

"Do you mind if I shower first? I want to take a quick disco nap, but I'd rather do that after I'm clean," Cassie says.

"Sure thing. I've got to figure out what I'm going to wear. It's my first benefit—of the season, I mean. I want to look my best."

"Good idea. You never know who you're going to run into at

these things. Out of seven hundred people, you're bound to bump into someone you know."

"I doubt that's the case for me. I don't know too many people out here."

"Well, it's always good to be prepared for anything," she cautions as she shuts the bathroom door.

Hamptons Unwritten Rule #17:
Charity-Schmarity. Before you do
anything else, claim your swag bag.

Stacy, as it turns out, is dead-on right. We pull into the makeshift parking lot on the grass of Luna Farm at seven-thirty and it's already three-quarters full. Now that she has proved her credibility, we decide to listen to her other advice about turning in our claim tickets for our gift bags as soon as we get there since, she warned, they always run out.

I follow the girls over to the gift table, which is swelling with large tote bags filled to capacity. Once we have our Scoop-branded bags in hand, our swag-reconnaissance team makes a surprise pit stop at a garbage can outside of the tent. I watch them as they expertly start digging through the bags, yanking out unwanted items, such as brochures for teeth whitening, hair removal, and information about the charity, to toss them in the bin. Only after the bags are rid of the extraneous goods, leaving only the "good stuff"— such as MAC cosmetics, a $50 gift certificate to Henri Bendel, a Cole Haan leather key chain, a DVD set of the latest season of *Entourage* from HBO, bottles of Voss water and the like—do we proceed to the car to lock our bounty safely away.

"The VIPs get even better swag," Stacy tells me on our way back into the tent. "My sister said she'd try to get me one if there are any left."

Cassie, who seems to have sized up the scene in about seventeen seconds, tells me she's going to say hi to some people she knows. Why am I not surprised that my favorite Socialista heads off in the same direction as the VIP section? I have a feeling she's more likely to end up with a VIP goodie bag than the hopeful Stacy, but I keep this thought to myself.

The party atmosphere is slow in building. Instead of mingling and dancing, people are stuck waiting in the various lines for their gift bags, the bar, and the buffet. Soon we have devised a plan to help us divide and conquer: some of us will save a table, some will get drinks, and the rest will procure food. It's a beautiful evening, so we table savers commandeer a table just outside the tent, under the gathering dusk as the stars begin to dot the inky sky. I happily accept a champagne cocktail brought by our designated drink-getters. The food is cold and not so good, so the bubbly becomes my primary source of nourishment for the evening. My housemates seem more at ease than I've ever seen them, probably because for once they're off duty from the party chase.

Cassie comes to join us a little while after we're settled.

"Cassie, I've saved you a seat," Leah offers, indicating the chair next to her.

"Thanks, but I'm not sure I'm ready to sit down quite yet." Cassie moves next to me and leans down to whisper in my ear. "A bunch of people I know are here. Why don't you come over with me so I can introduce you?"

I really want to join her, but Alice's admonitions about not blowing off my housemates are still ringing in my head. Besides, I would feel guilty about so obviously ditching at this moment, especially since I can feel Leah watching us. "You go ahead. I'll join up with you in a little bit."

"Promise me you will. It's always good to meet new people. I'm sure you didn't pay all this money for a ticket just to hang out with the housemates when you can do that at home for free. Come find me soon, okay?" She glides away from the table, the yellow and green chiffon ruffles of her dress floating in the breeze as she disappears into the crowd.

Hamptons Unwritten Rule #18:
If Manhattan is small, the Hamptons are minuscule.

Jackson surprisingly has threatened to make me dance with him once the party really gets going even though usually he keeps the lowest profile of all the housemates. He somehow manages to keep an eagle eye on the dance floor in anticipation of the first signs of life, while artfully ignoring the fact that Queen Leah is watching *me* like a hawk.

After the food plates are cleared away and people start circulating again, the DJ finally gets the party started. Jackson gives me a devilish look, and—cutting off Leah midsentence no less—grabs my hand and leads me into the tent toward the dance floor. There aren't many people out here yet, but a brave few are warming up to Beyoncé.

"Hey, you're pretty good," Jackson appraises.

"You sound surprised!"

"Not at all. Why do you think I chose you as my first partner?"

"I see. I'm just the fluffer. Don't worry. I don't mind that you're just using me to get your groove greased so you can show your real moves to your *second* partner."

"Damn, I hate being so bloody transparent. At least now you know where you stand with me."

A new song comes on with a faster beat. More people make their way toward the dance floor. Leah and Andrew appear next to us, clearly at Leah's urging. But after his initial reluctance, I'm surprised to see Andrew demonstrate more than passable dance skills. Soon a small but strong contingent of Andrew Admirers is slowly but surely edging Leah out of the way. Michael, who until now has been standing on the edge of the dance floor chatting with Stacy, jumps in to take Andrew's spot as Leah's partner. Leah stops, appears to be thinking about it, and then shrugs her approval. After I see how Michael dances, I have to admit, her hesitation becomes instantly understandable. I look back to where Stacy was standing so I can signal her to join Jackson and me, but she is gone. Poor thing.

After a long stretch of really good songs, the music abruptly switches over to an unrecognizable techno beat, which none of us can follow, driving most of the housemates back to the bar.

I'm looking for the nearest bathroom when I see a familiar face. Well, a profile of a familiar face.

Peter.

My stomach starts doing some hip-hop moves I didn't know it had. Peter is standing maybe twenty yards away. It doesn't seem like he's seen me yet. He's with a few people I don't know, most notably a pretty blond woman who is laughing and grabbing onto his arm. My feet feel like they're in quicksand, the pointy heels of my sandals literally sinking into the grassy earth. Even though I know that weird thing that happens when you stare at people—that eventually they can feel your eyes on them, which makes them turn to look at you—I can't take my eyes off of the two of them.

What the fuck is Peter doing in the Hamptons? What the fuck is Peter doing at a charity benefit in the Hamptons? Who the fuck is that girl hanging all over Peter at a charity benefit in the Hamptons?

The last time I even spoke to Peter was in the Taxi of Broken Promises and Shattered Dreams.

He never got in touch with me, unless you count the UPS box I received exactly two days later with the few toiletries, sleepwear, and random sundries that I'd left at his apartment. There was no note. I didn't even hear a peep out of him on my birthday, which was only a week and a half after he broke up with me. I read his lack of note and his lack of any additional contact loud and clear: *it's* over and now *you're* over. I was too stunned, hurt, and humiliated to reach out to him. Besides, what could you possibly say to someone who has just told you they don't want to marry you? Give him a point-by-point analysis of how great you are and why he should change his mind? If he didn't already know all those things after a year and a half, a follow-up phone call wasn't going to be the thing to tip the scales. If anything, you'd probably wind up looking like "The Girl Who Just Didn't Get It the First Time and Needed to Hear That Rejection Once More—for the Cheap Seats." No thanks. The most retaliatory thing I did was to block his screen name on my AIM Buddy List. Take that, you bastard! Now you can't see when I come online and go off-line! How does that feel?!

Because there was no verbal follow-up to his Taxicab Confession of any sort, I spent a lot of time afterward reflecting on every word he said, or didn't say, as the case was, during the three minutes it took him to decimate our relationship. The fact that the year and a half of us sharing our lives together only warranted what sounded like a canned speech hurt the most. It made me feel like we must've had the most generic relationship in the world if it didn't merit more time than it took to get from Twenty-third to Fourteenth Street. Or worse, that I was so generic *to him*, that I made no emotional impact or lasting impression that stood out enough to make it into his closing remarks in any significant way.

To be perfectly honest, it was for the latter that I hadn't been able to forgive him—or myself.

And now Peter was heading in my direction. I could easily slip into the crowd, avoid this encounter. But it's a car crash happening in slow motion and I have to find out who the casualty is. Even if it's me.

He's walking . . . he's walking . . . but he doesn't seem to be looking at me. But then he is. Looking at me. A look of surprise flashes across his face, followed by fear mixed with dread, maybe, and then a smile, that seems forced. I blink, and he's Peter, the guy I used to love, familiar and welcoming as my own bed. The Peter whose lips were cold when he kissed me outside my door on New Year's Eve. The Peter who used to spoon me every night before falling asleep. The Peter who used to leave me funny little messages on neon Post-it notes when he left for work before I did in the morning. The Peter who bought me a DVD player, hooked it up, and rented me every chick flick he could get his hands on when I was sick as a dog for a week.

I blink again and he's a complete stranger.

"Tori! Hi!" I flinch at his use of my name. What was I expecting? That he would still call me "honey" after all this time? "Wow, you look so . . . so different! I mean, you look amazing. How are you?" Peter is standing in front of me, handsome and tan, more curls to his wavy dark hair than I remember. Is it longer? A different cut? I'm still studying his hair when he leans over to kiss my cheek. The familiar scent of his Aveda shampoo is like a slap across my face. It sends me spiraling back to the first time he spent the night at my apartment. When I went to bed the following night, my pillows smelled of his shampoo and I lay there intoxicated, making me think that I might be in love for the very first time.

"Peter," I finally manage to say. "What . . . what are you doing out here? I thought you hated the Hamptons." I thought I'd finally be able to start a new life here, I want to say, a new life without you. A new life in a place that I thought you would never be, that you were never a part of. How could you be here, right now, in this place, with your hair waving perfectly and smelling exactly the same as it did two years ago when you were mine?

"God, it's been so long. Tell me what's going on with you. Are you doing a house out here? How are Alice and Scott? Is she pregnant yet? You must be president of Dream Job TV by now. Where are you living these days? Still on Astor Place?"

I notice that he has avoided my question. And it's funny that even after having no contact with someone for so long, all of their little quirks and cues are still as fresh as the first time you discovered them. I suddenly remember that when Peter had something important to say, he always started rambling. Strangely, it occurs to me now, the only time he didn't do that was the night he broke up with me. The early warning system had failed . . . that's why I never saw it coming. . . . But now, I am as attuned as a state-of-the-art satellite dish. And the mortal fear of the spiral, of the slope I slipped down so easily and had to work so hard and so long to climb out of, propels me to face this fear or be doomed to the pit below the surface of life forever.

"I'd love to pretend it's no big deal running into each other, but I'm just not there yet. It's pretty clear you have something to tell me, so maybe we can just cut to the chase."

He looks at me, surprised. I also imagine him to be surprised that despite the fact that he thought he had erased me, I still *know* him, and he can never take that back. This thought makes me suddenly feel strong, though at the same time the nearness of what used to be is practically choking me. "I, uh, I'm here with someone. Her name is Michelle Fortunato. She's on the benefit committee." Since I don't say anything, he continues, nervously filling the void. "Her family has a house in East Hampton. We come out to visit on weekends."

We. It stings. I can't look at him.

"So, you? How about you? Are you doing a house out here? Amagansett again? I know you loved it there the one time you guys did it. . . ."

"Sagaponack."

"Cool," he says, shifting his feet and looking around nervously, probably for someone to save him.

Someone does. "Sweetie! Did you make it to the bar yet? I'm dying for a drink!" The pretty blond woman, who I'm assuming is the other half of the "we," the much ballyhooed Michelle herself, appears at his side, latching onto his elbow with both hands.

I notice that I'm standing directly in his path to the bar. And so the truth hits me, hard: he didn't come over to say hello. He didn't come over to say he was sorry. He was simply on his way to get drinks. For him and Michelle. *We.*

My eyes dart down to her left hand, which is clutched around his elbow. I'm almost blinded by the light emanating from the emerald-cut rock lodged between her pinkie and middle finger. They're engaged.

It's just like Peter to bury the lead.

While I was alone for two years, he was falling in love with Michelle. While I was home watching *Planet's Funniest Animals*, he was out on the town with Michelle. While I was being cajoled into the backseat of Alice and Scott's car for yet another trip to the Berkshires, he was hopping into the Fortunato family car and spending weekends in East Hampton with his future in-laws. While I was *desperately* trying to convince myself I was better off in the long run, he was picking out a ring—correction, a rock— for Michelle.

"I ran into an old . . . friend," he now manages to answer.

Michelle turns to face me. "Oh, how nice. It's *such* a small world. I'm Peter's fiancée, Michelle. And you are . . . ?"

"Tori." She doesn't flinch, she doesn't blink, she doesn't make any sign whatsoever that she has ever heard of me before. It's one thing to *think*, to *harbor the belief* that you didn't make a lasting impression on someone's life, but to be given proof of it is entirely something else. Maybe she didn't hear me. "*Tori Miller*," I repeat.

Nothing.

"Well, Tori, it's nice to meet you. Thank you for supporting our cause. Love Heals is a wonderful charity. I've been with them since the beginning. It's so important to give back, don't you think?"

I'm about to ask her to *give back* my boyfriend when suddenly, I feel someone come up behind me, a hand on my back, and then an arm draping low across my waist.

"Darling, did you lose your way?" It's Jackson. "They finally changed the music back to something recognizable, since a massive horde of outraged dancers stormed the DJ booth, firing quite a hailstorm of expletive-laden complaints. Or maybe that was just me. In any case, ready to get back to it?" He turns to Peter and Michelle as his hand reaches up to rake through his hair. "Oh, so sorry! I didn't mean to nose my way in. How utterly ill-mannered of me. I'm Jackson Morton, Miller's dance partner, among other things." He laughs and extends his hand toward Peter.

Peter gets a confused look on his face. "*Miller's* dance partner . . . ," he says slowly. A second later, he regains himself and shakes Jackson's hand. "Peter Bernstein. Nice to meet you. And this is my . . . Michelle." Jackson and Michelle nod at each other and say hello.

Jackson gives my waist a squeeze. "Darling, we really should get going. Peter, Michelle, it was a rare pleasure. Enjoy the festivities." And with that, he turns me around and steers me toward the other side of the tent, his arm still firmly around my waist.

First it seems like he's going to lead me back toward our group, which is downing drinks by the side of the dance floor, but he must see tears start to flood my eyes just about the same time I even notice that my vision has blurred. He quickly changes course, directing me out the side of the tent into the night.

Once we're a safe distance away, he turns me around to face him, taking my hands in his. "Let me guess. An ex?" I lower my head and nod, big fat tears plopping onto the top of his rough hands. "*The* ex?" I nod again. "The ex with his new . . . ?"

"Fiancée."

"Ah. And I would venture to say that you didn't know he had a new fiancée? Or that he was going to be here?" I shake my head no, sending more tears flying onto his floral button-down. He sighs heavily. "Is that your first encounter since the breakup?" I nod. "And that was how long. . . ."

I hold up two fingers. "Years," I gasp. The crying sound rumbles up from deep within, finally catching up to the flowing tears, the way thunder follows the lightning.

He folds me into his chest, wrapping his arms around my goose-bumped shoulders and rocking me from side to side. "Wretched, miserable heartbreak! Shhhh. It's okay. It's going to be all right," he soothes.

Suddenly, I pull away from him, an anger I've never felt before, not even right after Peter broke my heart, welling up inside me. I am enraged. Finally. "That fucking fuck!"

"Whoa!" Jackson takes a few steps back.

"I can't believe he's engaged! 'I'm with someone.' *With* someone! That's the understatement of the new millennium!"

"So, who is that blond bird?" He takes out a cigarette and lights up with a silver Zippo.

" '*My Michelle!*' How revolting. I can't believe this! I come to the *one* place on earth I think he would never be and *he's* here, with his fiancée no less!" I begin pacing in the dark damp grass, not caring that clumps of dirt are getting caught between my toes and are probably ruining my new sandals.

He takes a long drag on his cigarette. "I hate to tell you this, but I've found the Hamptons not to be the best hiding place."

"Hiding! Oh, I've done plenty of hiding. Believe me, I'm finished hiding!" I stop pacing and face Jackson. "I will not let him do this to me again! I will not go back there again!"

"Back into the tent?"

"No! To where I was, to where he left me! He bailed on me without warning—there were no signs at all!—and what he actually said could barely be considered an explanation. And then he acted like I never existed. After he broke my heart into a million pieces, do you think I got a letter, a late-night drunken-dial, a regretful e-mail, a

Far Side birthday card? Nothing. And she didn't even know who I was! Was I that unimportant to his life that I didn't even warrant a mention to the woman he is going to marry? I was with him for a year and a half! I was hardly a blip on the screen. Do you know how that feels?"

"It must be awful, I have to admit, but maybe she knows *exactly* who you are but was playing it cool. You know, pulling the 'I'm the new Alpha-Female' move. You New York women can be pretty harsh to one another. I've seen the women in my office treat one another like they're on an episode of *Dynasty*. It's brutal."

"Possibly, but you know, that's not even the worst of it. The real kicker of the whole thing is that I was a wreck for two years! I could barely leave my house!"

"I don't believe it. You? The last time I saw you actually sitting still was out by the pool Memorial Day weekend, and that was only because you were hung over. You're the girl on the go as far as I've seen."

"Believe it. You wanted to know my dirty little secret, now you know." Jackson, however, doesn't look as if he's relishing his victory. "The worst part is that I let Peter get away with it! He made me invisible—and I let him. And then I spent the next two years proving him right." I start pacing again. "Well, I allowed him to ruin two precious years of my life, but I'll be damned if I'm going to let him ruin one more fucking minute!"

"Do you want me to go find him and give him the what for?"

I stop and face Jackson. "No, screw him. I am *not* invisible. I am *not* a nobody! I am *somebody*, goddamn it! For Christ's sake, last night one of New York's most eligible bachelors—who owns a house on the beach, I might add—kissed *me*! You know what Peter can kiss? *My ass.* That piece of shit better have left this party, and his little dog too!" Am I cackling?

"You're cackling, my dear," Jackson says. A crooked, conspiratorial smirk spreads across his face. His eyes flash. "I like it."

I stop making whatever awful noise is coming out of my mouth. We stare at each other, listening to the bass line of the music wafting out from inside the tent. We both blink at the same time, uncertain of what might happen next.

If we were in a movie, I would grab his face and pull his lips to mine. I would kiss him deeply with excruciating passion, and he would take me in his arms, yielding to my intensity, feeding off of it.

But we're not in a movie. We're in a summer share together. And if I've learned anything over the last several weekends, it's that you follow the rules, particularly the unwritten ones. And you don't mess with the August First Rule, especially when it's only June.

I wipe the back of my hand across my tear-soaked face. I yank my compact out of my purse, swipe away the thickly smudged mascara under my eyes, and slap on some translucent powder. "Come on," I command, grabbing his wrist. "I need a drink!" I whip around and head back into the tent, dragging Jackson behind me. I know I'm cutting the line but I don't care. I get the attention of a bartender and beg him sweetly, if not a little maniacally, for two drinks. He is about to tell me to wait my goddamned turn when he sees my face, which must look not a little frightening. He looks around furtively, since people have become more cutthroat about procuring cocktails as the alcohol supply dwindles, and throws together two cups full of cranberry and vodka, and hands them to me. I palm him a crumpled ten-dollar bill even though it's an open bar. "Keep 'em coming."

I return to Jackson, who is standing a bit apart from the throngs surrounding the bar, and thrust a drink into his hand. "Wow, that was fast," he says.

"From now on, my friend, I am all about getting what I want when I want it."

"I'll say."

"Here's to driving the bus!" I say loudly, smashing my plastic cup against his with a little too much force.

"Driving the bus," he repeats uncertainly. He takes a swig and makes a face. "Christ, Miller! This drink is practically all vodka!"

"Is it? Good!" I swig mine down in a single pull and then grab his cup out of his hand. "I'll get you a beer instead. I've got an in with that bartender. Then, we're getting back on that dance floor."

7.

Drunk Bus Driving

Hamptons Unwritten Rule #19:
A thorough Party Postmortem is just
as important as having gone to the party
because that's how you find out what
really happened.

"Nice of you to show up to our meeting," Jimmy says the minute I walk through the door. "We have a ton of stuff to go through that we never got to on Friday because *somebody* wanted to leave early. Wait, why do you look so horrible?"

It's Monday, the Day After the Day After. I spent most of yesterday in the throes of a colossal funk-slash-hangover, hiding out in the yellow room, even though it was a gorgeous day and the housemates spent it at the beach (probably sleeping off their own hangovers, but still). When I could finally move beyond my bed, I arranged for a taxi to take me to the Hampton Jitney bus stop and slunk out of the house while everyone was still at the beach. It seemed easier than explaining my behavior on Saturday night. Not that I remember most of it.

I reach for a Krispy Kreme to go with the dwindling remnants of my iced skim latte. "I think I'm still hungover. Is that possible?" I lay my head on my arms.

"What happened?" Jerry asks.

I lift my head so I can see their faces when I tell them, "I saw Peter." They gasp, suitably horrified. "And there's more. He's engaged."

"Start from the beginning," they say simultaneously.

"Before we get to Peter, I should probably start with George. . . ."

"I almost forgot all about the big Friday night date! Hopefully there's some good news to be mined out of that story, please God?" Jerry asks.

I nod and launch in. Forty-two minutes, several gasps, and two doughnuts later . . . "Okay, so you don't kiss Jackson, which hello!, seemed like the *exact* right thing to do at that moment. Oh, well. Then you get trashed on no-name vodka—after having mixed it with what was probably cheap champagne, I might add—and then what?" Jimmy prods.

I sigh and keep going. After I slugged back the drink Jackson rejected, he and I rejoined our housemates on the dance floor. Jackson stayed close, which, by the look on Leah's face, made her none too happy. Despite the threat of instigating her wrath further, I was not about to give up my English man-nanny when I needed him most, so I didn't let Man Poppins leave my side for a second. Nor did I ever join Cassie in the VIP section. I had already thoroughly embarrassed myself in front of Jackson; I wasn't about to do the same with anyone else, especially the always-appropriate Fashionista Socialista.

But there were at least a couple more humiliations for me to endure.

As I danced, I remained on full alert, a lethal combination of anger, rejection, and alcohol still boiling just under the surface. I couldn't help but scan the crowd, looking for Peter. I wanted that awful feeling to go away, but no matter how much I drank or how fervently I danced, the feeling just dug its claws in deeper, reasserting its hold on my shattered heart.

My vigilance paid off: I finally caught sight of what looked to be the top of Peter's head on the other side of the tent. (Now I know what that stupid moth who was so attracted to the flame felt like.) I told Jackson that I was going to the bathroom and somehow convinced him that I didn't need a police escort. As I headed in Peter's direction, I saw that the evil Michelle was still attached to his arm and that they were slipping out of the side of the tent. I sped up and followed them outside.

It wasn't a very long chase. When my eyes adjusted to the darkness, I caught sight of them behind the back of the tent. There they were: Peter, substantially taller than Michelle; she was standing on her tiptoes, his arms were encircling her waist. He was bent toward her . . . and then it struck me: she's *mini. Mini-Michelle.* Peter always used to say he liked that I was tall, since he was six three, and he liked not feeling like a circus sideshow when we were out together. In fact, he once told me he made it a rule never to date women shorter than five six. But here he was, *engaged* to a woman whose feet probably didn't even touch the floor when she sat on the bus. They were kissing—not mauling each other—but giving each other tiny kitten kisses in between private, hushed whispers. They looked like they were deeply in love, like they didn't have a care in the world, and, in fact, weren't even taking notice that the world was going on around them. Or that I existed and was standing only a few yards away.

I don't know who I hated more in that moment: them or me.

I felt sick to my stomach. I stomped toward the Porta Pottis trailer but the torrent of my tears was blinding. My heels kept getting stuck in the grass, causing me to stumble several times. Sure, Stacy warned us about every other freakin' detail of the evening except for how much easier it would've been to wear flats or wedge heels!

Next thing I knew, I opened my eyes and realized I was lying in the backseat of someone's car, staring up through an open sunroof at the blurry and fast-moving stars overhead. Which made me nauseous. Which made me close my eyes again.

Then I remember spending some quality time in the North Wing

bathroom, gripping the porcelain tightly with both hands, relieved
to have a physical way to exorcise not only the high levels of alcohol
in my blood but also the fear, hate, and pain that still held too
tightly around my heart. I think I was crying in between the heav-
ing. Good times.

Sometime later I woke up in the yellow room, shockingly in my
own bed, in my pajamas. The room was filled with the murky light
of early morning and the sound of Stacy lightly snoring, so I knew
that I didn't die of alcohol poisoning, which, given how I felt all
day yesterday, might've been a more humane outcome. I tried to
turn over but my stomach heaved, making me too afraid to move
again. Thankfully, I fell asleep-slash-passed out and slept until almost noon, then threw myself in the shower to prepare myself for
the trip home.

"Oy vey." Jerry now sighs, shaking his head back and forth.

"But wait, you haven't even heard the kicker."

Jimmy learns forward, gripping the table. "Don't tell me: that
beyatch boyfriend stealer Michelle is preggers!"

"Nope. Better. Listen to this. Cassie called me at home last night.
She wanted to make sure I was all right, since she heard that I wasn't
feeling well from. . . ."

"Stacy, who else. Cassie didn't see you all shit-faced and passing
out, right?" Jimmy pleads.

"I don't think so. She didn't mention it. So, I asked her a bunch
of questions about her evening so we wouldn't have to talk about
mine. She was telling me that she had a great time except for this
annoying girl she's known forever who's on the charity committee,
who was going around showing off her engagement ring and her fi-
ancé, *in that order*."

"Let me guess: Mini-Ms.-M. and Peter?" Jerry asks.

"Could the Hamptons *be* any more incestuous?" Jimmy says. "I
thought the Pines were bad."

"Cassie said, 'I actually felt bad for the guy! He didn't say much, but Michelle kept sending him off for drinks, not just for her, but for anyone who wanted one, like he was a waiter. He clearly hasn't caught on to what Michelle is all about.' You know how her name is Michelle Fortunato? Cassie said a lot of people who know her call her 'Michelle Certifiable.' Apparently, she's one of those girls who think her parents' money automatically makes her a great person, but what she doesn't realize is that her parents' money is practically her only redeeming quality and pretty much the only reason that anyone tolerates her."

"She's insane, shallow, and lives off of Mummy's and Daddy's money? That's awesome!" Jimmy says.

"Cassie said she actually began to wonder for the first time whether Michelle was smarter than she thought because she trapped someone who seems normal or whether he must be stupid for not seeing that she's completely insane. And get this: they've only been together for like seven or eight months!"

"Well, at least they weren't dating when you were with him. . . ."

"Jimmy!" Jerry and I admonish at the same time.

"What? It's not outside the realm of possibility that Peter, air-quote, released you because he had met somebody else!"

"Sweetie, just ignore him," Jerry suggests. "Continue."

"Where was I? Right, Cassie said the scuttlebutt is that Michelle pressured Peter to propose before the summer, and some people were saying she even threatened to break up with him by Memorial Day if he didn't seal the deal."

"Woah, that's some story. So now, you're . . . what? Okay? Upset? Freaked out?" Jerry asks, brows furrowed for the first time in weeks.

"Sad and hurt. Because this just confirms that not only did he not want to marry me, but also that I didn't mean as much to him as I thought I did, or as much as he meant to me. Which actually makes me feel foolish for having wasted so much time mourning our so-called perfect relationship. It clearly wasn't all that perfect, especially if he'd rather marry someone like Michelle than me."

"They ain't married yet," Jimmy points out.

"Or," Jerry says, removing his glasses and rubbing his eyes, "you could think about it this way: if they do end up married, then Peter gets to lie in the bed of his own making, or whatever the saying is, which from what Cassie reported, isn't going to be all that pleasant. While you get to do whatever you want, with whomever you want, whenever you want, for as long as you want—or not."

"Driving the bus . . . ," I mumble.

Jerry continues. "Starting with a very fine candidate, one Mr. George Daniels, Bachelor Extraordinaire. So, you tell me: who's getting the better deal in all this?"

Is it possible that the answer is finally me?

. . .

"Michelle Fortunato?!" This is about the eighty-seventh time in the last forty minutes Alice has repeated something I've said in that irritating, exaggerated, incredulous tone that only gets more irritating as it continues. I cringe when she does it for the eighty-eighth time: "They're engaged?!" Before I can finish the story—which I'm telling her at the outside tables at Friend of a Farmer on Irving Place because she actually said she was sick of sushi, a veritable first, I think—she's already begun her "Alice to the Rescue" bit. "Maybe you should take a break from the Hamptons for a little while. You could come up to the Berkshires with us this weekend."

"Thanks, but I'm fine, really. I'm totally looking forward to the holiday weekend. I already have some plans that sound—"

"You know you don't have to do the stoic-girl routine for me. I can only imagine how devastating this must be."

"Al, listen to me: it's all good. I was talking to the boys about it this morning. The summer is whizzing by, and maybe this is just the thing I needed to commit to the moving-on-with-my-life process, so I don't waste another minute."

"Optimally that would be the case, but you've only just come out

of a two-year-long depression. You can't expect yourself to just snap
back into place without a couple of setbacks along the way. It's perfectly fine for you to be upset about this. It doesn't mean you're going to sink back into your hole again. I know you're scared about
that. But maybe it means you just take it easy for a few weeks, steer
clear of the house and those people for a while until you get your
head back on straight. . . ." She continues to talk at me as we pay the
check and walk onto the sidewalk into the dusky purple evening on
Irving Place, a low-key, short street between Gramercy Park South
and Fourteenth Street.

We're standing on the corner, Alice still talking away, when I notice that a restaurant across the street has closed. I feel like I was
there recently . . . yet as I stand here, I realize that I haven't been
there for almost three years, maybe more. I can picture it like it was
yesterday: Alice, Scott, Peter, and I had gone there one Friday night
to celebrate Alice and Scott's recent engagement. I vaguely remember being pissed at Alice by the end of dinner, which is not something I felt often toward my best friend. What could I possibly have
been upset about?

And then it comes to me: instead of talking about her and Scott,
their wedding plans, what they were going to do about their apartments and the like—as most newly engaged women do—she kept
grilling Peter about his job, the lease on his apartment, and his future plans. She never directly came out and asked if he was going to
propose to me, but with every veiled, falsely casual question, it was
obvious to me that was what she was getting at. Though Peter
didn't usually like people prying, we all had drunk a lot of champagne, and I could tell he was enjoying sparring with Alice (he was
well aware of her bossy tendencies and occasionally enjoyed egging
her on to see how far she'd go), so he answered all of Alice's questions, which upset me even more, while he shrewdly dodged the
very thing she wanted to know.

For the first several minutes, I was shocked because I had never seen her act like that before. Throughout the years she certainly never tap-danced around her own marital ambitions, but while I had known her to coax me behind the scenes—usually when it made pretty obvious sense for her to do so, even I had to admit—I had never seen her go for the jugular so nakedly when it came to my stuff, especially directly to my person, perhaps because I never had a "person" before Peter. After several minutes, I realized I wasn't imagining how outrageous she was being, but it was too late: Alice had become a pit bull, her jaw locked around something that she mistook as fair game.

At first, I was embarrassed. What if Peter thought that I had put her up to this? Then I was mortified, but on her behalf. She seemed to have no idea that Peter was playing her and just kept going. Finally, I was seething. It was one thing to talk with me privately about how great it would be if we were on the parallel marriage track, but quite another to put my boyfriend on the spot about it and in front of me to boot.

Peter and I had been moving at our own pace. I was happy and comfortable with where we were and how things were going. I knew we were serious in all the ways I hadn't ever been with anyone before, which seemed like a minor miracle in and of itself: we had exchanged "I love you's" and keys, not necessarily in that order; we had met each other's parents; we spent almost every night with each other and planned all of our vacations together. We had touched on the subject of marriage once or twice—we both wanted it (so he said at the time), but neither of us felt any need to run to the wedding registry at Bloomingdale's that minute. And I was good with all that. Not long after Peter and I started dating and all that stuff fell into place, I assumed Peter and I would end up together and so figured there was nothing to worry about.

Until Alice's Inquisition.

Her relentless interrogation was enough to irk me. But then, Peter's clever responses, never actually committing to a commitment—and, of course, why would he do so under those circumstances, it was none of her business until it was officially his and mine—had planted the tiniest little seed.

The seed turned out to be a weed. Of a creeping nature.

After that awful night, I never admitted to Alice my newfound, growing doubt about Peter, because I never actually admitted it to myself. I struggled not to think about it again—wholly (but silently) blaming Alice for being an inappropriate pain in the ass while fervently ignoring Peter's vague responses and what they might mean (after all, he was just giving her back a dose of her own medicine! I knew what his intentions were!)—until Peter actually hit me over the head with the Frying Pan of Truth in the Taxicab from/to Hell.

Turns out, hoping is not the same as knowing.

I brush away the unpleasant memory. Before me stands Alice. My best friend. My oldest friend. My surrogate sister. I study her face, virtually unchanged from the day I met her in humanities class freshman year, when she became the first person in my life who recognized something inside me that I didn't even know existed and instantly became the closest friend I ever had because of it.

Try as I might right now, I am hearing her talk, hearing her speak words and sentences, but I can't listen. I don't know why. All at once, I want to hug her, but just as much, I want to walk away as fast as I can.

She has suddenly stopped talking and has a strange look on her face. Have I magically willed her to shut up? "Is that your cell phone?" I rifle around in my bag to extricate my bleating cell, which, I suspect just to mock me, works perfectly in Manhattan. On the screen is a familiar unfamiliar number. "Go ahead, answer it."

I do. It's George. I ask him to hold on and press the mute button. "Alice, it's George and he's at the airport about to leave for an overnight business trip. . . ."

An inscrutable look flashes across her face. "Talk to him. I told

Scott I'd be home early anyway. Call me before the weekend." She kisses me on my cheek, squeezes me on the arm. "I'm glad you're good. Really."

Then we turn away from each other. She walks north, toward the subway to begin her journey uptown, while I walk in the other direction, heading downtown, toward home.

To: Jackson.Morton@fsgpublishers.com
From: miller@millerworks.com
Date: Wednesday, June 27, 2007
Subject: Jackson to the rescue

Jackson,

I just wanted to thank you for *everything* Saturday night. My behavior was appalling, but I'm so very grateful to you for:

1. Posing as my dapper, dashing British boyfriend ;-) to my former flame and the blond, clearly inadequate replacement

2. Letting me rant/rave like a lunatic

3. Dancing with me for what must've been hours

4. Finding me (passed out? pls. confirm) by the Porta Pottis

5. Throwing my (sorry, drunken) ass in your car and getting me home safely

6. Positioning me in the proper prayer position in front of the porcelain god

7. Managing to not only find my jammies, but also wrestling them onto what must've been a pretty uncooperative body (hope you didn't peek, not that I would know if you had) and depositing me in the horizontal position in the yellow room

8. And finally, being a true and discreet friend by *promising* me on your Great Grandmama's grave that you will never breathe, sigh, or utter a word of the gory details of the events outlined above, no matter how tantalizing, to a single housemate—or even, for that matter, to anyone older than two years of age or living within a 500-mile radius of New York City

You are the best!!! I owe you big-time.

xo, m.

To: miller@millerworks.com

From: Jackson.Morton@fsgpublishers.com

Date: Wednesday, June 27, 2007

Re: Subject: Jackson to the rescue

Miller, my dear, dear friend:

While there's nothing more that I love on God's green one than lavish praise—so much of which, it has to be numerically listed, which is a most welcome first for me, btw—I can't take credit where and when it is not rightfully due. I most humbly (ha!) accept your gratitude for Items #1–3. Regarding item #8, of course! I take it to my grave! Discreet is my middle name! (Well, Kingsley is my middle name, but in Olde English Kingsley means "scrupulously discreet." ;-)) Sadly—at least for me—I cannot lay claim to the remaining actions as outlined in Items #4–7. But you know I would've happily done those things if called upon in the line of duty.

I hope you're feeling back up to snuff, as July 4th weekend is almost upon us and the fun is not showing any signs of waning yet. Bully for us, no?

j.k.m. iii

To: Jackson.Morton@fsgpublishers.com

From: miller@millerworks.com

Date: Wednesday, June 27, 2007

Re: Subject: Jackson to the rescue

Oh. My. God. *Please* tell me you're joking. If it wasn't you then . . . who???????????

To: miller@millerworks.com

From: Jackson.Morton@fsgpublishers.com

Date: Wednesday, June 27, 2007

Re: Subject: Jackson to the rescue

All bets are now off. You must indulge me in a little good-natured ribbing. I've held off for this long in deference to your recent emotional trauma.

YOU MEAN YOU DON'T' REMEMBER THE WHOLE REST OF THE NIGHT, YOU DRUNKEN LUSH? I THOUGHT *YOU* WERE JUST KIDDING BY THANKING ME FOR THE SAFE RETURN!

Seriously, it was not me who ultimately saved you from your highly pickled demons. And if I were a less nice person, I would enjoy torturing you longer, but alas, I am a gentleman (or at least, my parents always demanded that I be), and I know that you have suffered enough for this lifetime . . . or at the very least, this summer.

So, no, it was not your favorite ("dashing, dapper") Brit who got you home, emptied out, hosed off, and put to bed. It was Everyone's Favorite All-American Boy, the one who resides in the palatial suite just down the hall from me.

P.S. Since my ego is very fragile (and super-sized like everything else here in America), perhaps you could not exhibit nearly as much enthusiasm when thanking him as you did with me. I'd like to maintain the illusion of my being your primary hero for as long as possible.

Reborn on the Fourth of July

June

Su	Mo	Tu	We	Th	Fr	Sa
					1	2
3	4	5	6	7	8	9
10	11	12	13	14	15	16
17	18	19	20	21	22	23
24	25	26	27	28	29	30

July

Su	Mo	Tu	We	Th	Fr	Sa
1	2	3	4	5	6	7
8	9	10	11	12	13	14
15	16	17	18	19	20	21
22	23	24	25	26	27	28
29	30	31				

Hamptons Unwritten Rule #20:
If you're not in fighting shape by the
July 4th Weekend Triathlon, then maybe
you should consider spending your
summers elsewhere.

Fourth of July weekend. The unfailing sign that summer is in full
swing. By early July, hot weather has become the rule rather than
the exception. Everyone is now settled into their summer situations.
Summer routines are no longer new, but not yet tiresome. The days
are long and languid; the nights are sweet and sultry, with what
seems like an entire nation of cicadas and crickets whirring and
buzzing away their brief hours of darkness. The ocean isn't as warm

as it'll be in August, but it's no longer as frigid as it was in late May, when it welcomed only the hardy and foolhardy.

Even though the calendar says we're not yet halfway through summer, we're solidly past the pregame show. As June comes to a close, my in-box is full of unmistakable signs that the pace is poised to quicken, e-mail upon e-mail solidifying plans for the weekend. The housemates have been grousing since the beginning of the summer because this year July 4th is on a Wednesday, meaning everyone is gypped out of a long weekend. But my clever friends and their Hamptons peers have figured out a work-around: instead of celebrating during one long weekend, the festivities will be spread over two. For the first leg of the July 4th Extravaganza, we're all going to a fancy invite-only soiree at Absentee Abigail's parents' estate in Southampton on Friday night, and the next night I am going with George to what sounds like an exclusive (meaning expensive) benefit while the housemates have reservations at Madame Tong's, a trendy restaurant in Southampton that turns into a dance club after the kitchen closes, which actually sounds like a lot of fun.

Let's get this bus in gear. It's Miller Time.

Hamptons Unwritten Rule #21:
Hamptons parents—especially wealthy ones—
are a breed unto themselves. And they know
how to throw parties.

It's a little after seven o'clock and our caravan has just arrived at the Greers' annual Fourth of July celebration. After being driven in golf carts from the valet station at the top of the long, hedgerow-lined driveway to the "property," we are met by Abigail, who seems to have stopped scowling for the first time since I met her, because standing next to her is her boyfriend, Graham, who is making his East End debut. She then introduces us to her parents. Mr. and Mrs. Greer are personable and gracious, despite the picture Abigail had painted of them during her one weekend in the share house as alcoholic, WASP-y, overbearing ogres. It's obvious that Abigail's mother is very well preserved through the wonders of plastic surgery and strategically placed injections, but other than that, as far as I can tell, she doesn't seem capable of falling down drunk, hitting on the waitstaff, or eating any small children, as had allegedly been Mrs. Greer's wont at other public events, according to her daughter.

With the pleasantries out of the way, the housemates shift into full-on party mode, first by immediately sussing out the food and drink situation, then dispersing to do a lap to see if any bold-faced names are in attendance. The crowd is a mix of wealthy older types, who are friends and neighbors of Abigail's parents; people in their thirties and early forties, who were invited by Abigail and her siblings; and a handful of people who are famous enough that you recognize them but who look enough like regular people when the cameras aren't rolling. The traditional house sits on an expanse of green lawn that slopes down to a glittering green pond.

"Are you taking a night off from your mayoral duties?" I say to Andrew, who has just brought me a drink from one of the many fully stocked bars that have been set out on the lawn. "I would think that July Fourth would be one of your busiest holidays, with the parades down Main Street and the town fireworks and all."

Andrew smiles. "My deputy is filling in for me. Tonight I'm off the clock, so I can relax a little, as long as there are no cameras here." He feigns dodging paparazzi. "Hey, let's go check out the pond. Lower profile down there." We head through the forming crowds of guests and walk down to the reedy shore. A few ducks are floating aimlessly on the surface of the water, quietly quacking among themselves.

"You know it's a funny thing about outdoor parties. All the

women get dressed up and wear expensive killer sandals, but then they end up standing in damp grass, heels sinking into the dirt like golf tees the entire time. You don't know how many pairs of shoes I've already ruined out here."

"No danger of that for you tonight," he says, eyeing my Rafē flat thong sandals, which are adorned with enamel and crystal sea-horses, purchased during a pre-July 4th multistore shopping spree with Alice.

I smile at him. "I'm smarter than the average bear."

"That's for sure, Yogi. I would say you're even above average in a lot of ways, and not just in smarts."

I look at him sideways. I'm not sure if he's teasing me or not. Is that a reference to last Saturday night? Ever since Jackson told me it was Andrew who took care of me after the event, though I know I should thank him—and I *want* to thank him—I've been avoiding saying anything to him about the incident. When I thought it was Jackson who had batted cleanup, I wasn't as embarrassed, since he had experienced the whole thing right along with me and promised to be discreet. But the fact that it was Andrew who did the dirty work, I'm just too mortified to own up to it to him, not only because he saw me in my worst possible light, but also because that would probably mean telling him the whole story, which would lead to questions, which would lead to another story, which would be . . . too much information. And being the consummate politician, he knows better than to behave like a stark-raving lunatic at public events. Unlike me.

So, I decided to take the grown-up approach of abject avoidance, but now I'm not sure if the Mayor is on board with that or not. "And what's that supposed to mean, Mr. Mayor?"

"You just seem different from most people out here. In a good way. Like there's something behind the brains and beauty, something deeper."

"I'm not going to touch the brains and beauty comment for the moment other than to say thank you for the compliment, but what makes you think there's anything important or unusual going on underneath the surface? I'm just like everyone else. What you see is what you get."

"That may be true for a lot of people, but not for you."

"How can you be sure about that? We've only been living in the same house together for a handful of weekends, adding up to what, maybe a dozen or so days total? What could you have possibly learned about me in that brief period that I haven't told you?"

He turns to look straight into my eyes. "I hate to tell ya, Miz Daniels, but a lot."

I laugh nervously. "Oh, yeah, Mr. Mayor? Go ahead, tell me what you know." I hold my breath. When I get my hands on Jackson, I am going to kill him . . . or was it the House Mouthpiece who succeeded in doing what she does best?

"You always eat the same thing for breakfast: nonfat vanilla yogurt and fruit, but you have a major weak spot for doughnuts. You take your iced coffee with skim milk. You don't sleep too late in the morning . . . unless you're hungover, which, has happened *on occasion. . . .*"

"Okay, big deal. Breakfast and sleeping habits . . ."

"I'm not done yet. I was just getting warmed up." He grins. "You manage to sneak in a fair bit of TV watching, but not to zone out like most people, but almost as if you're studying for exams. You're extremely clever and funny, but sometimes it seems like you hold yourself back—I'm not quite sure why. We've already established that I know you sometimes clam up and go inside yourself when you aren't comfortable in social situations, usually in the safety of a nice corner—I hope you're working on that."

"I'm at this party socializing, aren't I?"

"Well, first of all, there aren't any corners out here, and secondly, I wouldn't say hanging down by the pond with one of your own housemates is exactly socializing."

"Andrew, don't sell yourself short. You are hardly just a housemate. Arguably, you are one of the most popular of all the guests—"

He continues, wisely cutting off my tired teasing. "I know you catch yourself sometimes, like, when you finally begin to feel more at ease, or let yourself be happy and relaxed, you stop, like you're reminding yourself of something you forgot. Oh, and you don't realize how cute you are."

I blink at him. "Alrighty then, Kane, you can stop yanking my chain. This has got to be something right out of the Mayor Handbook. I bet you do this disarming-flirty-nice-attentive-guy bit with all the girls."

"All who girls?"

"Yeah, Mayor. Good one. I think I'm going to believe you about as far as I can throw you across this pond."

He shakes his head, a wry smile on his face. "*And* you use humor to defuse serious conversations."

"Fine. You got me on that one. As for the other stuff, I can't possibly tell you if you're right or not."

"And why's that?"

I tamp my sandal down on the squishy sand, causing tiny air bubbles to pop open around my foot. "Because that would necessitate me knowing exactly who I am."

He leans forward to catch my eye. "You don't know who you are?"

I stare out over the rippling water, the setting sun behind us casting its long, warm light on the tips of the reeds that line the opposite shore. "No, I don't think I've figured it out yet," I say quietly.

"Maybe you know who you are but you haven't accepted who you are yet."

I turn to look at him. "I was kind of hoping there was still some flexibility there. You know, to make some last-minute changes before full-on acceptance. Do you think I could apply for an extension?"

He laughs. "Well, maybe some people are always a work in progress. I'm envious of that ability to keep changing. I think I lost that a long time ago."

"What do you mean? You don't feel like you keep growing?"

"No. I wish I did, but I think I might've missed my chance." He turns back to look out over the water. He looks sad. The sparks he usually has in his eyes have suddenly gone out. It makes me shiver, even though the breeze is warm.

I put my hand on his forearm. "Maybe you'll pleasantly surprise yourself. Being able to recognize things like that about yourself, having that ability to be introspective, is half the battle. If you know where you are and how you got here, maybe you can decide where you want to go."

He looks back at me, present again. "I hope so. It's nice enough where I am right now, but I wouldn't want to live here forever."

Before I can ask where "here" is for him, a huge seagull comes dive-bombing out of the sky, shrieking loudly and aiming for something not too far away from the content group of ducks. The bird dips down, clamps something in his beak, and swerves back up toward the sky. But the damage has been done. The ducks, caught unaware, quack and flap their wings noisily at the intruder, and then take off, one after another, into the air in search of another peaceful refuge. After a few minutes of staring out at the now-empty pond, Andrew turns to me, smiles, and takes my elbow, gently guiding me back to the heart of the party.

Hamptons Unwritten Rule #22:
Steamy July nights are the best breeding ground for nocturnal confessions.

"Miller! Wake up! I have to talk to you!"

I pull myself from the depths of sleep. "Cassie? Is everything okay?" I lean on my elbow, squinting at her face, which seems to be glowing in the predawn light. "What time is it?"

"Shh! It's almost five. Come into my room so we don't wake Stacy."

Since Abigail is staying at her parents' house for the weekend, I settle into the empty bed. I cover my mouth as a huge yawn tries to escape. For once, I'm not hungover, since I volunteered to be the D.D. in order to force me to pace myself, since the holiday weekend has only just begun.

"You won't believe what just happened to me!" She plants her hands on the bed and leans toward me. "Miller. I. Just. Met. The. Man. I. Am. Going. To. Marry."

"What? Where? When?"

"At Abigail's parents' party! Well, after the party I guess is more accurate." She sits down on her bed, knees curled up to her chest and arms wrapped around her legs. "I stayed late to hang out with Abigail and Graham after everyone had left. We were out back on the patio, sharing a bottle of wine, when a tall man appeared out of nowhere. We were all a little startled at first, but it turned out Abigail knew him. Miller, he's so handsome! You wouldn't believe. He literally is tall, dark, and handsome. Sort of a Pierce Brosnan look. Hair a little wavier, I think. . . ." She drifts off, smiling up to the ceiling. "And he kisses like a movie star. . . ."

"How did we get from tall stranger emerging from the darkness to kissing? And how do you know how movie stars kiss? Be kind, rewind."

"His name is Phillip Dunne. He's the Greers' next-door neighbor. He's divorced, well, divorced from his first wife and in the process of divorcing his second wife, or maybe they're legally separated. . . . I'm not totally sure, but his wife definitely doesn't live with him anymore. He has teenaged kids, but they only stay with him during vacations and some weekends. They're at tennis camp for the summer."

"Wait, how old is this guy that he'll have been divorced almost twice and has teenagers?"

"I think early fifties. If he's older than that, he doesn't look it. He's really athletic. He runs, bikes, and does yoga. He did a triathlon last year. He's a really successful hedge fund guy. He has been profiled in the Business Section of the *Times* and the *Wall Street Journal* a bunch of times, so I've read about him before but never met him. And he's writing a book!"

I have never heard of the guy, but that means zilch. "I don't think I'm following—why did he show up so late? Was he even invited to the party?"

"Yes, but he had a dinner he had to attend first. He was supposed to come afterward but the dinner ran longer than he expected and he couldn't get out of it. He felt terrible that he missed everything, so Abigail offered him a glass of wine." She giggles. "He told me later that he was happy to have an excuse to stay and talk to me, but if Abigail hadn't invited him, he would've stayed anyway. Isn't that sweet?"

"Very."

"So, the four of us talked for a while and then Abigail and her boyfriend went to bed. Phillip and I stayed outside for another hour or two, maybe? We couldn't stop talking! And he kept saying things like, if he had known I would be at the party, he would've ditched his dinner party entirely, and that even though he was pretty sure the party was finished when he got home, because he didn't see any cars in the street, he felt something propelling him to come over there. Isn't that wild?!" She's bouncing up and down like a little girl at a slumber party.

"Wild! Wow, Cass! And then?"

"And then he said he was dying to invite me back over to his house so we could keep talking, but he didn't want to seem inappropriate, so instead he suggested we have a real date first, but as soon as possible. So we're going to some big party tomorrow night, or, I guess, technically tonight. Then he walked me to my car and we kissed. He even called me on my cell a little while ago to make sure I got home safely and say good night again. I have never felt like this before. Anytime anyone's ever told me they fell in love at first sight, I always thought it was such bullshit. Didn't you? I mean, yeah, I could see knowing *early on* if someone is the one, but I never, ever believed in love at *first* sight. But suddenly I'm beginning to think it's possible. Maybe you don't believe it until it happens to you."

"Possibly . . ." The debate about love at first sight aside, what I'm having trouble believing is how this could be the same person who seemed untouchable when it came to men. The woman with the rotating roster of members from the International Bachelors Club has been clocked in the head with Cupid's arrow bag? Or is Phillip Dunne just the sugar daddy she was waiting for, the one Alice predicted Cassie would find? At the sight of Cassie's shining face, I push away the thought. "What great news. I'm so happy for you!" The yawn I'd been stifling for the last ten minutes finally forces its way out.

"I'm so sorry for waking you up! But I had to tell you the minute I got home, just to make sure I wasn't imagining the whole thing, you know? I should let you get back to sleep."

"Do you want me to stay up a little longer so you can tell me more?"

"You're sweet to offer but I'm sure I'll be talking your ear off about it plenty. Thanks for listening . . . and not hating me for waking you up." She gives me a hug. We're friends. Even in my delirious state of sleep deprivation, I'm happy.

Hamptons Unwritten Rule #23, Part One:
Do get caught in the act . . .

By the time George arrives to pick me up later that day for our second date, I notice how I feel one thousand percent better than I did this time only one week ago. It's amazing what a little attitude adjustment, retail therapy, a perfect holiday weekend soiree (with real fireworks, not the emotional kind), a seeming lack of repercussions from prior bad behavior, and having your closest summer friend falling in love can do to you.

"Miller, you look gorgeous," says George as I walk toward where he's leaning against his car in our driveway.

I'm wearing a new dress that I also scored during my shopping spree. It's a dusty rose pink silk number, spaghetti straps, kind of floaty where it hits right at my knee. It's the kind of dress that makes me happy that I don't have big boobs, since there would be no way to wear it with a bra. It's just me, the dress, and the baby pink mesh of my brand-new Cosabella thong that the Transformation Trio recommended I buy in every color to replace my serviceable yet decidedly unsexy Hanes for Her. "*Never* wear anything on your private hoochal area that you can buy in a *supermarket* unless it's disposable," Frederique had counseled. "Especially if there's a chance of it being seen."

When I reach George, he spins me around and then pulls me toward him for a very enthusiastic kiss hello. "Mmmm," he murmurs into my neck, which sends shivers down my back. "I wish we didn't have to go to the party."

The feeling is mutual. He's looking summer fresh in a pale green button-down, khaki linen jacket, white twill pants, and expensive tan loafers. His hair his still damp from a recent shower, and he smells like limes.

The front door of the house opens and a freshly showered, betoweled Andrew steps out. I reflexively pull away from George, both embarrassed to be caught canoodling in the driveway and self-conscious of the fact that my date is witnessing more share-house shenanigans, this time, my housemate parading around outside practically naked.

"Sorry, didn't know anyone was out here . . . just forgot something in my car," Andrew explains sheepishly as he tiptoes barefoot across the tiny white and gray pebbles of the driveway.

"No problem," George calls back. "Ready?" he asks me.

"Sure, let's go." George makes his way to the other side as I spy Andrew struggling to retrieve his bag from his truck and almost lose his towel in the process. When he turns around, he catches me watching him. He gives me a little wave and then disappears back into the house.

Hamptons Unwritten Rule #23, Part Two:
. . . and make sure there's proof.

George and I have arrived at the home of Alvin Schwartz—a very rich and powerful Hamptonite who happens to control half of the residential real estate agencies on the East End—for what looks to be quite the extravagant patriotic celebration. The guests are mostly other rich and powerful Hamptonites, with a few rich and powerful Los Angelinos thrown in for good measure. I scan the crowd, looking for evidence of Peter and his fiancée, since she is supposedly some socialite who could very well be on the same social circuit as George. I'm torn between wanting them to be here, for Peter to see me on George's arm, and being sick to my stomach at the thought that I might have to suffer a second run-in. The coast seems to be clear, though I stay on high alert for the rest of the evening in case they arrive later.

This event makes Abigail's parents' party—an authentic Texas BBQ for one hundred with a ten-minute fireworks display over the pond—seem like a seven-year-old's birthday. We're about to enjoy a four-course sit-down dinner for three hundred outside under the largest freestanding tent I've ever seen. There are several bars set up all over the property and a multiple-piece band playing on a stage.

"At least there's no ice sculpture of a swan," I say to George. "That would just be too over-the-top, don't you think?"

"Well, it's not a swan, that's for sure." I follow his gaze. Lo and behold, in the center of all the tables, stands a monstrous ice sculpture of the Statue of Liberty, out of which chilled vodka is flowing freely, available to anyone who grabs a shot glass at the sculpture's base. God bless America.

We spend the next half hour crowd hopping as George maneuvers us from one cluster to another. Luckily for me, some of the people here were either at George's party or at the painter's cocktail party last weekend or both, so as George makes conversation with the men, I chitchat with their wives and girlfriends.

"Is that Cassie over there?" I ask George as we are returning from one of the bars with refreshed cocktails.

"Where? Yup, that's her. Is she with Phillip Dunne?"

I give him a quick rendition of what I can remember from my early morning news flash from Cassie.

He laughs. "Cassandra *in love*? That'll be the day. I'll believe it when I see it. Cassandra Dearborn doesn't fall in love. She collects men like handbags."

"I haven't known her as long as you have, but maybe it has finally happened. It seems like the real deal to me from the way she was talking. And she certainly seems convinced of it."

We watch as Cassie and Phillip move closer for a kiss. Then George grabs my hand and pulls me to him. "Well, maybe it's just further proof that almost anything is possible during the summer in the Hamptons."

"You don't know the half of it. Let's go say hi, okay?" I release myself from his embrace and turn, gently tugging him behind me.

Instead of following me, he loops our held hands around the front of my waist and pulls me backward to him. "Anything you want, beautiful." Just as he's nuzzling his face into my neck, I'm blinded by a bright flash of light.

"Sorry to catch you off guard, George, but I couldn't resist such a great candid shot."

Through the white splotches that are now veiling my vision I can just make out a man with straight dirty-blond hair, wearing a blue blazer, standing before us holding a giant camera.

"Not a problem, Patrick. Good to see you," George replies.

"I was just on my way over to get some shots of Alvin, but I'll be back later to get your date's name." The photographer taps the microphone on the side of his camera, nods, and hustles toward the house.

"Who was that?"

"Patrick McMullan. He covers all of the big parties out here."

Suddenly I hear Cassie's voice. "Hey, you! I didn't know you'd be here!" She bestows a double air kiss on my cheeks, or at least near them.

"Hi, yourself! I didn't know this is where I'd be either. Actually, we were just coming over to see you."

"Cassandra, *quelle surprise* running into you here," George says drolly, dutifully leaning forward for his no-contact kisses.

"Well, you know me. . . ." she says with a smile.

"That I do indeed," George responds. "So, a little birdie tells me you've been bitten by the love bug."

"The birdie speaks the truth." She smiles. She is even more radiant than usual.

"Phillip Dunne, huh? Nice get, Dearborn."

"Why thank you. Have you met him yet?"

"I don't need to. I've been playing racquetball with that old fart at the club for years," George answers.

"Get out! Why haven't you introduced us?"

"You beat me to the punch, as usual. He's only been separated for about three minutes."

"Really? Is that true, Cass?" I ask.

"George is exaggerating. It's been at least a few weeks."

George continues. "Besides, I didn't think he was your type."

"He's tall, dark, devilishly handsome, and rich. What's not to like?"

"Well, for one thing, he seems to like getting married . . ."

"So? A woman can change her ways."

". . . and divorced."

"So? A woman can change a man's ways." She winks. "Here he comes!" Phillip Dunne is inarguably handsome, if you like that bordering-on-could-be-my-father thing, except for one detail: he has the evil eyebrow. I can't tell if he's happy or pissed off, because the natural arch of his dark eyebrows gives him a constant menacing look. I can see why Cassie was scared when he first popped out of the bushes last night: if I had to guess what the Hamptons Potato Field Killer looked like, Phillip Dunne would be it.

"Miller, it's a pleasure. I've heard so much about you," Phillip says.

"You have? In the course of the last eighteen hours?" I didn't actually mean to say that out loud.

Luckily he laughs, only he still looks pissed off even as he does. "Daniels, I'm surprised to see you standing upright. I thought I pretty much incapacitated you during our match last week."

"I see you've already met my *second* favorite Hamptons girl, Cassandra." He squeezes my hand, which he's still holding. I squeeze it back.

Phillip too chides George for not introducing him to Cassie sooner. This time, George keeps his snide commentary to himself.

"I usually like to leave these things up to fate," George hedges artfully.

"Fate certainly was doing his job in this case, that's for sure," Phillip says, pulling Cassie's wisp of a body into his imposingly large frame. "I thought I'd seen it all, done it all, done 'em all, at least the ones that were worth doing—heh, heh—but apparently, all of that was just amateur hour, target practice for the real deal." At that, they melt under each other's gaze, despite the scary-mean eyebrow arch thing he has going on.

Is love really that blind?

Hamptons Unwritten Rule #24:
Getting some is good; getting some
in a house on the beach is better.

Early Sunday morning, I'm woken up by the sound of ocean waves crashing just outside the open windows. I stretch languorously in the heavy, smooth white cotton sheets, yawning and sinking back into the pile of down pillows behind my head as the sheer cotton curtains flutter in the breeze. I look down and see an arm draped across my stomach.

It takes me a second to remember whose it is—George's—which in turn reminds me of where I am—his house on the beach. Whoever would've guessed even three months ago that I would be waking up in a house like this next to anyone, much less a guy like George? It feels strange, surreal, and good all at the same time. But most of all, it feels like progress.

After an enjoyable evening at the party, George asked me if I wanted to go back to his place. I stopped myself from blurting out "I thought you'd never ask!" and instead calmly replied, "That sounds great." Finally: the light at the end of the too-long tunnel of abstinence. That kiss in my driveway had certainly put unholy thoughts in my head that I hadn't been able to shake all evening, especially after spending a few hours in the company of two people who seemed to be falling in love right before our very eyes. The days, months, and years I spent without the pleasure of physical contact finally had backed up on me in a big way, and by the end of the party, especially after all of our casual, public-friendly romantic contact, I was practically vibrating with anticipation.

The time had come to break the safety seal, to de-virginize the re-virgin.

George must've been excited about us being alone too, because he drove about eighty through the dark back roads to his house. Then we practically sprinted up the wood steps to his front door. In a matter of minutes, we were horizontal on an extra-wide cushioned chaise lounge outside on the deck, the ocean laid out before us like a diamond-encrusted crazy quilt. With one smooth motion, he slid my dress up to my armpits. He propped himself up on his elbow so he could take in the length of my body, which was naked except for the fine mesh of my underwear. I shivered under his gaze, suddenly self-conscious and nervous. After what seemed like forever but was probably only a minute, he smiled. "Better than I even imagined," he said.

Talk about saying the magic words! I grabbed his head and pulled him to me. As we kissed, his hands roved across my body, grabbing my hip bones, lingering over my rib cage, and then moving up around my breastbone. At last, his hands went to my breasts, cupping, squeezing, pinching. Despite their modest size, he didn't seem disappointed. I felt myself go all slidey inside, melting from the inside out.

I don't remember whose hand ventured south first—he might've technically made contact sooner, since I still had to undo his pants and get beneath his boxers before touchdown—but then we were moving as rhythmically as if we were slow dancing, our hips swaying back and forth. After several minutes, I realized that he wasn't quite finding my T-Mobile HotSpot, but he was working it like a rock star, so I wasn't about to discourage his enthusiastic efforts. Besides, nothing kills the mood like a recitation of the instruction manual, so instead, I ratcheted up my efforts.

But then something kind of weird happened. He was clearly appreciating my two-handed attention until . . . nothing. It went away. As in, Mr. Happy became Mr. Sad. The even stranger thing was that he didn't seem to notice or care. He wasn't embarrassed or upset. He kissed me deeply, sighed, wrapped his arms around my waist, nuzzled his head into my shoulder . . . and promptly fell asleep.

Meanwhile, I lay there almost fully exposed to the Gulfstreams flying overhead on their way to the airport in East Hampton, Cosabella askew and damp, shivering slightly—and obsessing. Did I do something wrong or something he didn't like? Did I hurt it? Maybe I was so out of practice that my technique totally sucked. Maybe he wasn't attracted to me. The only bright side to my situation was that I wasn't lying there shivering, uncomfortably wedged into the chair, wielding a sticky, wet hand with nothing to wipe it on. I was, however, lying there shivering, uncomfortably wedged into the chair, which I tried to ignore for as long as possible until it felt like my spine was going to be permanently damaged if I didn't move soon.

Eventually, as in after I coughed loudly a few times and shifted around to the point of jostling him, he woke up. He hoisted himself up and then pulled me up as I pulled down my dress, which was tragically wrinkled beyond recognition. I followed him into his all-white bedroom, where he handed me a pair of pressed white cotton men's pajamas. Then he guided me to a sparkling clean guest bathroom and told me to help myself to the supply of new toothbrushes and other toiletries in the vanity. As I washed up and changed, I held on to the shred of hope that maybe I'd get a do-over before we went to sleep.

But when I came back into the bedroom, he was dead asleep, spread-eagled across the king-size bed. I carefully slipped in beside him, hoping that once he felt the weight of my body, he'd respond by moving closer to nuzzle. He didn't. I then spent the next several minutes debating whether I should try to cuddle up next to him— and risk waking him—or stay at the edge of the bed, where I had half a chance of finding a position comfortable enough to fall asleep in yet risk seeming standoffish in the process. Finally his body jerked and he sputtered awake. Before I knew it, he was covering me like an overly affectionate octopus. He kissed me on the cheek and whispered, "Sleep well, babe."

"You too." I smiled up at the ceiling and fell asleep, comfortable at last.

. . .

Now I run my finger along his jaw. His eyes open slowly, registering me and the morning light at the same time. "Waking up to the sound of the ocean is amazing."

"I'm glad you like it," he says, pulling me into a full-body embrace. "Mmmm. I could get used to this." His slides his hands beneath my pajama top as I turn toward him to give him easier access. Suddenly, his head jerks up. "Shit. Is that really the time?" I follow his eyes to the clock sitting on the nightstand next to my side of the bed. It's 9:20. "I almost forgot: I have a tennis game in forty minutes. I'm sorry, babe. . . ."

"That's okay," trying not to sound as disappointed as I feel.

"But I wanted to serve you breakfast on the deck. I have all these fresh berries from the farm stand down the road and I make killer waffles. . . ."

I smile. Another A for effort. "Next time."

He kisses me on the cheek and leaps out of bed. "You got it."

Hamptons Unwritten Rule #25:
Hold your head up high during the
Walk of Shame, Share House Edition.
You got some—wear it loud and proud.

When I walk into my house a half an hour later, wearing last night's dress, suspiciously more rumpled than when I left, it's as if my housemates have been lying in wait.

I'm greeted with a smattering of clapping, whistling, and whoops. The only housemates not sitting in the front row with popcorn are Cassie—who spent the night at Phillip's place and probably knows how to avoid having an audience witness her morning-after look much better than I do—and Andrew. Even though I didn't technically sleep *with* George, sleeping out—and the assumptions they've probably made as a result—seem to be more than enough fodder for their fun at my expense.

Stacy and Leah swoop in. "Sooooooo?" Leah wheedles. "Are you going to spill the deets or what?"

"How was it? Was it fun? Was he nice? What's his house like? Is he romantic? Did he make you breakfast? Do you think you're a couple now? When are you seeing him next? Is he going to hang out with us at the beach today?" Stacy gushes.

Though last night's activities weren't exactly the kind you brag about—not that I'm a bragger to begin with—the last thing I want to do is let on that I was a little disappointed or that it wasn't a perfect first encounter. In an attempt to dodge the inquisition, I walk into the kitchen, praying there's coffee left, since everyone seems to be wired on something this morning. But Leah and Stacy follow me, cackling like the witches in *Macbeth* and firing more questions at me. Andrew is standing at the counter with his back to us, stirring milk and sugar into his coffee. He hasn't looked in our direction, but I know he has heard everything.

I walk up to where he's standing and reach for a mug in the cabinet. "Hey," I say.

"Hey," he replies without looking at me. He turns away from the counter and walks out of the kitchen.

"Miller, are you glowing?" Stacy asks.

I almost snort in response but then snippets from last night flash across my eyes—kissing George in the driveway, George holding my hand the whole night, as if he wanted everyone to know I was his, speeding through the soft dark night in his convertible, him holding me in his arms this morning and saying "I could get used to this . . ."—and a mixture of happiness and relief begins flooding through my body. Physical malfunctions aside, all those things really happened. And it felt *great*. I turn and smile at my housemates. "Yes, I suppose I am. It was a wonderful night."

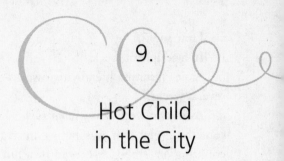

9.

Hot Child in the City

July						
Su	Mo	Tu	We	Th	Fr	Sa
1 ✗	2	3	4	5	6	7 ☹
8 ☹	9	10	11	12	13	14
15	16	17	18	19	20	21
22	23	24	25	26	27	28
29	30	31				

August						
Su	Mo	Tu	We	Th	Fr	Sa
			1	2	3	4
5	6	7	8	9	10	11
12	13	14	15	16	17	18
19	20	21	22	23	24	25
26	27	28	29	30	31	

"You are *not* going to believe this!" Jerry rips off his wireless headset and practically throws it across his desk—something he never does, no matter what kind of conversation he has just had. He's not the kind of person who would let something as trivial as emotions get in the way of being neat and orderly.

Jimmy shuts the office door behind us as I lay on the conference table the tray with the coffees we were out getting next to the Krispy Kremes Jerry brought. "What?"

"I just got off the phone with Ms. Percy. He's all aflutter because Hurrah! has just greenlit *Three-on-One*! The series is a go! They went into production last week."

"Wow, that's great!"

"That's not all . . . ," Jerry says. "The network wants to premiere it soon."

"How soon?"

"In a couple of weeks!"

"As in, meaning literally two weeks or at some point in the next several weeks?"

"As in two weeks *from tomorrow*. They need the series to replace something else that was failing miserably in the ratings. They're counting on *Three-On-One* to be a hit, so Hurrah!'s marketing execs have to throw as much as they can behind it—and fast. They're putting together a huge campaign to launch it as we speak."

"A hit, huh? I never saw the pilot but they really think the show could be that successful?" I ask.

"Percy said that they completely rejiggered the format to differentiate it from other makeover shows and play up its strengths. Apparently it's much edgier, with some surprise twists and turns."

At that moment, the most horrifying thought in the world crosses my mind. "Jerry. Please. Tell. Me. The. Pilot. Is. Not. Going. To. Air."

"Naturally, I asked Ms. Percy that very thing, and he said that since they changed the show so much, the pilot you're in is safely in the recycle bin. They don't think it's even good enough to air—no offense, sweetie."

I practically weep with relief. The pilot airing would not be good for my burgeoning social life. I mean, what could be more socially suicidal than having appeared on a reality show? I know! How about having appeared on a *makeover* reality show, in which you looked like *le crap on le cracker*?

"Okay, so wait. After we pitched the Hurrah! VP of on-air promotions two weeks ago, didn't she promise that if the show went to series we would get to do the on-air promos?"

"Well, boss-lady, you better get on the horn and see about that because"—Jerry looks at his watch—"the clock is ticking. And since we lost the BuzzTV branding project . . ." He raises his eyebrows above his glasses to finish the sentence.

Professionally, I was very disappointed that we lost the project. We not only could've used the money but also working on a branding package is a feather we have yet to put in our cap. Personally, however, I was relieved, though I didn't say that out loud. The client's deadlines were insane and most certainly would've gobbled up the rest of my summer weekends. It's not like I'm generally unwilling to work late or on weekends, but since we more than put in our time over the past year, I don't think it's unreasonable for me to hope for a few more weekends off. I know that's not the best way for me to be thinking as the founding partner of MillerWorks, but the summer is not that long, and weren't Jimmy and Jerry the ones who gave me the "Get a Life" marching orders in the first place, since clearly there was no life to get in this office? It's not like we're the interns at Seattle Grace. Besides, if we get this Hurrah! gig, it will carry us through Labor Day. Then we can gear back up again and hit it hard in the fall.

"I'm on it," I say, picking up the phone.

. . .

The good news: Hurrah! is making good on their promise to hire us to do the launch spots for *Three-on-One*.

The bad news: they want us to shoot original footage with the talent promoting the premiere to go along with the major national advertising campaign they're scrambling to put together.

The worst news: given the show's insane production schedule, this Sunday is the only time the Trio is available for us to shoot with them.

Which means: all three of the employees of MillerWorks will not only be working on July 4th itself, since it falls on a Wednesday, but we'll also be working this entire weekend.

As much as I'm excited about finally landing this assignment for which I surrendered myself mind, body, and soul, I can't help but feel pissy that this all has to happen just when things are getting interesting at the beach. But given we dodged the bigger bullet by losing the BuzzTV project, I know I have to suck it up.

I sadly send around an e-mail to the housemates informing them that I won't be in attendance for the July 4th Extravaganza Part Deux. Stacy replies that she will be "*so* totally bummed" I won't be there, but "please, please, please" can she invite a friend out to stay in my bed? (Yes, sure.) Leah responds in her usual verbose way: "okay." Jackson says, "Join the club. I have to crash out an edit on a manuscript this weekend. And it's supposed to be sweltering outside and my A/C is on the blink, so that ought to be great fun. Cheers." Cassie writes back to say that she'll miss me, but Phillip promised to keep her company. (She not only had her first sleepover at his house on Saturday night after the benefit, but also spent all day Sunday with him at his private beach club, flew back to the city with him on his G5 Sunday night, and is going out for dinner at hot spot Masa tonight. She's sweet to even pretend that she will miss me this weekend. Chances are she'll be so busy with Phillip, she won't even notice I'm not there.)

After neither speaking to nor seeing my own Hamptons beau since he dropped me off on the Sidewalk of Shame on Sunday morning, I find myself growing paranoid. Jerry has been assuring me that men over forty sometimes experience the Mr.-Happy-Becoming-Mr.-Sad-Syndrome and that it probably had more to do with the fact that George had been drinking and not that he suddenly decided he wasn't attracted to me. We also agree that it was better that I didn't end up having sex with him on what was only technically our second date. "Gives him incentive to stay in the game," Jimmy says, "not to mention, you don't want to seem slutty."

Then, much to my relief, I hear from George late Tuesday afternoon.

"I'm sorry I didn't call sooner, but I was blindsided by several deals I didn't expect to come through for weeks," George says. "I can't believe how busy I am! What happened to everyone taking vacation this week? I thought I was going to be able to plow through a few minor things yesterday and today and take off tonight or tomorrow morning and stay the rest of the week at the beach."

"I know, it's been surprisingly busy for us too."

"See what I mean? On top of that, all I can think about is seeing you again. When can we make that happen? How about Friday night?"

"George, I'm so sorry but I can't. . . ."

"How about Saturday night, then? I can probably move some stuff around if that's better for you."

"Unfortunately, speaking of being blindsided, I just found out that I have to work this weekend, so I'm not even coming out to the beach."

"Seriously? Can't you blow it off? I really want to see you."

"I wish I could, but we just got a big project from a brand-new client we've been chasing for months, and it's a total rush job. But the good news is that the spots we're making will be part of a national advertising campaign. They'll be seen on tons of different networks. It could put our business into a whole new league."

"Well, then, it sounds like you gotta do what you gotta do. Business before pleasure and all that."

"Hey, I have an idea. Why don't we do something this week? If you have to stay in town, I could get together later tonight or tomorrow night. . . ."

"I wish I could, but I'm trying to jam as much as possible so I can salvage at least part of the week. Besides, I'm much more relaxed and fun at the beach. I don't think you'd like the city-me nearly as much."

"I don't know about that. . . ." I wonder if the reverse would be true: Would he like Tori as much as he seems to like Miller? Would any of my new fair-weather friends? "I'm bummed we won't be seeing each other this weekend."

"Me too. I'll give you a call next week to figure out something for next weekend. Okay, babe, let me get going here. Someone just walked into my office. Good luck with your project. Stay out of trouble."

If only he knew how little risk there was of that for the city-me. . . .

Hamptons Unwritten Rule #26:
Inevitably you're going to eat one of your
summer weekends at the beach, and most
likely, it will be the hottest one of the year.

Outside temperature as of 3:30 P.M., Saturday, July 7, 2007: 96 degrees—in the shade. Humidity: 87 percent.

Inside temperature as of 3:30 P.M., Saturday, July 7, 2007: Do thermometers go up that high?

Saturday Afternoon Fainting Tally: One and a half. (Jimmy both times, but I think the second time was for dramatic effect and/or in protest.)

We're in a studio down in the far West Village to prepare for our shoot tomorrow with the Trio. And yes, they did bitch loudly about having to work on their one and only day off, especially since the show shoot schedule has been and will be almost nonstop for the next several weeks, effectively ruining the rest of their summer. Seems to me a small price to pay for potential national fame and fortune, but hey, I had my own tantrum on the phone with Alice while she was on her way up to the Berkshires in the air-conditioned comfort of Scott's Beemer, so who am I to talk. She clucked sympathetically about the inconvenient interruption and withheld what was likely her opinion about how much of a brat I knew I was being ("After all, it's one measly weekend and you are getting paid even more than you would under a normal deadline, not to mention it's a big job for a new client!" she easily could've said but thankfully didn't).

To up the insult-to-injury ratio, the air conditioner at the studio conked out about two hours ago, and the studio manager is still trying to find someone to come fix it. The shoot crew we usually hire totally laughed in our faces given the last-minute request (though typically the majority of shoots are either planned or changed last minute, especially when you're dealing with finicky talent and their amorphous schedules) and the fact that our shoot was going to be over the weekend. I can't tell you how many times I heard "Are you on crack?" this week. We finally scraped together enough people to work the shoot, but since they're not our regulars, everything is taking twice as long, and now with the lack of A/C, they hate us twice as much. We got here at 9 A.M. and were supposed to be done at four o'clock, which is looking more and more remote as the mercury inches farther up the thermometer.

Needless to say, tensions are running high. Except for Jerry's, who in times of extreme pressure, somehow manages to keep both his calm and his sense of humor, which is another important reason why I hired him.

"Look at it this way: you've probably lost at least three pounds of water weight today alone!" he says to Jimmy, who is standing in front of a wobbling, dust-encrusted window fan in the vain hope of drying his "perspiration-soaked" John Varvatos T-shirt.

The one bright spot of the day is a text message from Cassie: HEY, U! HOPE WORK IS GOING WELL. P. IS GREAT! THINK I'M IN LUV! MISS U MUCH! STAY COOL! XO C.

One more fainting spell (strangely, the Chinese food delivery guy who brought our dinner), two fights (me and the studio manager, the studio manager and the air-conditioning "repairman"), and seven hours later, we're done for the day.

As I command the taxi driver to close all of the windows and crank the A/C as high as possible, I pray that the air-conditioning at the studio gets fixed by our 8 A.M. call time tomorrow, or I'm going to have a very cranky Transformation Trio on my hands. That is, if they don't turn around and walk out when the wall of heat smacks them in their faces the minute they enter the studio.

. . .

"You are positively frying my 'fro!" Ms. Percy barks at the hair and makeup person we've hired for the shoot. "TO-mas! Where are you? This just isn't working for me. I need you to come right on over here and work your follicular *maj-eek*, ASAP."

TO-mas peeks his head out from behind the dressing room curtain. "Look, Tabitha, that's not how he likes it done. . . ."

"It's *Tabeetha*," the hair and makeup lady sniffs, hands on hips.

TO-mas, who is in zero position to give anyone a hard time about a name pronunciation, swallows what I'm sure would've been a hyperbitchy comment under other circumstances and replies, "Well, *Tabeetha*, if you just hold your horses until I'm done with wardrobe, then I can help you before you do permanent damage. We're going to be on *The View* in a week and a half, and we certainly can't afford for Ms. Percy to be all Richard Pryor, now, can we?" With a scowl on her face, Tabeetha puts down the hair dryer and the brush.

"Tabeetha, sweetness, why don't you help me out with the shine that's just now re-developin' on my forehead, huh? That will be very useful, thank you." Satisfied, Ms. Percy turns back to me. "Now, darlin', where were we? Oh, that's riiiight, you were telling me about your fabulous new life, courtesy of *moi*. Do continue."

I spend a few more minutes giving him the scoop, anxiously checking my watch as I envision the overtime dollars starting to mount, since we're already two hours behind schedule.

Thankfully, the air conditioner was fixed about an hour ago, but given how hot it is outside even this early in the morning and how big the studio space is, it's taking forever to feel the effects. Of course, that meant that the Trio didn't want to start with hair, makeup, and wardrobe to avoid what they were calling the "wilting factor." Their equally prima donna–esque creators/executive producers were no help at all. Typically, their sole purpose on these shoots (meaning, any shoot that they aren't in control of) is to stir up the pot with the talent and act haughty and disgusted in equal measure. And despite the fact that I had a special bond with them after they tore me apart and put me back together again for their pilot, which by the way, helped them get their show picked up for thirteen episodes, they unsurprisingly took the Trio's side, claiming that they would *never* subject their talent to these subpar conditions. Unfortunately for them, I know that is not true, since they are notorious cheapskates in the industry and have certainly put their talent in less than ideal situations to save a buck.

So, after plying the Trio and the creators/executive producers with no-fat venti mocha Frappuccinos (soy milk for TO-mas) and pretty much laying myself prostrate in front of them, I got them to at least start on hair, makeup, and wardrobe. I might've also promised them to try to end on time despite the two-hour deficit, which either means all three setups have to go flawlessly or we somehow are going to have to get our Hurrah! clients to let us cut one setup, which will mean MillerWorks will have to cut our fee by one-third, even though we already paid for all the props and wardrobe.

But we're not going to worry about all that right now. I just have to concentrate on keeping it all moving.

Now Ms. Percy, who is too busy preening at himself in the mirror to notice my agitation, says to me, "Well, it sounds like you're getting out there and having a good ol' time, just like I told you to."

"Surprisingly, but yes, it's been quite good."

"*I'm* not surprised. When we were done transformin' you, you definitely had the mojo working again. Woo, girl, it was like night and day! It's nearin' on impossible to tell by the way you look today," he says, eyeing me up and down with his lips pursed sideways, "but I hope you're keeping up with the Tried-and-True Trio Tips we gave you. Clearly they're working. I mean, just look at the difference we've already made in your life! I will bet you one-hundred-and-one-point-one million dollars that you wouldn't have gotten this handsome, rich, and successful George character to give you even a *first* look with those nasty-ass carg-OH pants." He shudders for dramatic effect. "Not to mention, that super plugged-in *Elle* friend of yours never would've brought you to the party in the first place—she can probably smell Old Navy from a mile away."

"Don't you think that *I* must've had a little to do with the outcome as well? I mean, I *am* the one who went into a house knowing no one and have made a whole new group of friends. And I'm the one who's been keeping George interested, successfully, I might add. Don't you think that can be attributed to me?"

"Nope. It's the fabulous, well-fitting clothes, the expensive haircut and color, and the flawless natural yet dramatic makeup. Personality aside—and yes, darlin', I do agree you have a natural abundance of wit, charm, and intellect—but let's be honest about this: they wouldn't have even let you step foot onto the Hampton Jitney if you didn't look like a card-carrying member of the South Fork Tribe. Trust me. It's all about fitting in and speaking the native language through your appearance. For instance, I dress differently in Palm Beach than I do in New York than I do on Fire Island than I do in Monte Carlo. You have to adapt to your surroundings. You've got to fit in so you can stand out, do you hear what I'm sayin'?"

"I think so. I just want a little credit for sustaining the whole thing, for not letting it all go to waste."

"Of course, darlin', Ms. Percy will concede a smidge of credit to you. Sure. Yes. You've been very convincing."

"What's that supposed to mean?" I walk over to the craft services table to grab us both bottles of water.

"You are playing a part," he says, accepting the water from me. "Just like I am. Just like TO-mas and Frederique are."

"But you guys are on a television reality show. That's your jobs, that's what you get paid to do. For me, this is reality. This is real."

"Reality show, reality, what's the difference? Darlin', don't you know it's *all* fake? Truly, Tori dear, don't believe everything you see or the way you're seein' it. I've been around the block—I'll never tell folks how many times, that's for me to know and no one else to find out—and I know: *nothing* is how it looks. So why shouldn't you get in on the fun? You seem very good at it, I'll give you that."

"Well, thank you. I do appreciate what you guys did for me. It helped me so much, I recognize that. I honestly do."

"I'm so very pleased I was able to help the cause. It's really why I do what I do every day. I just like to help people, to make a difference in their lives." He clutches the water bottle and sniffs, as if he is about to start crying.

"I thought you did it for the free stuff and deep discounts and invites to parties."

"Oh, darlin', that's just the low-fat whipped cream on the strawberry shortcake. You know how much I love being able to give back, since I didn't grow up with a lot of means."

I study him for a second. "Are you just practicing your spiel for *The View*?"

"Yeah. How does it sound? Sincere? Like I really care? Or was it obvious I was lyin' through my veneers? Oh goodness, I better work on that. . . . TO-mas! Mary Mother of God, how much longer are you going to *be*? I think my ass is starting to spread from sitting here so long!"

· · ·

A few hours later, we're cooking with gasoline, but thankfully not being set on fire in the process. We've knocked out the second setup in record time, and now it's our union-sanctioned one-hour lunch break. We're sitting in the lounge area, furnished with the standard black leather couches and low coffee table covered with niche hipster magazines no one has ever heard of. The Divas-in-Training are each eating the meals we had to special order for them. ("Come on, Madame President, did you *really* think we're going to eat cold pasta salad and lemon chicken that was made *hours* ago in *Queens*? Pu-leeze. That borough is hardly the hotbed of haute cuisine." Frederique sniffed at me in between setups.) Ms. Percy, who's purportedly watching his girlish figure, needed the "Lean & Mean" from The Pump Energy Food restaurant (though I've already seen him sneak two brownies from the craft services dessert tray); TO-mas, who is a "strict" vegan yet is known to have a soft spot for oysters, especially while on a hot date, required "Thai Mee Up" from the Angelica Kitchen in the East Village; and Frederique had a craving for BBQ, which required one of our production assistants to actually go to Blue Smoke, the only fine-dining BBQ place in the city, to pick up his Memphis Baby Back Ribs (lean!).

Jimmy, Jerry, and I are scarfing down the rubber chicken accompanied by the mayonnaise salad garnished with overcooked rotini pasta, half-listening to the Trio squawk back and forth to one another.

"No, no, TO-mas, I'll tell you which episode you looked especially good in. It was the one with what's her name, that butchy-girl who had no idea she was a lesbian? Remember her? Goodness me, the armpit hair on her, I think it was braided. . . ."

Frederique pipes in. "And the BO! I mean, *P*-freakin'-*U*!"

"She almost cried when she saw me wearing nose plugs!" The three of them cackle with glee.

"It was so *dis*gusting. I think I almost vomited in my mouth," Frederique adds for color.

"Ewww!" everyone within hearing distance protests.

"No, that wasn't the grossest. I'll tell you the grossest: I swear on my dear mama's grave that I saw a hairless rat in that other woman's apartment. Gina M., was it?" Ms. Percy asks.

"That wasn't a rat, you big queen!" Frederique answers, laughing. "It was her dog!"

Ms. Percy practically shoots Diet Coke out of his nose. "Oh my god, that's right! It was some new breed that's all the rage, the Chinese Crested Hairless! I hated that stupid thing! You know Ms. Percy loves all God's creatures great and small, but that thing was a mutant. I think I stepped on it at one point. I hope that didn't get on camera! I don't want PETA coming after me. I already have enough to worry about in the winter when I'm wearing my mink."

"Remember Gina M. had more clothes for the dog than for herself? She even had little pink rain boots for it. And little doggie diapers!"

"Because that dog was always peeing on itself out of nervousness!"

"We did a superhuman job on her, but she's still never gonna get laid. I mean, we fumigated that refrigerator after we found all of those open cans of fancy dog food piled in there, but the apartment still smelled like dog piss. She's going to have to move if she ever wants the chance of an actual man other than the Time Warner cable guy stepping foot in that apartment."

"Gina M. was *hardly* the worst, boys," TO-mas insists. "Remember the 'Weedwacker'? When I peeked into her dressing room at Barneys and saw that she hadn't mown the lawn, possibly ever? I think I might've even seen some small animals living in that jungle. I mean, didn't her mother teach her how to trim the bush? That waxing lady later told me that was the worst she had ever seen!"

I am practically choking on my chicken.

"Uh, TO-mas, that was, uh . . ." Ms. Percy cranks his head toward me.

Jerry and Jimmy move a millimeter closer to me, becoming the human equivalent of the Slomin's Shield. I'm about to say something when Jerry puts a hand on my knee.

"Tori, oh my god! I'm sooooo sorry!" TO-mas pleads. "You have to forgive me! I don't even know what I'm saying. We've been working so hard lately! Exhaustion makes me delirious, really, out-of-my-mind cuckoo-for-cocoa-nuts. You are hardly the same person you were then, so you can't take it as an insult, right? Because that was the old you, and now you're the *fabulous* new you, we all think so, you're practically our poster child for most successful transformation *ever.* . . ."

"Way to shove the second foot in the mouth after the first," Frederique says under his breath.

I force myself to swallow the bit of chicken that's been sitting in my mouth. "Wow, TO-mas. I don't even know what to say—"

Jerry interrupts. "Let's just forget about it, shall we? TO-mas admits it was pretty much the dumbest thing he's ever said in his entire life. Don't you, TO-mas? And hopefully he'll go home and feel terribly guilty about it, so much so he can't sleep and wakes up for his early call time tomorrow morning with very dark circles under his eyes."

Everyone gasps.

"Now, *Jerold*," Frederique retorts, deliberately using Jerry's hated full name, "there's no need to be intentionally *bitchy*. TO-mas didn't mean it. It was just an innocent mistake."

I have to do something before this escalates into the worst kind of catfight. I can't afford for this shoot to go south for many reasons, but I can afford to take a personal bullet if it will get us back on track. "Guys, it's okay! Sure, that was a little mean, but hey, it was accurate. I hadn't been taking care of myself, that's the truth. That's why I needed the Trio to transform me, right? If anything, I'm living proof of how good they are."

Everyone looks at me, trying to gauge whether or not I mean it.

TO-mas puts his half-eaten Thai Mee Up platter aside, gets up from the couch, and comes around to my side of the coffee table. He pulls me into a full-body hug. "I'm so, so sorry," he says.

I don't even care if he means it or not.

. . .

Twenty minutes later, I've managed to corner Ms. Percy on his way out of the men's room. "I need to talk to you. Now. In private." I lead him down the hallway to the studio manager's office and close the door. I point him to the black leather Barcelona chair while I assume the power position: propping my butt against the desk facing him. "That. Cannot. Happen. Again." I am barely holding it together.

"Please darlin', you have to believe Ms. Percy, TO-mas didn't mean it—"

"No, that's not what I meant. I couldn't care less about the insulting comments, though I have to say, those were beyond cruel."

"Then, what can't happen again?"

"Will you please talk to those two Queens for a Day and get them to *promise* to keep their guppie yappers shut about my being on the show? I'm counting on you, Percy. I really need your help with this. What happens when you're all yukking it up with those yentas on *The View*? Or with Matt and Meredith on the *Today* show? Of course the majority of the questions are bound to be about the most wretched victims you turned around, but I can't afford any slips, not even an anonymous mention. Not ever again. I am the nice girl who stays *behind the cameras* and does all of the on-air promotion spots and *that's it*. I was never, nor will I ever be, a victim on *Three-on-One. Capisce?*"

"I never realized it before but you are *très* sexy when you're angry! Look at that high color in your cheeks and forehead, so youthful—"

"Percy! I'm serious. Now that the gods watching over my social life have intervened and are keeping the pilot off the air, I can't have anyone else knowing I was on the show. The *last* thing I need is all of my Hamptons friends thinking that I'm some pathetic reality show wannabe."

Ms. Percy looked like I just told him that his Prada shoe collection burned to a crisp in a terrible fire. "O-w-chhhhh."

"No, I mean . . . you know what I mean! You guys are the stars! You're the talent! You're all bound for fame in a matter of days, trust me! But your transformation subjects, you know what I'm saying, people just have *opinions*, especially the Hamptons crowd. In LA, it's now practically de rigueur to have gotten your break on a reality show, but in New York, in the Hamptons especially. . . ."

His face softens. "I hear you, darlin'. No need to explain. I mean, you were pretty bad off in person before we transformed you, but the way they shot you for the opening segments, let's just say, on video, you look bad off times a thousand."

"Oh jeez. I never saw a cut of the episode. Did I really look that horrific?"

"Um, well, you were very, very funny. And witty."

"Wow, it's even worse than I thought." I slump back down onto the desk.

Percy puts his manicured hand on my arm. "Well, it doesn't really matter all that much now, does it? You're right. You've come such a long way! You are driving that bus straight to Destination: Fabulous and that silly pilot episode will never see the light of day if *I* have anything to say about it. *I* didn't even look good in that one. The whole thing was atrocious. But more importantly, I will talk to the boys. No one else will ever find out you were in the show. I promise. Mum's the word. BFF's again?"

"Yes." We hug. "Now let's get back out there and make the loss of our summer weekend worth it!"

10.

Slip of the
Tongue

Su	Mo	Tu	We	Th	Fr	Sa
July						
X 1	2	3	4	5	6	☹ 7
☹ 8	9	10	11	12	X 13	X 14
X 15	16	17	18	19	20	21
22	23	24	25	26	27	28
29	30	31				

Su	Mo	Tu	We	Th	Fr	Sa
August						
			1	2	3	4
5	6	7	8	9	10	11
12	13	14	15	16	17	18
19	20	21	22	23	24	25
26	27	28	29	30	31	

Hamptons Unwritten Rule #27:
It's all about who you know.

Monday, all three employees of MillerWorks spent the day—and a good part of the night—in the hermetically sealed, air-conditioned darkness of a rented editing suite, combing through all the footage from the shoot over the weekend. Given the imperfect conditions under which we had to shoot yesterday, it was a relief to see that not only was there no sign of any personal or heat-induced strife, but also that the Trio looked handsome, stylish, upbeat, and fun—all of which were the qualities we—and the on-air promotion and marketing execs at Hurrah!—were going for.

"Wow, our stuff actually makes the show look like it's going to be really funny and different from the ninety million other make-over shows out there," Jimmy commented as we found ourselves laughing out loud hearing the Trio read from the scripts that our own MillerWorks Trio wrote. Satisfied with a couple of rough cuts we managed to put together before we went into double-overtime on the studio fees, we left for the night.

After another half day of editing, we finally returned exhausted and not a little burned out to the MillerWorks headquarters Tuesday afternoon. The three of us retreated to the semiprivate spheres of our desks, eager for the semblance of a little personal space after being joined at the hip for three and a half days straight, to catch up on e-mails and phone calls.

"This is strange," I say to the boys. "Let me play this voice mail for you: *'Hi, this is Janice? From Lisa Gubelman Communications? I'm calling? Regarding your invitation to the event on Saturday night, July fourteenth? Please return at your soonest? 212-555-1924.'*"

"I thought all the Valley Girls died out when Nick Cage lost his hair," Jimmy comments.

"What's Lisa Gubelman Communications and what event is Valley Gal talking about?"

Jimmy says, "You're the resident party girl. Shouldn't you know the social calendar for the weekend? Maybe that boyfriend of yours put you on the list for something."

"Doubt it. Then the RSVP would be under his name."

"Isn't Lisa Gubelman Communications that PR firm that does parties and club and store openings?" Jerry suggests. "Didn't we go to something her agency put on last year for E!?"

"Yes! Wasn't Lisa Gubelman the bleached blonde with the fake tan and faker boobs and wireless headset who was bossing everyone around and kicking people out of the VIP section?" Jimmy adds.

"That could be. Did you get the same message on your voice mails?"

"I haven't gone through them yet."

"Me, neither."

I kneel down on the floor where we tossed the last several days' worth of mail. I rifle through the Jiffy bags filled with DVD screeners of pilots and scripts for series we're supposed to be pitching episodic tune-in spots at the end of the week that I forgot about until this moment, the many bills but fewer checks, duplicate J.Crew catalogs, and the monthly offer for a free chiropractic consultation from the quack in our building. Eventually I come to three identical thick sparkly white envelopes addressed to each of us individually. "Oh. My. God." I begin reading from the invitation. " 'Ready for our version of a ménage à trois? Come meet this summer's hottest new threesome—the Transformation Trio—stars of Hurrah!'s soon-to-be hit show, *Three-on-One*,' this Saturday, July fourteenth, nine to eleven P.M., The Star Room in Wainscott, The Hamptons.' "

Jimmy cackles. "A premiere party in the Hamptons? That's rich. They're sure pulling out all the stops. Well, Ms. Miller, as the highest-ranking officer of this company, of course you'll be attending to represent MillerWorks."

"And as the second-highest ranking officers of this organization, your attendance is required by the highest-ranking officer," I snap back.

"No-can-do, boss-lady. Jerry and I can't be there. We're hosting the Midsummer Night's Queen clambake with our housemates on Fire Island this weekend, and ever since that embarrassing incident in 1992 when that place was originally the Swamp, aka the gay dance mecca of the Hamptons, I have vowed never to step foot on the South Fork ever again, especially in that establishment. Duck, duck, *goose*!"

I pout at Jerry. He shrugs. "Sorry, sweetums. You're on your own."

"I'm not going," I say, dropping the invitation back onto the stack. "I'll just call Janice of Lisa Gubelman Communications and tell her thank you for the invitations, but unfortunately we can't make it."

"Hold it there, Quick Draw McMiller," Jimmy says. "You so have to go! Not only would Ms. Percy be deeply wounded if you don't, he clearly already knows you go out east every weekend, so there ain't no way for you to get out of it, short of contracting some life-threatening communicable disease by like, tomorrow."

"I hate it when you guys are right. Really. Hate it."

Jerry says, "Come on, it'll be fun. You can bring your whole little East End Entourage—I'm sure you can get them on the list. After all, you are one of the show's stars. How impressed will your house-mates be! A real live TV star, living in their midst."

I respond by throwing a J.Crew catalog at him.

Hamptons Unwritten Rule #28:
Don't buy into the Myth of the Midsummer Lull.

It's Friday night and Stacy and I are sitting at the table outside. She's keeping me company while I wait for George to pick me up. She and I were only going to have a quick glass of wine, but George just text messaged me to say he was running late so I tell her a refill is in order.

When George called during the week, I was relieved that he suggested we get together Friday instead of Saturday night. Not only did I not want to turn him down for the second weekend in a row, or worse, cut our evening short, but also I didn't want to mention the premiere party to him in the first place. I doubted going to such an event would be his thing, but just in case, I didn't want to risk having to explain why I couldn't/didn't want to bring him.

Stacy takes a sip of her wine. "It's that time of the summer." She sighs.

"What time is that?"

"When everyone starts to slack off on making plans. We've done everything and been everywhere at least once already this summer, so now it's like we all have sort of lost our momentum for going out." She settles back into her chair and starts flipping through this weekend's *Hamptons* magazine.

"You don't have plans tonight?" It seems highly uncharacteristic for my party-chasing housemates to be without anything to do. Even though more than half the summer is gone and practically none of them have missed even a single weekend out here, I wouldn't have predicted my housemates' appetites for making the scene would ever be satiated. The season isn't that long, and there always seems to be something going on somewhere. Like the stupid *Three-on-One* party tomorrow night, which I haven't mentioned to anyone in the house nor do I plan to, lull or no lull.

Stacy doesn't look up from the magazine. She only stops flipping pages long enough to reach for her wine. "No, we have something to do. There's some hip-hop CD release party at Flirt in East Hampton later. We didn't find out about it until a little while ago, because no one really took the lead in figuring out what was going on this weekend. Everyone has gotten pretty lazy. We weren't going to go at all because it is apparently invite-only, but Michael thinks he got us on the list."

"That sounds fun," I say, thinking that it doesn't and feeling grateful I have plans for which I didn't have to shoehorn myself into uninvited. "We're just doing dinner with some of George's friends at Nick & Toni's. I guess that might count as a lull for us, considering what we've done thus far on our other dates."

"See, what'd I tell you? The Midsummer Lull." She yawns. "God, I could use a nap, especially after this wi—" She stops mid-wine and then sits up to stare more intently at the magazine. Suddenly she squeals and starts laughing. "OMG! Miller!" She spins the magazine toward me and jams her finger on the page, pointing at a color photo of a couple. The dark-haired woman is looking down and away from the camera with a beatific smile on her face, while an equally dark-haired man nuzzles her neck.

"Oh yeah, that's my dress. No biggie. It's not like I could've possibly expected it to be one-of-a-kind since I bought it at Scoop."

"Look closer."

I gasp.

"What's everyone freaking out about out here?" Leah asks, flipping her freshly blown-out hair over her shoulder as she strides outside in the most spectacularly dangerous-looking bamboo wedge platforms I've ever seen. She grabs the magazine out of my hands. After a brief pause, she makes a sound that's a cross between a "hah" and a "hmm" and begins to read aloud: " 'Who is Gorgeous George's newest mystery lady, caught in the act at real estate mogul Alvin Schwartz's annual Fourth of July soiree to benefit the preservation of the Piping Plovers?' Oh and look, here's another one of you and Daniels with Cassie and . . . is that the Phillip Dunne? That must've been quite the double date."

Stacy catches the magazine as Leah drops it back onto the table. "Well, *I* think it's amazing. Miller, you two look so great together! You're the perfect couple, and now you're practically famous!"

"Who's practically famous?" Michael asks as he comes outside and grabs Stacy's glass, draining it in one gulp. Andrew trails out behind him. Stacy hands Michael the magazine. Andrew peers over Michael's shoulder to get a look.

"Are you sure that's you?" Michael asks.

"Yes, why?"

"Because you look hot."

"Meaning, hotter than usual or it can't possibly be me because I never look hot?"

"I don't know. I don't really think about my housemates, you know, as being hot or not."

Stacy doesn't bother to hide her disappointment at the slight she seems to have imagined Michael has given her.

Meanwhile, I look at Andrew, hoping for some kind of seconding of the hot motion or at the very least, a clever remark that Michael won't get but I will. "Nice work, Miz Daniels. Good for you." And he heads back into the house.

After a few minutes of chatter, the crowd disperses, leaving me alone outside with the magazine. When I'm sure no one's around, I can't resist turning back to the page for a private look. I do look pretty hot—and more surprisingly, happy. I suddenly wonder if Peter and Michelle will see the picture. That would be icing on the cake. Visual proof that I have moved on—and up. Just a few short months ago, I was a complete nobody with hardly any friends and zero social life. And now? I'm "Gorgeous George's Newest Mystery Lady."

The Social-Phobe turned Socialite.

Hamptons Unwritten Rule #29:
Remember where you came from.
And who got you there.

On our way to dinner, I wait to see if George mentions our debut in *Hamptons* magazine. He doesn't, even though he chats cheerfully about his week and tells me how great I look and how much he missed me last weekend. Given the response I've seen Stacy get time and again for her puppy-dog overeagerness, I decide as we near the restaurant it's probably better to play it Cassie-cool, as if this kind of thing happens to me all the time, since besides, the magazine is just "all so silly" in the first place.

After a pleasant dinner with a married couple George has known since college, he asks if it's all right if we stop by Flirt for the same CD release party that Stacy mentioned. "It's practically next door. We won't stay long, I promise. Besides, after two weeks of not seeing you, I wouldn't mind being alone with you sooner rather than later—that is, if it's okay with you that we go back to my place after the party."

"Sounds like a plan." When we arrive at the club, George takes my hand and directs us toward the entrance, which is swarming with activity. A gaggle of photographers are fiendishly snapping away at the people ahead of us. George, not cowed, continues leading the way into the limelight. Everyone begins shouting. "George, over here! George! George!" But then unexpectedly I hear *my* name— maybe one of the photographers figured out that I'm George's "newest mystery lady"? When I hear my name a second time, I look around and catch sight of my housemates, but they're on the wrong side of the velvet rope. I'm about to ask George if we can get them into the party when the flashbulbs start popping, completely blinding me. My eyes begin tearing madly. I try telling George I can't see anything, but he doesn't hear me over the ruckus. It is only by the grace of George's hand holding fast to mine and pulling me forward that I make it through the rabid paparazzi and into the front door.

"George, I just saw my friends outside and I was hoping we could get them—"

"Oh no, babe, your makeup is all smudged. Why don't you go fix it and I'll meet you at the bar? By that time, I'll have some champagne for you, sound good?" Before I can ask him again about my stranded peeps, he has disappeared into the diamond-encrusted throngs.

As soon as I get in front of the mirror, I have to gasp. "Smudged" was just George being kind. In actuality, my eye makeup has pooled around my eyes in giant raccoon rings, some of which has run all the way down my cheeks in long black streaks—all of which was probably caught on film. *"Who was that garish frightmare seen with Gangsta-Hottie George D. Friday night at Flirt?"*

"Honey, you all right? You look like you've been doing some serious crying." A tall woman with a huge beautiful Afro and gold eye glitter has just come out of the stall.

"I'm fine, thanks." I bet her makeup didn't budge when she ran the paparazzi gauntlet.

She clucks her tongue, shakes her head some more, and then reaches into her expensive-looking mini gold lamé clutch and pulls out a packet of Prada eye-makeup remover. "I always keep one in here in case of emergencies. If you ask me, this is an E-mergency! Take it! You don't want to be going out there looking like *that*." She thrusts it into my hand, gives me a golden-eyed wink, and disappears out the door. Even with the help of her expensive wipes, it still takes me several minutes to get my face into any kind of presentable condition.

As I come out of the bathroom, I come face-to-face with a life-size poster on the opposite wall bearing the cover art of the CD featuring a rendering of my golden-eyed friend amid four serious thug types wearing black suits and millions of dollars' worth of major bling between them.

Hopefully "Diva-Licious" wasn't too offended that I had no idea who she was.

I spend the next hour in an embarrassment-infused funk, slinking around behind George as he makes the rounds with the cadre of record moguls wearing black leather jackets and pinched-looking entertainment lawyers. Anytime my date releases my hand, I lift glasses of Cristal off of waiters' trays as they pass by and slurp them back. Matters begin to improve greatly around my fourth glass.

Finally, George yells over the ear-splitting hip-hop music that he's ready to go. When we leave, the only clamor out front is from the regular club-crawlers waiting behind a velvet rope off to the side until the private party is done so they can get in. Thankfully, the photographers are long gone.

And so are my housemates, whom I had totally forgotten about until now.

. . .

George and I are driving with the top down through the dark back roads, which cut across swaths of farmland that are interrupted with the occasional oversize McMansion. John Mayer's *Continuum*, which either is George's favorite CD or he hasn't bothered to switch out, plays on the car sound system as usual. Stars dominate the sky, and the breeze wafting over us is fresh and warm.

I'm buzzed off of what probably amounted to a magnum of

Cristal. And suddenly, I'm horny. I lean over the armrest so I can snuggle closer to my date. I lay my hands in his lap. "So, I hear you have a new 'mystery lady.' "

His body becomes tense. "Really? Who told you that?"

"Did you see the new *Hamptons* magazine, the one that came out today?" He shakes his head, eyes still on the road. "Well, there's a very nice picture of us in there, and according to them, I'm your new mystery lady." I move my hands up closer to his crotch.

"How interesting."

"I knew you'd think so." I lean in close enough to nibble on his ear, which causes him to swerve the car, propelling me right back into my seat.

"Maybe we better wait until we get home, mystery lady." He laugh-coughs then readjusts himself in his seat. We sit quietly for a few minutes, until George chuckles.

"What's funny?" I ask.

"So, that must've been why all those gossip columnists left me so many messages today."

"They called you about us, I mean, me? What did you tell them?"

"I'm not going to call them back, are you kidding?"

"Whew, what a relief," I say, realizing that suddenly I only half mean it.

Hamptons Unwritten Rule #30:
Nobodies can become somebodies overnight
if they know the right people . . . at least, temporarily.

"Here's to Miller," Jackson declares, lifting his Transformation-Tini glass into the air, "the Hampton's Newest All-Time Super-Duper It Girl! And to think: she lives in our very own humblest of abodes! A big thanks for getting us non-media-mogul regular folks into this happening bash!"

"Cheers!"

"Here here!"

"Long live Miller!"

Glasses clank together as most of my housemates and a few select hangers-on toast me loudly and for what must be the fourth time as we stand outside in the courtyard of the Star Room. So far, I've made it through the first hour of the *Three-on-One* premiere party without incident.

Since I had originally decided not to invite the housemates, I figured I'd just tell everyone I had a boring work obligation, borrow Stacy's car, and do a quick drive-by to say hello to the Trio, the producers, and whatever network folks were there, thus satisfying my professional duties.

The only flaw in that plan was my inadvertent dissing of the housemates at Flirt last night. When I got back to the house this morning from George's, somewhat hungover—both from the alcohol and the sex (after all, a girl can only hold back for so long, and two weeks was plenty)—I was ambushed.

The charge was led by Leah, who had clearly stirred up the pot in my absence. "I *know* you saw us. You just put down your head and walked in without even a second glance. We ended up standing outside for *another hour* after that. We thought *for sure* you'd come out and get us or have George tell them to let us in. I mean, how could you not?" Hair flip. "We wouldn't have left *you* standing out there if the situation was reversed." I tried to explain what had happened, but of course it sounded ridiculous, and Leah was not buying what I was selling.

I couldn't tell if my other housemates were also angry or if they were just staying out of the line of fire. Stacy pretended to inspect her manicure. Michael and Andrew mostly looked tired and out of it, but their silence added to the overall tense atmosphere. Jackson had just arrived twenty minutes prior and was helping himself to the coffee and muffins that were on the kitchen bar. Since he wasn't part of last night's angry mob, he wisely kept his nose out of it.

It was clearly time for me to resort to pulling out the emergency aces I had hidden in my pocket, namely, Jimmy's and Jerry's unused invites and our three plus one's.

Of course, I had to pretend that I had just gotten invited myself, because it would've looked way worse if they knew that I didn't extend the invite right away. But when I did, it was like I had just handed them all chocolate bars containing Willy Wonka's coveted golden tickets.

Suddenly I was the house hero. Everyone became visibly excited, especially after Michael had said he'd heard about some big star-studded premiere bash happening ("While I was waiting forever in line last night at Flirt," he had to add) but he couldn't dig up enough information to get the lowdown on what it was, much less score access. On top of their positive responses, Andrew and Michael asked if they could bring Jeff and Rachel—the infamous nonfollowers of the August First Rule they had told me about at the Pre-Summerhouse Dinner—and Hailey, a girl from Jeff and Rachel's current house. Adding them to the list required some fancy footwork on my part with my new buddy Janice from Lisa Gubelman Communications, but let's just say that my years in production, aka getting shit done any way possible, came in handy.

It turned out that Hailey, who is extremely blessed in the looks department, also happens to be a spinning instructor in East Hampton on the weekends. She has been teetering around the club in the strappiest high-heeled silver sandals I've ever seen and more notably, doing so without ever leaving the side of one Mayor Kane, who seems to be her single source of stability. A little while ago, the House Mouthpiece mentioned to me that this was not the first time Andrew and Hailey have shared nightclub booth-space.

All of this would be surreal enough, but to top it off, ever since I made the peace offering this morning, a very surprising someone has been glued to *my* side: Leah Brewster.

Even though I know *exactly* what the root cause of this 180-degree change of heart was, I have to say—and I'm scared to even admit this—it's been kind of *fun*, especially since Cassie has been AWOL since meeting Phillip. For the first time all summer, Leah invited me to sit next to her on the beach today and then proceeded to ply me with Diet Cokes out of her much-guarded personal stash, chatting away as if we've been BFFs since the dawn of time. She even summoned Stacy and me into her palatial lair to help her pick shoes for tonight (from, I must note, one of the most fabulous footwear collections I have ever seen in my life).

"So, I forget," Leah says to me now, "George is or isn't coming tonight?"

"Isn't."

"Why? What's he doing?"

Come to think of it, I didn't actually know what he was doing, but I wasn't going to tell her that—BFF or not. "I think he has a business dinner of some sort," I lie.

"That's a shame," she says, flipping her hair, the force of which combined with the number of Transformation-Tinis she has consumed cause her to totter on her high heels. I reach out to steady her. "He probably could've gotten us into the VIP section."

She's eyeing the balcony area upstairs that's being guarded by two WWE wannabees. I can just make out the over-the-top, brightly colored, neo-preppy coordinating outfits of the Trio, who gave me exaggerated hugs and sloppy kisses upon their grand entrance a half hour ago but were then whisked upstairs by their publicist with nary a backward glance, much to my relief.

"I think it would be fun to go upstairs, don't you?" Leah asks, clearly not letting it go. "Maybe your cute little Transsexual Threesome could get us in. . . ."

"Transformation Trio."

"Whatevs. They're the stars of the show, right? And what did you say, you're friends with them?" Apparently my new BFF doesn't listen too well because I've explained this connection to her

at least a couple of times already, leaving out the me-starring-as-the-
pathetic-jilted-loser-in-the-pilot part, of course.

"I guess I could *try* to get us in. . . ."

"Yes, do it! You know, if it's easier, we don't have to bring the
others. We can just sneak up there for a quick drink. No one will
even miss us. I think I saw a couple of the guys from *Entourage* go
up there."

After a quick chat with the VIP section bouncer, whom I have
somehow convinced to go fetch Ms. Percy for me (with the help of
a crisp twenty-dollar bill from Leah), we're in, sending my ranking
with Leah up and off the charts. Up here, there seem to be as many
VIPs as there are non-VIs, probably because the wrestlers at the foot
of the stairs seem to be steroid-filled suckers for slutty fake blondes
and/or real twenty-dollar bills.

Ms. Percy kisses me on both cheeks with his usual flourish. "Gii-
iiirrrrlllll! You look like a Hamptons Billion! And mightily more
fabulous than you did the last time I saw you, I might add. I was beginning to worry that all my hard work had gone out the window!"
I shoot him a warning look, which luckily he seems to pick up on.
"Isn't this far superior than sweating it out last weekend in that awful studio? I am so very honored that you came. Now tell me who
this gorgeous creature is!" He turns to Leah, who seems to have
been striking a pose in anticipation for her turn in the spotlight. "Is
this the fabulous Cassie you were telling me about?"

"*No, this is Leah*," I say through gritted teeth, "the *other* fabulous
housemate I was telling you about, remember?"

"Right, right! The even more fabulous Leah!" he convincingly en-
thuses, even though I barely mentioned Leah in the retelling of my
Hamptons fairy tale. "Now, Leah, you're exactly the kind of girl we
can't have on the show because you've already got the *whole thing*
going on!" He waves his hand in a circular motion in front of her as
she flips her hair and flashes a GoSMILE that's usually reserved for
hot-slash-rich straight guys and Jackson. Within seconds, the two of

them are immersed in a conversation about her outfit, focusing most especially on her shoes, which are these supersexy, whacked-out Christian Louboutin numbers with feathers and rhinestones. I don't know who's eating it up more: The Queen or the Queen.

"Isn't this just the most fantabulous party? They did a great job on such very short notice, but we really only have one person to thank for all this." Percy nods at me. "We were in a meeting with our publicist, and she said she was thinking that maybe we should throw a little soiree to help get the buzz going with the chattering class, which of course, the three of us thought was a spectacular idea. But as usual, Ms. Percy always knows how to improve upon a good idea to make it great, which is, of course, how I got to where I am today and where I'm *surely* going tomorrow, wink, wink. So, Ms. Miller, I suggested that we hold the fete in the Hamptons because, of course, as you so well know, everyone who is *anyone* is out here on the weekends. I have to give credit where it is rightly due, since last weekend you were telling me what a fantastic time you were having out here. You were my inspiration!"

"How nice. Glad I could help." Wait until Jimmy and Jerry hear this. They're going to laugh their asses off.

An unsmiling woman with a clipboard and a headset, presumably from the Lisa Gubelman Agency, appears next to us. "Percy, there's a reporter here from *Entertainment Weekly* who wants to talk to you and the boys."

"That's my cue!" Percy waggles his fingers at us and allows the publicist to whisk him away.

"I should probably go say hello to my clients from Hurrah! before we go back downstairs," I say to Leah.

"That's cool with me. I'll go wait for you by the bar. I think I see Adrian Grenier from *Entourage* over there."

After I make my obligatory rounds, I stop by the booth where Ms. Percy is holding court to say thanks. He's clearly wasted, despite the fact that he swore off alcohol earlier this summer because he claimed, "Partaking of The Drink makes my skin more Latte than Espresso." Percy grabs me and holds my face in his hands. "You so got it goin' on now, girl! I couldn't be prouder if I gave birth to you myself! I am a genius. Just look at you! You're a totally different person!"

I didn't notice that Leah has come up beside us. "Totally different from what?" I give Percy the death stare over Leah's shoulder. As sloshed as he is, I know he's getting my message loud and clear.

"Uh, well, I mean, she looks different than she did . . . earlier in the summer. She's so tan now." He has suddenly lost his thick southern accent.

Leah turns to face me. She cocks her head and gives me the up-and-down. She frowns. "Miller doesn't look that tan to me—"

"We should get back to our friends," I cut in. "We wouldn't want them to start worrying we ditched them!" Despite my BFF's protests, which she doesn't realize aren't echoed by her new recent former BFF, Percy, because he's too busy making the prayer-for-forgiveness sign to me over Leah's shoulder, I steer Leah by her bony elbow toward the steps—and me back to the safety of obscurity.

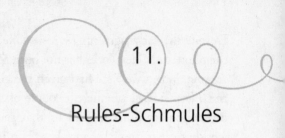

11.

Rules-Schmules

			July			
Su	Mo	Tu	We	Th	Fr	Sa
X 1	2	3	4	5	6	☹ 7
☹ 8	9	10	11	12	X 13	X 14
X 15	16	17	18	19	X 20	X 21
X 22	23	24	25	26	X 27	X 28
X 29	30	31				

			August			
Su	Mo	Tu	We	Th	Fr	Sa
			① 1	2	3	4
5	6	7	8	9	10	11
12	13	14	15	16	17	18
19	20	21	22	23	24	25
26	27	28	29	30	31	

"Hurrah! for Hurrah!! The cable net has struck gold again with its ab-fab new show, '*Three-on-One!*' The Transformation Trio is triple-handedly transforming the makeover genre one lady loser at a time."　　—*The New York Times*

" '*Three-on-One*' is going to put TIVO out of business as the pop-culture obsessed In Crowd—namely, EVERYONE ON THE PLANET—are going to be glued to their oversize plasma screens watching the show every Tuesday night in real-time or risk being decidedly out of the loop at the Wednesday morning watercooler."　　　　　—*Entertainment Weekly*

"Watch out, Fab Five! After only two episodes, Ms. Percy and 'her' cohorts are undeniably cable TV's newest 'It-Boys.' "　　　　　—*Us Weekly*

Despite the early signs of *Three-on-One*'s apparent runaway success, the phone at MillerWorks has not been ringing off the hook. Or even ringing. When we were first given the gig to do the launch spots for the *Three-on-One* premiere a couple of weeks ago, the VP of on-air promotions at Hurrah! told us that she was also assigning us the weekly tune-in spots because her team was too slammed with other work to do them. But after a few phone calls and e-mails from me over the last week that curiously went unanswered, she finally told me very late yesterday that they had miraculously figured out a way to keep the work in house. Though we got paid a nice chunk of change for doing the launch spots, we were also counting on the money we would've gotten for producing the episodic spots. Almost worse than the financial loss was the emotional distress, namely the resulting paranoia that perhaps Hurrah! didn't like our work as much as we had thought—or they had said. And since no other offers were pouring in as a result of our piece of what was clearly a successful marketing campaign, the natives were getting restless . . . and hungry.

"Maybe we should call Lisa Gubelman of Lisa Gubelman Communications to send out a press release to the industry trade magazines," Jimmy suggests.

"I don't think we can afford Lisa Gubelman of Lisa Gubelman Whatever," Jerry says, removing his glasses and rubbing at his eyes with the heels of his palms.

"What if we tell her that not only did we create the launch spots but also that their very first victim on the lost pilot episode is the founding partner of Mill—" Jimmy says.

I cut him off at the pass. "Don't even say it."

"Why so touchy? I was just thinking out loud. But it *would* make for a good story."

"I think I've already sacrificed plenty for the sake of the company, thank you very much. Besides, business is going to pick up. It's always dead in the summer." I get up to fill my empty Poland Springs bottle with water from our buzz-less watercooler.

"It wasn't dead *last* summer," Jimmy counters.

Jerry replaces his glasses and blinks hard a few times. "Instead of just sitting here quibbling, which I know you two enjoy, I have a better idea. Let's actually *do* something. I'll make dupes of the spots. Tori, you write a clever note, and Jim, why don't you take the review quotes and design an eye-catching postcard. Then we'll messenger the packages over to our top ten clients and top twenty prospects. Tor, you'll follow up the delivery with a call to try to get a lunch or at least a meeting set up. Sound good?" He looks back and forth between the two of us.

"Sounds good," Jimmy and I mumble, burying the hatchet, but only for the moment.

Hamptons Unwritten Rule #31:
You may be "the one" . . .
but probably not "the *only* one."

It's a rare occasion these days, but one I'm thrilled to have: Cassie is hanging with us, sans Phillip, for the first time in weeks.

Ever since she met her match, she has usurped Abigail's position as the Absentee Housemate by spending every minute of free time with her man, both out here and in the city. On the weekends, the lovebirds have taken to nesting at his place. And who could blame a fifty-six-year-old man (as in *twenty-one* years older than Cassie) for not wanting to stay in a room in a share house, barely out of earshot of several housemates hopped up on Red Bull? Except for the time Phillip and Cassie invited George and me over for cocktails before heading off in our respective directions for the remainder of the evening, we haven't seen them.

Luckily, Cassie e-mailed this week to ask me if I wanted to join her, sans ours beaus, at the premiere screening and party of *Leaving Loveland* Friday night in Southampton. I told her I'd love to go, but

my caveat was that I had made plans to do something with Leah, so
was there any way we could include her? Needless to say, Cassie was
fairly shocked, having plugged in to the inexplicable tension between me and the Queen, though she never talked about it with me
or involved herself in any way. But when I updated her on the little
lovefest that began two weeks ago at the *Three-on-One* premiere
party and has surprisingly flourished ever since, Cassie responded
that she'd be happy to get both Leah and Stacy on the list for
the screening as well. She also suggested that the guys meet us for the
after-party, since the movie was a chick flick they wouldn't be interested in seeing anyway.

As we're waiting for the movie to begin, Cassie and I flip through
the latest copies of *Hamptons* magazine that were left on our seats,
since they are title sponsors of the premiere. Leah and Stacy have
gone to get popcorn and Diet Cokes.

"Would you look at that," Cassie says. "Page seventy-three."

She has called out the Flash section, where the party photos from
the previous weekends are wallpapered across several pages. "Got it.
What am I looking—" My eyes lock onto a facsimile of George's
face, which is uncomfortably close, at least in my opinion, to the
smiling face of Pauletta, the supermodel.

I close my eyes and swallow. I open one eye, see George's face
again; open the other eye, and Pauletta is still there, smiling mock-
ingly at me. I read the caption: "The Hamptons' most-wanted bachelor and Manhattan real estate minimogul George Daniels, caught
canoodling with his date, Pauletta, fashion's most-wanted model."

His date? I read the fine print, which tells at what party the photo
was taken and when, so I can do the math: these pictures were take
two Saturday nights ago, as in the same night as the *Three-on-One*
party.

"That George," she says, clearly amused until she sees the look on
my face. "You're not upset, are you? It's just a silly photo in an even
more ridiculous magazine. Half the time the people photographed

together don't even know each other. The photographers just put
famous faces together to get a shot that will be picked up by the
wire image services and put money in their pockets. Trust me, I'm
in the magazine business. I know how it works."

"But it says she was his *date*."

"That doesn't mean anything. I bet some inexperienced intern at
the magazine made up the caption based on no facts whatsoever,
proud of his little parallel structure in under a hundred characters."

I'm not convinced, because as I scan the rest of the page, I come
across two more pictures of the two "Most-Wanteds," posing together with other party guests, arms around each other's waists.

As Leah and Stacy make their way past me into their seats, I slap
the magazine shut and let it slip to the floor, where it belongs.

. . .

The movie itself ended up being mediocre at best but served as a
passable distraction for two hours, or at least enough cover under
which I could secretly obsess. Cassie promised that the after-party
at Dune would be the highlight, so we left right before the lights
went up to avoid getting stuck in a long line at the club.

With my housemates' usual artful employment of mobile tech-
nology, Michael and Andrew arrive at the parking lot at the precise
same moment we do. We girls hustle into the line at the door, which
is getting longer by the second. The guys come in right behind us,
pissing off the people behind us, who think they are cutting.

"You guys remember Hailey, right?" Andrew asks.

"Sure, of course," I say, nodding hello. Hailey is wearing the
same exact pair of silver strappy sandals she was wearing two weekends ago, only her skirt is shorter, her legs seem longer, and the silver seems shinier.

"Hey, Miller," Hailey says, "I want to thank you again for, like,
getting us in to the *Three-on-One* premiere party. It was totally fun.
I think it's so cool how you, like, work on a television show."

"No problem, it was my pleasure. Though I think it's probably an overstatement to say that I work on the show. I do some work *for* the show."

"Isn't that, like, the same thing?" she asks, blinking her pretty long lashes at me uncomprehendingly.

Andrew puts his hand on the small of Hailey's back and guides her into the line behind us.

"How was the flick?" he asks me. Strappy Sandal Girl moves closer to Andrew and angles her body in toward him.

"You know, a typical chick flick: fluffy but entertaining."

"Good," he says.

"Good." I turn back toward the girls and concentrate on willing the check-in people to move just a little bit faster so I can get a drink already, goddammit.

The place is packed. Stacy, Leah, Cassie, and I manage to score a few stools at the bar and start indulging in the selection of free cocktails. With Cassie around, Leah isn't as attentive to me as she has been over the last couple of weekends, but our dynamic is still far better than it was at the beginning of the summer. Leah is regaling Cassie with the story of our adventures at the *Three-on-One* shindig, the highlight being how much fun she had in the VIP section meeting Ms. Percy, which of course carries that much more cachet, now that the show is a certifiable hit.

"Ms. Percy absolutely worships Miller," Leah is saying to Cassie. "You should hear the way he was talking to her. He kept raving about how great she looks. It was almost as if he was saying that she had been one of those ridiculously pathetic losers they transform in the show." She does a laugh/hair-flip combo.

"I can't imagine Miller ever needing any help in that department," Cassie says, sending a wink in my direction.

"Of course not," Leah adds. "Only desperate people go on those lame shows. Right, Miller?" She blinks at me.

"Totally." I begin waving madly at the bartender. Suddenly I feel someone kiss the back of my shoulder while hands slide around my waist.

"Look who it is: my favorite mystery lady."

"George! What are you doing here? I thought you weren't coming out until tomorrow." He begins reenacting our *Hamptons* magazine–worthy pose, nuzzling his face into my neck. I can smell alcohol on his breath. Stacy giggles, Leah stares, and Cassie simply smiles, probably thinking of Phillip, if I had to guess.

"My dinner in the city got canceled last minute, so I got a seat on the seaplane. I wanted to surprise you. Aren't you happy that you were the first person I wanted to see?" He grabs my hand and pretend-pouts.

Was he thinking of me as the photographer took multiple photos of him and his bold-ink-worthy date two weeks ago? But then again, here he is, making a special effort to see *me*. I suddenly become aware that our audience is waiting for my response. "Yes, of course I'm happy." He smiles and leans in for a kiss.

"Look what the cat dragged in," Cassie jokes.

"I wouldn't expect Cassandra Dearborn to be slumming it with the commoners these days, especially now that you're practically married to a billionaire. Where's the new hubby? You can't possibly have gotten him to agree to come to a cheesy nightclub. It would seem rather beneath him, wouldn't you say?"

"Well, *you're* here, George dear. What does that say about you?"

"Touché, Dearborn." He clinks his glass against hers.

"Phillip had some business in LA. He's taking the red-eye and should be getting out here crack of tomorrow morning."

"George, I don't think you've met Stacy and Leah, our housemates," I say.

"No, I haven't. Hi, nice to meet you."

"Actually, George," Leah says, extending her hand and a hair flip, "we met a few years ago at the Young Lions benefit for the New York Public Library." He squints at her, trying to remember. "I was with

Fabian Geller, Liam Oswald, and Trish Reinhardt." Nothing seems
to be registering with him. "I was on the benefit committee
and. . . ." She continues on for another minute trying to jog his
memory with more details.

"I'm sorry, Leah, but I just don't remember. But it's nice to re-
meet you. I'll try to not need to reremember next time we meet,
deal?" Leah seems satisfied with his response. George turns back to
me. "Babe, there's some people I need to say hi to. Can you girls
spare Miller for a little bit?" I look at Cassie. I'm torn—I *am* flattered George showed up, despite the unpleasant photographic revelation earlier this evening, but who knows when I'm going to get
some time with Cassie again?

"Of course! You two kids go do a lap. Catch up with us later,"
she says, gracious as always.

"Great. Nice meeting everyone. Have fun." George takes my
hand and leads me deep into the crowd. "I didn't want to say this
back there, but we're on the list for the VIP section. Now aren't you
glad I came?"

Soon we're on the other side of the velvet rope, hobnobbing with
the other hobnobbers, the stars of the movie and the ever-voracious
photographers.

Hamptons Unwritten Rule #32:
No one comes to the Hamptons to rest.
You can sleep when you're dead.

Not long after, the VIPs have all but disappeared and the paparazzi
have followed suit.

"I think I'm ready to call it a night," George says with a wide yawn.

"That's cool with me. Just let me say good-bye to my housemates."

"You don't have to leave. Why don't you stay and hang out with
your friends?"

"That's all right. I've had enough too. Besides, I think they're probably going soon. Can we get some food on the way home? I'm starving!"

"To tell you the truth, some of the guys invited me over for Cubans and whiskey. I don't think it'd be much fun for you. You'd have a much better time with your housemates. I'm sorry I hogged you tonight, but who could blame me?" He kisses my cheek. "I'd drop you home, but I don't have my car, and we're going in the other direction." He wobbles, causing him to lose his balance momentarily. "Not to mention, I'm probably not fit to drive at this moment. Maybe we could hook up later at my place."

"George Daniels! Are you asking me to make a booty call?" I tease. "Sounds very tempting, but I don't have a car, and even if Stacy let me borrow hers, I don't think I should be driving either."

"I guess I didn't plan my surprise very well. Sorry about that."

"Next time. I'll just get a ride with my friends. You go ahead. The cigars are waiting."

"You're the best. I'll check in with you tomorrow, okay?" He kisses me and then disappears into the crowd, which has almost fully changed over from party guests to professional club-crawlers.

I go in search of my posse, praying they haven't ditched me. They probably assumed I'd be going home with George. I know I did. After several minutes, I start to panic. There's not a housemate in sight, and Southampton is a good twenty-minute drive from our house. I fight my way toward the front door and outside, slamming right into Michael, who was too busy CrackBerrying to see me coming.

"Woah, Miller! Where's the fire?"

"Michael! Thank god it's you."

He snickers. "I haven't heard that from a girl in a while."

"Yeah, well . . . listen, do you know where the girls are?"

"They left an hour ago."

"What's up with your man? Everything okay?" It's Andrew. "I think I just saw him leave."

"He and a few guy friends were doing some male bonding over

illegal cigars. Not really my kind of thing. Are you guys going home? I could use a lift."

"Home?!" Michael answers. "It's early! We're just getting started. And you're coming with!"

"I don't know . . . I'm pretty tired."

"You can sleep when you're dead. Come on, Miller! The other girls wussed out. Be the cool girl. Come with the guys to Pink. It'll be the best time you'll have all summer."

"Just me and the guys?" I ask, looking around for signs of Strappy Sandal Girl but seeing none.

"See? It's your lucky night," Michael answers.

"Come with, Miller. Live a little," Andrew says with the slightest hint of a smirk. "We may not get into the VIP section, but we will get in."

"Especially if we have you with us," Michael adds.

"Now I get it. You're just using me because they won't let a bunch of guys in by themselves."

Michael shrugs but doesn't deny it. "Drinks are on us. And you can start with this," he says, tossing me a Red Bull.

"Are you kidding me? That stuff is nasty!"

"Not nasty, Miller. *Necessary*."

· · ·

We're finally on the right side of the velvet rope at Pink Elephant after waiting a solid thirty minutes in line until Michael saw the bouncer he knows. Inside it's wall-to-wall and about one thousand degrees. Someone hands me a Red Bull and vodka, which I gulp down in the hopes of cooling off.

I ask for another one.

· · ·

I'm dancing with Andrew, and we're cracking up uncontrollably. We're pulling out every cheesy bar mitzvah dance move we can

think of. The bump. The hustle. The funky chicken. The moon
walk. He can even cabbage patch. I can't stop laughing.

. . .

I have no idea what time it is. We've piled into a taxi minivan that
someone had the good sense to call. Michael and some random people who begged to split the taxi with us are up in front, singing
"Come On Eileen," which they've made the driver turn up to full
volume on the radio. Andrew and I called the "way back" and are
bouncing around slumped down in the backseat.

I think we've just kissed.

. . .

We've all just gotten out of the van. Michael has already gone inside. Andrew and I are standing in front of the house. We are kissing. More like, making out.

"Come on Eileen," he whispers into my mouth.

"My name is Miller, in case you've forgotten."

"Haven't forgotten. I know exactly who I'm kissing. Come on,
Miller, to my room."

"I can't! Everyone will know."

"No, they won't. The girls are sleeping, and Michael is too out of
it to notice." He pulls me by the hand as we walk inside. Michael,
Leah, and Stacy are in the kitchen, scavenging for food. Andrew
and I drop hands before anyone notices.

Stacy is wearing pajamas and full-on bedhead. "We're going
to grill some hot dogs. Want some?" Stacy is smiling more than
she should after being woken up, which I bet can be attributed to
the fact that Michael went in to sweet-talk her into making him
food.

I give Andrew a "what-do-we-do-now" look. He leans into my
ear and whispers, "Just come after."

"I don't know. . . ."

"Don't worry so much. They'll all be asleep or passed out, more likely. We can wait it out."

"But, what about the August First Rule, Mr. Mayor?"

"Miller, Miller, Miller. First of all, August starts in a few days. Second of all, everyone knows it's the one unwritten rule that was made to be broken."

Hamptons Unwritten Rule #33:
Just because you've gotten yourself
home safely doesn't mean that you
still can't get into trouble.

It's an hour later and the house has finally settled down. The problem now is that Michael and Stacy are in the living room, watching some terrible action movie, blocking the passageway between the North and the South Wings. Suddenly, my cell phone vibrates, signaling that I have a text message from Andrew, which is a minor miracle, since the phone is only showing one rather rare and lonely little signal bar. I take it as a sign from the Gods of Wireless.

IF U DON'T COME SOON, I'M GONNA COME GET U IN 10, 9, 8 . . .

Shit. How am I going to get over there without Stacy and Michael knowing? Then it comes to me: there's a door to the outside through the laundry room. It leads to the garbage area, but it's better than nothing. Then I can go the back way directly into Andrew's room.

I arrange my pillows and blanket to look like I'm asleep under my covers—even though the chances are higher than usual that Stacy might not end up sleeping in our room tonight—and tiptoe out into the hallway. Naturally, the side door in the laundry room is stuck from the humidity and lack of regular use. It takes two hands to yank it open, causing it to make a loud cracking sound as the door finally swings free from the swollen wood frame. I step outside and pull the door only partially shut, in case I need to use it to get back in. It smells like New York City during a summertime garbage strike. Some lucky raccoon must've had a feast of a lifetime earlier tonight because there's garbage everywhere. As I work my way around the trash cans, I step in something soft and gooey, which makes my flip-flop get stuck. I have to jerk my foot a couple of times to free it, ignoring the disgusting sucking sound it makes, and finally make my way out of the treacherous minilandfill. I'm now on the north side of the house. I need to make my way around Leah's bedroom, across the back of the pool area, which four of the six bedrooms face, and into Andrew's side door.

Leah's shades are up and only the light from her bathroom is on. If she looks out the window, she may see me, so I play it safe and crawl on all fours under the window line. After clearing her room and the North Wing, I begin to tiptoe at the edge of the field behind the house. I then hear some rustling, which makes me remember Andrew's impersonation of the Hamptons Potato Field Killer earlier this summer.

I break out into a run and sprint toward his door, tugging open the screen door and colliding into something tall and solid: Andrew.

"Ow!" We both say. I rub my forehead. He is rubbing his jaw. "Hey, you got your peanut butter in my chocolate!" I say, and then I start laughing, somewhat uncontrollably. He pulls me inside and closes the door, shushing me.

"Why were you running? I was just coming to check on. . . ." He stops to sniff the air and then sniffs around me. "What smells so bad?"

"You don't know what I went through to get here. I think I might've stepped in something . . . out by the garbage. . . ." I grimace.

"What were you doing by the garbage . . . never mind. I probably don't want to know." He leans down and has me step out of my flip-flops while I hold on to his shoulder for balance. He opens the door and flings my shoes out into the darkness. Then he starts wiping the grass and dirt off my knees, laughing to himself and shaking his head. "You're a total mess. But the most adorable kind."

We're kissing.

We're on the bed.

We're on the bed and kissing some more.

"I thought you changed your mind." He leans toward me, as if to kiss me, then pulls away, then does it again, and pulls away, teasing me, testing me.

"My mind? My mind didn't get a single vote in the matter. It's probably best if I leave my mind out of it entirely." I reach up to lace my hands around his neck, pulling him toward me. "In fact, I left my mind in my bed as my decoy. It's wedged between the pillows and the blanket."

"Good thinking, or, rather, good not thinking?" We both laugh, muffling it with a very delicious kiss.

. . .

When I notice the predawn light is creeping in though the skylights, I carefully try to untangle our bare limbs, so as not to wake Andrew or disturb the sickeningly high concentration of alcohol and Red Bull that's still swirling through my veins.

"Mumph. Where you goin'?"

"I should get back to my room before people wake up," I whisper.

"Don't go. Sleep now." He pulls me into him tighter.

"No, I can't. If we fall asleep, who knows when we'll wake up. I don't want to risk it." I try to sit up, but his strong arms, which are still around my waist, hold me down.

"Remind me again why we care if anyone knows? Come on, Eileen, just stay."

"Maybe you don't care, but I don't want everyone knowing all *my* business. They've already seen enough of it on the pages of *Hamptons* magazine." He flinches at the reference to George. Note to self: a man with whom you've just majorly fooled around doesn't want to be reminded that there is someone else with whom you regularly get naked.

"Right." He releases me without a struggle and turns over to fill the spot I've just vacated.

"I'm sorry." I lean down, kissing the space between his ear and cheek. "I . . . I didn't mean to. . . ." I pause. "I really enjoyed. . . . Sleep well, Andrew."

"Harumwah." Harumwah? But before I can ask him to repeat himself, he has fallen asleep, or at least has pretended to.

I collect my clothes as best I can from around the dim room, slip them on, and tiptoe back out the screen door into the warm, still morning. I pick up my dew-covered, smelly-gunk-covered flip-flops from the grass and steal back around the house to the laundry room door. As I carefully make my way around the garbage cans, I realize that I'm a complete moron, for not one but two reasons: (1) leaving a mostly naked Andrew in bed alone, and (2) not just walking through the house back to my room.

It is now confirmed: the Hamptons are destroying my brain cells.

. . .

I hold my breath all day, waiting for the other flip-flop to drop, meaning waiting for Andrew to give me some indication one way or the other, e.g., more or less attention than usual, to acknowledge that *something* happened last night. But after an uneventful morning of everyone following their usual routines—except me, as I try to limit any extraneous movement in order not to throw up—a typically lazy group beach outing and everyone, including and most especially Andrew, acting completely normal, I'm finally able to relax.

During a private moment in our room, Stacy confides in me that much to her disappointment, nothing ended up happening with Michael. Before the movie ended, he passed out beside her on the couch—granted, with his head up against ("not on," she takes the pains to clarify) her shoulder, which I agreed was a good sign. But after twenty-seven minutes (according to the cable box clock) of sitting completely still and listening to him snore, she finally gave up, left him there, and went back to bed. She doesn't say anything about noticing a body double occupying my bed or hearing/seeing/sensing me sneak back into the room, so at least that part of my covert operation was successful, even if the rest of it eventually proves to be a disaster.

Tonight turns out to be just as uneventful. Some of us go up to Sunset Beach, a trendy restaurant and motel on Shelter Island owned by hot hotelier, André Balazs, Uma Thurman's on-again off-again boyfriend, for cocktails. The "us" however doesn't include Andrew, since (I found out from Harriet the Spy) he was invited to Jeff and Rachel's house for dinner, which makes me wonder if Strappy Sandal Girl can't be far behind. The skies cloud over and the air turns cool almost as soon as we get there. The place is empty, as if the other potential patrons checked the weather in advance and thought better of coming. We end up leaving after only one round. It is already raining by the time we reach the ferry. We make a stop at World Pie and are home by the extremely modest time of ten-thirty. Given that I had about twenty minutes' sleep last night and am still a little hungover, I'm thrilled to have an early evening. Leah, Stacy, and I watch the end of *Bridget Jones's Diary* on TBS then call it a night around midnight.

Hamptons Unwritten Rule #34:
Geographical desirability isn't only about
having a house south of the highway.

I'm woken out of a deep sleep by our bedroom door opening inches away from my head. I look up, but the light from the hallway is shining right into my eyes.

"Cassie? Is everything okay?"

A damp, cold hand reaches in and grabs mine, pulling me out of bed and into the hallway. When my eyes finally adjust to the light I see Andrew standing in front of me, his hair and jacket wet, his cheeks red, and a wide grin across his face. "Come on Eileen," Andrew whispers, smelling like an intoxicating mix of beer, rain, and sea air. "Before anyone sees us. It's raining too hard for a trip through the garbage tonight." As I tiptoe behind him, I peek fearfully around every corner, dreading running into a housemate-turned-somnambulist.

"What time is it?" I stand in the middle of his room, rubbing my eyes as he takes off his wet coat and shoes in his walk-in closet.

"One-thirty, I think."

I stretch and yawn. "I was sleeping so well!"

"Is that a whine I hear? Are you whining?" He comes up close to me, warming his hands on the small of my back.

"A little, yes."

He tsks at me, shaking his head. "You know the house guidelines, Miller. You can only enter a housemate's room unless you're expressly invited, but once there, there's no whining, especially in Andrew's room."

"There were a lot of rules, but I don't remember that one."

"The rule wasn't worded exactly that way. It was on page twelve, Appendix three, paragraph Q, subsection C-one. Did you not get that far? It states, 'Andrew's room is the Happy Zone. Only people who are happy to be there are allowed in his room.'"

"I'm happy to be here. It's just a little weird, right? We barely talk all day or hang out tonight and then you come pull me out of bed for a rendezvous?"

"Ah, but Miller, you were the one who was worried about the housemates knowing. I was just keeping up my part of the bargain by maintaining a high level of discretion throughout the day."

He looks crazy cute. The rain has made his hair curl up around his ears. Suddenly I have the urge to nibble on his left lobe. His room feels like a cocoon with the rain falling rhythmically against the skylights. It's like we're a world away from Leah, Stacy, Captain CrackBerry, George. . . . "Oh, I see. I'm just here because I'm geographically desirable."

"No, not exactly." He kisses me. His lips are cool and wet. "Just the latter part." He walks forward, causing me to back up until I reach the foot of the bed. He gently lays me back onto the comforter as he climbs up to sit astride my waist.

"Are you drunk?" I ask.

"Not enough to not worry about what I'm doing and just enough to be enjoying what I am."

"You need to be buzzed to be with me? You really know how to flatter a girl."

"It's not what you're thinking. Believe me, if you knew why, you'd be flattered." He leans in to nibble on my neck—only my favorite erogenous zone ever—tripping every sex sensor on my body.

"I would, would I?" I stretch my neck longer to give him more surface area and let myself relax. "You know, I think I'm beginning to remember that rule now. . . ."

. . .

This time when I creep out of his room around seven in the morning, leaving him fast asleep, I use his bedroom door. Since there's no chance anyone is up this early, especially with the pouring-down rain, I figure I can risk taking the direct route. After a quick peek down the empty hallway, I tiptoe through the house back to the North Wing. I slip back into my room and slide into my chilly bed. Stacy doesn't even stir. I pull the covers up around my chin, shiver, and promptly fall asleep to the sound of the rain pattering against the shingles.

Hamptons Unwritten Rule #35:
What happens in the share house stays
in the share house . . . for better or worse.

When I finally wake up, I amble out into the living room and am
surprised to find that the common rooms are alive with activity,
despite how much today is so obviously not going to be a beach
day.

"Michael is making us pancakes!" Stacy calls out, motioning me
into the kitchen. Despite how inconceivable that statement seems,
lo and behold, Captain CrackBerry is futzing with a fancy-looking
griddle attachment for the Viking stove.

"Good morning, sleepyhead," Leah says to me. "What's with you
two, anyway?"

"Us two who?"

"You and Andrew." My stomach drops into my pajama bottoms.
Does she know? "The two of you are the last ones up this morning.
I was just going to come wake you up so you wouldn't miss break-
fast. Guess I'll have to go kick his ass."

I silently congratulate myself for having the good sense to return
to my room earlier this morning. Leah discovering us together in
Andrew's room would not have been good. "Right, yes. Kick his ass.
I'm already up." That's all the invitation our resident Queen Bee
needs to buzz off in the direction of the South Wing, her cork
wedges clomping loudly down the hallway. "Can I help?" I say to
the Sagaponack chapter of the Breakfast Club.

"Dishes!" Stacy calls, hauling down a heaping stack of plates
from the cabinet, the weight of which nearly pitches her tiny body
backward.

"Morning, sunshine," Jackson says to me from a stool at the
kitchen bar. "Don't worry. I'm a fellow sleepyhead, as I was still in
bed until a few moments ago, before I was ambushed on my way to
the loo."

"Let me guess who did the ambushing."

He raises his coffee mug to me in confirmation.

"The first batch is ready!" Michael calls out. "Everyone sit down! These things get cold really quickly."

"Warmed real maple syrup? Nice touch, Michael," I say. "Does anyone want some of this?"

Leah clomps back to the dining room and sits down. "Andrew's just washing up, he'll be right out. Oh, and *someone* must've left *these* in his room last night." She opens up her right hand, dropping a baby lime-green mesh Cosabella thong in the middle of the dining room table.

Oh. My. God. I'm about to reach out to grab them when I stop myself just in time, realizing that doing so would immediately reveal me as the guilty, thong-less owner.

"Eww, gross!" Stacy squeals.

"Top Two Moment of the Summer!" Michael exclaims, trying to high-five Jackson, who gives him a scornful look while continuing to butter his pancakes.

It suddenly occurs to me that if anyone has done the quick calculation I've just done in my head, they will realize that they've heard denials from two out of the three possible female owners. I avoid Jackson's gaze. I know he must be super good at the new math.

Andrew appears at the table. "What's going on?"

"Oh, I just found a little something in your room that I thought might belong to someone else." Andrew looks confused until she nods at the incriminating evidence sitting in an embarrassed heap between the OJ and the syrup. "I found these hanging from the lamp next to your bed."

"Dude! Way to go!" Michael tries for another high five, this time with Andrew, who returns it, but unenthusiastically.

Andrew calmly reaches down and scoops up the thong, tucking it into the back pocket of his jeans. "I'll make sure these get back to their rightful owner. Thanks for finding them, Leah." He sits down but thankfully not next to me. "I'll take as many as you got," he says to Michael, holding out his plate.

"I'll bet. You obviously worked up an appetite," Michael snickers.

Hamptons Unwritten Rule #36:
The Code is uncrackable.

I'm hiding in my room after the outing of my underwear, when I see Leah standing at my door. We exchange a couple of pleasantries about the inclement weather, which is fitting, since at the moment, I'm not feeling so sunny about my BFF.

She sits on the end of my bed and crosses her long tan legs. "So, I wanted to tell you that I know that the thong is yours."

"What are you talking about?"

"I *know*, Miller. About you and Andrew. Friday night, last night . . . I'm sorry about the underwear thing. I wasn't trying to embarrass you. I thought you would think it was funny. I mean, everyone *knows* you can't keep secrets in a share house, so I figured there was no way that you could've seriously thought that no one would find out. But then I saw your face and saw how mortified you looked. . . . Well, I just hope you don't hate me."

"I don't *hate* you, Leah." I just want to throttle you every once in a while, but I wouldn't call it *hate*. "So, I guess everyone else figured it out too?"

"Pretty much. Look, I know we haven't been as close all summer as we've become more recently, but I'm not just your housemate; I'm also your friend. And being in the house together just makes our friendship that much deeper, especially because of, you know, the Share House Code."

"The what?" If it's anything like the August First Rule, then I'm in big trouble, since I clearly botched that one. Twice.

"The Code!" she says, somewhat impatiently. "It means that we look out for one another, watch each other's backs. And it's even more important that we female housemates follow the Code, especially when it comes to guy matters, even if it has to do with guys in our own house. Do you hear what I'm saying?"

"I think so. Sure." I have no idea what's she talking about.

"Here's the thing. I'm your friend. I'm on your side. I would hate to see you get hurt or end up being disappointed. You're a great girl, but I just don't think it's going to happen."

"What's not going to happen?"

She sighs and recrosses her legs. "What I'm saying is that Andrew is not a long-term, exclusive-relationship kind of guy. I've known him for close to three years, and this is my third summer living with him. You learn a lot about someone when you've spent that kind of time together. He doesn't let a lot of people in, but we've gotten close. I'm probably his best female friend. He's a great guy—one of the greatest, really—and in most ways, he's a total catch. Who could blame you for going after him? You'd be crazy not to try. He's got it all. But the thing is, Miller, he's just not there emotionally. Unfortunately, I just don't think he's ever going to settle down— with *anyone*."

"Woah! Who said anything about settling down? We just spent a couple of nights together . . . it was fun . . . no big deal . . . I wasn't thinking anything. . . ."

"I know it's early days and completely none of my business what you do and who you do it with, but I've seen this before. More than once. You might think you're just having fun, but I bet deep down you're hoping it will turn into something else, or if you're not there yet, you will be. But considering what happened with him, chances are it will be a dead end."

"What happened with him?"

"When he was married? In his twenties? You knew about that, didn't you?" I shake my head. "Ack. I knew I shouldn't have opened my big mouth." She purses her lips. "I always do this . . . maybe he should be the one telling you this."

"No, go ahead. Tell me."

She gets up and pushes the door closed. "All right, but don't tell him I told you. He is supersensitive about this stuff. But at the end of the day, I do think you're better off knowing. Andrew married his college girlfriend the summer after they graduated, even though they were going off to graduate school in different cities in the fall. He went to Yale Law School and she went to Wharton in Philly. Not long after that"—she lowers her voice to a whisper—"she found out he was cheating on her."

"Wow."

"But they were so young, so it's not entirely surprising. What are the odds of it working out when you get married at twenty-two? It probably made Andrew realize, too late of course, that he was too young to settle down, so he divorced her. After he graduated, Andrew was recruited by one of New York's biggest law firms, and from then on, he became a classic workaholic. He made partner a couple of years ago—earlier than most of his class—and you know what that does to a guy's ego." She makes the exploding gesture with her hands. "Most people would say—and he would claim—that he has just been too busy working and building his career to get involved in a serious relationship, and that may be part of it, but I suspect that he has never been the settling-down type and probably never will be. Some guys are just like that."

"How do you know that he hasn't or won't change?"

"Of course I don't know for sure, but he hasn't had a serious relationship with anyone since I've known him. Every once in a while, he'll hang out with someone for a little while, but no one girl is ever around for too long. I know you've seen that firsthand at least a couple of times this summer. . . . His career comes first and women are just . . . entertainment."

"That's quite a story."

She runs her finger along the quilting on the bedspread and then looks up at me again. "So, it's good I told you, right?"

"Yeah, sure. Thanks, I guess."

She stands up and smoothes out her miniskirt. "At least it's not like you've lost anything—not even time. And you're still dating George Daniels, right? I love Andrew, don't get me wrong—he's a great guy to be friends with—but *George Daniels*. If you can snag him, that's like winning Mega Millions."

I wonder if she has seen the pictures of George with Pauletta. "I'm not sure that I'm trying to snag anyone."

"Still. You're better off with George, if for no other reason than because he's not in your house. It's so much . . . cleaner. Why do you think God invented the A.L.D. Rule?"

"The A.L. whatty-what?"

"Come on, Miller, I can understand you not knowing the Code, but the After Labor Day Rule? It's Hamptons House 101. Never, under any circumstances, should a girl fool around with anyone in her house until *after* Labor Day. Why do you think Jackson and I aren't together yet? If it weren't for that, he and I would be all over each other. But A.L.D. is like the quintessential golden rule!"

"I thought the August First Rule was the golden rule?"

"What's *that*?" I tell her. "Are you kidding me?! That just sounds like something guys made up so they conveniently could fool around with girls in their houses before the end of the summer without having to put in any of the actual effort of dating them. Men are always looking for ways to eat their cake and have it too. Who told you about that?"

"Michael and Andrew. At the Pre-Summerhouse Dinner."

"Figures." She shakes her head. "See what I mean, Miller? God, if there's anything I've learned it's always to consider the source." She clomps toward the door, opens it, and swings her hair in a wide circle as she turns back to me. "The August First Rule. Ha! Price-less."

Priceless indeed.

. . .

Since hiding in my room failed, I lock myself in the bathroom to take a long shower. Everything Leah said about Andrew is spinning in my head. Her story seems reasonable—after all, I *have* seen the Mayor in action, first with Blonde, then with Hailey, and who knows who else—but something isn't quite gelling for me. By telling me she always "considers the source," it's like she suggested that I not only question the validity of what Michael and Andrew tell me but also—perhaps inadvertently—that I also question *her.* How could I have absolute faith in Leah as the source of this new information, no matter how much sense it seems to make, when she has been my so-called friend for only about five minutes?

To give her the benefit of the doubt, Leah could just be someone who is prickly to people she doesn't know and then warms up to them as she gets more comfortable, which would explain her semi-frigid behavior to me at the beginning of the summer. She would have to be downright evil to deliberately misinform me, or at least have cause to be evil, which now, more than at any point earlier in the summer, she doesn't really have. Given that, it's quite possible she's telling the truth.

And regardless of whether or not she's being honest or not so much, this morning's thong incident was not even remotely in my "Top 2" favorite moments of the Summer of 2007. The notion behind the A.L.D. Rule, especially now that I've been burned by the August First Rule (would waiting two more days until the of-ficial start of August have made any difference?), is far from out-rageous. Do I really need to complicate my life in my own house while serving as free-on-demand entertainment for my house-mates? And even though Pauletta has reared her pretty head as a factor in whatever-it-is-I'm-doing with George, I shouldn't just jump to conclusions about our situation. Cassie wouldn't have introduced me to him if she thought he was just looking for a fling, would she? Also, I can't really go to Cassie at this point for verification about Andrew. First of all, she may not know, but more importantly, what would she think about the fact that I'm fooling around behind her friend George's back? She has known George longer than she has known me—ultimately her loyalty may lie with him. Besides, she did say that George and Pauletta probably weren't even together. . . .

Twenty minutes of washing, rinsing, and repeating hasn't cleared my head of all the confusion, but as I watch the water spiral down the drain, I realize that there is at least one thing that I know I need to pull the plug on.

. . .

After getting dressed, I march down the hall to pay a visit to the Mayor. I knock, but there's no response. "Andrew? It's Tori . . . I mean, Miller. Can I come in?" I press my ear up to the door, but all I can hear is muffled music. I ease the door open a crack. The music is on, not loudly, but the lights are off, the shades are down, and since the rain is still coming down, it's dark. "Andrew?"

A lump beneath the blankets moves and a head pops up from the pile of pillows. One eye opens and squints at me. "Friend or foe?" The head disappears again, replaced by an arm sticking up in the air, motioning for me to come over. I approach the side of the bed and stand there hesitantly when his arm swoops out and pulls me down into the crook of his shoulder. "Mmm. Nap with me."

I wriggle around to face him. "We have to talk."

"No talking, napping. Napping is good."

"Andrew, seriously. I just wanted to make sure we're cool."

He props himself up onto his elbow and pries his eyes open. "Cool?"

"Yeah, cool together, cool separately, cool about what we did, what we've been doing the last couple of nights. . . ."

"I'm pretty cool with all that. Nap now?"

He looks really cute with his hair all mussed up. I have an urge to stroke the blond hair on his forearm just above his Rolex, but I resist and press on. "I think given the fact that we have to live together for the rest of the summer, it would be better to, I don't know, manage the expectations up front, instead of giving either one of us any room to assume anything. If we figure things out now, then we're better off. There'll be no misunderstandings, and no one will get hurt."

He rolls onto his back and drapes his arm over his forehead. "Shit. You're freaked out. I knew I shouldn't have—"

"No, I'm not freaked out. I've just been thinking, and to keep things simple we should just forget about the August First Rule and instead follow the tried-and-true A.L.D. Rule."

"A.L.D. Rule, huh."

"Yeah, don't you think? I don't want it to be weird around the house or when we're out with . . . other people."

"Like George, you mean."

"Like whomever. Come on, Mayor. It's not like you're not racking up some quality time with the ladies. I'm not blind. I see how girls flock to you everywhere you go."

"*And* guys."

"Well, that part's just none of my business," I joke, trying to lighten the mood. He still looks grim. "None of it needs to be any of my business, actually. Look, we're friends and housemates first, and feeling comfortable here, where we live—where we've paid a lot of money to live—is the most important thing, right? Let's just pretend it never happened, okay?"

He props himself up on his elbow to look me in the eye. "Is that what you want? Or is that what you *think* you should want?"

"I think it's what we should both want."

Suddenly, there's a bang at the door. "Kane! Are you in there?" It's Michael. "Dude, I scored us an indoor court, but we have to leave now!"

"I'll be there in a minute!" Andrew shouts toward the door.

"Looks like you have to go," I say, getting up from the bed.

"Yup, sure does." He pulls back the covers and slips out of the other side. "Miller, wait." I turn around. He tosses something to me. I open my hands to see what I've just caught.

The green thong.

12.

Secret Society

August						
Su	Mo	Tu	We	Th	Fr	Sa
			①︎	2	✗3	✗4
✗5	6	7	8	9	10	11
12	13	14	15	16	17	18
19	20	21	22	23	24	25
26	27	28	29	30	31	

September						
Su	Mo	Tu	We	Th	Fr	Sa
						1
2	3 Labor Day	4	5	6	7	8
9	10	11	12	13	14	15
16	17	18	19	20	21	22
23	24	25	26	27	28	29

Hamptons Unwritten Rule #37:
Though it may not seem like it during
the season, your Hamptons social circle
actually does exist outside of the East End.

"Can you pass me a napkin?" I ask Jimmy.

Jimmy, Jerry, and I are sitting on a bench in Madison Square Park on a stunning Monday afternoon. The rain that plagued the Northeast most of the weekend finally stopped a few hours ago and left dry and clear conditions in its muggy, soggy wake, so I suggested we have a late, thoroughly unhealthy lunch at the Shake Shack, despite its notoriously long lines.

"I'm confused," Jerry says, as if we were in the middle of having a conversation about the weekend, even though hours have passed since our Monday morning meeting and my exhaustive review of all the strangeness that ensued over a mere forty-eight hours. "I thought you *liked* George. So, what I still don't understand is why did you sleep with Andrew? I guess you could make the argument that you were drunk and maybe a little pissed at George on Friday night, and so you were acting out by being with Andrew. But that doesn't explain why you were with Andrew again on Saturday night, when you were sober."

It's not as if I haven't wrestled with this very conundrum all weekend, but I'm quiet for a moment as I choose the words that can best explain what I haven't fully figured out for myself. "I like George and am attracted to him, but I don't think we're falling in love."

Jerry's eyebrows knit even farther together with the strain of understanding. "Then why are you still dating him?"

"Because I like spending time with him. He's fun, he's a gentleman, he's attentive. . . ."

"He brings you to nice parties, gets you into the VIP section, pays for everything, has a hot car and a beautiful beach house . . . ," Jimmy adds with a surprising lack of snark.

"Well, yes. The package doesn't suck, that's for sure. But it's more than that. It makes me feel good to be with him."

"To be with *him* or to be with a guy who also happens to have all of these bells and whistles?" Jerry persists.

"I don't know, Jer. Maybe it makes me feel good that he wants to be with me or even that someone like him wants to be with me. It's nice to wake up knowing that there's a guy out there—not just any old guy but someone I'm interested in—who's going to be calling me and making plans with me. I look forward to hearing from him and seeing him. Besides, is it the most terrible thing in the world for me to date someone I enjoy being with but is probably not my future husband? I can't be the first person to have ever dated someone with that intention. Men certainly do it all the time." As I say this, I wonder if by "men" I mean Peter. "And if you think about it, George is technically my rebound guy," I joke.

But Jerry's not having any joking at the moment. "Unless Andrew is your rebound guy and you have just been too scared to let yourself fall for George because of what happened with Peter."

"That sounds feasible, I suppose, but I really don't think that's it. . . ."

"But what if George is falling in love with you? What if the Pauletta thing was just a fluke, like Cassie said, and he's got feelings for you, not just for you as his standing Friday night beach date?"

I frown and look off into the distance to chew on that idea and my cheeseburger for a second. Could George have feelings for me? I guess it's possible. . . . "Woah, hold the phone! Is that Jackson over there?" I nod toward a big tree at the edge of the park.

"That handsome guy over there kissing that older woman?" Jimmy peers over the top of his sunglasses. "Remind me why we didn't kiss him when we had the chance at the Love Kills Benefit Debacle?"

"Who's the lucky lady?" Jerry asks.

"Based on hair color alone, it's certainly not Queen Leah."

"Are you going to say hi?" Jerry asks.

"I don't know. Should I? They sort of look like they're having a private moment."

"Yes, of course! Aren't you dying to know who that woman is? I am."

"I'll be right back." Jackson and his very own mystery lady are holding each other's hands and talking. As I get closer, I get the feeling that they're *hiding* behind the tree. I'm about to retreat when Jackson spots me.

"Miller?" Not only is it strange to see someone from the Hamptons outside of that microcosm, but it's also odd to hear the use of my last name here, where I've always just been "Tori."

Jackson quickly drops his lady friend's hand and whispers something to her as her eyes meet mine. She pats down her hair and wipes her lips, which are smudged with dark brown lipstick.

"Hi! What a coincidence! I was sitting over there having lunch with my friends and I thought that was you. I didn't mean to intrude."

He leans forward to give me a double-cheek air kiss, rakes his hand through his floppy hair, and then pushes his crooked glasses back into position. "Miller, this is Margaret. We work together. She's the editor in chief. Margaret, this is Miller. She's one of the sane ones in my crazy summer share."

"Pleased to meet you, Margaret. Is your office nearby, or did you just come up here in the vain hope of having lunch at the Shake Shack?"

"We're down on Union Square but we, ah, had a lunch meeting in the neighborhood."

"But they didn't serve any milk shakes where we went, so I think you made a better choice," Margaret says, nodding toward my cup. Margaret is a tall and slim but not dainty woman. She looks to be in her early forties with short, dark hair that she wears tucked behind her ears, dark eyebrows and pale skin. She could pass for an older Audrey Tautou. She's wearing a crisp white button-down blouse, a black pencil skirt with a silver chain belt, and seriously expensive-looking pumps. She's wearing a ring on her left hand, but it's unclear whether it's a wedding band or not.

"I'm sure you two need to be heading back up to your office, and my friends are over there, so. . . ."

"Miller, it was good to see you off campus. We should make it a point of doing so sometime soon, you know, far from the madding crowd." Jackson bestows two more air kisses on either cheek.

"I'd like that, especially now that we have proof that we each actually exist outside of the Hamptons." He laughs. She doesn't. "Margaret, it was really nice to meet you."

"And you, Miller. Have a good rest of the summer."

I head back to the boys, who have been craning their necks in our direction the whole time like baby chicks demanding to be fed. I risk a glance back over my shoulder to catch sight of Jackson grabbing Margaret's hand before disappearing down Fifth Avenue together.

"So???"

"Jackson is having an affair with his boss."

"Well," says Jerry, leaning back and rubbing his neck, "at least you're not the only one leading a double life."

Hamptons Unwritten Rule #38:
For some Hamptonites, there's no
such thing as over-exposure.

I'm with George on Friday evening. It's only eight o'clock and we've already hit a cocktail party at London Jewelers in East Hampton for the launch of a new luxury watch brand followed by a reception for a cookbook written by a hotshot local caterer at Book Hampton down the street. At each event, George glad-handed the various guests of honor and acquaintances in attendance and posed for some pictures (given my negative reaction to flashbulbs, he has begun to grant me reprieves from joining him for the photo ops). Then he and I would sip some champagne while we ostensibly looked at the new watch or cookbook for twenty minutes before finding the right opportunity to sneak out.

"So," he says as he hustles me to the car while checking his watch, "we'll get a bite at the bar at The Lodge to refuel and catch a minute to ourselves and then we have to be at Boutique by nine for the other thing."

"What's that one for again?" I say, struggling in my spindly heels to keep up.

"Uh . . . ," he says, pulling out his BlackBerry to scroll through it, "the launch of some new vodka brand." He opens the passenger door for me.

"Remind me why we're going?"

He pulls the car out into the steady Friday night east-bound traffic on Main Street, which is also technically Route 27 as it winds through town, and makes a left onto Newtown Lane, passing Calypso, Scoop Beach, Theory, Catherine Malandrino, Jonathan Adler, J.Crew-at-the-Beach, John Varvatos, and a host of other upscale boutiques. "My publicist thinks it's a good idea if I do a drive-by."

"Which publicist?"

"My personal publicist."

I can't help but turn to stare at him. "You have a personal publicist?"

"She's a genius. I've only been working with her for the last couple of months, but the exposure she's gotten me has instantly raised my profile, which has already made a tangible difference to my business."

"You're kidding, right?"

"Not at all. She arranges everything for me but is very strategic about it. She decides which events I should attend based on what kind of press coverage they're expecting to have so I don't waste my time going to the wrong ones. She's the one who insisted that I go to that Diva-licious CD release party a few weeks ago, because she knew there would be a red carpet and some national press there, plus it would be good for me to mix it up with some different folks."

"There was national press there that night? That's just great. I certainly didn't put my best face forward for *Star* magazine," I say, recalling my makeup malfunction.

"I wouldn't sweat that one too much. When I'm not with anyone famous, the national books usually only use pictures of me."

"That's a relief, I guess. What else does this person do for you?"

"Her name is Jodi. Sometimes I have her organize who I go with too. It helps guarantee coverage if I go with a 'face,' like models mostly, since so many of them live in New York. Occasionally she puts me together with an actress when a good one comes to town from LA to shoot a movie or for a press junket."

"Jodi arranges *dates* for you with models and actresses?"

"It's not like the woman is running an escort service, Miller. Some she coordinates through their publicists, and some of them I set up on my own because I'm friends with them. It's just another part of my marketing strategy. It's great for the residential side of my real estate business. I deal in a lot of very expensive properties, so the PR helps attract potential clients, especially younger ones who can be repeat clients down the line. And if the models and actresses buy from my company, then Jodi can get the sale picked up in the newspapers. It works out very well for all involved."

It suddenly occurs to me that this must explain the Pauletta thing, which would mean Cassie was at least partially right: George was in fact technically out with Pauletta, but for purely opportunistic as opposed to romantic reasons.

"You've been a great sport letting me drag you around to all these things. I know it's not exactly the most relaxing way to spend an evening, but for the most part it's been fun, right? And you are much better company than all the models or actresses put together."

We've just pulled into the parking lot at the restaurant. As soon as we get out of the car, I grab him and plant a big kiss on George's lips, which he returns enthusiastically.

Hamptons Unwritten Rule #39:
Inevitably, there's a hidden quid pro quo.

As has been his habit, Jackson arrives at the house on Saturday morning just as George is dropping me off from our marathon date, which ended with the promised farm-fresh breakfast on the deck and a walk on the beach. As we walk inside, Leah announces that the train is leaving for the beach in ten minutes before the small parking lot at Gibson gets full, since it's only eleven-thirty and already eighty-four degrees with off-the-charts humidity. Jackson and I dash toward our respective rooms to throw our beach gear together.

As opposed to the way the housemates travel at night, i.e., in as many cars as possible, when it comes to going to the beach, an economy is employed in order to minimize parking hassles. We jam our stuff and ourselves into two cars, Andrew's being one of them, and drive the mile and a half to the beach. Beyond Andrew inadvertently catching my eye in his rearview mirror, since I'm sitting behind him in the backseat of his Rover—Leah has commandeered the front seat, natch—with a look I couldn't decipher, we've had no contact since our talk last Sunday.

Later at the beach, Jackson, complaining loudly and often that Englishmen were not made to withstand this kind of heat and humidity, asks me if I'm daring enough to try out the waves with him. We take leave of our human sundial to walk down to the edge of the surf, where the air is refreshingly cooler, thanks to a light breeze coming off the Atlantic.

"Well, my dear," Jackson says, "now we're even. First I had dirt on you, and now you have dirt on me. Though mine is far juicier than yours, if I may be so bold."

"What dirt? I don't have anything on you, juicy or otherwise."

He looks at me sideways. "Are you really going to make me come clean?"

"You were the one who said you were dirty."

"Touché." He sighs, buries a toe in the wet sand. "All right, then, if I must. As you probably surmised from what you witnessed the other day, I'm shagging my boss."

"And?"

"*And* she's married, which is why I don't come out to the beach until Saturday mornings, because Margaret and I spend Friday nights together in the city, while her husband, who is much older and semiretired, is at their house in Southampton."

I raise my eyebrows, impressed by these new details. "And?"

"Wow, you're tough. *And then* we drive out together, and I drop her off at her house before coming here."

"I see. How long has this arrangement been in place?"

"Nine months, give or take. Though not the elaborate summer weekend scheme. That is obviously a newer development—my brilliant plan, of course." He takes off his straw hat, rakes his hand through his mane, and holds it back while he replaces the hat. "We're in love, if that makes any difference."

"I'm not judging, Jackson. Believe me, I'm not one to judge."

"She's his second wife. He cares more about his booze, his boat, and golf than he does about her."

"Then why doesn't she leave him?"

"These things are complicated. . . ." He frowns.

"Is he rich?"

"Yeah, very."

"And you're . . ."

"Not. Among other things. I'm assuming I can count on you to return the favor of discretion? After all, a person who has a lot of secrets of his or her own is always the best one to trust with your secrets."

"So, no one else knows, I mean, like any of the housemates?"

"That's right. And I think it's much simpler to keep it that way."

We walk for a few moments, our feet making imprints in the wet brown sand.

"You respected my privacy, I can certainly respect yours. But as your friend—despite how little time I've actually held that position—I have to ask: aren't you worried Margaret's husband will find out? Or someone at work? Isn't it kind of risky, at least from the professional standpoint?"

"Funnily enough, as unsexy as book publishing tends to be, on top of its notoriously pathetic lack of intrigue and scandal, everyone at work knows and seems thoroughly indifferent to the whole thing. And they've all met her husband, so if anything, our colleagues seem silently supportive of our affair. Or maybe it just gives them all something to have a laugh about in the photocopy room." He smiles ruefully. "But you're kind to worry after my well-being. I don't know what the answer is just yet, but I've gotten myself out of trickier scenarios in the past without too much bloodshed, so I think I'll be fine."

We walk for a few minutes as I screw up my courage to ask him the question that's been weighing on me since my Leah Talk last weekend. "So, do you have any scoop on Andrew? Do you know if he and Hailey . . . have they ever . . . ?"

Jackson stops and gives me a sly look over the top of his aviators. "Could it be that the web you've been weaving over the course of the last several weeks has gotten a little too tangled up with pink thongs, my dear?"

"Can you just answer the question, please?"

"Well, it depends. Do you want to know what I've seen or what I've heard?"

"Both."

"I've *heard* the words *elusive* and *heartbreaker* bandied about in reference to our All-American Hero. I've *seen* plenty of fine young ladies put themselves in Mr. Kane's path, as I'm sure you've observed as well. But I've also seen one particularly tenacious woman actually succeed in crossing over—other than you, of course."

"Hailey."

"Yes. But I have not personally witnessed anything beyond public socializing as of late, but you also have to take into account that I am not out here half the nights the rest of you crazy kids are, so my knowledge base when it comes to Andrew's romantic activities is incomplete, at best."

"Right. Well, thanks. That's just what I needed to know."

He turns his head toward the cloudless sky and chuckles to himself. "Look at us, will you? Two peas in a goddammed pod. When I first met you, I knew you were going to be interesting, but I have to admit, you've succeeded in amazing me beyond my wildest imaginings."

"Well, keeping you entertained wasn't exactly my top priority this summer, but glad I could oblige. How about we take that swim now? I seemed to have worked up a bit of a sweat."

13.

Birthday Bashed

August						
Su	Mo	Tu	We	Th	Fr	Sa
			①1	2	✗3	✗4
✗5	6	7	8	9	✗10	✗11
✗12	13	14	15	16	17	18
19	20	21	22	23	24	25
26	27	28	29	30	31	

September						
Su	Mo	Tu	We	Th	Fr	Sa
						1
2	3 Labor Day	4	5	6	7	8
9	10	11	12	13	14	15
16	17	18	19	20	21	22
23	24	25	26	27	28	29

On Tuesday morning, I'm at the office alone. Jerry, who is a bit of a hypochondriac, is at yet another doctor's appointment, and Jimmy has his personal trainer on Tuesdays. The only lunch appointment I was able to set up as a result of our mailing was supposed to be to-day, but there's an e-mail from the woman at the Culture Channel in my in-box already, which I know means she's canceling without even having to open it. Instead I start reading through a string of e-mails that started with one from Andrew providing details around his highly anticipated annual birthday party at the house this Satur-day night and the ensuing offers of help and questions from the housemates about the guest list.

The phone rings and it's Alice telling me that she's just seen a pic-ture of George that was taken at a Central Park Conservancy benefit last night on "Page Six" of the *New York Post*. Luckily, Jerry is a tabloid addict, so he has the *Post* among other local papers delivered to the office. I grab today's edition and turn to the gossip section. It's a very good picture of George, except for the fact that a stunning young woman named Muffy Von Harrington-Schroeder, who is referred to as a "baroness," is standing beside him. With their arms around each other.

"Okay, I admit that it's weird to see him with another woman, but he explained the whole thing to me." I tell her about Jodi the Publicist and the business strategy. "I'm sure this is just part of the master plan."

"Tori, you're not only dating a guy who has a personal publicist—which, hello, isn't that kind of weird enough in and of itself—but also you've pretty much given him the green light to date other people while he's sleeping with you."

"Alice, he's not dating other people. They're appearing at events together, that's all."

"Are you sure? Did he say that, or are you just extrapolating that from your conversation?"

I suddenly feel a twinge of guilt thinking about my dalliance with Andrew two weekends ago—both because it's something I decided not to tell Alice about, since she seems to have something negative to say about everything these days, and because ever since Jerry planted the idea in my head about George perhaps harboring real feelings for me, even though we haven't discussed our status, it's not out of the realm of possibility that *he* thinks we're exclusive, or at least, isn't sleeping with anyone else. "No, I suppose I could be *extrapolating* about where he stands on the matter."

"So, that means he could be actually dating at least one, if not more than one, of these women."

"I doubt it. He really made it sound like being seen with them was purely work related and that he was with me because he likes me, not because I will further his career."

"And that's okay with you?"

"Well, it's not my favorite thing in the world, but it's not like I know for sure that I'm ready to be exclusive with him, so until I decide that, it's really not worth driving myself crazy about this whole thing. We're having fun and getting to know each other."

"It's one thing if two people wait before deciding that they want to be exclusive, but usually that doesn't entail one of the people *parading* around in the press the other women they're seeing."

"Things are different from when you were dating, Al, and they're especially different in the Hamptons, or least with this crowd. Cassie said that noncelebrity people having personal publicists isn't that uncommon these days. It doesn't make George an asshole just because he wants to be a successful businessman and will do what he needs to do to achieve that, does it?"

"Doesn't it?"

"Christ." My head is now in my hands.

"Look, I know I'm being a complete pain in the ass, but it's only because I love you and think you are the most special, wonderful, unique, and charming person in the world who deserves a man who will worship the very ground you walk on. But I can't help wondering if maybe you're not being honest with yourself about being more hung up on this guy than you're willing to admit." How is it that Alice and Leah are accusing me of the exact same thing but about two different guys? Did everyone sneak off to Mind-Reader Camp when I wasn't looking? "It's just not like you to be talking this way, Tor. Maybe this is your cue to realize that your dalliance with George was fun while it lasted but now it's time to say good-bye before you really get humiliated or hurt."

"By him or you?"

She sighs heavily. "Fine, I'll drop it. What do I know? I'm just an old married lady. . . ."

"And a terrible drama queen. You really need to work on that. Maybe Jimmy could give you some lessons."

"Funny. By the way, Scott's been asking when you're going to spend the weekend with us. It's already August. Maybe this is the perfect time for you to take a break from the craziness out in the Hamptons and come to the Berkshires, where it's normal."

"And boring," I say under my breath.

"E-mail me which weekends you think would work best. I'm assuming Labor Day is out, so pick another one so I can check with Scott—not that we have any other plans."

After promising to send her my schedule, I quickly get off the phone. I look at the picture of George and Muffy Von-Baroness one more time before slapping the newspaper shut and depositing it in the office recycle bin, aka the trash.

Hamptons Unwritten Rule #40:
Since temptation abounds, resisting it is (usually) futile.

My ear is pressed up against Andrew's closed door. It's almost 2 A.M. Friday night. The closest I've come to explaining to myself why I'm here—insanity aside—is the inalienable right to behave badly-slash-stupidly when one is jealous and spent the night drinking margaritas.

Even after Alice read me the riot act earlier in the week, I was still feeling fine about my situation with George. I was just as happy as ever to speak to him on Wednesday when he called, until we started trying to figure out plans for the weekend. He offered to make me dinner at his place on Saturday, since he was going to be out fishing all day and wanted to do something mellow afterward. Since I had Andrew's party on Saturday, I asked if we could do something Friday night instead. That's when he told me he couldn't because he had to escort Little Miss Muffet to an important event that Jodi had mistakenly arranged. ("I told her that if I have to make appearances on the weekends that I much prefer to do them with you, but she must've forgotten," he had explained.) So instead of not seeing him at all, I invited him to come to Andrew's party, even though I knew that wasn't exactly the relaxing night at home he originally had in mind. He said he would try to make it to the party after fishing, especially when I told him that we had gotten Cassie to commit to coming with Phillip.

As the week went on, I began to have a hard time getting Alice's finger-wagging out of my head. Out of curiosity, I started hunting around online to try to figure out what publicity-driven event George might be attending that would necessitate him going with the socialite over me, at least in his publicist's mind. But based on my preliminary research, there didn't seem to be anything of note going on at all on Friday night. After getting off the Jitney earlier this afternoon, instead of grabbing a taxi, I walked down Main Street in Bridgehampton until I found the latest issue of *Hamptons* magazine in the doorway of Bobby Van's to check the events calendar. Nothing. It occurred to me that maybe they were going to a private event that wouldn't have been listed, but then why would his publicist have arranged for him to go with the Muffster if there wasn't going to be any press coverage? "Because they're on a date-date," Alice's imaginary answer rang in my head. "Yeah, but then why would he tell me he was going out with her? Huh?" I shot back to the disembodied Alice voice.

I fought silently like this with Alice for the rest of the night, even while some of my housemates (not including Andrew, whose absence was never explained) along with a few of Michael's friends from his old house sucked down margaritas and stuffed our faces with fish tacos and chips at Almondito. My paranoia only increased as the night went on, which in turn raised my Grump Factor, so I asked Stacy to drop me home on her way to wherever they were going after. I was hoping to turn off my hopelessly overactive monkey mind by passing out, which I managed to do for an hour or two, until I found myself staring up at the ceiling, stewing in margarita juices and dying of thirst.

Which is how I've come to find myself standing in front of Andrew's closed door.

I have stopped breathing, in the vain hope of hearing what's happening within Andrew's suite and of not being discovered stalking by my housemates. I can't hear a thing. He's got to be here—his car is in the driveway. But is he alone? Knock or don't?

"Miller?"

I jump, banging my nose on the doorjamb in the process.

"What are you doing?" It's Andrew. Behind me. I whirl around. Thankfully, he's alone.

"I, well, I was just, you know, I thought maybe . . . but, I didn't know if . . ."

He smiles. He walks past me to open the door that's been my nemesis for the past several minutes. Inside it's completely dark except for a shaft of moonlight, which, I swear to God, is coming through the skylight and illuminating his bed. He walks in and disappears behind the door.

A hand reaches out, grabs my wrist, and pulls me in as the door shuts silently behind us.

Hamptons Unwritten Rule #41:
Most things never live up to their hype.
Though on rare occasions, some things
actually far exceed expectations.

As if ordered in advance in honor of the Mayor's big birthday party, Saturday is one of those picture-perfect summer days: dry, warm with a slight wisp of a breeze, and what could possibly be the bluest sky of the summer. Because it is so stunning out, everyone is up early, hurrying to get exercising out of the way so we can go to the beach and still have time to get the house—and more importantly, ourselves—ready for the party. We're practically the first people at

Gibson, but within an hour, dozens of multicolored umbrellas polka-dot the landscape, groups of friends and families fanning out from beneath them.

The ocean, which is usually quite rough, with waves crashing close to the shore, is amazingly calm, tiny waves turning over themselves, lapping languidly at the wet sand. More people than usual avail themselves of the tranquil surf, wading out on sandbars to stand in the knee-high water.

I'm standing alone by the edge of the water, squinting out at its shiny expanse when I feel a warm, strong body come up behind me, gently pushing me forward.

"You know what I want for my birthday?" Andrew murmurs into my ear.

"No, what?"

"I want to throw you in."

"Really? That's all? Then I guess I can return the very expensive present I bought you."

He pushes me forward, his legs behind mine, propelling me into the water. "You bought me a present?"

"Yup. How could I be a guest at the Mayor's birthday party without bringing a gift?" We splash into the delightfully warm ocean. We first sink in to about the height of our waists, and then as we start walking up onto the sandbar, the water lowers to about midthigh.

"True. It would be rude to show up empty-handed." He slides his hands onto my hips and turns me to face him. We are close enough to kiss. "Present time!" Before I can escape, he has grabbed me by the waist and flung me over his shoulder as he begins walking out into the deeper water.

"Andrew! Stop it! An-drew!!!!"

He flips me backward to dunk me and then dives under the water himself. He resurfaces with a huge grin on his face as I make a big deal of sputtering the salty brine.

"Drama queen!" he accuses. I drag my hand over the surface of the water and splash him in the face. "Okay, fine: let's call a truce."

We swim around for a few minutes in silence. "Are you excited about tonight?"

"I'm looking forward to it, yeah."

"Everyone in the house has been telling me that your party has the reputation for being the bash of the summer, which, of course, didn't surprise me in the least."

"I don't know if it can quite live up to that title, but it has been known for getting a little wild in the past."

"Like everyone-skinny-dipping, leaving-without-their-shoes, someone-always-ends-up-arrested wild?"

"No, more like, dramatic things always end up playing out during the course of the night. People hook up, break up, get mad at each other, fall in love. The whole panoply of interpersonal human drama."

"Impressive—both the word use as well as the legacy of your party."

"Why, thank you. It's never dull, that's for sure. So I can promise you won't be bored."

"Didn't even enter my mind that any event you hosted could be dull."

We swim a little more then stop to bob around. "The party is always fun, but I think the best thing I did last summer was stay out here the last week of August. The weather was like this almost every day. I spent hours on end at the beach, read, played a ton of tennis, grilled up some amazing food, and went to bed early every night. Are you planning to take any time off before the summer is over? Sounds like you've earned yourself a vacation from what you've told me about how hard you've worked over the last year."

"I hadn't really thought about it, actually, but I don't know if I feel right dumping everything in Jimmy's and Jerry's lap for a full week."

"Well, you should seriously consider it. Barring any unforeseen

emergencies at work, I'm going to be out here the week before Labor Day."

"Are you now?"

"Yes, ma'am."

"Well, I just feel bad for the Deputy Mayor. He'll be stuck covering your ass while you get to lollygag in the sand and surf."

The Official Response from City Hall? Another birthday dunk-
ing of Miller.

Hamptons Unwritten Rule #42:
August is prime time for getting bitten
on the ass—and not only by mosquitoes.

A palpable air of excitement fills the house as the party preparation
hum rises. The caterers Andrew hired have taken over the kitchen,
busily readying both warm and cold hors d'oeuvres; the bartenders
are setting up stations around the pool; and the DJ is hooking up
his top-of-the-line music equipment outside. This afternoon we
helped get the place party-ready by neatening up and placing
citronella-filled tiki torches and luminaria all around the backyard
and front of the house. As the blue sky turns deep purple with the
growing dusk, the house starts to glow, flickering expectantly with
candlelight.

As I'm showing the DJ where there might be more outlets outside, Andrew flies by me on his way inside to check on the caterers'
progress. "It looks like it's going to be a great party," I say.

"Hope so. You look amazing, Miller." He squeezes my hand and
continues on his way toward the kitchen.

. . .

By nine-forty-five, the party is jamming. There are people all over
the house and out by the pool, plastic cups of planter's punch in

hand, greedily scooping hors d'oeuvres off the servers' trays before they even get halfway through the crowd. The DJ has started kicking up the music to match the mood. So far, there's no sign of George, but he did say that since he'd be out on his friend's boat all day, he wasn't sure what time he'd get here. I will myself to not give in to the anxiety that's inexplicably growing in my belly.

As opposed to making the bar their first stop, as 99 percent of all partygoers do at every other fete I've ever been to, Andrew's guests make a beeline for the Birthday Boy. Andrew graciously accepts birthday presents, kisses cheeks, and shakes hands, all while flashing his campaign smile as he skillfully redirects his well-wishers toward the bars to make room for new arrivals and keep the flow of guests moving.

Jackson appears next to me with a cute brunette server who looks seventeen. "I've convinced Chloe here to give us first dibs on her delicious treats." If she weren't concentrating so hard on holding her tray of hot tiny sun-dried tomato quiches level, I bet she'd be swooning.

"Thanks, Chloe," I say, plucking a couple of quiches off her tray. "And thank you, Jackson. This liquid diet I've been on for the past couple of hours probably isn't the most balanced." I pop a quiche in my mouth. "I take it Margaret won't be stopping by tonight?"

"You take it correctly. I never mix business with pleasure. Or at least not publicly." He winks at me just as a hand clamps down on Jackson's shoulder from behind.

"Old Man Morton, for the life of me, I will never understand why your faux English charm always works so well on the ladies. Don't they know you're nothing more than a penniless pauper with a good vocabulary?"

Jackson turns around to face a WASPy blond guy who looks like he just stepped out of a Ralph Lauren ad circa 1985, replete with the classic blue blazer, khakis, crisp white oxford. "Of course they know, but I keep telling you, my popularity with the opposite sex has nothing to do with my English charm." They do the guy hug—banging opposite shoulders, slapping each other's back with a cupped palm—and pull apart, grinning like mischievous schoolboys. "James Cheever! Good of you to show! I didn't think you'd make it."

"You're very lucky to have me. Ever since I finished that endless revision on my manuscript, I've become rather smitten with the slower pace up on the North Fork. Plus, it's the only place I can afford until I get the rest of my book advance, so you better approve my changes and get that damn thing into production. This is my first and probably only time down on the South Fork all summer. Do you know that I had to take two ferries to get here? I see now, however, that perhaps I've been missing out," he says, giving me the once-over. "The girls aren't nearly as pretty up north as they are down here on the South Tine. Maybe that's why the Hamptons are so much more expensive."

"This happens to be my favorite housemate. Miller, meet James Cheever. Cheever, Miller."

James shakes my hand. "Mr. Morton here is my brilliant—yet cruel and task-master-ish—editor. It's entirely his fault that I missed out on half the summer."

"That's right," I say to him, "I remember hearing about you. You know Leah as well, right? I think Jackson meeting Leah at your book party is how he ended up in the house."

"Someone's been doing her homework," James says, giving me an approving look. "You better watch out for this one, Jackson."

"Believe me, I have been. She's had my number from the first time I met her."

"You mean, zero?" he replies. They both hardy-har-har.

"Well, if it isn't James Cheever in the flesh. I'll be damned." Queen Leah is standing before us in all her glory, as if she were posing for her Red Carpet money shot.

James whistles long and low. "God, you are even more gorgeous than when I saw you last!" Leah responds with a signature hair flip.

"I've been stuck in the city toiling away, eating my heart out listening to Morton here go on and on about how the two of you have been romping around this hedonistic playground all summer."

Leah blushes. "Well, it could've been the *three* of us romping around all summer, but you blew it."

That receives the kind of guttural cough-laugh that only men who are extremely turned on can give.

"Please, darling Leah, please, you're absolutely twisting the knife that is already lodged in my heart. How could you be so cruel? At least tell me that this old windbag here was your second choice."

Leah sidles up to Jackson and wraps herself around his arm, holding his hand in hers across the invisible strike zone at the front of her expensive-looking pleated chiffon miniskirt.

"Sorry, Cheever. Sloppy second's all I got for you."

Just then, I see George. I excuse myself from the highly charged tête-à-tête-à-tête to go meet him. "Miller, you look great, as always." He leans in for a kiss.

"George, what's that awful smell?" Not only is he completely disheveled and covered with the remnants of god-knows-what gook, but he also reeks of a toxic combination of fish, sweat, and beer. I bat him away before he can touch me.

"I know I'm a mess. Sorry, babe, but we just got off the boat an hour ago in Montauk, and since your place was on the way back to my house, I thought I'd just come directly here rather than wasting another hour going home to shower and change and then schlep all the way back."

"I guess that makes sense. Do you want to take a shower here? Or I could hose you off out back?"

He smiles. "Thanks, but I don't have any clean clothes with me, so it's not really worth it. But I could use a drink!" He reaches out his hand. "Don't worry, I washed them like ten times. Promise." I take his hand and follow behind him as he leads me toward the less crowded bar on the other side of the pool.

As we're waiting for our drinks, Andrew comes up behind us. "Miller, I've been looking all over for you." I turn toward him, just in time to see his eyes jump from me to George. His smile disappears. "Oh, uh, I didn't know you were. . . ." His voice trails off as he stares down at my hand clutched in George's.

I try to disengage my hand and begin waving it à la Vanna White. "George, I don't think you ever officially met Andrew. Not only is he our host this evening, but it's also his birthday today."

"Tomorrow," Andrew says quietly, looking down and away.

"What?"

"My birthday's *tomorrow*. Nice to meet you, George. Glad you could, uh, make it." I see Andrew's nose wrinkle almost imperceptibly as he moves closer to shake George's hand. Just then, the bartender hands George our drinks, so George winds up leaving Andrew hanging. "Look, I have to go. I'll catch up with you . . . later." Before I can stop him, Andrew has disappeared into the crowd.

"What's eating that guy?" He takes a sip of his drink. "Finally! Some normal people. Cassandra! Phillip! Over here!"

"Hey, you!" Cassie says, enthusiastically giving me a double-cheek kiss. I'm shocked to see that Cassie doesn't look like her normal radiant, beautiful self. In fact, she looks downright bad. She seems much thinner than usual and has dark circles under her eyes. "God, it's been forever since we've seen each other, hasn't it? I'm so glad the party's still going. We were stuck at this dinner that just went on and on. They hadn't even served dessert yet by the time we left!"

Phillip, by contrast, looks as if he's somehow gotten bigger and stronger, which in turns makes him seem even scarier than usual. "I haven't been to a party in a share house in a hundred years. I thought I was done having to drink out of plastic cups and eating defrosted hors d'ouevres."

"At least there are no kegs," George quips.

"Not that you've seen," Phillip adds.

As George and Phillip amuse themselves trading derisive comments about the party, I pull Cassie to the side out of earshot. "Cass, are you okay?"

"Of course! I'm great. Why?"

I eye her hand, which is shaking as she moves a strand of hair out of her face. "I don't know, you just seem, a little nervous or upset, maybe?"

"It's nothing. Really, I'm fine. We've just been so busy the last few weeks, running from one thing to the next. You know how it is. Sometimes when you're on the go, even though you're exhausted, you don't sleep as much. But it's nothing, truly, don't worry about me. Everything is great. I couldn't be happier. And Phillip is really taking care of me."

It doesn't really look like that's the case, but since Phillip and George are signaling us to rejoin them, I don't press it.

. . .

"We really should get going," Phillip announces not too long later. "We've been on the go since four this afternoon, and we still have a long drive back to Southampton." Cassie told me that Phillip has a full-time driver on weekends, so technically he doesn't have to do the twenty-minute drive back to Southampton himself.

"Phillip, so soon? I haven't seen Miller in weeks." He answers her with an evil-eyebrowed look that seems to say, We talked about this. "Phillip's right. We have an early tennis game tomorrow and a brunch after that."

As much as I want Cassie to stay, I can see how out of place Phillip seems and how jumpy that has made her, which is making me jumpy. I make a mental note to call her this week to make sure that everything is copacetic.

"I'm going to head out too, then," George says.

"Oh, no, George, do you have to?" I hear the hint of a whine in my voice.

"I'm sorry, but I stink to high heaven and I'm beginning to feel tired and uncomfortable."

"I could come with you—it would only take me a few seconds to grab some stuff. . . ." I have this sudden urge to go home with George and burrow into the cocoon of his white bedroom.

"No, you don't have to do that. Besides, I'm beat—I don't think I'd be good company tonight. I have a feeling I'll be asleep before I even hit the sheets."

After we've said our good-byes, I can't help feeling like Cinderella only backward: instead of being left behind at home while everyone else heads off for the big ball, I'm left stuck at the big ball while everyone else goes home—without me.

I'm standing amid hundreds of strangers who have overtaken my house, not a familiar face in sight, when I spot Leah, deep in conversation with James Cheever. I'm about to head over there when they both look up and see me—her eyes filled with something akin to fury. Before I know it, she has risen, smoothed out her minuscule skirt and is stomping over in my direction, practically pushing people out of the way to reach me.

"Hey, Leah! Are you having fun?"

"You bitch!" she spits out at me.

"Ex-excuse me?"

"You're such a fucking two-faced bitch!" Her voice rises perilously, catching the attention of a few surrounding guests. "I can't *believe* you! You made me look like an asshole! After all I've done for you!" Her face is red and her fists are balled up by her sides, looking like they're ready to take a swing at me at any moment.

"I truly have no idea what you're talking about, but whatever it is, I'm sure you're mistaken." I try to catch James Cheever's eye for help or a clue or something, but the minute I do, he looks away.

"No, there's no mistake. I know what you did to me. You are evil! I welcomed you into this house! I invited you to everything! I even watched your back, and what do I get in return? You just sit by and watch me make a fool out of myself in front of everyone!"

Fear rises up within me as the truth starts to dawn on me. "Leah, I can't apologize or take responsibility if I don't know what the hell you're talking about!" My voice is shaking. Even though the music is quite loud, the people immediately surrounding us have stopped talking and aren't bothering to hide the fact that they are hanging on every word.

She must notice, too, because she gets right in my face. "Jackson. I'm talking about Jackson. You *knew* that he's been fucking his boss! You knew he was leading me on the whole summer! You knew I liked him, and you never said a word to me!"

I stand there stunned, as if she has physically slapped me. "I . . . I . . . didn't know!"

"That is such fucking bullshit, and you know it! James Cheever just told me that you ran into Jackson and his *girlfriend* while they were together in the city *weeks* ago!"

"It wasn't *weeks ago* . . . it was just last week, just the other day, really. But Leah, it was just . . . just none of my business. I swear, I wasn't keeping it from you—"

"Oh, *really*? What would you call it, then?"

"Look, it wasn't my place to talk about it. If he wanted you to know, then he would've told you." Do I tell her that he told me not to tell anyone? Would that make it worse? Better? "Shouldn't you be taking this up with him? Isn't this about him, not me?" I just want this to stop. Preferably, before I throw up on myself.

"He's just a fucking *guy*, Miller. *You're* supposedly my friend! I would expect a friend to be *honest* with me, just like I was with you about *your little situation*. I would expect a friend to be watching my back, not stabbing me in it! I can't believe I was concerned about you and reached out to support you but the minute the situation was reversed, you just left me hanging! You pretend to be all nicey-nice, everyone's favorite new girl, but really you're just using everyone and doing whatever you want while you clearly don't give a shit about who you hurt."

Who is she talking about? That's not me. Is it? "You have it all wrong, Leah. Really, I didn't mean—"

She relaxes her stance as she surveys the enraptured crowd. Then she looks back to me and narrows her eyes. "You know, maybe you're right. I did have it all wrong. Very, very wrong." Hair flip. "I thought you were one of us, but as it turns out, you're just another wannabe. A wannabe of the worst kind. Was it worth it, Miller? Going on a national TV show as a total loser to be made over in front of millions of viewers for what, a hosing down and a few free outfits? Isn't that what the Transformation Trio gave you? That and a serious bikini wax, from what I heard. Yowch."

A snigger rises up from the crowd. "How . . . how did you find out?"

"Be real! Now you're acting like you *didn't* want everyone to know? If you really wanted to keep it a secret, then why on earth would you bring all of your housemates to that stupid premiere party? After your gay Trio friend opened his big mouth, it wasn't hard to find out the whole story. But you see, Miller, that's a case in which discretion is actually the right thing to do. I wasn't going to tell anyone and embarrass you any more than you'd already done for yourself. Too bad I can't say the same for you. Enjoy the rest of the party." She wheels around on her spike heels, making her pleated miniskirt do a Marilyn-like flutter, and stalks off, the crowd parting to let her through.

I am shaking. All I can think of is splashing some cold water on my face—that is, if the earth won't do me the kindness of opening up and swallowing me first. I turn away from the spectators, who have erupted into loud, gossipy tones, and practically sprint into the house.

Where I run smack into Andrew.

"Thank god! A friendly face!" I grab his arm and pull him into the empty back hallway. "You were so right about this party! It's crazy! You won't believe what just—"

"I heard."

"I mean, what the hell is her problem, right?" I search his face for sympathy. It's not there.

"Miller, I hate to say this, but maybe you're the one having the problem."

"What?"

"Well, I can't say that Leah handled her issue with you in the most discreet way, but is it possible that maybe she isn't too far off?"

I feel like I've just been slapped on the other cheek. "Are . . . are you taking her side?"

"I'm not taking anyone's side. I'm just speaking from my own experience with you."

"Which is?"

He sighs. "Maybe you don't always consider other people's feelings. Whether that's intentional on your part or not, I was hoping it wasn't. But I'm beginning to wonder if maybe it is."

"Are we now talking in general or specific to you?"

"Both."

"How have I not considered your feelings?"

"You honestly don't know?" I shake my head, unable to dislodge the lump that has taken up residence in my throat. "First of all, you bring that Daniels guy to my party. My *birthday* party. Not only is he barely even polite to me, but I heard he was dissing the party the whole time he was here. He looked like he didn't even bother to take a shower, for Christ's sake. I mean, I know this isn't the Maidstone Country Club but at least take a shower, wear some clean clothes."

"You're right. It was rude of him to come and behave like that. I'm sorry. But he had been fishing and didn't get a chance to—"

He lays his hand on my arm. "No, Miller, you're not hearing me. It wasn't exactly polite of you to invite him to come, made less polite by the fact of his appearance and his attitude. But my personal beefs aside, he's apparently going out with every supermodel he can get his hands on and flaunting it in every rag in town. Don't you see? *He's walking all over you.* I have no idea why you're even giving this guy the time of day, much less inviting him to the party, especially after last night. . . ."

"That's just rich, Andrew. What's the ratio of women to men here, huh? You've been surrounded by the entire female contingent of your fan club all night, and Hailey has practically been surgically attached to you since she got here!"

He shakes his head slowly. "You know, there are some real pieces of work out here in the Hamptons, but you, Miller, you take the cake."

"What's that supposed to mean?"

"Every weekend you *flounce* out of the house dressed to the nines for your fancy dates with Mr. M6 and make out in the driveway, or worse, bring him to *my* birthday party to shove him in my face and you have *the nerve* to be jealous of who I talk to at my own party?"

"Jealous? You think I'm jealous? Give me a break, Andrew!"

"Yes, I think you are and won't admit it."

"That's crazy! I have nothing to be jealous of! And you've known since the beginning that I've been dating George. I have not hid that fact from you for one single second. I haven't been flaunting or shoving or anything. I *live* here. And at least I've only been with one person the whole time. As opposed to you, Mr. Mayor. Who knows how many acolytes you've bedded this summer. How many notches on your bedpost are you up to now? Seven? Ten?"

He looks stunned. "Wow, is that what you think?"

"What else am I supposed to think?"

"I've just been playing by the rules—*your* rules, actually. The 'A.L.D. Rule'? You kept that one for what, two weeks, before you showed up at my bedroom door? As far as I can tell, you should have no complaints."

"I . . . I don't . . . That's not . . ."

"I think I've had enough for one night. I guess I gave you much more credit than you deserve. It's a shame. I'm usually a better judge of character." He begins to walk away.

"Meaning what, exactly?"

He turns back around. "I was *hoping* that eventually you'd be able to see the truth. But now, I can safely say, that hoping isn't the same as knowing." He lets the back door slam on his way outside as I rush off to the North Wing to the sanctity of Cassie's empty room.

. . .

I wake up with a start. I must've dozed off. It takes me a second to remember everything. A wave of nausea wells up, and I stumble out of the bedroom to a thankfully empty bathroom, the appalling sight and smell of which actually reverses my impending sickness. I open the door slowly, hoping to avoid whoever is next in line to tell me off or gawk at the resident pariah, but then I notice that the house is suspiciously quiet. I go down the hall to poke into the living room/dining room/kitchen. Empty, except for the remaining catering and bartending staff who are packing up. I head in the direction of Andrew's room, but before I even get down the hall, I see his door is wide open, revealing only a still darkness beyond. I speed back down the hallway and out the front door, where I catch sight of the last remaining partygoers, who are walking down the long narrow driveway.

Andrew is one of them. I walk a few steps down the driveway and am about to call out to him when I see that he's with a group of people, which most notably includes Strappy Sandal Girl herself. The group laughs loudly as they try to fit seven adults into a two-door blue Mercedes, like the reverse of the clown car circus gag. Andrew is the next to last to slide into the backseat. I hear his laugh waft across the almost empty parking lot as Strappy folds herself onto his lap. Someone yells out that it's after midnight and now officially Andrew's birthday. They begin a rousing but off-key rendition of "Happy Birthday to You." Andrew, laughing, pulls the door shut as the car is already in motion, crushing the green grass beneath its heavy, unforgiving wheels.

. . .

That Tuesday, due to the overwhelming popularity of the show, the pilot episode of *Three-on-One,* featuring the old Tori before she was transformed and soon thereafter became known as "Miller," is launched as a video download on iTunes.

Normally, this could easily pass under the radar, but Hurrah!, in the interest of furthering their partnership with iTunes as well as making a little additional revenue, promotes the hell out of the exclusive episode during their Tuesday night airing of a brand-new current episode on the network. Even though they don't air the full pilot on TV, the promotional spots, which ran at least once in every commercial break, show my face about five times. Oh, and my greasy hair, lack of makeup, and closet full of cargo pants.

The episode itself is reported to have something called a "Wax Cam," which not only shows "Before" and "After" close-ups of my bikini area, but also bonus footage of the "During," courtesy of a hidden camera I had no idea they used at the spa where they had taken me.

The audience for the show on Hurrah! that Tuesday night that would've also seen the promos: 3.5 million viewers.

The number of downloads for the pilot episode on iTunes: 106,371 people.

And that's just as of Wednesday morning.

"Please tell him to stop calling," I beg Jerry. "I want to be left alone."

Jerry has his hand cupped over the mouthpiece of his headset. "But Percy is desperate to talk to you. He says he's absolutely beside himself about this whole mess."

"Just say the same thing we've been telling the press all morning: No comment."

He opens his mouth, as if he's going to say something else but instead gives me a resigned nod. "Percy, we'll have to call you back. Uh-huh, yes, I know. I'll tell her. Okay, thanks." Jerry releases the call and removes his headset. "He sounded as if he were about to cry."

"What does he have to cry about? The fact that they showed his hair in a different style in the pilot versus the rest of the series?"

"Come on, you know he feels sincerely awful for tipping off Leah at the launch party. Everything is moving so fast for him, with the show getting picked up and going right into production. He was overwhelmed and exhausted by the time the party happened. He fully admits he drank too much that night. He said he was nervous. It was a big deal for him. He didn't mean to—"

I put up my hand and gesture for him to stop. "I *specifically* asked him—my supposed friend and self-proclaimed personal guru—not to breathe a word to anybody. And not only does he then shoot his mouth off the first chance he gets, he does so to the absolute worst possible person. And yeah, yeah, yeah, I know he didn't exactly spell it out for her that I was in the show, but he certainly gave her enough fodder to go digging around for more info. Whatever his excuse—he was drunk, giddy, overwhelmed—I don't care. I did him a *huge* favor by agreeing to be in that stupid pilot at the eleventh hour, the least he could've done was honor my simple request."

The boys are silent. Without even looking at them, I can tell they are speaking to each other with furtive looks across the room.

"But, sweetie," Jerry says quietly, "Leah and your housemates would've found out anyway. The video download, the press coverage . . ."

A tear plops out of my eye, appropriately landing on the *M* on my keyboard. "I know. It was inevitable. I was an idiot to do the show in the first place, it's just . . . he could've . . . I begged him not to . . . It was so humiliating, the way she screamed at me in front of all those people . . . the nasty things she said about me . . . they were all looking at me like I was a freak. . . ." I'm officially sobbing.

Jerry rushes over to put his arms around me. I cling to him, pressing my face into his stomach. Jimmy appears on the other side of me with a wad of tissues. When he stuffs them in my fist, I squeeze his hand hard and don't let go as I finally let it all out.

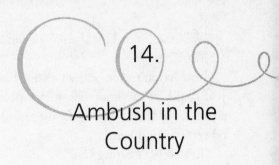

14.

Ambush in the Country

August						
Su	Mo	Tu	We	Th	Fr	Sa
			(1)	2	X3	X4
X5	6	7	8	9	X10	X11
X12	13	14	15	16	X17	X18
X19	20	21	22	23	24	25
26	27	28	29	30	31	

September						
Su	Mo	Tu	We	Th	Fr	Sa
						1
2	3 Labor Day	4	5	6	7	8
9	10	11	12	13	14	15
16	17	18	19	20	21	22
23	24	25	26	27	28	29

"Tori, you really need to get me the scripts for those public service announcements," Jimmy says to me in the office the following afternoon. "You're holding up the process. You know I have to begin working on those graphic elements ASAP."

"I told you this morning to go ahead and start," I reply. "You can figure them out without my exact copy."

He sighs dramatically. "Do you at least have a draft of the scripts for me to work from?"

"*Yes*," I lie. I've actually been playing Scrabble online with my new game buddy, ScrabChamp84. Luckily, since our desks all face toward the center of the room, Jimmy can't see my computer screen. Still, I minimize the browser window and reopen the empty script document.

"Well then, can I see them?" he persists.

"*No.*"

"You haven't even started them, have you? Okay, fine. Maybe you could let me know when you plan to start doing some work again. Until then I'll just take the rest of the summer off like everyone else around here."

"Jeez! What's eating you?"

"All we have in the pipeline are these pathetic PSAs, which we're doing for peanuts by the by, and not only have you not gotten those done—which I know you can do with your eyes tied behind your back or whatever the saying is—you haven't lined up anything else in weeks."

"Jim, it's not like I haven't been trying to win new business. It's not my fault that what's-her-name from the Culture Channel canceled lunch on me."

"Maybe not, but it *was* your fault that we lost the BuzzTV project earlier this summer," he retorts.

"How can you possibly pin that one on me? I contributed just as much as you two did, and I didn't miss a deadline or hold up the process for a single second."

"True, but you can't claim that you've had your head in the game since the summer started, and personally, I think it showed in that pitch. It wasn't nearly as strong creatively or strategically as our other pitches have been and *that*, my friend, is your bailiwick. I'm glad you've been having fun at your MTV beach house, truly I am, but *seriously*, it's time to get back to work."

Suddenly I'm fighting back tears that have instantly sprung into my eyes for what seems like the billionth time this week. Could my life be unraveling any faster? What is this, the "Big Slide 2: We Mean It This Time"? "What do you expect me to do, exactly? Start calling prospective clients the day after the video clip of my bikini wax became the number one viral video of the day? Can't you cut me a little slack? You know I'm going through a lot right now."

"You're not the only one going through a lot right now." He looks up to the ceiling and then back at me, his eyes now watery. "Did you even know that Jerry and I had to take out a home owner's loan to pay our bills?"

My mouth drops open. "Are you kidding me? I had no idea. I'm so sorry. Why didn't either of you tell me?"

He narrows his eyes at me. "Jerry didn't want to ruin your summer."

Just then, Jerry walks in with our afternoon order of caffeinated beverages that it was his turn to fetch. "What are you two bickering about now?"

"Nothing. Nothing at all," Jimmy says, grabbing his coffee off the cardboard tray and striding past Jerry and out the door.

Hamptons Unwritten Rule #43:
Though you can't imagine it in the beginning
of the summer, there will come a point
when you will need to take advantage of your
Hamptons Hall Pass, so be sure to keep
it somewhere safe.

"Tori, are you ever going to come out of your room?" Alice complains at my bedroom door.

"Probably not, no." It is Saturday morning. I've finally taken Alice up on her invitation to join her and Scott in the Berkshires for the weekend.

Last Sunday morning, aka Andrew's actual birthday, I hid in Cassie's vacant room until the house went quiet (it was another beautiful day, so it didn't take too long for everyone to scatter) and then called for a taxi to take me to the Jitney.

I haven't spoken to or heard from anyone from the beach since—not even Jackson, who I was hoping would at least call or e-mail to apologize for getting me into that shit storm with Leah in the first place. When I called him at work, his voice mail said that he was away at a writers' conference for the week and would only be checking messages periodically. On Thursday night after my fight with Jimmy, which sealed my decision to get the hell out of Dodge and escape up to the relative obscurity of Massachusetts, I e-mailed Stacy to let her know I wasn't coming. The notoriously Chatty Cathy responded with an uncharacteristically brief reply, "Thanks for letting me know. Enjoy the country."

Even the talker was barely talking to me. The Miller Freeze-Out was now complete.

Alice now opens the door, clearly sick of speaking to painted planks of reclaimed wood. I respond to the invasion by pulling the covers over my head. "Come on, it's a beautiful morning. Scott and I want to get to the farmers' market before all the good stuff is gone. And I know you love to pick out the pie, so you have to come."

"I don't care about pie. Just let me lie here and wallow in the failed social experiment that was heretofore known as my life and my newly failing business venture. I want to see if I can become one with the sheets." I didn't lay down the whole sad story of last weekend, including the previously unmentioned hookups with Andrew, on Alice until the car ride up to the house yesterday, even though my ever-astute best friend knew something was up with me all week; especially after I e-mailed her the press release about the *Three-on-One* pilot being available on iTunes for only $1.99. She was pissed I hadn't told her about the Mayor stuff sooner and basically said as much, but when she understood the full extent of how my life had completely imploded, she heeded my plea not to judge or provide commentary but just listen, as the last thing I needed to hear was a rendition of the "I Told You So" theme song. The one point she couldn't help making was, "So, you're finally coming out with us to the Berkshires because you're avoiding your housemates and the Hamptons in general." There was no denying that one, so I didn't even try. I just said I was sorry.

"Really, huh," she now says to me through my sheet tent, "you don't care which kind of pie I get? What if I choose wrong and get cherry peach or worse, pecan?"

"At this point, I'm not even worthy of my favorite kind of pie, so I leave it to the pie fates and your discretion."

She doesn't say anything. Then I hear her sigh and walk out, half-slamming the door behind her.

Great, another country heard from.

. . .

Alice and Scott stay out of the house long enough to let me stew in my own miserable juices, finally become antsy, get myself showered and slightly more perked up (thanks to multiple muffins Scott had picked up from the local bakery earlier this morning and leftover but still delicious coffee).

When I hear them come home, I meet them in the kitchen to help unpack the groceries. "You bought enough food for an army! The three of us can't possibly eat this much tonight." I remove ten fragrant heirloom tomatoes and pile them in the wooden bowl on the counter.

"Actually, we're going to be four."

"How do you get four? Me, you, and Scott."

"And Joe."

"Who's Joe? By the way, good job on the pie: strawberry rhubarb. Thanks."

"Joe is a friend of Scott's. He works in the Boston office. He rents a weekend house here with a few friends, but as you know so well, there isn't much of a social scene, so we invite him to dinner every so often."

"Having dinner with a married couple counts as a social life for this guy?"

"Hey, thanks a lot!" She whacks me with her now-empty reusable canvas shopping tote. Alice is very green in the country. "He's really into riding mountain bikes, so he likes coming here instead of the Cape. He's a nice guy. Decently good-looking."

"Way-way-way-way-wait. Is this a setup?"

She trims the stems of a bunch of wildflowers and arranges them in a ceramic vase. "No, not really."

"Is he single?"

"Yeah."

"And the rest of his housemates aren't coming?"

"No."

"So, if it looks like a blind date and it smells like a blind date. . . . When were you going to tell me?"

"I just did," she says, blinking innocently at me. Unfortunately, Alice is really bad at playing dumb, so I know immediately that this is more calculated than she's trying to make it look.

"Only after I saw the huge quantities of food you bought."

"It's no big deal. I thought it would be fun. He's a super nice guy. Late thirties. Down-to-earth. Normal. An adult."

"The implication being?"

"No implication, Ms. Suspicion Pants. The summer is almost over. I'm just thinking ahead."

"Ahead to what?"

"To when you're ready to be you again." Alice closes the cupboard and exits the kitchen, leaving me to contemplate the pie.

. . .

The afternoon turns dark and gray, as much inside as outside. The rain starts not long after the sky clouds over, so left with nothing much to do and not a lot of space to do it in, we each pull out our books and sink into reading-slash-nap time in the living room until it's time to start prepping dinner. And more importantly, drinking wine. Which I begin to do, heavily, around six o'clock.

I come into the kitchen to refill my glass and find something to nibble on.

"Aren't you going to change for dinner?" Alice asks me, doing an uncanny imitation of the person who gave birth to me thirty-three years ago.

"Why? Is there some new dress code out here in the sticks that I wasn't aware of?" I steal a slice of tomato from the cutting board.

"I just thought you might want to put on something a little less ratty. Isn't that the T-shirt we bought at Target like five years ago in the junior section for four dollars?"

"Yeah, so? I found it in my room. I must've left it here last year. If you can't be comfortable in the Berkshires, where can you be? It's not like we're in the Hamptons."

"That's for sure," Alice mutters. There's a knock at the front door. "That must be Joe."

Joe, as it turns out, is a Regular Joe, top to bottom. He's tallish and has retained most of his dirty blond hair (despite a bald patch forming on the crown of his head), which is buzz-cut short. I would say he is dressed less "Country Casual" and more "Casual Friday": pressed, pleated khakis (which, by the way, I hadn't seen once in all my weekends in the Hamptons), a worn, blue button-down shirt that says "work shirt that should've been donated to Good Will but now I wear it on the weekends," and the kind of outdated brown leather fringed loafers with a too-short instep, but luckily no socks.

After Alice and Scott welcome Joe and take his umbrella, they part like the Red Sea. Awkward doesn't even begin to describe the scenario. I can almost hear the heralding trumpets as Alice waves her arm in a wide arc and announces, "And! This! Is! Tori!" No one cheers, much to my disappointment.

"Nice to meet you, Tori." He extends his hand, but I have the wineglass in my right hand. I hold it up to signal "Sorry, no-can-do on the handshake," but he doesn't get the message and stands firm, which means I have to switch the glass to my other hand so I can shake his. "Sorry, it's a little wet. From the glass."

"No problemo," Joe says.

I hate him already. Alice is a close second.

Then we stand across from each other, neither of us knowing what to say. It suddenly occurs to me that Alice must've told him about me, so instead of only me knowing that this is a setup, we both know, which is about one thousand times worse. I speak first, desperate to end the silent mutual scrutiny. "It's nice to meet my replacement."

He looks confused. "Replacement for what?"

"I'm not sure if you realized this, but you took my place as the adopted singleton this summer."

He looks at me as if I've just spoken Sanskrit, backward.

Alice laughs nervously. "Tori came out here a lot the last couple of summers to spend weekends with us. Joe, let me get you some wine. Red or white?"

"Why don't you all take a seat at the table?" Scott suggests. "Everything's about ready to come off the grill."

Scott and Alice bring in plates filled with grilled herb-encrusted steaks, vegetables, a plate of gorgeously ripe local heirloom tomatoes and fresh basil, drizzled in balsamic vinegar, and a giant bowl filled with ears of corn grilled in their husks. After some ooh's, ahh's and "this smells delicious," we clink glasses in Scott's honor for braving the steady rain to grill up our feast and greedily begin eating.

"So, Tori, if you used to come to the Berkshires a lot, why haven't you been out this summer until now?" Joe asks.

"I have a house in the Hamptons. I go there every weekend."

"That must be nice. I've never been."

I practically choke on my steak. "You've never been to the Hamptons? What planet do you live on?"

"Not *everyone* has been to the Hamptons," Alice says.

"The Hamptons sound great, but the Berkshires are more accessible from Boston," Joe explains. "I couldn't make it down to the Hamptons every weekend. Way too far, plus all that traffic. I hear it can be a nightmare."

"The traffic can be pretty bad but after a while, you get used to it. You should try it sometime. It's really social. There's always a party or a club to go to. It's got to be better than hanging out in the middle of the sticks waiting for your married friends to import a single woman from Manhattan who probably wouldn't have much in common with you anyway," I say. "Trust me." I give him a wink, which he returns with a blank stare and a noticeable bob of his Adam's apple.

"More wine, Joe?" Alice leans over to fill his glass without waiting for a response. She doesn't fill mine, so I reach for the bottle after she has replaced it on the table.

While Scott launches into a long conversation with Joe about work, Alice and I concentrate on eating our food and not looking at each other.

After devouring dinner, I clear the table, bring our empty plates into the kitchen, and preheat the oven to warm the pie. By the time we start on dessert, Scott has run out of work tidbits. Feeling a slight bit of remorse for torturing the boring guy—after all, it wasn't his fault that he got pushed into the Alice/Tori crosshairs—I pull out the fail-safe topics of television, movies, and books, trying to direct questions toward Regular Joe, who by this point isn't exactly enthusiastic about answering my questions but is too polite not to respond at all.

Joe eats his pie in record time and then excuses himself for the night, claiming he has to be up early for a bike race in the morning.

"Even if it rains?" I ask.

"I ride rain or shine."

"Good times. Well, nice meeting ya, Joe." I extend my hand, which he looks at as if I had just thrust a pile of poisonous snakes at him.

He shakes my hand reluctantly. "Have fun in the Hamptons."

"Thanks, and if you ever come out that way, look me up," I say, mostly for Alice's benefit, so she can see I'm trying. But she has gone into the kitchen.

After Joe leaves, I head into the kitchen. "More pie?"

She turns from the sink to face me. "I'm . . . just . . . speechless."

"I didn't eat *that* much tonight. I'm just taking another smidge."

She throws down the dish towel. "I cannot believe you. You were such a bitch to Joe!"

"Oh, come on. Maybe I wasn't as nice as I could've been, but I thought I made up for it pretty well at the end there."

"Too little, too late. Seriously, Joe didn't deserve to be treated like crap. You could've at least been polite."

"*I* could've been polite? Really? You know what really would've been *polite*? If you had bothered to ask me if it was all right to have this guy over before you foisted him on me!"

"What, all of a sudden I'm not allowed to invite whomever I like to my house for dinner?"

"Of course you are, but I came up here to relax and hang out with you, not to be served up like a piece of herb-encrusted steak to some boring banker. Not to mention the fact that you know how much I loathe blind dates, yet you totally blindsided me!"

"It wasn't a blind date. I just thought you'd appreciate meeting a nice guy for once."

"In case you weren't listening yesterday during the two-hour drive out here, I am already involved with *two guys* at the moment."

"And your involvement is what? Huh? Fucking two guys who couldn't care less about you on alternate nights?"

I stare at her. Then I say, struggling to control my voice, "That's not how it is, and you know it."

"No, I don't know it. I seem to be the last one to know anything about you these days. It took you how long to tell me about Andrew? Half the time, I feel like I don't even know who you are anymore. Ever since you started going to that stupid summerhouse, you've completely changed, and guess what, it hasn't been for the better. Where has the Tori whom I know and love gone? The one who has worked her butt off to build a successful business for her and her close friends, despite recent but surely temporary setbacks? Who just bought her own place? Who is always there for her friends? Who did the hard work of turning her life around, bouncing back so amazingly when the going got tough? Who is real and down-to-earth and not swayed by superficial things or people?"

"She is standing right in front of you! I'm still that person!"

"Are you sure? I've been wondering if you've turned into one of those selfish, self-absorbed shallow people you've been telling me about, when you even bother to tell me anything, that is."

It's one thing when a bitchy diva who barely knows you says this to you, another when a guy whom you barely know even though you're sleeping with him says this to you, but when your best friend in the whole world says it . . . you have to look at that. Later.

"Alice, have you forgotten that *you're* the one who sent me—no, *forced* me—out there in the first place? You lined up the share, handed me the money, and then practically pushed me out the door at gunpoint! But not before you and the boys ambushed me in my own home, I might add, and coerced me under duress to go on that stupid makeover show that seems to have done more harm than good! What did you expect me to do? Sit under a beach umbrella in a caftan, drink purified water, and contemplate my navel? Did you just want me to go there and continue being the loser I've been for the last two-plus years? Not fit in? Not make friends? Not date?"

"Of course not."

"It was sink or swim for me out there. And I thought I did a pretty damn good job of swimming with the sharks. Well, at least until last weekend, but still. But this whole time, all you've been doing is judging me, making not unmean comments about my new friends, about the guys I'm dating, about how much I drink, go out—everything—as if you don't approve. And if you're not doing that, you act like I can't handle it or anything for that matter. But it's *my life*. And at least I'm living it now instead of sitting paralyzed on the sidelines. Can't you just give me credit for that instead of tearing it apart every time we talk about it?"

She turns back to the sink to begin rinsing the dirty dishes. She says something I can't hear.

"What was that?" I ask.

She turns off the water but doesn't turn around. *"I'm pregnant."*

"Wow, Alice! That's amazing! Congratulations! I can't believe I didn't figure it out sooner, what with you not having any wine tonight or not letting us eat sushi most of the summer. I didn't even know you were trying. How far along are you?"

"I just went off the pill a few months ago, so even Scott and I were surprised that it happened so fast. It's still early days. Eight weeks or so. Not out of the woods yet."

"But still, that's great!"

She turns around from the sink. There's a tear streaming down her cheek. "I don't know. Is it?"

"Of course it is. It's your dream come true! Scott must be thrilled!" A fresh tear plops from her face onto her shirt. "Alice, what's happening here? Isn't this what you've always wanted? The husband, the apartment on the Upper East Side, the cottage in the country, and the adorable bouncing baby something?"

"I thought it was. But now, I'm not so sure. . . ." She picks up the dish towel to mop up her soggy face. "All along I thought that this is what I wanted, but now that it's happening—it's not just an idea but reality—I'm really freaked out about it. And now, with you . . ."

"With me what?"

"Well, I'm losing you. I've barely seen you all summer. This is the first weekend you've even come out here, and it's already almost Labor Day. And when I have a baby, we're going to be even further apart. You're going to be out at fabulous parties, dating tons of exciting men, hanging out with cool people, and I'm going to be all alone, wiping snot and butts."

"Alice, that's so not true! You're not losing me! You *haven't* lost me. I promise. It's not like that. What, do you think I'm going to drop you the minute you have the baby?" She nods like a little girl. "That's ridiculous. I'm going to be an auntie!" She gives me a small, grateful smile. "But you have to understand, and maybe even accept, you're where you are and I am going to be wherever I am."

"We were supposed to be doing this together." Her lip quivers.

"I know. But Peter kind of fucked us on that one. Oops, I didn't mean to swear in front of the baby!"

She smiles weakly. "I guess that's what the whole Joe thing was about tonight. I thought that maybe I could introduce you to a guy who really wants to settle down so you could catch up to me. Joe has been dying to meet someone, so I figured . . . it was dumb. I knew you wouldn't like him. Scott told me not to do it, isn't that funny? I guess lately I've been thinking, what if you really enjoy your new lifestyle? Then we really will never be doing this together." She rubs her still flat belly.

"But it's not like you're doing it alone. You have Scott, who loves and adores you and is the model husband."

"I know, you're right: technically I'm not alone. I love Scott so much, you know I do. But he's just not a talker. Maybe it's just the hormones, but I've been feeling so lonely lately. And obviously, Scott and I talk about it all the time, but our conversations are pretty much relegated to logistics. He's very excited to be a dad, and I know he'll be a wonderful father. He's so patient and kind and attentive. But when it comes to talking about what it feels like to actually be pregnant, that we're going to be the sole caretakers fully responsible for a helpless being, he just doesn't know how to engage with me on that level."

"I'm sorry, Al. I can appreciate how that must feel. You know you can always talk to me. I may not know what it's like firsthand, but I will listen."

"Thanks, that means a lot to me."

"But it's not like I'm purposely diverging from the path. Being single at this point in my life wasn't exactly where I expected to be either, but I'm here now—wherever here is—and I've finally accepted it and even embraced it. I had to because it was my reality. I had to stop holding on to what I had *hoped* would happen. It was hard, but I did it. You and I both experienced how bad me not accepting my reality was and what damage it could do. And the thing is, to be honest, Al, your chosen path has never really been the path I wanted. Maybe it seemed that way when I was with Peter, but for the majority of the time we've known each other, we've always wanted different things or at least have approached our lives differently. That's always been true, hasn't it?"

She nods. "Yeah, I guess you're right about that."

"And so, now it's still true, but it doesn't mean we will stop being friends. But I do need you to support me. You don't have to love all of my choices or even agree with all of them, but you have to support me. And I have to support you. And I will."

"Thank god for that." We hug tight. And now, all that's between us is a little tiny baby, who, without even having been born yet, may have already brought Alice and me back together.

15.

Rescue 911

Su	Mo	Tu	We	Th	Fr	Sa
			①	2	X3	X4
X5	6	7	8	9	X10	X11
X12	13	14	15	16	X17	X18
X19	20	21	22	23	X24	X25
X26	27	28	29	30	31	

August

Su	Mo	Tu	We	Th	Fr	Sa
						1
2	3 Labor Day	4	5	6	7	8
9	10	11	12	13	14	15
16	17	18	19	20	21	22
23	24	25	26	27	28	29

September

It's Monday morning and Jerry has arrived at the office solo.

"Where's Jimmy?" I ask. These two rarely travel without each other, and when they do, there's usually a very good reason. Or a very bad one.

He puts the Krispy Kreme box on the conference table and busies himself with digging for something in his backpack so he doesn't have to meet my gaze. "He's out sick today. One of his famous migraines."

"Really?"

He looks at me as if he's deciding how to answer then says, "I knew you'd know I was lying." He slumps into a chair. He looks exhausted. I can relate.

We sit quietly for a few moments, unsure of how to break the awkwardness of the moment. "I feel awful," we say at the same time.

"You shouldn't feel awful," I say. "It's not like you were the one who called me on the carpet last Wednesday."

"No, but I did have a feeling that Jimmy was about to have one of his freak-outs, and I should've spoken to you before he blew." He rubs his hands briskly across the top of his head. "He feels terrible too, if it's any consolation. He knows he was way out of line. I've lived with him for a long time, and believe me, I've been the recipient of his periodic tirades myself. I'm not excusing him, because how he treated you was uncalled for, but I usually chalk up those outbursts to him being more visually than verbally oriented. Sometimes he just doesn't think before he speaks or hear how what he's saying might sound to someone else."

I open the box and take a doughnut, but then decide I don't feel like eating it. I put it on my napkin and begin twirling it instead. "Yeah, I know he didn't intend to be mean. But it wasn't like he was wrong. I've been very distracted this summer, and I haven't been taking my work—our work—seriously enough. I thought about it a lot over the weekend and I've learned my lesson: when you have your own business, there's no coasting, and it was unfair and immature of me to think I could. I'm really, really sorry, Jer. I had no idea that things were so financially dire for you guys."

He shakes his head. "Please! How could you? We purposely didn't tell you because we didn't want you to worry. But the truth of the matter is it's not all because work has been slow lately. He was wrong to make it sound like our financial issues are your fault. Jimmy doesn't exactly love having to stick to a budget, as we've had to do this year by coming to work here, which we did knowingly and by mutual choice, so don't start getting all worried that I coerced him into doing this. But between the summerhouse and Jimmy's shopping sprees at the various Paul Smith and John Varvatos sample sales, we've fallen behind more than usual. But it's all going to be fine. We have some stuff of our own to work out, as you can imagine."

"Yes I can." I get up and walk around to where Jerry's sitting and hug him from behind. "I love you, Jerry," I whisper, my tears soaking his collar.

"And me you, my love."

Hamptons Unwritten Rule #44:
Despite claims to the contrary, there's no
such thing as a shortcut in the Hamptons.

As the musty-smelling taxi turns down Sagg Main Road late on Friday afternoon, I comfort my returning-to-the-scene-of-the-crime-induced nerves with the thought that in less than an hour, George is going to pick me up at the house and whisk me away somewhere hopefully fabulous, fun, and distracting.

I can handle fifty-three minutes in my own summer share, right?

Yes, especially when there's not a single car in the driveway when we pull up. And even more especially when I have to fish out the house key from under the potted plant on the porch to open the door because no one has even arrived from the city yet.

At least they didn't change the locks on me. That's a good sign.

. . .

With George, I've decided to take the military approach to touchy subjects: "Don't ask, don't tell." With any luck, he didn't hear Word One about the dressing-down Leah gave me at Andrew's party a couple of weeks ago. Plus—and more importantly—he doesn't watch TV, so there's a chance—slim but still fighting—that he hasn't heard about my appearance on *Three-on-One*. Unless Jodi the Publicist saw the press release.

But by the semidistracted way he kissed me—on the cheek—when

I slid into his M6 fifteen minutes ago and the intensity with which he's now flicking his thumbs around on the keypad of his Black-Berry, I can't shake the feeling that he might've changed his tune—and I'm not talking about the John Mayer CD on his car stereo—while I was gone. We're at a small dive bar I didn't even know existed in Sag Harbor called Murf's. It's completely empty, except for the cranky bartendress and a couple of seafaring types who are likely regulars. I'm hoping that this is only a layover on our way to greener pastures.

At long last, he puts away his BlackBerry and looks up, as if he had been transported here without his prior knowledge or permission. He takes a sip of his untouched, melted Jack & Coke, as if confirming that's in fact what it is, not some poisoned concoction meant to make him pass out so the regulars can hold him down while the bartendress rolls him for his cash and car keys.

"What exciting happenings does Jodi have on the agenda for us tonight? A fabulous shindig on somebody's yacht docked in Sag Harbor, perhaps?"

George clears his throat. "Babe, I think we're done here."

"Good, because you don't really look like you're enjoying your drink, and to be honest,"—I lower my voice so the barmaid doesn't hear—"mine is kind of nasty."

"No, I mean, I think we've completed our *relationship*."

"We have? What makes you think that? Honestly, I was just kidding about the drink. I can hang with the locals as well as any girl. Want to shoot some pool?"

He doesn't laugh. For that matter, he doesn't even smile. "What I'm trying to say is that I think our romantic acquaintance has run its course, but I'd like for us to part as friends."

He's not joking. He's firing me.

Could this fucking summer get any *worse*? Was it really so unrea-sonable for me to think that I could make new friends, date a cool, happening guy, and flit around the Hamptons like all the other social butterflies? Are these things really so far out of my reach that I shouldn't have even been reaching for them in the first place? Maybe this is how it works in the Hamptons, maybe this is just another unwritten rule that they don't tell you about until you break it: if you're a newbie, you get one brief peek inside Fantasy Land, but after the novelty has worn off, they push you out and slam the door in your face.

Adding insult to all the other injuries, this guy is now *dumping* me? Anger starts bubbling up inside my chest. Who does he think he is? Why does he get to call the shots? I refuse to let this one get off so easily. If he wants out, he's going to have to *tell me why*, not give me some lame, canned excuse and then disappear. If there's anything I learned from the whole Peter thing it's that there are no second chances to say what's on your mind, to ask your questions, to demand the answers that might help you let go and move on. And the only one who is going to stick up for you is . . . you.

"Is this because it's almost Labor Day or is it something else?"

"Well, timing has a bit to do with it, I guess. But honestly, it's you."

"Huh, really. Wow, I don't even get the feigned politeness of an 'it's not you, it's me'?"

"Come on, babe. You and I both know this isn't going anywhere. . . ."

"Do we? You recently made it sound like you were into me and preferred me over your rented models and actresses."

"Look, I admit I've been having fun with you. But recently it's become clear that we're in different places."

"You mean, on different levels."

"I just really can't be seen spending time with, uh, well, quite frankly, someone who is on a reality TV show."

"Unless I were Heidi Klum or Tyra Banks, of course." He gives me a blank stare. "Technically I'm not *on* the show. I was on it *once*, as a favor to some friends. And as a way to secure an important new client for my business. You of all people should understand having to do something for the good of your career."

"Yes, of course, one has to make sacrifices. . . ."

"Which is why you're sacrificing me." He doesn't say anything. "Did your fabulous publicist tell you to throw me overboard? Is that how you found out about me being on the show?"

"It came up, of course, but Jodi doesn't make those decisions for me."

"That's a relief. But she probably suggested that you don't do the dirty deed anyplace where there might be a photographer lurking, am I right?" I make a show of checking under the bar and stools. All I see are dozens of multicolored mounds of hardened gum.

He sighs, looks up to the ceiling, and mutters, "I knew I should've done this over the phone."

Suddenly I hear another voice in my head: Andrew's. *He's walking all over you. I have no idea why you're even giving this guy the time of day.* As I look at George's unsmiling face and eyes that I've never seen sparkle or fill with authentic emotion, not even in our most so-called intimate moments, I wonder to myself: *Why indeed?* To take the edge off of my loneliness? To prove to the world—or at least my corner of it—that I matter because George Daniels thinks I might?

"Don't sweat it, big guy. I'm done giving you a hard time. I don't even know why I'm getting upset in the first place because it's not like we ever really got beneath the surface with each other. You may think of me as just a lowly, bottom-of-the-barrel reality TV star wannabe, but I'm probably the most real person you've ever dated. Maybe I haven't shown it lately, but deep down, I know it's true. But 'real' doesn't seem to be what you're looking for. And you know what? I don't actually want to *be* the kind of person you're looking for—someone who cares more about being seen than about *being*. It was fun while it lasted, don't get me wrong. But ultimately, it's just not me."

He stares at me blankly. He clearly has nothing to say.

Funny: even when you try to get someone to go deeper, deeper doesn't always exist.

"Just do me a favor and answer one question: Muffy Von Harrington-Schroeder?"

"What about her?"

"A Red Carpet Special courtesy of Jodi the Publicist or a Voluntary Companion?"

He shifts uncomfortably. "Both, actually."

I nod slowly, understanding so much all of a sudden.

. . .

In bed alone that night in Cassie's abandoned room (she moved all her stuff to Phillip's place because she's staying there for the rest of the summer), I'm flipping through *Hamptons* magazine, when an item in the gossip section catches my eye:

Mystery Solved!

Not only have we finally learned the identity of one of **George Daniels's** *mysterious summertime sweeties, we've also discovered that she is one of the legions of reality TV stars who have been invading our formerly pristine East End shores as of late. As it turns out,* **Tori Miller** *(pictured at left with Daniels at the* **Alvin Schwartz** *July 4th party), has not only appeared on a "lost" online-only episode of* **Hurrah!***'s blockbuster summer hit,* **Three-on-One,** *but was also its very first victim for its maiden episode. We think the* **Transformation Trio** *did a bang-up job making this ugly duckling (pictured bottom left in a "Before" shot) worthy of a Hamptons hottie like George Daniels, don't you?*

At last: I've become a **bold-faced name.**

Hamptons Unwritten Rule #45:
Your allies are only your allies until they need
to sacrifice you for a higher cause: themselves.

"Are you going to hide in here until Labor Day?" Jackson has just
pushed his way into Cassie's room, where, in fact, I've been camped
out all morning.

"Just the man I've been wanting to see—the only man, actually.
So, I assume you got my e-mail from the other day? And the three
messages I left on your work voice mail that you never bothered returning?"

He shuts the door behind him and comes to sit on the bed across
from me. "Yes, indeed. As requested, I came straightaway. Just
pulled into the driveway, in fact. Now what's this nonsense about
changing your name from Miller to Mud?"

"Well, aren't we both personae non grata now?"

"*We?*"

"Yes, we. Leah will barely even look at me, much less speak to me.
This morning when I went into the kitchen to get some coffee, she
gave me the death stare to end all death stares. My coffee mug almost
shattered in my hand. You must be getting it much worse, though."

He shrugs. "Actually, she's been fine with me."

"Talking to you civilly and everything?"

"Sure. I haven't seen her yet today, but we hung out a bit last
weekend. Everything seemed normal. She didn't paw me as much
as usual, but that could've been attributed to the fact that it was a
fairly tame weekend drinking-wise, relatively speaking."

"I just don't get it. Did she mention anything about the incident
to you? Tell you she was mad at you, spit, take a swing at you?
Nothing?"

"No, no, no, and no, nothing."

"And you didn't initiate a conversation about it?"

"The topic of which would've been . . . ?" He blinks at me
through his smudged wire-rimmed glasses.

"For starters, you could set the record straight. Clear my name. Tell her that you asked me not to say anything to anyone about Margaret, including and especially her."

"Now, why on God's green earth would I go and do something like that?"

"Are you kidding me?"

"No, my dear, I'm afraid I'm not. It's a very delicate situation. I'm sorry that you got caught up in the crossfire, I truly am, but I'm not going to offer my head to be the second one on the already bloody chopping block. Besides, I can't afford to raise Leah's ire any more than I have already. Literally, can't afford it. Even though she had it coming. . . ."

"What *ever* are you talking about, Jackson?"

"Oh, my poor sweet, naïve Miller, I hate to poison your young, unadulterated mind with the tales of such shady backroom dealings, but perhaps if you understood this in context, maybe you would think twice about asking me to lay myself prostrate in front of her highness."

"I got all day." I lean back against the pillows, knees up. "Clearly, no one is banging my door down and demanding my time. Go ahead and defile me. So to speak."

He sighs and rakes his hand through his shaggy head of hair, which looks more unkempt than usual. "The truth is: I sold my soul to the devil to be in this house, the devil being none other than the long-legged, well-shod Leah Brewster herself. When Abigail and Leah approached me about joining the summer festivities, I couldn't afford to pay my way. But they wanted me in, badly. They were after me for weeks. Finally, Leah gave me a deal. It was an offer I couldn't refuse. I love Margaret and all, but hanging out solo in the city on the weekends wasn't exactly my idea of a smashing good time. So, since I couldn't be with the one I love, I figured why not be with the one I'm with? Figuratively speaking, of course."

"Am I understanding this correctly: Leah *paid* for you to be in the house and you agreed to keep her, uh, company in exchange?"

"Now, Miller, I'm not the British version of Richard Gere from that horrid 1980s gigolo film. Give me *some* credit! It was never an explicit deal. And she didn't exactly *pay* for me as much as charge me far less than market value."

"So, if she's not paying for you, who is?"

He looks away and rakes his hand through his hair again. "Well, truth be told, you are. And Stacy, and Michael, and Cassie . . ."

"I don't get it."

"In order to make up for my discount, you're all paying a little bit more than you would be otherwise."

"Are you shitting me?! Not only are we carrying you, but you got your own room to boot?"

"Shhh, keep your voice down! No one else knows. I'm telling you all this in the strictest of confidence."

"Great, another secret that I didn't want to know in the first place that's going to come back and bite me on the ass. Does Andrew know, at least?"

"Nope. And I know Leah would like to keep it that way. It's the least I could do at this point, given that unfortunate leakage of information by my talented yet inebriated author, James Cheever."

"That arrangement of yours kind of sucks for the rest of us. I don't know whether to be pissed at Leah for secretly overcharging or pissed at you for taking advantage of everyone. It's not like I could afford my share by myself, you know. MillerWorks isn't quite in the black yet."

"It's not exactly my fault she gave me a deal. How could you blame me for taking it? I think whatever blame, fault or what-have-you rests squarely on her. Too bad you can't throw it back in her face. Then you'd really be even. Regardless, you've already sworn yourself to secrecy, remember?"

"I don't recall my promise to keep mum about Margaret standing as a blanket agreement."

"Well, after six P.M. on Labor Day, when the rights to the house revert back to the owners, you're free to do as you will with the information. However, I would urge you to think twice about telling Leah that you know. If the others find out, the repercussions against Leah could be quite serious. I can't even begin to imagine how Mr. Kane would react to being duped by Leah and being a party to duping everyone else, for that matter. Your supposed slight against Leah in reference to me will be dust in the wind as soon as the lease ends, but you outing Leah's indiscretion will turn everyone against her. Likely, permanently. And as far as I can tell, the old gal doesn't have hundreds of friends waiting to move up from the B Team, if you know what I mean."

Now that he mentions it, I haven't heard of Leah having any close pals other than Abigail. Leah seems to think of Stacy as a pesky little sister more than as a friend. Leah hasn't brought out a single guest, nor do I ever hear her talking on the phone to anyone other than house people. And clearly Cassie did not evolve into her newest best bud. No wonder she has had the time and energy—and interest—to keep track of everyone's whereabouts and whoseabouts. We *are* her friends. With the exception of me now, it seems.

"I'll take that under advisement. I shouldn't even ask you this, because I really don't know if I can take any more, but I can't help myself: you and Leah, did you ever, you know?"

"No. Not technically, no. I had to keep up at least part of my end of the bargain. And, of course, she is fairly ravishing, so it wasn't hard to pay the girl a bit of attention from time to time. And as you know, I'm a natural-born flirt, so it was actually fun, believe it or not. But no, I do truly love Margaret, and even though our arrangement is a bit fucked-up, shall we say, I'm not interested in being with anyone else."

"So, James Cheever just *happened* to let it slip to Leah about your affair? Or was that, *shall we say*, a more calculated move, to get the blond monkey off your back?"

He rises from the bed. "I think I might need a cigarette. Care to join me outside?"

I yank his sleeve and shove him back down on the bed. "Oh, no you don't!"

He sighs. "Miller. Really. What do you think?"

"I think you knew all too well about the A.L.D. Rule and wanted to ensure that you wouldn't be formally pursued once the house arrest was over. So you gave James the green light to spill the beans. But what you didn't anticipate is that he would end up dumping out the whole can on *my* head."

He takes out a cigarette and taps it on the box. "My, my, my Miller. You do have a very active imagination."

"Do I? See, I think I'm finally getting savvy to the ways of the world. Or at least, the way things are done in the Hamptons."

"And if you ask me, it's high time."

Hamptons Unwritten Rule #46:
Many of the East End emergency workers
perform their duties on a voluntary basis.

It's official: I'm sick. And not just in the head.

After Jackson left me earlier today, I fell asleep, and when I woke up around three, I found that I could barely swallow and my whole body was aching. I thought maybe I had just gotten too much sleep, so I forced myself into a hot shower—during which I nearly passed out—and made myself some tea with honey. But almost four hours later, I'm feeling just as craptastic, if not more so. Stacy was the only person who was nice enough to ask if I needed anything (probably because I kept her waiting to use the bathroom, and when I finally emerged, she was all but forced to ask after my well-being after I sneezed in her face). I told her I was fine, but before she scurried away, she insisted on leaving me with a few tabs of extra-strength flu medicine she got when she was in London visiting friends last spring.

Since she left, I've been dozing on and off, miserable in every possible way. At around seven-thirty my cell, which gets slightly better reception in the Absentee's room than in the yellow one, rings. It's Cassie.

"Hey, you." Her voice is shaky.

"How are you?" I sneeze into the phone, which makes my eyes start to leak.

"I'm all right but you sound awful."

"I'm sick. I think it's the flu."

"What a drag! You poor thing!"

"On top of that, George broke up with me." I start to recount last night's dumping, but a couple of minutes into it, I can tell she's not listening. Then I hear snuffling, as if she's crying.

I hoist myself into a sitting position. "If anyone should be crying it's me."

She laugh-cries in response but then begins sobbing in earnest.

"What's wrong?"

"It's . . . no, it's nothing. I'm sorry. Here you are sick and dumped and I'm. . . ."

"Talk to me." I silently berate myself for not calling her after I saw how out of sorts she looked at Andrew's party. I got so caught up in my own drama that I completely forgot to check on her.

She sighs. "You know, I'm just being silly. Phillip and I are having this dinner party tonight—I would've invited you, but it's mostly his business associates—and we just got into this huge fight."

"Why? What did you fight about?"

She laughs ruefully. "What *didn't* we fight about. It wasn't so much of a fight as much as him screaming at me all day for every little thing that's gone wrong. First, all the linens were stained, so we had to find a place to get them dry-cleaned with a four-hour turnaround—no easy task out here on a weekday, much less a Saturday, let me tell you—then the caterers were a half hour late, despite the fact he had me call them five times to confirm the time, then someone canceled last minute and we had to change the seating arrangements. . . ."

"But those all sound like normal mishaps—and not your fault. Why was he yelling at you?"

Her voice catches. "I . . . I don't know. Everything was going so well until we started planning this stupid. . . ." I hear muffled voices and lots of shuffling. "I gotta go. I'm sorry for bothering you with all this."

"Are you sure you're okay? I can come there if you . . . achoo! . . . need me."

"No, I'm fine, really. It's just been so stressful lately, I think I just needed to vent and hear a friendly voice. Look, the caterer just told me the first guests have arrived, and my face is a total mess. I'll give you a call tomorrow. I'm sure everything will go back to normal after this dinner is over. Feel better!" And she's gone.

. . .

"If she says she's fine, then I'm sure she is. She was probably just overreacting. I've never known Cassie not to be able to take care of herself."

I'm in Andrew's room, leaning against the dresser for support and shivering despite the blanket I have wrapped around me. Ignoring the fact that we haven't said more than two words to each other since our fight at his party, I tucked my tail between my legs—along with my pride—to come ask his advice. I've just summarized my conversation with Cassie as well as my observations of her at his party.

"Even so, I think I'd feel better going to check on her. She really sounded, I don't know, like she was scared to be around him."

He moves about the room, getting ready for a night out. He takes off his T-shirt, tosses it on the bed, and goes into the walk-in closet to retrieve a light green button-down. Despite my watery eyes and muddled brain, I still manage to register how good he looks bare-chested and then how the shirt brings out the color in his eyes once he puts it on. He takes his wallet and car keys off of the dresser.

"I guess you're taking your truck. Because if you didn't have to, I was wondering if maybe I could borrow it, just for tonight."

"You're clearly sick as a dog, so you shouldn't be going anywhere, much less all the way to Southampton. Not to mention, being in this weakened state is probably making *you* overreact. Go back to bed and get some rest. I have some NyQuil in my bathroom if you need it. I've got to get going." He walks toward the door and stops. "Miller, she's fine. Okay?"

I nod slowly as I watch him walk down the hallway and disappear around the corner.

. . .

The taxi for which I waited over an hour and paid almost forty dollars including tip, drops me off in front of an imposingly large Spanish-style stucco house, next door (separated by what seems like at least a few acres) to Absentee Abigail's parents' house. More than a dozen expensive foreign cars flank the circular driveway.

After my conversation with Andrew, I still couldn't get Cassie's voice out of my head. I tried to fall asleep, but I kept having visions of Phillip's evil eyebrows narrowing at Cassie as he screamed at her for the white wine not being chilled to the perfect temperature. So I downed the pills Stacy gave me and called a cab. I was so consumed with the challenge of getting here, trying to remember the directions through a maze of confusing semiprivate back roads and not sneezing in the direction of the surly driver, that I didn't have much of a plan for once I got here. Not to mention, the flu stuff Stacy gave me has made me not only feel as if my illness has magically disappeared, but also feel a disorienting combination of being spacey and wired at the same time.

It's now almost ten o'clock. I spy a gate off to the side that looks like it leads to the backyard. As I walk through it, I begin to hear voices and music. When I get around the back corner of the house, I find myself standing in front of a long table with at least thirty people seated around it. The conversation all but stops as thirty heads swivel toward me.

"Miller!" Cassie hops up from her chair, knocking the table as she does. "What a surprise!" She looks nervously at Phillip, whose face I can't see. Everyone else goes back to their conversations, except for one person: George. His eyes linger on me as Cassie extricates herself from the linen tablecloth that has wound itself around her legs. He nods his head almost imperceptibly before returning his attention to the party chatter. Then he leans to the left to drape his arm around the shoulder of his neighbor: none other than Miss Muffy herself.

If George had any second thoughts about jettisoning me, I have most certainly just erased any doubt.

As Cassie comes near, I see how much worse she looks than even two weeks ago. Despite best efforts with makeup, a professional-looking updo, and a gorgeous dress, she looks gaunt, wan, bleary-eyed, and bone thin. She takes my elbow and hustles me back around the corner of the house, out of view of her dinner guests and more importantly, Dr. Evil.

"What are you doing here?" Instead of looking relieved, she looks pissed. And not a little scared. "I thought you were home sick!"

"I was, but you sounded so awful on the phone, I thought you might need some moral support, so I took some drugs and tried to get here as soon as I could. I asked Andrew what I should do but he said. . . ."

Her bloodshot eyes widen at me, and a flush rises up her throat. "You told Andrew? Christ, Miller! Now Phillip's going to know I called you! This is just great." She looks over her shoulder to check that no one is behind her.

"Shit, that never even occurred to me. I guess I'm not thinking too clearly."

"I appreciate your concern, Miller, I really do, but you have to leave." She steers me toward the driveway.

"What will you tell Phillip?"

"I don't know. I'll figure something out."

"Cassandra? Where are you? Our guests are waiting. . . ." It's Phillip.

"Please," she whispers to me, "just go. Okay? I'll call you tomorrow." She rushes back the way we came to catch Phillip before he clears the corner. "I'm coming, darling!"

Naturally, my cell phone has no signal, so I start circling the driveway to see if I can pick one up. Nothing. Now what, brainiac? Think. Maybe I can sneak in the front door—there's got to be a land line close by. It's a big house, and from what I can tell from looking in the windows, the front rooms are empty. It's not a great plan, but it's a plan.

As I suspected, the front door is unlocked. I tiptoe down the hallway. The first room on the right is a study with a cordless phone standing like a beacon on the desk. Bingo. As I'm fumbling with my cell to find the taxi number, I overhear voices speaking in furtive tones from the next room. I edge closer to the other entrance to the study that adjoins an empty, dark living room.

"I'm going to ask you again: what the hell was she doing here?" Phillip roars.

"Darling, please keep your voice down," Cassie responds nervously. "I told you—she was devastated by what happened with George and she just wanted someone to talk to. I told her that we were having guests tonight, but I think she was really upset and she's sick, so she must not have been thinking straight. . . ."

Being represented as a love-crazed lunatic wouldn't have been my first choice of an explanation, but I have to give Cassie credit for thinking of something credible on the fly under these circumstances. I just wish it wasn't so believable.

"Cassandra, I cannot have this sophomoric behavior in my

house, especially tonight. Do you realize how embarrassing it was to have her show up looking like a crazed homeless person in front of my guests? Do you understand who these people are? I thought I made myself very clear about how important this night was for me. And still you couldn't do one fucking thing right."

"Phillip, please—"

"Linda used to be able to pull off this party without batting an eyelash. Frankly, I'm beginning to wonder why I left her in the first place."

"Are . . . are you thinking of going back to her? Is that why you haven't begun divorce proceedings yet?"

"I am not going to answer that question. I've told you a hundred times: it's none of your goddamn business!"

"Phillip, I love you so much. I can do better. Just give me a chance. . . ." I hear some scuffling and then a small crash, like glass breaking. My heart is beating like crazy. What if he's hurt her? Should I go in there? What if he hasn't hurt her but my going in causes him to go over the edge?

"Goddamn it!"

Before I can decide what to do, I hear him stomp away, followed by the *clack-clack* of her heels scurrying behind him. I steal through the dark room and peek around the corner. As I suspected, there is a spray of shattered glass glittering on the floor. But then someone approaches, so I duck back around the wall and hold my breath. After a second, it's clear that it is only someone who has come to sweep up the mess. I just pray Phillip didn't make Cassie do it as her penance, but I don't hear any sniffling or crying, so hopefully it's just one of the catering staff.

I clearly can't go now. What if he's waiting until everyone leaves to unbridle the full extent of his wrath? What if the next time he throws a glass he doesn't miss?

I retrace my steps and slip out through the front door, closing it carefully behind me. I spot Cassie's convertible in the far corner of the driveway, hemmed in by several other cars. I decide that's as good a place as any to hide out until the guests go. I feel a sneeze coming on. I stifle it, but my ears feel like they're exploding from the pressure. I pull a tissue from my bag as I jog across the gravel, ready to make myself at home in Cassie's vintage Mercedes for the next couple of hours.

I am awakened by a yelp. I swim out of my trippy hallucinogenic dreams and struggle to open my eyes. Cassie is standing with the car door open, hands over her mouth. It takes me a minute to remember where I am: in Cassie's car in Phillip's driveway. "What are you still doing here?" She is surrounded by bags stuffed haphazardly with clothes, shoes, and purses, as if she has just been on a wild shopping spree at Saks. She sinks down into a squat, face buried in her hands. The clock on my cell phone reads 1:36. I must've completely crashed from those crazy drugs I took. I didn't even hear all the dinner guests or the catering van leave.

"*This* is what I'm still doing here. Why do you have all your stuff?"

"It was awful," she whispers in a hoarse voice. She immediately straightens up as if she's been given an electric shock. "We should get out of here. If he finds out you're still here, who knows what he'll do."

An image of a sawed-off shotgun comes to mind. "Great idea. Let's get your stuff in the car. Give me the keys." I sneeze into my own outstretched hand.

"No, you're sick and clearly on some kind of major barbiturates. Besides, my car is really quirky and has been acting up lately. I'll drive."

We manage to stuff all the bags into her tiny car and tear out of the driveway, two bats out of hell, gravel spitting behind us for good measure. Soon we're riding through the dark streets, lit only by the tiniest sliver of moon and our headlights, the warm breeze wafting across our faces, as if we're out for a romantic late-night drive instead of fleeing from Cassie's evil boyfriend. I stay quiet except for the occasional sneeze, sensing that Cassie isn't ready to talk.

"What's that smell?" Cassie sniffs at the air.

"I don't smell anything, but then again, pretty much none of my senses are in working order." I sneeze to prove it.

A billow of thick, black smoke is rising up from beneath the car hood. Then the engine begins making sounds as if it's choking. Cassie pulls over onto the grassy shoulder by the side of a spooky-looking cornfield and turns off the car. We stare at the smoke until it disappears into the starry night.

After a brief discussion, we decide it's not worth the risk to turn on the car again, so I recite the number of the taxi service to Cassie, which she dials into her phone. As she waits on hold, she starts crying quietly, so I take the phone from her and cover it with a clean tissue. After ten minutes I get taken off hold. I explain our situation and try to give our approximate location to the dispatcher.

"I'm sorry, we can't make a pickup unless you're at an actual address," the dispatcher says. "'A cornfield somewhere on Mecox' is hardly an address. Maybe you'll have better luck with Triple A," she suggests in a sarcastic tone.

"Look, we're really in a dire situation. . . ." I sneeze for dramatic effect. "I'm probably running a fever, and my friend was kind enough to get out of bed and pick me up."

"Fine, I'll send someone but, hon, it's Saturday night. The soonest I can get anyone there is in about ninety minutes."

"Ninety minutes! That's ridiculous!" I protest. Cassie, who has stopped crying to listen in, buries her head in her arms, which are crisscrossing the steering wheel. "Okay, you know what, that's fine, but if there's any way you can prioritize us, we'd very much appreciate it. We'll make it worth the driver's time, if you know what I mean."

"That's what they all say, and then they somehow conveniently forget when it comes time to pony up. Ninety minutes." She hangs up. I call information to get numbers for more local taxi services, but each one I talk to gives me the same hassle and same wait time or longer.

"Guess we're going to be here for a little while," I say as I stifle a shiver.

"It's over. We . . . he broke up with me." She says this staring straight ahead, as if she can see him standing on the edge of the cornfield. "I can't believe it. I worked so hard to pull off this stupid party, but it was absolutely impossible to satisfy him. I did everything he asked me to do and then some, but it was never enough. I just don't know what happened. No matter what I did, he was angry. It's like he has this uncontrollable rage."

"That's pretty obvious." Cassie looks at me. I would tell her I heard her fight with Phillip in the house—even though technically, I suppose, you could say I was snooping—but I don't want to risk making her feel embarrassed on top of everything else. "I mean, it sounded that way from what you told me earlier on the phone. So, was he just being so difficult and demanding recently because of the party? He hasn't always been this way, right? At the beginning he seemed to be treating you like a princess."

"The first month, he was a dream, I told you. It was wonderful. We got along so well, as if we had known each other our whole lives. We even joked that we probably were together in a previous life." She's quiet for a minute, perhaps savoring the memory. "Thinking about it now, though, I did see him lose him temper every so often before, but never this bad, and when he did, he'd calm down immediately and then apologize profusely for behaving that way. I never thought anything of it, to be honest."

"But was he freaking out about things *you* were doing, or weren't doing, as the case may have been?"

"Actually, until recently, his blowups never had anything to do with me. They were always because of something more random— like work things, which, considering how much money he deals with and how much pressure he's under every day, was somewhat understandable—but occasionally he'd act out about trivial stuff, like a hostess trying to give us a bad table or his driver being late. It was only in the last few weeks, when he told me about this dinner party and asked me to help him, when he started losing his temper more often—and *at* me."

"What happened after I burst in unannounced and uninvited? Did he ask you why I was there?"

"Yes, and he wasn't pleased. I told him you came because you were upset about George breaking up with you and needed to talk to me." She purses her lips. "Sorry about that, but it was all I could think of. And, by the way, I'm sorry that you had to see George there with Muffy. Phillip has some business connection to Muffy and her family, so that's why she was invited, and of course, she brought George. . . ."

"You don't have to apologize or explain. Truly. So, did Phillip buy your story?"

"It seemed like he did, but he still found a way to blame me for it. He yelled at me right after you left."

"I feel truly awful about adding insult to injury . . . I had no idea that would make matters worse."

She waves her hand, dismissing my apology. "But then we had to go back into the party like nothing had happened. It took me a long time to calm down and get myself together, but the really scary part was that Phillip was immediately cheerful and normal, just like that." She snaps her fingers. "It's like the whole thing didn't even phase him! He was even affectionate with me in front of everyone. It was so strange, not to mention confusing."

"Very Jekyll and Hyde."

"Exactly! Anyway, after the guests left and the caterers finished up, I was still so upset. I just had to say something. So I told him that I thought he could've treated me a lot better not only tonight but also about this whole event and he said . . . he said . . ." She chokes up, takes a deep breath and starts again. "He said that if I hadn't fucked it up so badly, he wouldn't have had to yell at me in the first place."

"Woah."

"Pretty horrific, right? Actually, that comment is tied for Most Horrible, Hurtful Comment of the Evening with the one he said to me earlier about how Linda—his most recent wife—used to pull off that dinner party flawlessly. Do you know that they're not even legally separated?"

I play dumb. "I thought you told me weeks ago that they were already in the process of getting a divorce?"

"Nope. Can you believe it? Almost from the minute we met, he had said he was going to put the divorce into motion. But then, nothing. He and his wife are definitely not together, but whenever I asked about where things stood, he would just say that he loved me and wanted to be with me, which I naturally thought meant marrying me. But when it came up a couple of weeks ago, he told me to butt out of his personal life." She laughs bitterly. "I mean, we've spent almost every night together since July Fourth! I practically live with him, both out here and in the city, but somehow that doesn't actually make me part of his life. Part of his staff, maybe."

A pair of headlights turns onto the road, heading toward us. The car turns out to be a Porsche. As if to rub salt in the wound, it speeds up as it whizzes past us, throwing dirt and sand into our faces, which Cassie doesn't even seem to notice.

"So after I made that comment, he went ballistic, ranting about how clingy, needy, and possessive I was. You haven't known me for that long, but believe me, the idea of me being clingy is just ludicrous! I've never been that way before. But then I realized that with him, especially the last few weeks, it's been absolutely true, because he makes me feel so insecure. I've been completely on edge dealing with his temper tantrums, tiptoeing around all the time trying to please him, which seems to just irritate him more. I suggested that we try slowing things down so he could have some space to wrap stuff up with Linda. Then we could be free to focus on us. That's when he kicked me out."

I was hoping she had walked out on him, but I keep that thought to myself.

"He said that he was sick of women trying to 'own' him. Then he started running around the room, grabbing my things and stuffing them into bags. I kept waiting for him to realize the lunacy of what he was doing. I just stood there like an idiot and cried, hoping he would stop and apologize. But he didn't. He didn't . . . stop." She starts crying again.

Talk about being in shock. How could this have happened? My strong, independent, smart, confident friend Cassie has been emotionally abused by her insane boyfriend for the last several weeks and then thrown out of his house like trash in the middle of the night? What kind of psychotic maniac would do that? And I was too busy being caught up in my own bullshit to do anything, even though I could tell something was very wrong the last time I saw her.

Maybe Leah and Andrew weren't far off about what kind of person I am, or at least, have become.

Another car that isn't our cab goes by. I sneeze and start shivering, feeling feverish once again. I still have Cassie's phone in my lap. It's almost 3 A.M. But that doesn't stop me from dialing. I pray as I count the rings—three, four. . . .

"Hullo?"

"Andrew? It's Miller. Did I wake you?"

Cassie sits quietly watching me, too tired to protest.

"Where the hell are you? Why are you calling from Cassie's phone?"

"I'm with Cassie, actually. We, uh, had to leave Phillip's kind of quickly, and her car broke down. We're in Bridgehampton off of Mecox. We called a taxi, but it's taking forever."

"Tell me exactly where you are. I'm on my way."

. . .

Andrew carries Cassie's bags to her room as she and I shuffle behind him, exhausted (both of us), sick (me), and heartbroken (her and me on her behalf). As he turns to go, he touches my elbow and whispers, "I left the NyQuil in your bathroom. Take twice the rec-ommend amount. And let me know if you need me." I nod as he slips out.

She looks helplessly at all her belongings. It's as if we can hear the screams of all of her beautiful clothes as they become more wrinkled and rumpled by the minute. "I know I should unpack these right now, but I'm just so exhausted." She flops onto the bed. That's when I notice it: a purplish blue bruise on her right cheek, unmistakable in the light of the bedside lamp.

"What happened to your face? Did he hit you?"

Her hand flies up to her face. "No, not exactly. He didn't mean to hurt me—as awful as he has been, I know he didn't mean to. . . ." She curls herself into the fetal position. "Really, he didn't hit me. He shoved me and I fell—it was my fault. I got in his way. . . ."

"Got in his . . . ?! Christ, I had a feeling . . . let me get you some-thing for that." I rush out of the room and return quickly with an ice pack wrapped in a washcloth.

"Thanks." She flinches as she presses it gingerly against her face.

I sit down on the bed next to her. "Cassie, I really need to apolo-gize to you."

"No, you don't. This didn't happen just because you showed up to help me."

"No, I don't mean for that. I mean for everything else. I'm sorry you had to go through this whole nightmare to begin with, but even sorrier that you had to go through it alone. The truth is that I didn't believe that everything was fine when I saw you at Andrew's party, but I let it go. Maybe I could've helped you sooner, prevented this . . . I guess I didn't even think that you needed someone. You just always seemed so. . . ."

"In control? Yeah. I'm a good actress. Turns out, I'm a bit of a mess. I just always thought if I kept moving quickly, no one would really notice." She laughs ruefully. "Welcome to the real me."

I cover her hand with mine as we both look outside to see the sky brightening with the coming dawn. I am scared for her—for what happens next—but make a silent pledge to be her friend, her real friend, from now on.

16.

The Peter Principle

In my wildest dreams, this is the last place I could ever imagine being right now, but considering how things have been going the last couple of weeks, I guess I should've started to expect the absolute unexpected.

I am sitting outside at a cocktail table at Bread Bar by Madison Square Park across from Peter. Yes, that Peter.

He left me a message at the office on Monday morning, but since I had stayed home sick, I didn't get it until Tuesday. I called him back, dialing the number that was still familiar all this time later. After very little preamble, he asked if we could grab a drink this week. I thought, life can't possibly get any weirder than it has been—or can it and will it no matter what I do anyway—so I said yes. A mere thirty-something hours after our phone conversation, we're sipping white wine as if not one second has passed since we were last together.

He clears his throat. "You look great."

I wonder if he can tell that in the time-honored tradition known as "Making Your Ex Eat His Heart Out," I got a blow-out and a mani-pedi during my extended lunch hour, downed as much Emergen-C as I could stomach, and covered my sallow skin with layers of bronzer and blush. I'm still not feeling 100 percent, but certainly much better than I have in days. "Thanks. You do too."

Though, in fact, he looks tired and older than he did when I saw him in June.

"It must be pretty obvious to you that this isn't a casual 'so, how's it going?' get-together," he says.

"Yeah, I guessed as much."

"I didn't want it to be this whole dramatic thing, but I guess it inherently is."

"There's no getting around it, so we might as well embrace the drama."

"Good advice. Let's embrace—I mean, embrace what it is, not each other. You know what I mean." He takes a deep breath. "I've been thinking about you and us a lot lately and realized that there were some things I wanted and needed to say. And just talking on the phone or sending you an e-mail didn't seem to cut it. Though you should know, or, I just want to confess, I was about to do both a million times, both right after we ran into each other at that benefit a couple of months ago and over the course of the last two years." He stops, as if he's waiting for a response. Does he want a medal because he *thought* about calling me after he dumped me? Or because it only took him two and a half years to get up the nerve to sit across from me and explain himself? He's going to have to do a lot more than that to get Brownie points from me. I've already granted him a concession by being here. The rest is up to him. I nod as a signal to continue.

Peter looks to the heavens, which are obscured by the navy blue umbrella hovering above our table, for his inspiration or courage. "Michelle and I are no longer engaged." He takes a too-long swig of wine. "Correction: I broke off the engagement a few weeks ago." Now I take a gulp from my glass. "I should probably back up a little: Michelle and I met and got engaged very quickly. I know the gossip is that she pressured me, but in truth, it was a combination of things.

"After what happened with you and me, I was pretty freaked out, or more accurately, I had freaked myself out. For a long time, I was in shock that I had broken up with you. Eventually, I got over it by convincing myself that our relationship just wasn't the right thing for me." He looks at me, aware that he has just said something hurtful. I drain my glass, and he signals the waiter to bring us another round. "I'm so sorry. To be honest, I don't even know what I told myself to be able to buy my own rap. Whatever it was, it was bullshit to convince myself that I did the right thing and I wasn't some horrible cliché of a commitment-phobe.

"While I was single, most of my friends had gotten married." He mentions familiar names—some surprising, since they had professed to be dedicated bachelors when I knew them, some not, since they were in serious relationships while Peter and I were together. "So then I met Michelle, and she was very clear from the get-go about what she wanted: marriage, kids, the whole nine. Actually, she reminded me of Alice in that way. Instead of running from Michelle and her desires, I let myself get caught up in them. I jumped right into being integrated into her family, friends, and lifestyle. That's what normal people do, right? Or, that's what I told myself.

"There seemed to be this tacit agreement that if we were still together and things were still going well after six months, then we'd get engaged. And when the time came, I thought I was ready. I was going to be turning forty soon, and how much longer could I possibly keep dating without looking like one of those ridiculous bachelors? And not only were most of my friends married, but they were also already moving on to the baby stage. So we got engaged on Memorial Day weekend, and surprisingly, I felt relieved, as if I had crossed some kind of finish line and was done. The problem was I was naïve to think that a woman who wanted to get married that badly would chill after we got engaged, to just enjoy it, to—quite frankly—get to know each other a little more. What was it you always used to say? About the four seasons?"

"That you only really get to know someone after you spend all four seasons with them, seeing what they're like at every time of the year, during every holiday, birthday to birthday. . . ."

"Exactly," he says, reaching out reflexively to touch my arm. When he realizes that he has done so, he pulls it away and gives me an apologetic look. "I even said that to her when she kept pressuring me to pick a wedding date. But instead she became obsessed: going shopping for wedding gowns, researching honeymoons, discussing venues, the whole bit. But a few weeks ago, I stopped sleeping. I couldn't eat. I became jittery and unable to concentrate at work, so much so that people started to notice. One night I woke up sweating and feeling like I was having a heart attack. I went to the doctor the next day just to get checked out. Of course, he couldn't find anything wrong. The doc asked me if I was experiencing any stressful situations lately. And then all of a sudden, it became clear: I didn't want to marry her. Not only that, but it seemed as if I physically *couldn't* marry her."

He looks pale, like he's having one of those panic attacks right now, so I push the sweating glass of water toward him. He drains it in one gulp. "The truth is . . . that if I was ever going to marry anyone, it would've been you. But even as great as you are, as great as *we* were—and we were, I know that now, boy, do I ever, no offense to Michelle or anything—I've recently realized that I don't think I can ever get married. To anyone."

I stare at him, shocked. I'm not sure if this confession is supposed to make me feel better or not. Mostly it makes me feel that familiar emptiness, like I just lost the one man I truly ever loved all over again. I take a few deep breaths and then finally manage to croak out the question that's been plaguing me since that fateful cab ride. The question I never got to ask. "But, why? I don't get it. You always seemed to love being a boyfriend and being in an exclusive, committed relationship, not just in general but with me. I thought you loved me. I thought we both wanted to share our lives together."

"I did, so much. All of those things were true. They really were. To be honest, ever since Alice's interrogation when we took them out to dinner to celebrate their engagement, I consciously tried to wrap my head around the idea of us getting married, but it wasn't gelling for some reason. Then we were at Scott and Alice's wedding, and something inside me just snapped. They seemed to be able to get there so easily. I couldn't understand where my resistance was coming from, but that night I knew no matter what it was or where it came from, it was real. I didn't want to lose you, but if I couldn't marry you, then it would be selfish and cruel of me to stay with you."

Tears are streaming down my face. I wanted these answers, didn't I? Didn't I need them so I could fully move on? "But you never even told me that you felt that way about marriage. The one or two times the topic came up, you made it seem that you wanted it too, and we'd figure out the details when the time was right. I was devastated. All I wanted was for us to be together. Maybe if we had talked about it, we could've figured out something else. I'm not Alice. I didn't necessarily want it all the way Alice had it . . . maybe it seemed that way at the time."

"I could've handled it so much better—I know that now. But somehow, as much as I didn't want to hurt you, it seemed easier to bail than to take a hard look at myself and admit something fundamentally frightening about myself that I didn't want to see. You have to believe me, it's not like I walked around secretly knowing that I never wanted to get married. I always just *assumed* I did— that when I found the right person, it would be a no-brainer. Looking back on it, maybe it would've helped to talk about it with you, but it felt like it had nothing to do with you and had everything to do with me. It didn't make sense to me. Still doesn't. But for what it's worth, I'm trying to figure it all out now, you know, more *formally*."

"Meaning?"

"I just started therapy." He looks sheepish.

"That's good," I lie. It's not that I don't believe in therapy, but I'm hurt and angry that he didn't take that step a lot earlier, i.e., before he broke my heart and ruined my life.

"I think Michelle is still hoping that I will snap out of it or get over my cold feet, but I'm worried that all therapy will be able to do is to help me come to accept who I am and teach me how not to hurt anyone else by being more up-front with them from the start or just not getting too serious in the first place."

We're quiet for a minute. Peter's eyes are watery. His voice cracks when he speaks. "The crazy thing is that at the time, I thought I was doing you a favor. By breaking it off when I did, I thought that you could bounce back and find someone who could give you what I couldn't. And when I ran into you at the Love Heals party, it seemed like you were with that British guy, and I sort of congratulated myself. Believe me, it felt weird to see you with someone else, but I felt better too, like I finally had proof that I had done the right thing." I don't clarify that I wasn't with Jackson the way that he thinks. "You seemed so much stronger and confident about yourself. And you looked amazing, almost as if you had transformed into a completely different person since I last saw you. I was sad for myself, but happy for you. But then a couple of weeks ago, I heard about the *Three-on-One* episode."

I grimace. "Oh no, tell me you didn't watch it. . . ."

"Yeah, I'm sorry, I did. It was pretty awful."

"Thanks, I already know I looked like an absolute horror show."

"No, I don't mean that. Besides, they totally exaggerated everything. Anyone who knows you would realize that they went out of their way to try to make you look bad and exploit the situation. What was truly terrible was the look in your eyes during your confessional bits. There was so much pain there. Then you referred to something really bad that had happened to you two years ago that sent you into a spiral, and I realized that you were talking about me. I did that to you. And I was stunned. I haven't been able to shake it ever since. I had no idea—"

"Peter." Now I put my hand on his forearm and leave it there. "You had something to do with it, yes. But honestly, I did it to myself. And I kept doing it to myself, until everything in my life fell apart. Should we have had *some* kind of conversation, preferably before you just walked away from me, from us, or at least after, so if nothing else, I could've understood and maybe found some peace with the outcome? In hindsight, yes, but I could've called you too. I could've demanded some kind of explanation, but I didn't. Instead, I completely withdrew. And let my life unravel."

He looks at me sorrowfully. "Even if you had asked me for an explanation, I doubt I would've been able to tell you anything useful. I was in complete denial, with a dash of self-loathing for good measure." He gives me a wry smile. "It may be one of the most trite explanations on the planet, but I guess they invented 'it's not you, it's me' for a reason." We smile sadly at each other. "But, Tori, you have to know, that you're still one of my favorite people in the world, maybe even most favorite. You were always so real, so good and true to the people you loved. I always admired it, tried to live up to it. And the truth is, in my life, I have fallen short. I'm deeply sorry, but I'm not looking for you to accept my apology. More than I want to figure out how to be happy for myself, I hope that you're happy. You were always the one person who seemed to know herself absolutely. With any luck—and some hard work—I can get there too. But I just hope—and think that perhaps—you're there."

"Maybe not there exactly, but I'm working on it. I am working on it."

Hamptons Unwritten Rule #47:
News may travel fast, but it doesn't
necessarily mean it's true.

I'm at home lying on my couch, thoroughly worn out—both from still being somewhat under the weather as well as the mild aftershock of just having seen Peter. I'm replaying our conversation in my mind, trying to figure out how I feel now that, after all this time, I have what could possibly be closure.

I'm fairly clear on how I *don't* feel: I don't feel like I'm about to fall headlong into another Peter-induced tailspin. Nor do I feel like I want to spend the next several weeks living in the delusional world of "Maybe": "Maybe therapy will help Peter. Maybe he'll figure out what his mental block about marriage is and move past it. And he said it himself: if he was going to marry anyone, it'd be me, not Michelle, so maybe. . . ." I don't feel sorry for myself, but actually, I do feel a little sorry for Peter: it makes me sad to think that he might not be able to figure out how to get out of his own way and be truly with someone. It would be a real shame, because ultimately, I think he's one of the good ones, possibly great ones, except for this, his one Fatal Flaw.

And while we're at it, I don't feel too bad that George "completed" our relationship, though does it ever feel too good to be dumped? Was his attention flattering? Yes. Was it fun and at times exhilarating to live the glamorous life even for a couple of months? Yes. Did I enjoy being "George Daniels's Newest Mystery Lady"? Sure, until the mystery became, "Why does George Daniels have all these *other* ladies?"

Did I really think that Jerry could be right, that it was possible that George was falling in love with me? Deep down, no. But neither was I. And frankly, I think I was nearing the expiration date on our "acquaintance" as well. I don't think I could go on much longer pretending that having semiregular sex and running around to a zillion parties meant that we were becoming emotionally intimate. This closure conversation with Peter (which, even after all this time, still had the vestiges of true emotional intimacy) has brought it even into sharper focus that that's what I really want—what I *need*.

I don't want a relationship that just looks good on the outside. It's more important that it feels great on the inside.

But there's something I'm still confused about: Peter said, "It's not you, it's me." George said, "Honestly, it's you."

Who was right?

Could both of them be? With Peter, I was my true self—or at least who I was then, at that stage of my life, but I wasn't pretending to be anything that I wasn't—but then that self got rejected lock, stock, and barrel. Then I thought, Well, that self must've sucked, if the greatest guy in the world doesn't want to marry me. So, what did I do? *I* rejected that self.

And then I *reinvented* that self, perhaps even invented a whole new self. With the help of three crazy, fame-seeking gay guys, $5,000 worth of free clothes, hair and makeup, a summer share—and a new name.

And that's who George rejected. And that's who almost screwed things up with her best friend, Alice. And actually, come to think of it, that could be who Andrew isn't so pleased with at the moment, which would mean. . . .

My phone rings. It's Cassie. "Hey, you. I'm sorry it took me so long to get back to you. But I'm doing a lot better. The bruise on my face actually started to look worse, so I called in sick this week. Taking a little time to heal, both inwardly and outwardly, I guess."

"I'm glad to hear you're taking care of yourself. I was worried about you, hence my zillions of messages."

"You're sweet for checking in on me. I think I needed to be alone with my thoughts for a little while—I wasn't really up for talking to anyone—but it was nice to hear a friendly, concerned voice. I also wanted to thank you again for taking that insanely early Jitney with me on Sunday morning, even though you were beyond sick and we got no sleep the night before. I just wasn't quite ready to face the housemates—or have them see my face, for that matter."

"I was more than happy to get the heck out of there myself and be home in my own bed, but please, I would've done it regardless. I didn't want you to be alone after everything that happened."

She tells me that she hasn't heard from Phillip since he threw her out, which she's now thinking is just as well. There's really nothing he could say or do to make up for how he treated her. She knows that she's better off without him, even though she can't help but miss him—who he was at the beginning—and the potential of what she thought they had. I tell her how strong she is not to be tempted to go back, to get out while she can—before anything even worse happened—and move forward.

"On to bigger and better things and all that, I suppose," she agrees. "Though I'm thinking that maybe I should take a break from fraternizing with the opposite sex for a little while, figure out some things. But you know who did call me: Andrew. I spoke to him a little while ago."

"What did he have to say?"

"Not much. He just wanted to make sure I was all right and that I didn't need any 'protection,' as he put it. He even offered to come back from the beach and sleep on my couch if I was worried that Phillip might show up. You didn't tell him anything more, did you?"

"No! I haven't spoken to him, and even if I had, that's all your business. But he might've noticed your face when we got home, and well, given what he did already know, it was probably sort of easy for him to draw some conclusions."

"I'm sure you're right. I still can't believe you managed to get yourself to Phillip's house and then stayed in the driveway that whole time! I thought you were crazy. But I'm so grateful you were. Not to mention, how nice it was of Andrew to come rescue two crazy women, no questions asked. I'm sorry I freaked when you told me you shared your concern about me with him. Out of everyone in the house, I trust him the most. You made the right choice. He's a total mensch. Always has been."

"You mean a total player, don't you?"

"Player? Andrew Kane? Uh, not really . . ."

"That's not what I've been hearing, experiencing, or seeing for that matter. Actually, I need to tell you something." I recount the highlights of my saga with Andrew, including the information about Andrew's history that Leah told me about him cheating on and then leaving his former wife, up until the ugly discussion at his birthday party.

"I have two things to say about that," she responds. "First of all, Leah has a warped sense of reality, so I'm not shocked that her version of history is completely askew. The truth is *Natalie* left Andrew—that is, after cheating on him while he was in his last year of law school and she was working in Manhattan."

"Woah, really? Not the other way around?"

"I know it for a fact. I met Andrew around that time because I was friends with some people who worked with him. Everyone knew that it was *she* who had cheated on *him*—and not just with one guy, apparently. Andrew was so absolutely ruined by it that I don't think he's ever really gotten close to someone since. To the women who have tried to date him since then, I can see how he might've come across as a player, because they never got past go in any meaningful way. Why do you think Leah has that take on him?"

"What? No!"

"Yes! *Of course* she wanted to go out with him when they first met—I think she thinks they actually did date—but he never engaged with her on any other level beyond friendship. So naturally she was going to go around blaming it on the fact that he was a player who couldn't settle on one woman rather than admit that he wasn't into her. Especially now when he seems genuinely interested in someone else."

"I'm in shock. But I guess I shouldn't be, given what I've been learning about her lately."

"Leah is biased! Call Anderson Cooper! Get the camera crews on the scene!" We both laugh. "But to those of us who knew him right after his divorce, it's fairly obvious that Andrew has just been too scared to put himself back out there emotionally. His ex-wife was one of those charming, gorgeous, smart, and wildly sexy women who was also completely out of her mind. He wanted to believe the best about her, but at the time, he was too smitten to see the truth."

"Was she also, perhaps, someone who only thought about herself?"

"Completely."

"So, one could say, he has a special sensitivity, perhaps aversion, to selfish women?"

"One could say that, yes."

"Ah, very interesting. So, what's your 'second of all'?"

"Huh?" I remind her that when we started this whole Andrew discussion she said she had *two* things to say about it. "Oh, yes, that's right. Second of all, it sounds to me like Andrew Kane might finally be in love again."

"Oh yeah? Who's the lucky girl to finally win the heart of our beloved Mayor?"

"You, silly. It's you."

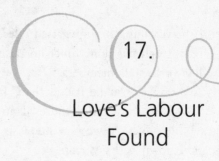

17.

Love's Labour
Found

August						
Su	Mo	Tu	We	Th	Fr	Sa
			1	2	3 ✗	4 ✗
5 ✗	6	7	8	9	10 ✗	11 ✗
12 ✗	13	14	15	16	17 ✗	18 ✗
19 ✗	20	21	22	23	24 ✗	25 ✗
26 ✗	27	28	29	30	31 ✗	

September						
Su	Mo	Tu	We	Th	Fr	Sa
						1 ✗
2 ✗	3 ✗ Labor Day	4	5	6	7	8
9	10	11	12	13	14	15
16	17	18	19	20	21	22
23	24	25	26	27	28	29

Hamptons Unwritten Rule #48:
If you listen hard enough, you can hear
not only the ocean, but also the truth.

I've called an emergency session of our morning meeting, even
though it's Thursday, to fill them in on What Peter Said and the
couple of bombs Cassie dropped on me last night. Ever since our
little blowup, Jimmy and I have studiously been pretending it never
happened, though things have been different, in a good way, since it
did: he has been a lot kinder and less snarky to me during the last
couple of weeks, and I've been trying to focus more on and at work.
To help matters, an old colleague of ours who is now perma-lance at
USA Network called out of the blue and asked us to work on a sizzle

reel showcasing a big integrated sales campaign they've just completed, which has done much to raise the collective morale of all MillerWorks staff members.

"No way! Cassie did *not* say that!" Jimmy says.

"Way! She thinks that Andrew is in love with me—or at least in heavy like—which, we now know, is not usual for the Man Formerly Known as the Mayor."

Jerry's brows are deeply furrowed. "Did Cassie make the love-slash-like statement based on all the stuff you told her or because she knows something or because Andrew said something specific to her?"

"Mostly based on what I told her, but she also said that when she and Andrew spoke, he asked Cassie if I had gone back with her on the bus, because there was something he wanted to talk to me about."

"The already thick-ish plot becomes thicker!" Jimmy says.

Jerry takes his glasses off and rubs his eyes with the heels of his hands. "Okay, so: Andrew is out at the beach house on vacation this week. Is anyone else in the house taking this week off?"

"Yes, apparently Leah's there as well."

Jimmy gasps. "You don't think . . . she isn't there to. . . ."

"She had her chance. If he's not into selfish, never in a million years would he go for her, especially now," Jerry says.

"Though she might be taking advantage of this time to spread her venom about you to him . . . ," Jimmy posits.

"Well, that's not good." I sink my head into my hands. "I'm such an idiot. He practically invited me to be out there this week with him and I blew—"

Jerry shoves his glasses back onto his head, as if doing so will help him hear better. "Stop. Say that thing again."

"I told you that. . . ."

"Uh, no you did not."

"Uh, yes I did. I told you how when Andrew and I were at the beach the day of his party he was talking about spending the last week out there and asking me if I was going to . . . Oh, my god. No, you're right, I never told you because I totally forgot about it because I'm a complete and total clueless idiot! *He was asking me to take vacation with him!* Could I be any dumber?"

Jimmy and Jerry just look at me, pity filling their eyes at my sheer and utter stupidity.

"Act-u-a-lly," Jimmy says slowly, "you could be dumber if you sit here one minute longer instead of high-tailing it home, packing your bag full of your sluttiest lingerie, shaving your legs, and getting your ass on the next available bus. Dur, *Miller.*"

"But we have to go through the materials that USA sent. . . ."

"We can totally cover it," Jimmy volunteers, surprising both Jerry and me.

"But what will you guys—"

"Tori," Jerry says, "despite recent conversations about the state of our business, the summer is over in about three minutes, and nothing's going to happen between now and then. Jimmy and I can take a first pass on the sizzle reel and have something to show you on Tuesday and we'll still be on schedule. So there's no work-related excuse for you not to cut out early this week in the name of trying to reverse this whole thing with Andrew. The only excuse, and I don't even consider it a real one, is if you're not ready to take a chance on someone who actually might deserve it."

"Andrew?"

"No, my little kumquat. You."

. . .

As the sold-out Jitney (luckily I got a seat off of the standby list), which has been crawling its way east for the past two and a half hours, turns from Route 111 in Manorville onto Route 27, a major wrinkle in my plan suddenly occurs to me.

The wrinkle has a name, and that name is Strappy Sandal Girl.

I totally spaced re: her. Andrew never denied actually being with

her. I did see Senorita Strap curl herself onto Andrew's lap in the car
the night of his birthday party. On top of that, so to speak, I don't
know if he came home at all that night. Then, who knows what
happened the weekend I was in the Berkshires—she could've
moved in for the kill. When I called him to pick up Cassie and me
last Saturday night, maybe he wasn't in bed alone! What if, after the
debacle with me, he invited *her* to join him for his vacation week instead, and that was what he wanted to talk to me about, to just give
me a courtesy heads-up in case I had decided to take the week off?
That would be something he would do. As opposed to me, who
thinks nothing about bringing one paramour to another paramour's
birthday party.

I start sweating even though the A/C is blasting. I can't call anyone because the Jitney attendant will come over and yell at me for
breaking the "No Cell Phone" rule, as she just did to a woman two
rows ahead of me who was yakking away at full volume. They do allow you three minutes for an emergency call. This counts as an
emergency, does it not? If it's a true emergency, how can you possibly limit your call to only 180 seconds? I can't exactly call Andrew
and say, "Hi, I'm coming out to apologize for being such a shit to
you and maybe you'll forgive me so that we can live happily ever after Labor Day. But, by the way, is Miss Strap-A-Lot lying tan and
naked in your California King by any chance?"

Abort! Abort! I could get off in Southampton and get on a bus
going west, have Stacy pack up my stuff and bring it home, and
never, ever set foot in the Hamptons ever again.

I start looking around for the attendant. And then I see it: the bus
driver. The man who is *driving the bus*. Calmly, confidently, casually even.

A sign from the universe if there ever was one. Sure there's tons
of traffic and idiots cutting him off and minivans going too slow
right in front of him and cars stopping short to make unexpected
left turns . . . there's all that and more. I guess the point is that you

keep driving the bus no matter what crosses your path, even if you take a wrong turn or reach a dead end every once in a while.

So, I decide to stay on the bus and see where it takes me.

Hamptons Unwritten Rule #49:
If you cross the Resident Alpha Female
you will bear the consequences—
for eternity, if not longer.

Around six-thirty, I arrive at the house. There aren't any cars in the driveway. All is quiet inside, providing me with ideal snooping conditions. Andrew's door is somewhere between open and closed, so I enter, flagrantly disregarding House Guideline #2. I spy definitive evidence of habitation: a pair of upended sneakers on the floor, an imperfectly made bed, a couple of half-drunk glasses of water— free of lipstick stains and both on the same nightstand—and a newspaper on the floor. However, I don't see evidence of *cohabitation*, such as underwear hanging from lamps, strap-laden sandals peeking out from under the bed, or any other obvious signs of a female foreign body.

As I make my way toward the main part of the house, the front door opens.

"Miller!"

"Leah, hi."

She clomps in, hair a-swinging, front door a-slamming behind her. "Jesus! You scared me! I didn't know anyone was here."

"Sorry about that. But isn't Andrew out this week too?"

"Yes, but his car isn't in the driveway and that's usually an indication of whether someone who owns a car is home or not." I guess she hasn't forgotten that she hates me.

"Is he at the beach?"

"Nope."

"At the gym or playing tennis maybe?"

"Nope and nope." She gives me a big flip and then begins walk-ing toward the kitchen. I follow her. She pours herself a glass of water and turns to face me, her eyes full of challenge. Go ahead, Miller, ask me anything you want, but I'm not handing you a thing, you Share House Code Traitor, you.

"Do you happen to know where he is?"

"Actually, yes, I do know."

"Look, Leah, I know I'm not your favorite person on the planet right now, but it would be really helpful if you could tell me where he is."

"Why should I tell you anything that might be helpful to you? After all, you had the opportunity of doing me that courtesy but you obviously couldn't be bothered to help me." Her eyes are as fiery as when she confronted me at the party. She clearly hasn't let even an ounce of it go. When she was ignoring me, I could deal. But now that she seems to be demanding a second round, it's a dif-ferent story. As much as I wanted to avoid this—and her—this weekend, something tells me that if I face her now, à la Dorothy standing up to the as-it-turns-out-not-so-nice Wizard at the end of the yellow brick road, I just may be able to pull back the curtain and find something there other than a purely evil bitch. At least for her sake, I hope that's a possibility.

"Leah, you've been giving me grief for most of the summer, and for the life of me, I still can't understand why you felt the need to treat me that way from practically the first minute we met, but now I'm going to give you a little tip: you really should stop fucking with me. You have officially gone too far. I've been holding myself back because, honestly, I don't feel the need to trot out every skele-ton I know is hiding in that gigantic walk-in closet of yours the way you did for me."

She flips her hair and crosses her tanned arms in front of her chest. "Really? What could you possibly know about me?"

I channel my inner Kirsten Dunst from *Bring It On* and take a few steps toward her until we're standing only inches apart. "Plenty. But the question you have to ask yourself now is, 'Is it really worth pushing Miller to the edge to find out whether she's bluffing or not?' But I guarantee you, I'm not bluffing. I'm not that good of an actress. And there are several people who I know will find what I have to share with them very interesting. In fact, five other people, to be exact."

When she blinks, I know that I've won. She backs up against the counter, trying to appear casual as she leans against it and crosses one tawny leg across the other. I summon all my resolve and move just one more step closer, putting a hand on my hip and the other on the marble countertop.

"The way I see it, Leah, we only have four more days to deal with each other. I'm not saying you have to be my best friend or even like me, but you have a choice. If you choose to stay out of my face, then I will stay out of yours. Then boom, it's Labor Day and the 'FFFTS Rule' will officially no longer be in effect."

She takes the bait. "What's the 'FFFTS Rule'?"

"Come on. Are you seriously telling me you don't know what it is? You of all people should be on top of this one. It's the 'Fake Friends For The Summer Rule.' Won't it be nice to finally stop pretending? I know I'm done with the charade. So, what do you say? Are you going to tell me where Andrew is or not?"

She gives me a look that is far from filled with love, but the flame that was burning bright only seconds ago has definitely been lowered to a flicker. "Fine. If you really must know, he's in the city. He had to go back this morning for a work emergency."

"Is he coming back out?"

"He said he was going to be there 'as long as it takes.' He didn't elaborate on that for me, so I have nothing else to give you." She drains her water and clunks the glass down on the counter. "I imagine we're done here, unless you are in need of any other information."

"Nope, I'm good."

"I'm so glad to hear it." Leah clomps off toward the North Wing. When I hear a door slam a few seconds later, I know it's safe to breathe again.

. . .

I call Jimmy and Jerry from the house phone, hoping that the Queen Bee-Yatch doesn't pick up the extension in her bedroom. I give them the Andrew update.

"Well, I say kudos to you," Jimmy says. "I'm really proud of you for taking the risk. No matter what happens, you were true to yourself and chose to do the brave thing."

"Very well said, sweetie," Jerry says softly to Jimmy, with a rare show of affection for his partner in life.

"Thanks, guys. Um, you know I love you both with all my heart and don't know what I'd do without you, right?"

"We know," Jimmy says.

"Right back at you, boss," Jerry adds.

"And, Jimmy, I'm so sorry—"

He doesn't let me finish. "Tor, I'm the one who's sorry. I am so ashamed of my behavior, you don't even know. I've been kicking myself ever since. You didn't deserve any of those vile things I said. I promise never to talk to you like that ever again—either as a colleague or a friend—or take out personal problems on you."

"Apology accepted. And I promise not to fall asleep at the wheel ever again."

"Especially when you're driving the bus as fast as you are right now! That could be dangerous!" he quips. We all laugh, putting our issue to bed in the most fitting way.

"Anything interesting happen since I left?" I ask. "Did USA get you all the support materials they promised?"

Jerry says, "Yup. All set. And Jim found some really great music to use. It's going to be kick-ass. But otherwise, you haven't missed a thing. The phones and e-mail have been quiet. People must've started their holiday weekend early. Although, someone called and asked for you—a guy. I told him you were out of town for the rest of the week, but he wouldn't leave his name, and when I asked him if I could help him with something, he said 'Thanks, I don't think so' and hung up."

"That's odd. I hope it wasn't someone calling about a rush job who got frustrated because I wasn't there to do it."

"I wouldn't worry about it. It was probably a telemarketer," Jerry says.

"So, what are you going to do now?" Jimmy asks.

"I guess I'll just settle in for the night. Clearly Leah and I aren't going to paint the Hamptons red tonight or anything, so I guess I'll just wait and see."

"You could call him . . . ," Jimmy suggests.

"I thought of that, but if he's in the middle of a work crisis, it's probably not the most opportune time to bug him."

"Makes sense. Good luck, sweetie."

"Thanks, Jer. I hope I won't need it."

. . .

To kill time and distract myself, I decide to take a long hot bath, accompanied by a glass of white wine. When I get out and dressed, Leah is gone, hopefully for the night.

Without a car, I'm at the mercy of what's in the kitchen for dinner, which amounts to some stale crackers and leftover hunks of cheese and olives. I pour myself more wine and dig in. I get caught up in watching Plum TV—a Hamptons-centric local station—but then the re-airing of that day's live morning show is over. The gardening show that follows it is a bit of a snooze, so I flip around, trying to find something else until I remember from my earlier snooping that Andrew has a bunch of good DVDs in his room. I select an indie flick about a dysfunctional upper-middle-class family living on the Upper West Side and return to the living room. For some reason, I can't get the DVD player to work, so I take my bottle of wine and head back to Andrew's suite, breaking every "guideline" in the book at this point. It's already almost ten o'clock, so chances are he's not coming back tonight, and when I'm done, I'll make sure to leave everything the way it was, so he'll never even know I was there.

Hamptons Unwritten Rule #50:
Ultimately most, if not all, unwritten rules,
are meant to be broken. Or at least, ignored.

The room fills with light.

"Jesus, Miller!"

I squint toward the doorway, my eyes trying to readjust to the light. There's Andrew, looking like he just saw the Hamptons Potato Field Killer. "I have a reasonable explanation for why I broke a house rule. I was watching a movie because the DVD player in the living room wasn't working. I'm sorry I trespassed."

He flips off the glaring overhead light and comes over to sit on the side of the bed, switching on a much more humane—and flattering—lower wattage lamp on the nightstand.

"What time is it?"

"After eleven." He shakes his head. "Miller, you never cease to amaze me."

"I know it must seem like I've got a lot of nerve coming in here and using your stuff when we're not exactly. . . ."

"No, I mean you've been a pretty big pain in the butt lately, and today you definitely outdid your previous record."

"Well, I'm nothing if not a type A achiever, always trying to improve myself."

He laughs. "When did you get here?" I tell him. He shakes his head, a half smile on his face. "So, I was there and you were here."

"Sounds that way. Crisis averted?"

"Not really. There was nothing I could accomplish there so I came back. But now it seems like I might be able to make some progress."

"That's good. But isn't it kind of a bummer that you have to work on your vacation, even if it's out here?"

"Who said anything about work?"

"Leah did. She told me that you had to go back to the city for some work emergency. Was she not telling me the truth?" And if so, that means she had the nerve to lie to my face even after I told her to back the hell off. . . .

"She wasn't lying per se, but she wasn't exactly telling the truth." He signals me to slide over so we're sitting side by side, our backs against the headboard.

"I knew it!"

"I told her I had to deal with something that came up at work. You didn't really expect me to announce to her that I went into the city to see you, did you?"

I turn to stare at him. "That's funny. Because I came out here to see *you*."

He smiles. "Just what I said: progress." He lays his hand on top of mine. It's warm and soft. It feels like safety.

"I wanted to say that I'm so sorry . . . for everything. . . ."

"You don't have to say anything," he says softly.

"Yes, I do. I've been an asshole and an idiot, among other things. That's not who I really am, at least, not who I ever meant to be."

"Why do you think that happened?"

"I blame the Hamptons."

"Really. It's the Hamptons' fault?" He looks amused, which I take as a sign to continue.

"Well, the combination of me plus the Hamptons—turns out: not so good. Before the summer, I was fine. I was me. I didn't have the most exciting life ever, but it was real. And then it was Memorial Day, and almost immediately, all these things that I had never even imagined having were suddenly available to me. I let myself get caught up in it all. But then I became incapable of telling the difference between what—and who—was real and important and what wasn't." I tell him about Peter, the breakup, the ensuing months of letting my own life slip away, the intervention, and the Transformation. He listens intently as I talk, his fingers gently rubbing my forearm at the sad parts. "Being made over by the Trio gave me what I now realize was a false sense of confidence. It gave me self-esteem, but for the person I was trying to be, not the person who I really was. Does that make sense?"

He nods. "Totally. I think we're more alike than you may have realized."

"You've been on a reality TV show too?" I tease.

"Yeah, *Survivor: Sagaponack*." We laugh.

I tell him how I began to think that it was only the New and Improved "Miller" who could thrive in the Hamptons. She was the one making new friends, dating, going to parties, and socializing like a pro, whereas Tori got dumped by the love of her life, then could barely shower or get herself out of the house except to go to work. Clearly Tori couldn't get her act together, so why keep her around? But that recently, it became readily apparent that I was in danger of throwing one too many babies out with the bathwater. "So, I came out here to ask you to A, forgive me, and if you would agree to A, then I'd ask for B: for you to give me another chance."

He narrows his eyes. "Which you? The New and Improved version or the other one?"

"Neither, actually. How about the Older and Wiser one?"

"I don't know . . . is she cute?"

I play-punch his arm. "And there's something else: George and I . . . well, we're no longer a George and I. It took me awhile to see that one clearly for what it was, but let's just say when I finally did, it was a rude awakening. I've had a lot of those lately." I turn to sit cross-legged, facing him. "I was wrong to make all of those awful assumptions about you and to listen to other people's opinions. Turns out not everyone or everything are as they seem."

"Funny how that happens. And sometimes when they are, you just let in outside noise and you don't even realize what you're hearing is interference, not the original thing you were listening to."

I stare at him, surprised. "Exactly."

"And how I know that is because I did the exact same thing. It just seemed easier than really examining what was going on. Because once you do that, you not only have to take a good, hard look at the things outside of you, but you also have to look at yourself, which is even more difficult."

"So, what did you figure out was going on?"

"That I was falling for you, and that revelation terrified me."

My heart does a somersault. "Why?"

"Because my preferred MO—which, by the way, has been in practice much longer than your three-month personality detour, so I've got you way beat—was to avoid any and all romantic attachments. I couldn't bear being hurt again the way I was when I got divorced, so I just steered clear, never got close to anyone. I think I compensated by becoming acquaintances with tons of people, so in that respect, the nickname you gave me was apropos. But when you came along, you not only put a match to my MO, you were the first person to truly call me out on it. You really had an effect on me. All of a sudden, I was in new territory and highly uncomfortable being there, in case you couldn't tell."

"How do you mean?"

"You're telling me you didn't notice how the only way that I could express my interest in you was to behave no better than a horny college kid? You honestly thought that getting drunk at a nightclub, dancing like Elaine on *Seinfeld*, and then making out in the back of a taxi van was me putting my best foot forward?"

"You're selling yourself short. You're a much better dancer than Elaine."

He laughs. "Seriously, though, I hadn't been intimate with anyone for so long that I became a complete bumbling amateur around
you."

"But it was fun. And frankly, I don't know how I would've re-
acted to a more straightforward approach, so maybe it worked out
for the best."

"Well, until it didn't. When I realized how much I had been
telegraphing 'summer house hookup' instead of what I was really
feeling, it all began to fall apart."

"So the weekend of your party . . ."

"I thought we were getting somewhere. Even though you had
laid down the A.L.D. Rule on me, you came to see me that Friday
night, so I got my nerve up to ask you to spend this week out here
with me, which I realized after, I wasn't exactly clear about either."

"And then I brought what's-his-name to your birthday party!
Ugh. I'm such an idiot, like I said."

"How could you possibly know how I really felt? Besides, I was
hardly the model of good behavior."

"Can I ask you something? I don't want to pry but . . . what's the
deal with Hailey?"

"She's a great, fun girl and we have spent some time together, but
honestly, she wasn't for me. A few weeks ago I told her I wasn't interested in anything serious. And then it occurred to me that I had
been clearer with her than I had been with you. Dumb, huh?"

I shrug. "Who am I to say?" He smiles. "But what I still don't understand is what made you change your mind about me. I gave you
every reason to believe I was a Class-A Selfish Bitch."

"What you did for Cassie . . . that was huge. You were a true
friend to her. I've always been extremely fond of her, but she's been
a notoriously flaky friend, not intentionally, but just because she's
always flitting around doing her own thing, which is sort of part
of the bargain with her. But the minute she needed someone, even
though she hadn't exactly been a reliable friend to you, you were
there and did whatever it took to help."

"I take it Cassie told you about my failed rescue attempt?"

He nods. "Sounded pretty successful to me. She might not have left him for good if it weren't for you."

"I didn't even think of that. By the way, thanks for rescuing *us*."

"It was the least I could do after I totally discounted what you were trying to tell me."

"Yeah, you should listen to me more often!" We smile at each other. "What else did she tell you?"

"She also maybe perhaps let it slip that you and Daniels were no longer."

"That little sneak!"

"More like, instigator, but in the best possible way. I think she had our number."

"Speaking of number, did you call my office today?"

"Yes. They said you were out of town. I thought maybe you had decided you were done with the Hamptons insanity and went to spend the weekend in the Berkshires again. But then here you were, in the last place I expected you to be, or to ever be again: in my bed." He slides us so we're completely lying down, facing each other. His arms encircle my body. He looks into my eyes. "I was thinking . . . we should get rid of the nicknames. If it's okay with you, I'd like to call you something else."

"Yeah, what's that?"

"Something pretty radical: Tori."

18.

No April Fools

"Here's to the Peanut!" I toast.

"To the Peanut!" everyone echoes, clinking glasses, sloshing champagne into one another's flutes and onto the tablecloth.

"I love that you're drinking champagne!" Cassie says. "You're such a renegade mama-to-be!"

"I haven't had a single drop of alcohol or caffeine or a piece of sushi since the day I found out I was pregnant, so I figure, what harm can a little bubbly be since I'm a few days past my due date? The Peanut's got to be fully baked by now." Alice takes a big, flaunting gulp and then wipes her mouth with the back of her hand.

"You better not drink much more of that Veuve, *Grande Dame*, or I'll have to report you to Dr. Spock," Jimmy warns.

Alice burps loudly in his direction, and everyone laughs.

We're at Alice's favorite nonsushi restaurant, Hearth, celebrating Alice and Scott's last few hours of being able to go out without paying for child care. Jimmy and Jerry are already competing for the Favorite Uncle/Aunt Award, having brought an over-the-top care package they put together for while Alice is in labor that is bursting with expensive anti–stretch mark potions, a giant can of Evian Brumisateur facial spray, blue cashmere slippers, a designer swaddling blanket (light green, appropriate for either sex), and of course, a stack of the latest trashy celebrity gossip magazines. Cassie gave Alice a gift certificate and the private phone number for the newest high-end spa for which even celebrities have to be on the waiting list, making Jimmy pout in the face of his imagined defeat. I bought the mom-to-be a portable iPod speaker so she can play music in her hospital room, and my boyfriend got from his sister, who has two kids, a list of every CD of music for babies ever recorded and bought them all. In the card he included a handmade coupon that entitled the recipients to a personal visit during which he would rip all the CDs onto Alice's iPod.

"Scott, do you have the proverbial overnight bag packed and sitting by the door like all the expectant dads do in the movies?" Andrew asks, refilling everyone's glasses with champagne.

"Actually it's more like a steamer trunk," Scott answers. "I've already put the doormen on alert that I'll need at least two guys to help me get that thing downstairs and into the car." Alice swats at him as he leans in lovingly to kiss her big belly. She rubs his head and beams with happiness.

"Looks like impending fatherhood has given ol' Scott the Boring Banker a much-needed infusion of personality," Jimmy mutters in my ear. I elbow him in the ribs and reach for my champagne to cover up my giggle.

I look around the table and am filled with gratitude that I'm surrounded by these people, my favorite human beings on the planet. Only months ago, I was in serious danger of driving them all away and running my business into the ground. But thankfully I came to my senses on all fronts and was able not only to redeem myself and turn our company around in the nick of time, but also to integrate the two seemingly disparate parts of my life—and parts of myself—more naturally than I ever would've imagined.

Despite Alice's original snobbery about the Hamptons and disdain for my too-fancy friends, she got on board before summer officially ended. Either the pregnancy mellowed her out (after she got over her initial panic, that is) or hearing about Cassie's unfortunate relationship debacle with Evil Eyebrow Man gave her a newfound compassion, or both; regardless, Alice ended up taking to Cassie like the mother hen that she has always wanted to be and is about to legitimately become.

In fact, the mutual lovefest was almost immediate. After meeting Alice and Scott for the first time, Cassie declared them one of the coolest couples she had ever met. The deal was sealed after Cassie, Andrew, and I went out to the Berkshires one weekend in October. Cassie fell so deeply in love with Alice and Scott's cottage that she put in a call to one of the editors at *Elle Decor*, who then arranged for the house to be shot for the May "stylish country living"–themed issue. Jimmy and Jerry, of course, worshipped the ground Cassie walked on from the moment they met her, not only for her exquisite fashion sense but also because she has introduced them to a whole new division of the Gay Mafia: the fashion and shelter magazine boys.

As for Cassie and me, our friendship grew and took on a whole new depth after I "rescued" her, as she called it, from the Peril of Phillip. She still does plenty of flitting and isn't the easiest to pin down for plans, but she never completely flies away and makes a point of staying in regular, meaningful contact. More importantly, she always comes through for me when it counts. She has, however, definitely slowed down on the guy front, having let her membership in the International Jet-setters Club expire. For a while, she didn't go out with anyone, despite the band of her usual suspects calling every time their G5s touched down on the tarmac at Teterboro Airport. Eventually she went out with a few people who were more in her age range, but when those petered out, she explained that she wasn't all that anxious to jump into something serious just yet.

Now Jimmy is trying to get Alice, who is loopy from her single glass of champagne, to spill her top name choices. "As Peanut's favorite uncles and aunts, don't you want us to like the kid's name so we can use his or her proper designation instead of 'Peanut'?"

"You'll have to like the real name Scott and I choose no matter what. That's the one requirement of an uncle: unconditional love."

"That and lots of presents," Jerry adds.

"And letting him or her have girl-boy parties at our apartments without you guys knowing," I say.

"And buying him or her beer before he or she is of age," Andrew chimes in.

"And taking the kid for their first wax," Cassie says.

"What if the Peanut is a boy?" Scott asks.

"Then Jimmy or Jerry will take him!" Cassie answers.

"As long as there are no hidden cameras!" I add. The table breaks out into a roar.

"To Peanut's first wax!" Jimmy cries, raising his glass, prompting the rest of us to do the same.

. . .

A little while later, I come out of the unisex WC to find Andrew standing against the wall.

"Hiya, hot stuff." He pulls me to him for a kiss.

"Hi there yourself, handsome man. Are you loitering here because you have to use the facilities or did you just miss me?" He blushes and buries his face in my neck. I weave my fingers into his hair and think about how it feels as if Labor Day were only seven seconds—not months—ago.

When it became spring a couple of weeks ago, it occurred to me that now I've known Andrew for four seasons. Granted, we spent most of the summer in limbo, but since we did technically meet last spring, we have completed one full cycle. And it's been amazing— not perfect, but amazing. I'm actually glad of the nonperfection because that has made our relationship feel more grounded, solid, and real than what I had with Peter, which just cruised blithely along, deceptively perfect, until it crashed and burned in a fiery wreck.

One of the best parts of our relationship is the fact that we truly communicate. Our pre–Labor Day heart-to-heart set the tone going forward, since the whole summer was one huge case in point that

making assumptions and not talking things out could lead to disas-
trous results. There's nothing that I've ever felt that I couldn't say to
him, good or not so, and I think he would agree that the reverse is
true. On the flip side, we don't overdo it on the talky-talk. After all,
Andrew Kane is still a guy, which works out quite well for me in
more ways than one.

Not surprisingly, Andrew had Jerry, Jimmy, Alice, and Scott at
"hello." All those years as the Mayor definitely left their mark, the
difference now being that we knew his charm was a natural, authentic trait, not a put-on to gain more votes in the Most Popular
Man about Town category. Alice, to her credit, has kept her desire
to be matron of honor to herself and has contented herself with seeing me so happy not just with Andrew, but also in all aspects of my
life.

"Have I told you lately that I love you?" I now whisper into his
ear, moving an errant curl back into place.

"Do two hours ago count as lately?"

"I suppose. . . ."

"Have I told you lately that you're the best thing that's ever happened to me?"

"Do two hours ago count as lately?" I lean in for another kiss. A
door to another WC opens and an older lady emerges, seemingly
annoyed to find us canoodling by the bathrooms. We separate to
give way. "Are we the most disgusting lovey-dovey couple on the
planet or what?"

"I sure hope so," he says.

"Perhaps someday we can stop speaking in song titles." I take his
hand and start leading him back toward our table.

"Hopefully only because we're really old and can't remember any
more songs." He squeezes my hand as we walk. I don't even have to
turn around to know he is smiling.

After we settle ourselves into our main course, the talk turns toward summer plans.

"I just put in for a leave of absence at work," Cassie announces. "I applied to an artists' colony in New Hampshire, and I got in, so I need about a month off."

I'm not the only one who drops their fork or stops chewing so we can stare at her.

"I'm a painter." She smiles self-consciously. "I mean, I used to paint but I stopped doing it a long time ago. Other things began to seem more important, but after everything that happened last summer, I realized that I had lost touch with a really integral part of myself, so I started working on some pieces and remembered how much I loved it. I recently met someone who told me about this artists' colony, so I applied and got an invitation for August."

We congratulate her and tell her how amazing it is that she's doing this. She now smiles widely, obviously glad for the support from her new friends.

"Well, you two will be back in the Hamptons," Alice says, pointing her fork at Andrew and me. "Clearly, no one will want to do a house with Leah this year after her white-collar shenanigans last summer."

I never outed Leah's price gouging to Andrew or any of our housemates. I didn't have to. After Labor Day, Leah asked Andrew for his help figuring out the remaining expenses and the amount of everyone's rebate from the security deposit. From that, he discovered that not only had she overcharged everyone for their share to cover the majority of Jackson's portion, but she had also *under-charged* herself! Apparently, she and Andrew had agreed to pay the most, given the size of their rooms and the fact that they weren't sharing, but Leah hadn't kept her end of the bargain. Instead of telling everyone that Leah had cheated them all, Andrew rebated the money to the housemates, covering the discrepancy out of his own pocket and apologizing for what he called an "accounting error." Whether or not the others had figured out what she had done, Leah was such a colossal bitch to everyone during Labor Day weekend, that most of them were turned off by her anyway. When she sent an e-mail to us and the former housemates a couple of months ago saying that she had rented the same house again, as far as I know, no one signed on for another round, not even Stacy.

I now say, "Actually, Andrew and I were thinking that maybe we'd try somewhere different this summer."

Eyebrows go up all around.

"Really, is that so?" Jimmy says. "I thought the Hamptons were the *only* place to be between Memorial Day and Labor Day weekends. If you're not going back to the scene of the crime, where could you two possibly be going?"

Andrew and I grin at each other. He squeezes my hand under the table as a signal.

"The North Fork."

Acknowledgments

My name may be on the cover of this book, but without the real people on this page, *LoveHampton* would not exist on any map—including my own.

I am so happy and grateful for:

Andrea Schulz and her intelligence, incisiveness, good humor, and bionic speed-reading ability. She helped me get this book under way and then stepped back from the page to see the book from the eight-hundred-foot view so I could figure out how to finish it.

Everyone at The Creative Culture, especially my agent, Mary Ann Naples, whose decisiveness, savvy, creativity, guidance, and vision have made all the difference and meant so much.

The smart, creative, and enthusiastic team at St. Martin's Press, especially Jennifer Weis, Hilary Rubin Teeman, Stefanie Lindskog, Anne Marie Tallberg, Ellis Trevor, and Shelly Perron. Thank you for seeing the possibilities.

My early readers, who took time out of their busy lives to plow through various drafts of this book: Suzan Colón, Marissa Rothkopf Bates, Jennifer Robinson, and David Hirshey.

Mary Matthews for knowing the exact perfect way to bring this book to life as poetic moving images. And for those who participated in various aspects of the production of *LoveHampton:* The Videos: Eric Price, Hal Brooks, Mark Melrose, and Scott Stein. For Jeff Rabb for making my Web site so much more than a registered domain name. And for Michael Falco and Pam Geiger for helping me put my best face forward in my photos.

Everyone at the Virginia Center for the Creative Arts for introducing me to my first true community of writers and artists and providing me with a truly special place where I could put the finishing touches on this book and start my new one. And for 71 Irving Place, my local writing annex.

The Rifkin family, whose support and love I feel, even across the many miles that separate us: my parents, Sam—who always told me that I had "good expression"—and Grace, who passed on her love of fiction to me; my brother, Alan, and his wife, Hilary; my nephew and niece, Ben and Hannah, who all cheered me on while I was "making a book."

And all of my behind-the-scenes players who rallied every time to offer encouragement and, just as important, listened when the story needed untangling, including Stefanie Ziev, Anthony Schneider, Melissa Lipman, Jay Dubiner, Marci Weisler, and Julie Merberg.

I am so happy and grateful to have all of you in my life. Thank you.